WITCHWORK

BETWEEN THE RAVEN AND THE DOVE

SOPHIA KINGSHILL

Published by Accent Press Ltd 2017

www.accentpress.co.uk

ISBN 9781786154804
eISBN 9781786154682

Printed in the UK by Clays Ltd, St. Ives

CONTENTS

CHAPTER ONE
DANGER

They're getting closer.

I can feel it, I mean physically, through the floor. The boards I'm sitting on are thin: every time someone opens a door down below, I can feel the movement.

I'm in the attic, with Grace. We're not moving, not speaking; we're completely still. It's late afternoon, and the sun's slanting through the skylight in the roof.

I can hear voices, but not clearly. They haven't started up the last set of stairs yet. They're still searching the second floor.

Soon there'll be nowhere else for them to look but where we are. If they find us ... if they find us ... I don't know what happens next, but whatever it is, it mustn't happen.

I've only been in the attic once before that I can remember, and I wasn't supposed to be here then either. The floorboards might be rotten. Dad was furious: 'If you fell through, you could have broken a leg.' It was his fault, because the door's supposed to be kept locked.

I can hear a noise from the stairs. Creak … creak … very slow.

Someone's coming up.

I look at Grace, sat on the floor in her dressing gown and slippers. I want to tell her, *Keep still*, but I mustn't make a noise. I want her to look at me, so I can put my finger on my lips to show we've got to be silent, but she's staring at nothing, like she always does. She won't say anything. She never says anything.

We mustn't let them know we're here.

Creak … creak. The footsteps reach the top of the stairs, and the door handle starts to turn.

*

I'm awake. My heart's hammering, and I'm sweating and cold at the same time.

It was a dream. It didn't happen; it wasn't real. I'm safe in bed. Just a dream.

So why do I keep having it every night?

It's not even a nightmare, not really. The people looking for us are Dr Sykes and my own dad. They're not frightening. If I was really in the attic, what's the worst that could happen? Sykes'd have a go at me for being irresponsible, and Dad might clip me one. No big deal.

How come Grace is there too? What in the world

would I want with Grace up in the attic, or anywhere else?

Just because we're the same colour, it doesn't mean I want to hang out with her. I'm used to being around white people; there's hardly anyone I know who isn't white. Even Dad's white. Anyway, if I was looking for a friend, I'm not going to choose a middle-aged woman who doesn't talk, who's autistic or whatever.

There's no point trying to make sense of it. It's a dumb dream, that's all. But I've had it so many times now. Always the same, always Grace and me in the attic, always that we've got to hide, be quiet, be still, or else they'll find us. So many times, it has to mean something, doesn't it?

I should ask Sykes, I guess. It'd be just his box of tricks. He's interested in dreams and stuff, how your mind works. It's his job, after all, messing about with people's minds.

Maybe that's why I haven't told him. I don't want my mind messed with.

It's very early, but I don't fancy going back to sleep, so I get some clothes on and grab a towel. It'll be cold for swimming, but that might clean the dream out of my head.

Tiptoeing along the passage, I pass the other rooms. All the doors are shut; everything's quiet. Everyone's asleep but me. I stroke the wooden banisters on my way down the stairs, till I get to the carved eagle at the bottom. Back in the day, the Residence used to be some old country-house type's country house, and it still feels pretty grand if you don't look at the institutional carpets and the scuffed paint. When I want to show off, I tell people I live in a mansion, but everyone at school knows what the place is now, and they tell me if I live in a nuthouse, that makes me a nutter. Maybe they're right about that.

It's not like, you know, a secure unit where they lock up maniacs – just residential for people with whatsit, behavioural problems.

Yeah, Mag, it's still a loony bin. Who are you kidding?

I look into the empty canteen. Dad hasn't wiped the crumbs off the tables from last night. He cooks for the patients and staff, plus he's supposed to fix whatever goes wrong around the place, though he's not very good at technical stuff. He can change a fuse, but if something major gets bust, it tends to stay that way till Sykes gives in and calls a proper electrician.

I unbolt the side door and pull it to behind me. Any burglars up at this hour deserve what they can get.

Outside, the air smells fresh and salty. Here on the Island, you're never too far from the sea, and we've got our own little bay behind the house. There used to be a boat, and there's still a wooden landing stage, which is smoother to sit on than the pebbles. Down the south end of the Island there are sandy beaches, but round us it's just cliffs and rocks and gulls.

I thought I had the world to myself this morning, but as I come round the bend in the track, I hear I've got company on the shore. The sound of a flute's drifting, swooping like a gull. A little closer and I can see Temple, cross-legged on the jetty, serenading the sunrise.

My, isn't that romantic?

She's pretty good, though, and I stop where I am able to listen.

Temple's the carer at the Residence, which means she does everything that's too skilled for Dad and too menial for Sykes. There are nine patients, which she says is small for a residential unit, but if there were any more of them, I guess Sykes'd have to hire extra help. As it is, she's hard at it most hours of the day. Maybe dawn's the only time she gets to practise her music.

When she arrived, a couple of years ago, I didn't click with her at first. She's into yoga and nature and watching birds: she wanted to take me camping in the woods. In the end it was less trouble to go along, and I actually kind of enjoyed it, apart from the insects down my neck. She told me a bit about her mum, who she never got on with, and I said maybe I was lucky not having a mum at all. She said she always wished she had a sister. It seemed mean to turn her down, so now she's White Sister, I'm Black Sister, and the flute's the third member of the family; she's Silver Sister.

I've got used to having a sister around. Dad still complains about her diet: she tried to get all of us macrobiotic, which was one fight she lost, but there's a shelf in the kitchen full of weird sprouty things she lives on, like a rabbit. She looks ever so slightly rabbity, too, when she smiles, because there's a gap between her front teeth, but she's a cute rabbit, skinny and blonde, in her twenties.

The tune she's playing now is a kind of ballad. She sang it when we went camping, and I remember the words:

> *I know a lady lives in a tower*
> *Her face as fair as the lily flower*
> *Her smile as sweet as the crimson rose*
> *That in her secret garden grows.*

She's winding up on a melancholy trill, when a ferry out in the open sea lets off a long, rude cartoon *PAAARP*, like it's blowing her a raspberry.

I start laughing, and she turns quickly.

'Who's there? Oh, it's you.'

'Morning, White Sis.' I spread out my towel next to her. 'Coming for a paddle?'

'It'll be freezing.'

I dip a hand off the edge of the platform and lift it out fast. She's right, though I'd rather not admit it, and I flick a drop of water at her.

'Couldn't sleep?' I say. My idea is for her to ask me the same, and then I can talk about the dream. She'll probably tell me it's to do with finding my inner path, or being in harmony with the universe, but at least that'll give me something to disagree with.

She doesn't reply. Looking sideways, I see her eyes are red.

'Temple, have you been crying?'

'I had a fight with Eron.'

'Is that all?' I'm relieved: for a second there, I thought it might be something serious. 'Listen, everyone fights with Dad. For me it's like brushing my teeth. If I skip it, I know all day there's something missing.'

She stares out to sea. From here it's waves all the way to wherever. Geography's not my best subject, that's along with all the other subjects that aren't my best, and I don't know what the next land is, but you can't see it.

'Mag,' she says, 'do you want to come away with me?'

'Where to?'

'Wherever we end up. Take a boat. Take a plane.'

Wow, there really is something wrong. Or is she joking? 'Well, yeah, I'd love to see the world sometime.'

'I mean … today.'

I stare at her. She's not smiling.

'Temple, I'm thirteen. I can't go away, I've got school.'

'There are other schools.'

Well, sure, and a few of them have got to be better than Beckwood, but that's hardly the point, is it?

'I've got, you know, like, a father.'

She's playing with the fringe of my towel, tying knots. 'He hits you.'

'Not that often.'

'Once is too often. I told him.'

'Was that what the row was about?'

'That was the start of it. I also said he should talk to you about your mother.'

'Uh-oh.'

'He behaves as if there was never any such person.'

I shrug. 'She's been dead a long time.'

'You've got a right to know,' she insists.

'Know what? It's not like I remember her.'

'It's not good for him, keeping it all bottled up. If he loved her, he should let himself talk about her.'

'Try telling him that. Oh yeah, you did, didn't you? Look, maybe he didn't love her. Maybe she was a cow.

There are kids at school who hate their mums. I mean, how about you with yours?'

'That's different.'

'Of course it is. You've got one, and you couldn't wait to get away from her. You don't need your mum; I don't need mine. We are family – I got all my sisters with me,' I chant tunelessly. I'm trying to cheer her up, but it doesn't seem like I'm doing a great job. She's looking down at the edge of my towel, her fingers still plaiting the fringe, and what I can see of her face looks miserable. 'Don't fret about Dad. You leave him alone, and he'll leave you alone. Whatever you said to him, he'll be over it by now.'

'It's not him, it's Dr Sykes.'

'What's it got to do with Sykes?'

'He said … it'd be better if I moved on.'

'Moved on?' I repeat.

'From the Residence.'

'Hang on. Are you saying you've lost your job? Sykes is booting you out because you ticked Dad off?'

'He's getting me a new posting.'

'Where?'

'I'm not sure yet.'

I start getting up. 'I'll talk to him.'

'There's no point. It's settled. I'm leaving.'

'But …' I sit back down. I feel like I've missed a step in the dark. 'You'll be back, won't you?'

'I don't know. I don't think so.'

'For holidays?'

'I might be going a long way from here.'

'There are still planes.'

'All right, let's say I'll come back. But I don't know when.' She looks at her watch, and sees what she's been doing to my towel. 'Oh, I've wrecked the fringe.'

She has, too. It's kind of dreadlocks now. 'That'll ruin my beach cred,' I say.

She stands up. 'Mag, I've got to go. The cab'll be waiting.'

'What – you're leaving *now*?'

I scramble to my feet.

'Temple – were you not even going to tell me you're going?'

'I didn't know what to say. I don't know what to say now.' She sounds furious, and I take a step back, though I guess it's not me she's angry with. 'You can't come too, either, I know that. I shouldn't have asked you. It was stupid.'

'Stupid's the new smart,' I say, which is a line I made up for myself at school after I failed the history test three times.

She starts up the track, the pebbles scrunching under her sensible nurse's shoes.

I trot after her. 'Look, we'll stay in touch, won't we? As soon as I get a chance, I'll come and visit. You can show me round wherever it is.'

I can't believe she's going; it doesn't feel real. Could I still be asleep and dreaming? I know I'm not, though, when I see the taxi idling on the gravel, and the cases waiting in the porch.

The driver loads her bags in the boot. She gets into the cab, but leaves the door open.

'Mag, keep this.'

She's holding out the flute.

'Don't act crazy,' I say. 'I can't imagine you without her.'

'I want you to have her.'

'Absolutely not. Silver Sister lives with White Sister.'

'You could learn to play.'

'Yeah, right. Like it was such a success when you tried to teach me recorder.'

She looks at me. 'Black Sister ...'

I don't want either of us to start crying, so I say, 'Goodbyes suck.'

She gives me a rabbity smile. 'Yes,' she agrees. 'They really do.'

Then I close the door on her and her flute, and watch as the car drives off. For a while I can hear the sound of the motor.

Now that's gone too, so I go back in the house. I'm thinking I never did get the chance to ask her about the dream.

*

Dad's in the kitchen, loading cutlery onto a tray. 'Hi-ho, hi-ho, it's off to work we go,' he's whistling. It's his favourite tune, and it suits him, because he's a bit of a gnome, with a wide mouth and a big nose. Unfortunately, apart from the colour, I'm a dead ringer for him. It's like I got scanned in a darker tone.

'You're up with the lark,' he says. 'Been seeing Temple off?'

'You knew she was going. You didn't tell me.' I could do with an argument, and he's usually up for one of them.

'She only said last night. You'd gone to bed.'

'You might not have got on with her, but you didn't have to get her thrown out.'

'None of my doing, girl.'

'But it was because you had a row, right?'

'Sounding off about what's none of her business,' he grumbles.

'You could have just got her a warning.'

I'm expecting him to get mad, but he looks sincerely puzzled. 'All I did was tell Sykes what happened.'

'Dr Sykes,' I correct him automatically. We both have a problem calling people their proper titles: Sykes doesn't seem to mind, but it got us a complaint from the Health Inspector last visit.

'Yeah, whatever. I wouldn't have even done that,

except he heard me shouting and asked what was going down. Next thing I know, she's taking the high road. Coulda knocked me down.'

'I wish.'

He doesn't get it for a second; then he coughs and shoves his hand in his pocket without noticing he's still holding a fork. I see the points poke through where the stitching's loose.

'I'm trying hard with my temper. You know that.'

'Yeah, you could do good with practice,' I say, meaning it sarcastic, but he looks pleased. Then he tries to get his hand out of his overalls, and can't think what's gone wrong. 'You stuck a fork in there,' I tell him.

He's got to be the clumsiest guy on the planet: he'd do more damage if he was massive, but luckily he's quite compact. He's also going a bit bald, and his socks don't match.

'I'm sorry about Temple,' he says. 'She's got a good head on her shoulders. I didn't want to lose her neither. Lord knows what they'll send us instead.'

'Let's hope a gorgeous chick with a taste for short, ugly chefs,' I say, and duck out the kitchen when he throws the fork at me.

*

We'll stay in touch, won't we? That's what I said to Temple, and it's not like I haven't tried. I've texted,

13

tweeted, looked on Facebook, rung her number and all I get is *The person you are calling is not available, please try again*. Some days I'm sure she's had an accident, drowned or been in a crash or a terrorist attack, except that would have made the news, wouldn't it? Other times, I think she's just forgotten us. I can't decide which I like less, really, so I tell myself she's lost her phone, that's all.

Instead of her, we got Bella Cole, who's fat and forty and a dim Kiwi. All right, perhaps that's unfair. She could be mid-thirties.

No, ok, if I'm being honest, there's not much wrong with Bella except she's a bit cuddly for my taste. She's got these enormous warm, soft bosoms, and when she puts her arms round you, which she does all the time, it feels like death by duvet. But at least she can have a laugh.

She's not the only new arrival, though, and Gordy Shaw is a real five-star pain. He's called an Intern; he's meant to learn about psychiatric care and help out while he's at it. His hair's straw-coloured, cut long on top and short at the sides, his feet are enormous, and in between he's tall and healthy and bulging with biceps. He talks like he's auditioning for the House of Lords.

Dad thinks the reason I stay out of Gordy's way is because I'm shy.

'I guess you like him more than you let on,' he chuckles.

'Dad, Gordy's nineteen. To him, I'm some little infant who doesn't know how to wipe her own nose yet.'

'So show him different.'

'What, blow it and give him the snot?'

He starts whistling, 'Hi-ho, hi-ho.'

'All right, you're a dwarf,' I snap. 'Do I look like Snow White to you?'

He blinks at me. He didn't even know he was making a noise; it comes automatically.

'You've got a real attitude on you these days, Mag. Want to watch yourself, or you'll never get a boyfriend.'

I can't decide if I should give him a lecture on feminism or just go for him with the bread knife, so instead I stomp out of the kitchen and up to my room. When I sit on the bed, it feels so comfortable I could just lie down and close my eyes, though it's only the middle of the afternoon. Dad's got a point. I am cranky, and I guess it's because I'm short on Zs.

I'm still getting the dream.

Sometimes I get a night off, and then I sleep so deep and sound I feel even dopier than usual in the morning. Next evening I hope for the best, I start drifting off, and there I am, back in the attic with

15

Grace. You'd think I'd get used to it, but the thing is, while it's going on, I don't know it's a dream and I don't know I've had it before; it's all fresh and I'm terrified all over again.

Suddenly I think, Why not do it for real?

That's a crazy notion, Mag.

Well, is it, though? If I did take Grace to the attic, then just possibly that might sort me out.

Yeah, and possibly I'll get an earful from Dad and Sykes.

At least that'd only happen the once.

I don't let myself discuss it any more. I go straight to Dad's room while I know he's in the kitchen, and find the attic key. That's something I've never done in the dream, but I'll need it to get in there.

Now comes the bit I'm really not sure about: Grace.

The thing is, I get on ok with the rest of the patients. I like them better than any of the kids at school, that's for sure. Grace, though, she's the odd one out. It's not just that she doesn't talk, or that when she goes into a strop she starts dribbling and shaking. She's also got this thing like she's better than everyone else, and don't ask me how she gets that across without saying anything; it's the way she looks at you, or through you.

I'm wary of her, to tell the truth, and I'm half hoping she won't be in her room. If she's downstairs with the others, then I'll give up the plan.

Well, Mag, no one's making you do this. Simple enough to put the key back, and go get a cup of tea.

I'll just see if she's there.

I push the door open and my nerves twang. She's sitting on a chair by the window, like she could be waiting. What goes on in her head? Is it nothing, or is there a lot that just doesn't get out past her eyes? That's kind of a frightening thought.

'Grace, come with me,' I say.

Sometimes she pays no attention when you speak, sometimes she does what she's told like she can't be bothered to argue. Now she gets up, and though she's still not looking at me, she starts shuffling towards me in her slippers.

Here we go then. I'm feeling a bit breathless as she follows me down the corridor, back past the other patients' doors, past their bathrooms, then my room and Dad's room and our own bathroom. Just after that, there's a door that looks like a cupboard, but when you open it, there are the steps going up. This isn't the door that's locked; there's another one at the top.

I'm about to start up the stairs when I realize Grace is walking straight on past me. I shoot out a hand to grab her arm, and she stops, swaying a little. I don't think I've ever touched her before. Her wrist feels kind of dry, thin and bony and hot.

'Up here,' I whisper.

Creak … squeak … the steps give a little, and groan under our feet. The noise is just like in the dream.

Now we're at the second door, and I fit Dad's key in the lock. It's stiff, but it turns. The door opens. Here we are in the attic.

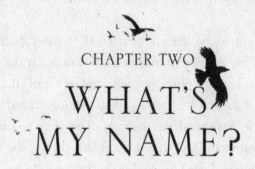

CHAPTER TWO

WHAT'S MY NAME?

It's a big room, runs the whole length of the building, and it's full of stuff Dad might be going to mend if he ever gets time or learns how. Chairs with bust seats, tables with broken legs, a sofa with the stuffing coming out. A couple of old computer units. I don't know why anyone's kept those; it's not like Dad can make them compatible. Everything's thick with dust, and there's a musty, dusty smell.

I shut the door and lock it. When I turn round again, Grace is perched on the mouldy sofa. There's room for two, but I'm not sure I fancy cosying up to her, so I squat on the floor. It's no dirtier down here than anywhere else.

It's dead quiet. There are a couple of pigeons somewhere, chanting oo-coo, oo-coo, and a flutter that makes me jump. They must be nesting in the roof. A plane goes over, high up, a distant hum that fades into silence.

I can almost hear the dust settle.

We've got to wait, haven't we? What are we waiting for?

I've got to be dreaming after all. I must have lain down in my room and dropped off. I'm not waking up, however hard I pinch myself, but it's got to be a dream, it has to be, because I'm getting scared now, like I've always done before. The fear's stirring, tightening round my throat. And like always, the really scary thing is, *I don't know what I'm frightened of.*

It's a dream. I don't have to be frightened.

I concentrate on breathing: slow, normal, calm. Grace isn't making a sound. Has she gone to sleep? No, her eyes are open. She could be watching the dust float and sink in the sun slanting down through the skylight.

How long have we been here?

I'm starting to hear noise from downstairs. Feet moving, doors opening and closing, voices calling.

'Grace! Grace, where are you?' That's Bella.

'Grace, you mustn't hide from us.' Sykes's voice is muffled, two doors and a flight of stairs away, but it's clear what he's saying. 'You need your injection.'

Of course, it's well past time for her jab. What happens if she doesn't get it? I glance up at her. Her head's on one side and her eyes are staring at the beam full of dancing dust. Her mouth's half open and she's drooling slightly. Is she going to have a fit? Could she die?

I have to tell them where we are.

I don't move.

It's a dream; that's all it is.

'We've had enough runaround now, Grace!' Dad barks.

If he loses his rag, I don't want to be the one he gets his hands on first.

'It's all right, babe. We're not angry with you; everything's fine,' Bella sings out. 'We just need to find where you are, that's all.' It's Grace she means: if they knew I was hiding too, they'd be angry sure enough.

The voices get a lot louder suddenly. Someone's opened the door at the bottom of the attic steps.

'I'll check up here,' says Gordy.

'She couldn't have got in,' Bella calls after him, but the steps are creaking – he's coming up.

What if I didn't turn the key all the way?

'Don't move,' I mouth to Grace.

The handle rattles. My heart's thumping so loud I'm surprised he doesn't hear it on the other side of the door.

'Nope, it's locked.'

His big feet go away again down the steps, crash-creak.

'She must have gone outside,' says Bella, and the

21

door at the bottom of the stairs shuts with a click. Their footsteps move off along the corridor; their voices mumble into distance.

I take maybe my first breath in ten minutes.

'So what now?'

I say it out loud.

Grace looks at me, and the dust moves in the air between us.

'No injection.'

What?

'No injection.' She's shaking her head, side to side. 'No. No. No injection.'

She's talking.

I kneel up beside her. 'What's wrong with your jab? You have it every day.'

Her eyes go sideways – a cunning look. I'm in an attic with a madwoman. *Jane Eyre* meets *The Curse of the Zombies*. I try not to think about any horror film I've ever seen.

'Grace. Do you know what's happening? Do you know why we're here?'

We're here because I'm dreaming we're here, or because I want to stop dreaming we're here. Which makes less sense? I'm asking a woman who can't talk. But she spoke to me just now. Did she?

I'm seeing her properly, I guess for the first time. Her eyes are big and wide apart, over curved cheekbones. Her forehead's high and round, the hair cut short, and her mouth's a pretty shape, though her lips are dry. She could have been good-looking once, and she's not as old as I thought, either.

She swallows. 'Maggot,' she says.

'That's not my name,' I tell her. Which is true, though it's not the first time I've been called it. 'Now listen, Grace—'

'That's not my name.'

Is she just repeating what I said to her? I realize she's looking straight at me, really looking.

'That's not my name,' she says again, and her voice is clear though it's quiet. 'Not my real name.'

'Grace is the only name I know for you.' Well, apart from *awkward cow* and such.

'Margot,' she says – *Mah-go*.

Now I'm really surprised, because although that actually is my name, nobody ever uses it. I'm not sure how she'd even know.

'Yes,' I whisper.

'Margot, do you remember your mother?'

Whatever I was expecting, it wasn't that.

'No, I don't,' I say. 'She died when I was little.'

'What do you know about her?'

'Not a lot.'

'You haven't got a picture?'

I shake my head. I've wondered. I mean, Dad's got

to have photos, hasn't he? You wouldn't throw them away. But I've learnt not to ask.

'She was black,' says Grace.

'Well, yeah.'

That doesn't take much working out, as Dad's white. It's kind of a pity we're so identical in other ways – I wouldn't mind not being short and chunky, with a mouth that seems to go halfway round my head when I smile, which is one reason I don't often do it. Still, maybe my mum was no oil painting either.

'Black like me,' says Grace.

'I guess so.'

'I'm your mother, Margot.'

I know I'm dreaming.

'I'm your mother,' she says again. 'You're my daughter.'

People don't lie in dreams. I don't know – do they?

Physically it's possible. She's about the right age, I guess. She's the right colour. No, it's *not* possible.

'What about Dad? He hasn't noticed?' I say.

'Poor Eron. He didn't want to upset you. He thinks I've forgotten, you see. He thinks I'm mad. Who wants a mad mother?'

Not me, lady.

'Look, I'm – I'd like to have you as a mother,' I lie. 'But, well, she's dead. I know she's dead. There's a place where the ashes are scattered and everything.'

24

'You'll know it's true, sometime. Don't worry about that now.'

'Fine, I won't.'

She almost laughs. 'Mouthy kid, aren't you? Listen, we might not have long, and I've got a lot to tell you. Shut up a bit, and remember what I say. I probably won't get a second chance.'

Everything's quiet now below stairs, Sykes and the rest must be out searching the gardens. The sun's going west, the skylight's shading into red.

'It happened ten years ago,' she says. 'You were three.'

'That was when my mother died.'

'No, she didn't. I didn't. That's what I'm telling you. I was part of a – a group.' She hesitates. 'A sort of secret society. There weren't many of us, but we had a lot of power.'

I'm only half-listening. I'm staring at her, wondering if there's any chance she's on the level. Could she be my mother?

'Margot,' she's saying, 'do you believe in magic?'

'Do I what? No.'

She smiles. 'I was a witch. The group I'm talking about, we were witches.'

And it seems stupid, but I don't have a problem with this. Even though I don't believe in magic, and even though I don't think she's my mother, I take the

25

witch bit on like she just told me she used to be on the board of school governors or something. I'm like, ok, she was a witch. And I kind of know it's weird that I don't think it's weird. How weird is that?

'It was called the Bureau,' she goes on. 'We all worked together, to help people.'

'Witches don't help people,' I interrupt.

'That's what you think, because you've been brought up like a normal person. You're not a normal person, and you're going to have to change the way you think.'

Other people have told me I'm not normal, but the way she says it makes it sound as if I'm better that way. For the first time, I feel I might get to like Grace.

'Witches can be good or bad, like anyone else,' she tells me. 'You'll find that out soon enough.'

'Which sort were you?' I ask.

'What do you think?'

I catch myself thinking how nice she looks when she smiles, and I catch myself smiling back.

'Best of the best,' I guess, and she high-fives me.

'I had an enemy. Nilas was his name.' She stops and corrects herself. 'Nilas *is* his name. He still is my enemy. He's a strong witch and a cruel one.'

'Don't you call it a wizard when it's a man?' I want to know.

'A wizard's a wise person; a witch has magic. You

26

can be both. Nilas might be wise but he's wicked. He wanted to take my magic away from me, and he worked a spell. I had to stop him taking my magic.'

'How did you stop him?'

She leans closer to me, looking straight into my eyes. 'I sent it to you. All my power, all my knowledge, all my skill: I sent it all on to little three-year-old Margot.'

I sit back from her. 'I don't have any power or whatever.'

'Not yet,' she agrees. 'You haven't started your periods, have you?'

A good answer to that might be Mind your own business, but I say 'No.'

'But it'll be soon. And when you do, then you'll start to find your powers. That's the way it works. Nobody knows they're a witch before puberty.'

When I come on, I'll be able to do magic? I can't believe I'm believing this.

'I had to do it,' she says. 'There wasn't any other way. But you see, when Nilas worked his spell, something went wrong. We both got hurt. I lost my memory. I didn't know what had happened; I didn't know what had become of my magic. I didn't remember anything.'

I see her frown in the fading light.

'Then they brought me here. The Residence belongs

to Nilas.'

'It's under the District Health Authority.'

'It doesn't matter what it says on the notepaper. Nilas is a witch, remember? A master witch. He runs what he likes. He runs this place.'

My tummy rumbles. It must be suppertime. Down below, the other patients are probably getting their plates and spoons, sitting round the tables. Now Dad's got to know I'm missing too. Will they realize we're together, me and Grace? What'll they do about finding us?

'Go on,' I say.

'But I do have friends, and they did what they could. They've sent someone here to help me, and that's how I've got my memory back.'

'Your memory, but not your magic?'

'That's right. I haven't got my magic, but at least I know what I did with it.'

'You sent it to me.'

She reaches out and takes my hand. And when her fingers slide into mine, just at that second, something happens.

'Mummy,' I say, without meaning to, and I grip her hand like I could fall off the floorboards into space.

She smiles. 'That's right.' But she's not answering the Mummy thing, she's carrying on with what she was

28

talking about. 'That's right, I sent it to you. And one day, soon, you'll start to get it. And then you'll be able to give it back to me.'

She's my mother. She really is. I'm having difficulty concentrating on what she's trying to tell me. 'Give it back. How will I do that?'

'You need to know your name. Not your human name, but your real name. All witches have a name, tied up with their power and their knowledge. You've got to look for your name, Margot, as soon as you can. And then when you know it, you'll be able to give my power back.'

'What if I decide to just hang on to the power?' I ask. 'I might like being a witch.'

Suddenly she's right up close to me, kneeling right in front of me, holding my shoulders with both hands. 'You must come to me *as soon as you can*, Margot. You must find your name *as soon as you can,* and then you must come to me *at once*. Because until you do, you're not safe. I've put you in danger now. Do you understand?'

Not really. I shake my head.

'Nilas could know we've talked. He's got his spies everywhere. He'll guess you know something if he knows you've talked to me. And if he thinks you know something – something that he wants to know ...'

She doesn't tell me what then, but I get the idea it's

not pleasant.

'So you must not mention this, what I've told you, to *anyone*. Except Gordy, if you like.'

'Gordy? Why would I want to talk to him?'

'He's the friend I told you about, the one who's been helping me remember.'

Well, he wouldn't be my choice for sorcerer's apprentice, but I suppose she had to take what was on offer.

'What about Dad?'

'Don't say anything to him.'

'How much does he know, about you and magic and stuff?'

'He never knew I was a witch. There are not many people who can understand when they've got no magic themselves. So I didn't try to tell him, because he wouldn't have believed me. He thinks I had a nervous breakdown and never got over it.'

'But he does know you're you?'

'He took this job at the Residence so he could carry on looking after me.'

Well, if that's true, it's true love for sure.

'Why didn't he tell me who you were?'

'I suppose he thought it would be better for you not to worry about me, wondering if you were going to turn out the same way, getting distressed because I didn't recognize you. Till Gordy started helping me, I didn't know I even had a child.'

That kind of upsets me. Wouldn't you remember having a child, even if you'd forgotten everything else?

'The jabs,' I say, 'the injections. What do they do to you? Why do they give them to you?'

'To keep me quiet. You see, before I got my memory back, if I wasn't sedated, I'd get hysterical. Because all I knew was that I used to be strong and now I was weak. And that I'd been tortured.'

'Tortured!'

'Nilas thought I knew, you see. He thought I had to know – what I'd done with the magic.'

'If you'd remembered, do you think you'd have told him?'

She sounds like I've hurt her.

'Never. Never. That was why I sent it to you – so I'd never never tell.'

Ok, that's the way mothers are meant to feel about their children. I'm not entirely sure I believe her, though, which is odd when you look at what else I'm believing. I mean, if you're being tortured, you're going to say just about anything, aren't you? I know I would.

'Every time I went to sleep …'

I can hear her breathing. It's almost night now; I can barely see her face in the darkness, just the pale grey of her dressing gown.

'Every time, there he was … staring at me … with

31

his one eye …'

'One eye?' That's horrible, somehow.

'He was injured when he worked his spell on me. He was crippled and lost half his sight. But he could see me well enough.' I can hear her swallow. 'Sitting at the end of my bed … watching me … listening … and I knew … it was going to begin again …'

I try to touch her, to comfort her. Her hand's cold. 'That's just dreams,' I say.

She pulls away from me and bursts out laughing. It's more like yelling – a mad witch cackling.

'Just a dream! Just a dream!' She's gasping. 'You don't know anything. Just a dream! *That was the torture*, stupid girl. Every night, every night, do you know what someone can do to you in your dreams?'

I've jumped up to get away from her. The noise she's making – I can't bear it.

'No escape, no way out, never wake up …' She's sobbing, lying on the floor with her fingers in her mouth.

I've got to get out. I fumble with the lock, open the door and stumble down the steps. I can hear people running down below too: someone's heard. I trip and pick myself up and keep on. I've got to get away.

Then there's Dad and Bella and Gordy, and Dad's caught me.

'Don't be frightened,' says Bella. 'It's all right, you're

safe.'

I wipe my eyes and nose on my sleeve. 'I'm ok.'

But I'm wondering if I'm safe anywhere now.

CHAPTER THREE
THE HOLLIES

What happened up there? And what happens next? I don't know what's real and what's my imagination, I can't tell the difference any more.

The night after, I don't get the dream. I sleep like the dead.

When I wake up, I go looking for Grace, but she's back to normal, or not normal, whichever it is. She just stares over my head, and when I take her hand, it's like holding an empty glove. I guess if I'm going to talk to her again, I'd need to get her off the sedatives or whatever they give her, and it's not like anyone's about to take my advice on her meds.

I'm in trouble, of course, but that's nothing new, and I don't say anything about dreams, or witches, or mothers. I just let everyone think I was being naughty, hiding in the attic, messing about. That makes me look like an idiot but it's the best I can do, and Bella gives me spam about being childish – you don't play games when it's a patient's treatment, blah blah.

Dad's trickier. I say I didn't mean to cause trouble, and I won't do it again, and he says I'd better not, but none of that really means anything. It's like both of us are talking to hide what we're thinking. He doesn't get rough with me. I have the idea he might be too worried. Then again, maybe I'm just thinking that, because now I know what's going on in his mind. Or do I? I try every way I can invent to get him to tell me about Grace and if she's really my mother – everything short of asking him straight out. I can't do that. It's too important. What if it isn't true? Then he'd be, like, sorry for me.

After Dad, I go to see Sykes. I usually spend a couple of hours with him every week; he calls it a tutorial. It's not exactly lessons – he doesn't teach me anything – but we listen to music and look at pictures and do word-association, that kind of thing. I think it's to help my development. With what I know now, I wonder if it's anything to do with Grace. I mean, if Dad thinks she's mad, maybe he's worried about me going the same way and has Sykes keep an eye on me. Maybe I am going mad; maybe that's what's happening.

This time we don't do any of the usual stuff; we just have a chat.

'What took you up to the attic, Mag?'

'I wanted to explore a bit.'

'Why was Grace with you?'

'She tagged along.'

He swivels his chair, like he can't think what to say, and takes his glasses off and puts them on again. I notice he's got thinner. He used to be a portly gent, but these days his jacket hangs loose on his shoulders. His beard's gone a bit moth-eaten too.

'Have a biscuit,' he says.

I'm not hungry, but I take one for good manners. It's got a foil wrapper I can play with. That might help keep me awake. His room's very warm and quiet, with thick dark red curtains over the windows, and plenty of times during our sessions I've dozed off, especially when he plays classical music.

He clears his throat. 'It must have been a disturbing experience, seeing Grace become, ah, disturbed. Would you like to talk about it?'

'Not really.'

The silence gets long. I'm wondering if maybe I should tell him because he's the oldest person I know and the cleverest, and he's always been kind to me. I try to look at his eyes, but his glasses reflect the light so you can't really see what's behind.

He starts again. 'I wondered whether, perhaps, she said anything to you before she ... while she ... if she said anything. People with psychiatric problems can have strange delusions, you know that very well, of course. And perhaps she might have said something that worried you.'

What does he know? What does he guess? Grace said not to tell *anyone*. If she was mad, really, she might say that anyway. But if she is really mad, then none of it's true and there's no point telling him, is there?

I shake my head. 'She didn't say anything.'

He sighs. 'I'm getting old.'

Well, yeah, he's ancient.

'I should be able to tell …'

'Tell me what?' For a second I think he might say Grace is my mother.

'No, never mind. Just remember, Mag, if there ever is anything you'd like to discuss, anything at all, I'm always happy to …'

He doesn't finish the sentence, but I get the drift.

'Thank you, Dr Sykes, I really appreciate it,' I say politely, and that seems to be it, so I go away. Poor old Sykes, I'm thinking, he's getting past his sell-by, isn't he?

*

If Temple was here, she could tell me what to do. I hold my phone, wondering if it's worth one more try.

What would I say if I got through?

Hi, White Sister – it's me. Listen, you know you said Dad should tell me about my mother? Well, turns out she's not dead after all. No, he didn't tell me that, she told me herself. Wait for it – she's Grace. Yeah, that Grace. I know – but she did talk to me. She told me she used to be a witch, and pretty soon I'm going to be a witch too.

Even Temple wouldn't believe that.

How come I believe it? Do I believe it?

In the attic, when Grace held my hand, I didn't have to think. I knew.

But now?

I click on Temple's number.

It doesn't even ring. I just get the unobtainable signal.

*

So that leaves Gordy. Grace said he was the only one I could talk to, but when I set eyes on him, I can't bring myself. I've got to do it, though, and it better be this weekend because Tuesday I'm back to school.

I go for a swim, trying to get my brain in gear, and when I come back from the sea, I'm absolutely going to find Gordy and get this out on the table. But before I can even dump my towel or shower the salt out of my hair, here's Dad.

'I need a word.'

I tense up. What's coming? Is he going to tell me about Grace?

'Come in here.' It's called his office, but really it's just a big cupboard off the kitchen with a laptop and a phone and that – sometimes he has to order supplies. I sit on the stool and he hitches his bum on the edge of the desk. 'You've got to go to school,' he tells me.

Like I might have forgotten? 'Day after tomorrow,' I agree.

'Different school.'

'What? You're kidding.'

He's looking sullen, not meeting my eyes. Bad sign.

'You can't make me change school with two days' notice,' I say. Not that I'm in love with Beckwood, but at least I know the score there.

He gets up, puts his hands in his overall pockets, stamps about with his shoulders hunched up. 'It's not the school; it's being here. I got a letter – social services sticking their oar in. *Not an appropriate environment*,' he quotes, articulating like he's having tea with the vicar. 'I guess they've got a point.'

'But wherever I go to school I'm going to be living here. Unless it's a boarding school.'

'Uh-huh.'

I stare at him. '*Boarding* school? Where?'

'Crossbeams.'

I'm silent because I think somebody is pulling somebody's leg.

'Yeah, I know.' He coughs, scratches his ear. 'I thought the same, April Fool. But I rang them up and all. Seems on the level.'

'Are they asking you to *pay* for it?'

Crossbeams is the rich kids' school. They wear blazers.

'Full grant. Special circumstances.'

'Dad, it's not – is it anything to do with what happened, you know, in the attic?'

It does mean something, I can tell from his expression.

'You know I told you I wouldn't do anything like that again,' I go on, 'you know I promised.'

Steer clear, I warn myself urgently. He doesn't want to talk about it. But if I push him a bit further, maybe now I'll find out?

'If the problem's me being here, at the Residence,' I say, 'we could both go, couldn't we? I mean, you could get a different job. We don't have to stay here.' Except he does if it's true what Grace said. He can't leave her, can he?

'You think jobs grow on trees?'

'You're a good cook. Sykes'd give you a good reference,' I insist. 'We could go anywhere. I could carry on at Beckwood or somewhere else but, like, an ordinary school. I mean, Crossbeams? Hello? Dad, think about it.'

'I'm thinking you don't know how lucky you are.'

'Yeah, but I don't *want* to,' I say desperately. 'Doesn't that mean anything? What I want?'

His face is stony; he thinks he's not giving anything

away. 'You gotta try it out.'

'If there was another reason,' I probe, 'why you should stay here – if you just tell me – I mean, if it was, like, Mum made you promise or something—'

I'm crashing red lights here.

'I've heard enough – you stop this talk now.' He's scowling.

'What the hell's wrong with that? If Mum wanted—'

'No call for that kinda language!'

'What language? Mum's not a bad word!'

He kicks over a wastepaper bin. 'You'll do as you're told!'

'I just want to get told the truth!' I yell and stand up: mistake. Next thing, I'm on the floor.

'Are you surprised they want to take me away from you?' I mutter, but I've got a hand over my mouth and he doesn't hear.

'It's not me, all right?' he shouts. 'I'm not sending you away. It's them, it's, you know, the government. They tell you to jump, you jump. Doesn't matter what Sykes says either. He's got to play by the rules too.'

'Ok.' I pick myself up. I guess I haven't proved anything. Sometimes when I behave badly, he's upset because he thinks he's not bringing me up right. If that's the official word now, it'd be enough to get him on the boil without dragging Mum into it. 'I hear you,' I say. 'But Dad – it's Sunday. Am I meant to go on

Tuesday? I'll need uniform. I'll need books. I mean …'

'I know. I told 'em we'd want a bit more time, but they wouldn't stretch it. Said you can't miss the start of term. Get all the gear when you're there.'

'Did they only just let you know?'

'Got the letter this morning, been on the phone ever since.' He stretches out a hand, strokes his finger down my cheek, not quite touching it. 'You ok?'

'Yeah.' My face isn't hurting much where he slapped it, though I've hit my knee.

'I'll come with you Tuesday.' It's not an apology, but at least it's a gesture – he'd probably rather pull out his own teeth than set foot in a posh school. 'It's, you know, an opportunity for you,' he adds.

'Going to Crossbeams? You don't think they've got the idea that I'm, like, a genius or something?' If so, man, are they in for a surprise. 'Or you reckon I'll meet a millionaire and get married?'

He laughs, and that seems like a good place to leave it. I'm not going to get any more out of him.

*

I don't want to go. I'm not going to go. If I've got my mother now, I can't go. All right, she's a patient in a mental home, but I can kind of get to know her, even though she can't talk to me since she's back on the drugs. She looks at me different from how she did before. Ok, she doesn't, but I look at her different.

What made me go with her to the attic? I haven't had the dream since I did it.

Dreams don't mean anything.

Do you know what someone can do to you in your dreams?

Don't think about that.

Could Dad have fixed it, just to get me away from her? I don't think so. How'd he get the school to agree? It's not like he's got money to bribe anyone.

Or is it a plot? Is it her enemies separating us?

Stupid: that magic stuff, that's a fantasy, that's all it is. Mad people make up stories.

But she wouldn't have made up that; she's my mother. Would she?

I'm going to talk to Gordy.

*

He's making beds, but when he sees me hanging round the door he puts down the pile of sheets.

'Come outside,' I say.

'Sure thing.' He grins at me like a toothpaste ad. He always looks so clean and wholesome – he makes me feel grubby. 'I thought you might want a chat.'

We go out in the garden and sit on a bench. I'm not sure how to start this conversation without sounding like an idiot.

'Is it true?' I blurt out.

'Yep, all true.'

'Grace is really my mother?'

'Oh, that? Yes, sure.'

'What do you mean, "that"?'

'I thought you meant ...' He stops and looks at his feet. There's plenty there to look at. 'I don't know how much she told you.'

This is where it could get ridiculous. 'Witches,' I manage to say.

He looks relieved. 'Witches,' he agrees.

'Spells, magic ... I'm going to be a witch myself?'

'All of that.'

'Yeah, but Gordy, I don't believe in it. Magic, it's like, it's not *real*. Next thing you'll tell me Father Christmas is coming down the chimney.'

'Wrong time of year.' He nudges me. 'I'm kidding.'

Give me patience.

'Look, Mag, I know how you're feeling. But once you, well, once you get your own magic, then you won't have that problem. You'll know it's true.'

That happens when I start my period, according to Grace. 'How does it work for boys?' I ask, without thinking, and then my own face goes hot when I see him blush. 'No, ok, don't answer that. I know you get a change too.'

'Happens to us all,' he mumbles. 'Listen, have you talked to anyone else, about what she told you?'

'Nobody.'

'Eron? Bella? Dr Sykes?'

45

'Sykes asked if Grace said anything, and I said she just went funny and started crying.'

'Did he believe you?'

I shrug. 'He stopped asking.'

'Fair enough. You did pretty well.'

'Cheers.' I don't need Gordy's approval.

'Pity they got to know you were up there at all.'

'Oh, like I could do a lot about that!' I don't need constructive criticism either. 'She was going into one, it was really …'

'Yes, of course. It must have upset you.'

'Gordy, is it always going to be the same? I mean, either she's getting the drugs, and she just sits and stares and doesn't talk, or else she's throwing a wobbly?'

'She's been on that stuff ten years.' He makes a face. 'Mind control. Give us time and we'll get her straight.'

'How much time?'

'You can't make a date with fate.' He nods like he's said something amazingly profound. 'It's not going to happen right away.'

'The thing is, I've been told I've got to go to boarding school. Dad got some letter. I'm supposed to start the day after tomorrow.'

'You happy with that?' he asks.

'Happy? Sure, I'm walking on sunshine.'

He looks surprised. 'Good you're feeling positive.'

Someone didn't take A-level sarcasm. 'I mean I'm *not*,' I explain. 'I have to stay near Grace, don't I? If I've got to look for my name or whatever, and give it back to her, then ...'

'Calm down, dear,' he says, which annoys me because I wasn't shouting. 'It might not be such a bad thing if you weren't around for a while. If you're here, you're going to want to check on Grace, see how she's getting along. And that's going to look unnatural, because why would you suddenly take an interest? You can never be sure who's watching.'

I thought it'd make me feel better, talking to Gordy about all this. Instead it's giving me the creeps.

'But what if someone wants to get me away from her? Can it just be coincidence, so quick after I find out she's my mum and everything?'

'What did the letter that Eron got say?' he asks.

'Basically, how I shouldn't be living at the funny farm.'

'Let's call it a care home.'

'Let's call it Disneyland if you like.'

'Well, I suppose it's not exactly a normal way to bring up a child.'

'According to Grace, I'm not a normal person. Can you imagine how well I'm going to fit in at Crossbeams?'

'Crossbeams!' He opens his baby-blues wide.

47

'That's the school they're sending me to.'

'Ok-a-a-ay.' He's screwing up his face like he's doing sums in his head. Two and two could be his limit, not that I'm one to talk.

'I mean, that place costs a fortune. They're giving me a grant. Why would they do that?'

'Shh,' he says.

'Don't shush me!'

'I'm thinking. Listen, Mag, did Grace mention to you someone called ...' He pauses, glances over his shoulder, and whispers, 'Nilas?'

I swallow. 'Yeah. So I'm not just being paranoid? You think it's down to him?'

'There's no sense taking chances.' He claps his hands like he's calling the meeting to order. 'You did the right thing to come to me. I should be able to sort something.'

I look at him, long and fair and muscly. He'd probably be ok in a punch-up, but I guess right now I'd prefer a touch of cunning, brainpower, something sneaky. I mean, it's magic we're dealing with, isn't it?

'Can't we get some extra help?' I suggest. 'What about the group Grace was in, what was it, the Bureau? Do you know who they are? Can you get in touch with them?'

'Mag, you don't understand the situation.'

'So how about you try explaining?'

He stands up. 'That'll have to be another time. I've got things to do, calls to make.'

Hello, it's Executive Gordy.

'You'd better play along, do your packing. Make out you're going to Crossbeams all serene. Come on, let's get moving.'

'Yes, *Sir.*' I stay sitting. 'Excuse me, Sir, did I mention you're a prat?'

He turns back and leans down, putting one of his huge hands on the bench each side of me. 'Listen, I'm guessing what could have happened is that Nilas heard you were with Grace.'

I wriggle to get away from him. 'You're in my sun,' I say, but I know that's not why I'm feeling cold.

'If that's so, perhaps he wants to talk to you. Maybe you're cool with that, maybe not. Maybe he's going to try again with Grace too. Get the picture?'

'Full colour.'

He lets me go, with another well-flossed smile. 'Except I'm in charge of protecting both of you. Don't worry. Leave it with me.'

Don't worry? Yeah, that's going to be so easy.

*

When Gordy said he'd sort something, did he mean I won't have to go? He didn't exactly say that, but I don't see what else he could have meant.

Still, he said to do my packing, so I'm doing it. If I was going to boarding school, what would I take?

I wear a big T-shirt in bed; they're all a bit manky. I bet everyone at Crossbeams has pyjamas.

Do I take Little Bear? Yeah, if I want everyone calling me Christopher Robin.

Oh, like I'm going to be Ms Popular if I just don't take my teddy.

At Beckwood, the school I'm at now, I'm the reject, the one nobody talks to. They don't exactly give me a hard time, but that's only because I can kick. They call me Maggot.

When I was just starting there, everyone had to write what they were called. I wrote M-A-G-O-T. Mrs Chinch laughed; she said, 'I don't think that's your name. Do you know what a maggot is?'

Even my dad calls me Mag.

If I go to Crossbeams I can be Margot. *Mah-go*.

But I'm not going to Crossbeams. I hope I'm not. I wish I knew what Gordy was planning.

Parrot puts her head round my door.

'Hi, Parrot – I'm packing.'

'I'm packing!' she repeats. She comes and sits on my bed and watches me. She's left the door open, and whenever someone goes past she calls out 'I'm packing!' Then they have to come in and watch too. Before long I've got a roomful of Hollies.

The Hollies are what we generally call the patients because that used to be the house's when this place was a house, and there's still a faded old sign for The Hollies behind the shiny one that says The Residence. There aren't any holly bushes, though, not any more. Dad says there must have been once, and he tried planting a couple, but they didn't take. It would have been handy for Christmas decorations.

Anyway, saying Hollies is kind of nicer than inmates, or nutters, or whatever. They're all right, you know, they're pretty sorted for mad people. I wouldn't exactly call them my friends, but they're probably my family, seeing as I've lived here ever since before I can remember.

'Are you going away?' asks Chough.

He's my favourite Holly. He's big and bald with three pink chins; he's cuddly and gentle. Nobody ever gets his name right – you say it 'Chuff'.

'Boarding school. I'll be back next holidays.'

'Back next holidays,' Parrot consoles me. Parrot's not her real name, obviously. She looks a bit like one, though, as well as the repeating thing: she's got this crest of hair that sticks up on top of her head, and she loves bright colours. Today she's wearing a yellow nightie and an orange fire blanket.

'One, nine, seven, sixty-three.' Mrs Frisch is counting my socks. She's happy – she likes numbers.

Chough puts Little Bear in my case. I take him out again.

Abram and Lewis come in. Lewis is very white and Abram's very black. Abram strikes a pose in the doorway.

'I am MAD!' he announces.

'Join the gang,' I invite him.

'Nobody here is mad like I am. I am entirely lunatic.'

'Excellent, shut the door.' He doesn't.

Lewis gets a piece of chalk out of his pocket and starts scribbling on the wall.

WILL YOU WRITE TO US? I'LL WRITE TO YOU.

'You're writing to me now. Stop it – I'll have to clean it off.' He writes on everything: windows, tables, his own arms, other people's arms if he can get them to sit still long enough.

IT IS LOVELY WEATHER HERE. HOW IS IT WHERE YOU ARE?

'Lewis, we're in the same room.' I might as well save my breath. He's starting on one of his poems:

> SUN BRIGHT SUN LIGHT
> OUR EYES REACT TO BURNING RAYS
> LIGHT IS ONLY IN THE MIND
> AND DARKNESS TOO

'Twenty-nine, three times ten, eighteen,' says Mrs Frisch.

'Did you know I'm the King?' Chough asks Little Bear.

'I have a first-class degree in blue underpants,' says Abram.

I chuck Abram and Lewis out, but almost at once I get Jennifer and Perkin and Betsy. They've been cooking or something; they're covered in flour.

'Go away, you're making a mess.'

'We'll miss you,' says Chough.

'Miss you!' Parrot starts crying, and Perkin joins in, though he doesn't know why.

'I'll miss you too.' It's true, I will. Except I won't because I'm *not* going to Crossbeams.

Thin little Jennifer comes up close and starts whispering. 'Are they taking you?'

'I'm going to a new school.'

'Be careful, oh be careful! They're always trying to take me. It's because of who I am and what I know. I have to be on my guard all the time.'

She's spooking me. What if she's right? I could say the same thing and everyone would think I was mad. Maybe I am. How would I know?

Chough sees I'm looking worried. 'Good girl!' he shouts. 'Good boy, good girl!'

I think he used to have dogs.

Betsy decides now is a good moment to start taking off all her clothes. She likes to strip, and she has a song to go with it, 'Ba-boom-ba … BOOM,' which starts quite quietly so sometimes you don't notice for a bit, till she's down to her undies.

*

The rest of the day and all of Monday, I'm trying to get Gordy on his own and find out what's happening, but either I'm not lucky or else he's avoiding me. In the end, late Monday night, I go to his room, but the door's locked.

'Gordy!' I whisper, tapping on the panel. 'Gordy, it's me! Let me in!'

Nothing.

Where is he; what's he doing? I'm kicking myself I didn't ask him more questions when I had the chance in the garden yesterday.

I can't hang round his door all night; it's going to look really weird if anyone sees me. I go back to my own room, and sit up awake in case he comes to find me, but now the sun's nudging up over the sea. It's Tuesday morning.

I go down to breakfast, and still no Gordy.

Any minute now, Dad's going to get my case and take me out to catch the bus to the other end of the Island. Everyone who lives here just calls it that, like there's only the one island in the world. It's not big, but it's got quite a lot of people, because the laws are different. If you run your business from here, then you hardly have to pay any tax, and the weather's nice too, so there are holiday cottages.

'Mag, babe, I've got sandwiches for you.' Bella gives me a plastic bag with chocolate in it as well and a thermos. It's like I've got a day's travel ahead of me, though actually the journey probably takes an hour. It would if I were going.

'Thanks.'

'You'll ring then, won't you, pumpkin?' She folds me into her breasts, and I stand very stiff because I'd rather not do anything stupid like start crying. *Where is Gordy?*

'Ok, let's get the show on the road.' There's Dad, carrying my case, and I realize suddenly what I might have known all along: Gordy's messed it up. Whatever he thought he could do to stop me getting sent to the new school, it hasn't worked, and that's why he's been keeping out of my way, because he can't admit he's not smart enough to sort it out.

I'm going to Crossbeams.

'Wait a sec,' I say.

Dad shouts something, but I've run off before anyone can stop me. It's early; the Hollies are all still in their rooms.

Grace is sitting on her bed in her dressing gown.

She doesn't turn her head when I come in.

'I'm going away. I've got to go to school.'

I'm standing right in front of her. She blinks, but her eyes aren't looking at me.

'I've come to say goodbye. I'll be back soon. I'll think about you.'

Can she hear me? Is she listening?

I bend down and kiss her on the cheek. I'd like her to hold me for a moment, but her hands lie still on her lap. Her face twitches a bit when I kiss her, but she doesn't move away.

CHAPTER FOUR
HUMPH

'Look, there's a squirrel.'

'Nice,' I say, though I haven't seen it. I didn't get any sleep last night and my eyes keep closing.

'Used to be loads of animals here.' Dad doesn't often get a day trip, and now on the bus he's like a little kid, taking an interest in everything. 'Hares, ferrets, badgers in the evening.'

We're on the main road. Down south, where we're heading, the Island's pretty built up, but round here it's mostly moorland and woods, with Mountbenet sticking up in the middle. Bella says it's not a real mountain, just a big hill, but I guess if you're from New Zealand, everywhere else looks dinky.

'Not so much wildlife since they started the Network building,' Dad goes on. 'Will you look at that thing?'

There's a huge double fence with spikes on top, cutting out a segment of the wood and disappearing into the trees.

'New since I was up this way.' Dad cranes his neck to get a better look. 'Security guards and all.'

Network's the big IT company. They're constructing here but there's been trouble ever since they started, people say there's a jinx. First the foundations turned out dodgy and they had to underpin. Then they hit water and the whole site was flooded out, and they just got that sorted when somebody broke in and torched the place. I guess they don't want anything more to happen.

'Crazy idea anyway,' Dad grumbles. 'Why build it in the woods? Just spoiling the landscape for everyone.'

I'm drifting off to the sound of his voice; I'm so sleepy I can't fight it any longer.

*

I'm dreaming. The bus is stopping. Everyone wonders what's happening. The driver gets out of his seat.

The door opens and somebody gets on. He's tiny, maybe four feet tall, with pointy ears and covered in shaggy brown hair.

'Stick 'em up!' he growls, brandishing a stick of celery.

I expect everyone to start laughing, but instead they're gasping and screaming, getting down behind their seats like it's a gun he's holding.

'Money on the floor.' It's hard to make out what he's saying, but people get the idea and start chucking their wallets down.

Dad's holding my hand tight and muttering to me. 'Don't be frightened, now, Mag. Don't worry; it's going to be ok.'

I realize I'm not asleep after all, and I open my eyes.

Now I can see why everyone's scared: the person who's got on is neither small nor hairy. He's a rifle-toting seven-foot mugger in a hoodie.

He swaggers down the bus, scooping up purses as he goes, and stops next to us.

He jerks his head at me. 'Off the bus.'

'Who, me?'

Why aren't I frightened? When there's nothing but footsteps on the stairs, I'm petrified. Now I'm on the wrong end of an Uzi, I'm like, hey, whatever. What is *wrong* with me?

I climb down to the ground. There's a mean black Harley rammed across the road just ahead of the bus.

'On the bike,' says the robber.

'Are you crazy?' Dad tumbles out behind him.

The robber ignores him and uses the gun to push me towards the bike. I make like the man says and get on. No point arguing with metal.

Dad sees it different. 'She's not going nowhere with you,' he declares, and takes a swing at the guy.

Next thing he gets the gun butt right in the stomach. He falls on his knees, gagging.

'Dad!' I go to jump off the bike, but I don't get a chance; the guy's on behind me, he's grabbed me round the waist, and he doesn't even kick the gas: the machine barks and leaps away up the road like it's alive.

*

I've never been on a motorbike before. I'm half-terrified, half-thrilled; I'm sure as hell not going to struggle, though my belly's aching for Dad.

The road flies away beneath us, and the wind scours my face. We head into the woods up a lane that turns into a track.

As we go on, I notice that the grip round my middle feels less muscular. I look down and see a furry brown hand, or maybe I'd even call it a paw. The roar of the bike is quieter, more rhythmic, more like ... panting.

What I'm sitting on isn't a seat – it's a back. Chrome handlebars shrink, sprout hair, flap in the wind: ears. We're riding a big black dog.

He's still galloping pretty quickly. He gets off the track and right in among the trees, jumping over fallen logs and diving under branches. I duck my head to keep clear, and after a few minutes the dog slows to a trot and pulls up.

Whatever's got hold of me lets go. I scramble down and turn round to look: correct, it's the Celery Gangsta.

We're under a big beech tree, with a clear space a

few feet all around the trunk. Beyond that the wood's thick, and there's no path that I can see. I'm looking at these two and they're looking at me, the dog with its long pink tongue hanging out.

'Who are you?' I ask.

The little guy, creature, whatever, twitches his whiskers. 'I'm Humph. This here's Bargus.' The dog wags its tail.

'Gets yer off of there no trouble, ennit?' The thing's voice is squeaky, not gruff like it was on the bus, and he's got an accent that goes up and down, like some of the old people on the Island, with furry 'r's. 'Come on down the cave.'

He doesn't wait for an answer: there's a big hole among the roots of the beech, and he pops into it like a rabbit.

Ok, I'm a sucker, but I have to find out what's going on. I follow him down, finding steps under my feet. There's just room for me to stand upright, and once we're at the bottom, the space opens out into a cave about the size of the Residence canteen.

The floor's hard earth; the ceiling's plaited twigs. At one side there's a hearth of stones with a banked-up fire keeping warm. It's all very tidy and clean.

Humph drags a couple of upside-down plastic crates next to the fire and sits on one of them. 'Park yerself, missy.'

I stay standing. 'How did you do that? You looked tall back there and, well, not hairy. You had a gun.'

'Shifts me shape, I do. Often comes handy,' he agrees.

'You hit my dad,' I accuse him. My own stomach's hurting still.

'Has to be done, ennit? Can't get yer out of it no other way. That being the point of the exercise.'

'I thought *that* was the point of the exercise.' I point to the pile of other people's wallets on the floor where he's dumped them.

'Oh no, missy. Hobs doesn't use no money.'

'You're a hob? What's a hob?'

'Never heard of hobs? Times is changing for sure.'

'If you don't want money, why did you hold up the bus?' I ask.

'Gets yer off of it, dunnit?' he says as if it's obvious. 'All me own plan, and don't let nobody tell yer hobs is thick. That's a smart piece of work. This way, see, everybody's looking for a robber, big man. Nobody's looking for no hob. Nobody's looking for *you*.'

'My dad's going to be looking for me.' My brain starts catching up with my ears. 'Hold on. Do you mean it's all about *me*?'

'Ain't nobody told yer?'

'Nobody's told me anything!' I'm feeling a bit dizzy and I sit down at last. Humph blinks at me: his eyes are small and round and very dark.

'Nobody ain't told me much neither,' he admits. 'Long time I ain't talked to no human. What does they call yer, missy?'

'Mag.'

'Happy to meet yer, Mag.'

'Yeah, you've made my day and all. Just tell me what's going on, and I'll kiss you on both cheeks.'

His ears go back in alarm.

'Give me a break,' I beg. 'Why am I here? What are you going to do with me?'

'I ain't gonta do nothing with yer!' He spreads his paws. 'All I knows is yer on the bus, I gets yer off of there and saves yer from the Bureau.'

'From the Bureau?' That's the group my mother worked for. Why would I need saving from them?

Humph's lip curls up, showing sharp little teeth. 'The Bureau's the witches wants to kill the Others.'

'What others? Other witches?'

'No, they doesn't kill no witches; they kills the Others.'

'*What* others?' This conversation's going nowhere.

'Two kinds, ennit? Humankind and Otherkind. Your lot and our lot.'

'Your lot are hobs?'

'Not all hobs, no, missy!' He snuffles: I think he might be laughing. 'Plenty more. There's brags, like

Bargus, there's little fellers lives underground, and there's big fellers lives in the cliffs. Then there's erls, and the green fellers in the trees, and mers in the water.'

He can't mean what it sounds like. 'All these people aren't human?'

'Humans is your sort, and witches – they're humans but smarter. Used to be we all gets on no trouble. We has our places and you has yours. Yer doesn't mess with us and we doesn't mess with you. Not much,' he adds.

'What do you mean, not much?'

'Well, there was the odd bit of hassle, time to time. Humans stealing treasure off of big fellers, erls taking human kids, always somebody can't keep their hands off of other fellers' stuff.' He catches me looking at the pile of wallets. 'Hobs doesn't use no money.'

'Yeah, you told me that.'

'Hobs and humans, we goes way back. Hobs likes best to live in human houses, used to keep things tidy and the humans done give us milk. Years it bin since I had a bowl of milk.'

'I've got some milky tea.' I get the thermos out of my bag. 'Want some?'

His ears twitch. 'Milk? Real milk?'

I get it open and pour him a cupful. He laps it up like a cat.

'Oh, ain't that the real stuff. Oh, ain't that sweet.'

'It's got sugar in. Go on about the Others.'

'Like this, see. Used to be room for everyone, plenty of space. We didn't mix, even the hobs only came round at night when the humans was in their nests.'

'Beds.'

'Beds! All comfy and white and blankets. I slept in a bed one time.' He sighs. 'So there ain't no trouble, them days, see? But the Others was always night-time fellers, so the humans didn't see us round, and then they got this new god who didn't like the Others and he said we ain't really there, or if we was, then we was naughty things, demons.'

I think he's talking about long ago in the past.

'Well, so the humans, they thought we was just stories, so they didn't need to take no care no more. They could build their houses where they liked, and roads too. Never no mind if it was the little fellers' caves or cutting down the trees where the green girlies live.'

I'm listening to something that isn't human, a hairy creature with wiggly ears, and he's telling me the world's full of things out of kids' stories: goblins and elves, mermaids and giants.

'Just up from here a ways,' Humph goes on, 'them woods used to be home for I dunno how many, but the humans been building and they's druv off a heap of us. Same story all over, that's what they says. Gets worse all the time. The humans doesn't want us no more; they doesn't give the hobs no milk.' His ears droop.

I offer him the thermos. 'Have some more.' I'm feeling a bit sick anyway; sweet, milky tea's the last thing I fancy. 'So where did the Others go, the ones who used to live in the woods?'

'They didn't go nowhere. They died. See, humans, they moves around, they likes to move, but the Others doesn't like to move. Us hobs, we can pack up if we needs, go to a new home, but we sooner stays put in one place. Most of the Others they can't do it no way. Yer land's where yer lives, see? If yer can't live on yer land, yer can't live nowhere.'

He breaks off and looks at me: I'm holding my tummy. 'Yer not feeling too clever?'

'Just a stomach ache. Go on.'

'So us Others got nervous first, and then we got narked, and some of us turned nasty. Trying to keep humankind off our land. Whoooh!' he shouts, waving his arms. 'Bogeyman! Clear off or the demons'll get yer!'

'And what's the Bureau?'

'Them's the smartest witches, them's who tells the rest of the witches what to do.'

'Like a government?'

'Like that maybe, ennit?' Humph looks doubtful; I don't think he knows what I mean.

'The witches still knows the Others,' he goes on. 'Even when most of the humans forgot we was ever real, the witches knew better. There's no shapeshifter can't fool no witch; a witch always sees yer real form.'

Maybe that's why I had that dream-that-wasn't-a-dream on the bus, when I saw Humph with the celery. But I'm not a witch, not yet anyway.

'There was times some of the witches was friendly with the Others,' Humph tells me, 'but the Bureau, they sees the humans was stronger, so they says, mates, we ain't gonta help the Others no more. We're human, says the Bureau, and we're on the human side, and we're gonta sweep the floor clean of them dirty Others, and then we can take all the land and keep all the milk.' He plays with the thermos.

'Finish it off if you want.'

There's still quite a bit left, but it all goes down. Humph up-ends the flask over his mouth to get the last drops out. 'Aah. That takes me back a ways, that taste.' He pats his stomach and burps. 'Pot's empty, hob's full.'

He leans back and his eyes start to close. I keep quiet: there's more I'd like to ask him, but I could do with some time to think.

Grace was a witch; she was with the Bureau. 'We

worked together, to help people,' that's what she said, and from what Humph told me just now, I'm guessing she meant they protected human beings from the Others. She said there are good witches and bad witches: the Bureau's the good ones, and Nilas is bad. He's got to have ganged up with the Others.

Getting me sent away to school, I thought that was Nilas. I still reckon he's got to be behind it, but maybe it's not the school that's important. Maybe the point was to get me on a bus out in the woods where the Others could get hold of me. And what'll they do with me, now they've got me? They'll hand me over to Nilas.

Humph starts to snore.

I can't quite believe he's going to give me up to be tortured. I know, I'm soppy about furry things.

But just because a few of the Others are friendly, like him, doesn't mean the rest of them aren't horrible. I mean, in fairy tales, there are kind of cute little leprechauns and stuff, and then there are ogres and werewolves and monsters. I can see why the Bureau would want to get rid of them.

Humph thought he was *rescuing* me. He doesn't know my mum was with the Bureau. Someone's been telling him lies; someone's told him I'm on the other side – the Other side. Who's lied to him? Nilas. It has to all come back to him because he's the one Mum and

Gordy told me to be scared of. The single reason anyone's interested in me is because of Mum, and her enemy is Nilas. And now he's got me where he wants me.

I get up and start tiptoeing gently towards the steps.

'Where yer off to?' I never heard him move, but he's standing up, fully awake.

'I was looking for the toilet.' It's not totally a lie, either.

'Toilet?'

'Come on, even hobs must go to the toilet. You know …' I try to think of a polite way of explaining. 'Do you just go in the woods?'

'Oh, that! Hole in back there.'

'Humph, how did you know I was going to be on the bus? Who told you?'

'Sylvian got a message from the witch feller.'

Ok, that settles it. I don't know who Sylvian is, but there's only one witch wants me in his party bag. I'm going to have to get out of here.

*

Humph's hole is just that, a pit dug in the earth. What's more, hobs obviously don't use toilet paper, so it's lucky I've got tissues in my pocket.

I undo my trousers and then realize I'm going to have to take them right off to get over the hole. It's while I'm getting undressed that I notice there's blood.

Where's that from? I wasn't the one who got hit.

Then I get it.

I've started my period.

That means I'm a witch now.

CHAPTER FIVE

IN THE WOODS

I've got tissues stuffed in my knickers and a plan of sorts in my head.

Humph is giving the stolen wallets a once-over; he's emptied out the contents and spread them around on the floor.

'Don't do that, you'll never be able to sort them out and give them back.'

'What for'd I want to give 'em back? What's these things would yer say?'

'Bank cards. People need them. You said you didn't want them.'

'No need for such; no need at all. Toys and rubbish.' He gets a box and starts putting everything away with care.

I'm not pushing the point; I've got other things to ask.

'You're very clever to be able to do that thing, what did you call it, shifting your shape,' I say.

'Ah, that's a knack.'

'I bet not many people can do it.'

'Brags can shift, like Bargus; he can run fastest too. Green fellers, they does it natural, but they only makes tree-shapes. Sylvian, she's a champion shifter.'

'Who's Sylvian? Is she one of the Others?'

'She's all of the Others, maybe.'

That doesn't make anything clearer.

'Can witches do it?'

'I never seen a witch shift, but I reckon they can learn. Smart fellers, the witches.'

Maybe I'll be able to change shape one day. I fancy being a motorbike, but I mustn't get sidetracked here.

'I shouldn't think anyone's much smarter at it than you.' I'm laying on the flattery as thick as I can. 'Do you just change the way you *look*, or is it actually the way you *are*?' This is important.

Humph has to think about it for a minute.

'How I am,' he says at last. 'If I'm a robber, then I'm strong like a robber. I ain't never gonta be so strong nor so fast as Bargus, maybe, but I can talk and he can't. So we changes, but there's things doesn't change.'

I'm not sure if that answers the question, but I'm going to have to take the chance.

'I suppose changing into something large like a robber isn't so very hard,' I say.

'Ain't it?' Humph bristles. 'Ain't so easy neither.'

'What I meant was, isn't it even more difficult to turn yourself into something very small? All that fine detail. I bet you have to be *really* clever to turn yourself into something tiny. Maybe you can't do that.'

'I can so.'

'I'm sorry, Humph. I didn't mean to make you feel, you know, stupid. Just because you can't turn yourself into something little like a snail maybe. I mean, you shouldn't be ashamed.'

'No, nor I ain't!'

One minute there's a hairy brown hob, next there's a shiny brown snail jutting its horns at me. The minute after that, I've popped the snail into the empty thermos flask and got the lid on, and then I'm running up the steps and putting my head out among the beech roots.

*

When I'm well away, I stop running and start thinking.

What now? Number one: find out where Dad is. Correction: number one – find out where I am. I wasn't paying too much attention when we were on the bike, or rather on Bargus the dog. I don't want to spend all day wandering about round here. It's starting to rain, and the wind's rising. Maybe I should head up the slope. That way I know I'll end up above the trees and I'll see what direction to go in, but I'm tired already.

Maybe I should ring Dad. He won't know where I

am, but at least then I'll know where he is. And where's my phone? I left it on the bus. Hey, nice one, Mag.

I'm not used to walking in the woods by myself. I wish Temple was here; she knows how to find her way. She'd tell me what all the different trees are, and we could sing.

Now it's kind of eerie – the way when I stop I can't hear anything except raindrops patting through the leaves, and the wind in the branches. I keep remembering what Humph said about things living here, Others. He said the humans drove a lot of them away, but obviously not all of them. I mean, he's still here himself, right?

Yeah, too right, I've got a shape-shifting hob in a thermos. I probably should have just dropped it in the cave, but I wasn't thinking straight. Should I dump it now? I can't do that; he'd die in there. So I'm going to let him out? What if he changes into something massive and mean?

There's a gleam of metal through the trees up ahead. When I get a bit closer I see it's wire mesh.

Probably this is another bit of the fence we passed on the bus. That means if I keep going round it, sooner or later I'll get back to the road.

That's not as easy as it sounds. It'd be ok if I could stick right next to the fence, because they've cleared the undergrowth for a couple of feet all along, but I don't want to do that. Every so often there are guards, and I don't like the look of them. They're hulking guys in grey body suits, and I guess they could be armed, unless those are just extra-big walkie-talkies.

So I'm trying to stay covered, keep the fence in view, and not fall over roots or get myself ripped to bits on the brambles. One way or another, I'm not a hundred per cent successful.

There's a real storm blowing now, which is a help in a way because I'm not exactly creeping along like a trained Girl Guide, and the wind in the branches covers the noise I'm making. The downside is I'm soon soaking wet. Leaves and twigs are flying off the trees, and there's mulch underfoot. I slip and come down in a puddle.

This is really no fun. I sit there getting my breath, and now the wind drops for a second, and I think I can hear a car.

Wow, I must be near the road. Yes, I can see clear through the trees: I'm almost at the edge of the wood.

There's some action here as well, too near for comfort. Just a bit further along the fence is an open gate, with three of the guards outside standing round someone else who's got their back half-turned to me. It could be a tramp; I can see a green beret with a feather, and a long shabby coat, brownish-green, coming almost down to the ground.

There's some sort of argument going on: it looks as though the guards are telling the tramp to clear off out of it, though I can't hear what any of them are saying.

The person moves round my way. It's a woman. There's curly hair tangled under the beret, and her face still looks like she could be a tramp, someone who's been out in all weathers for a long time and is maybe slightly crazy.

One of the guards starts shouting at her, and she takes a step back. Because I'm on the ground, level with her feet, I get a clear view of what happens next.

As she moves, her coat swings open at the bottom, and something – a little greyish animal – scoots out. I'd swear it came from under her coat. It runs through the gate.

None of the guards have noticed; they're making moves like they're going to get the woman's arms and maybe march her off. She puts out her hands – ok, no need to get heavy, that sort of thing – and starts to walk away.

There's an almighty explosion from somewhere inside the fence.

Everyone freezes for a second; then the guards start running through the gate, towards whatever's happening inside. Brave, I guess. I think if it was me, I'd be running the other way. One of them stops at the gate and looks back at the woman, but she's gone. I didn't see where she went, and I shouldn't think he did either.

The guard reaches into the holster at his belt. It's only a giant walkie-talkie after all; he trots off, yelling to it. Sirens are going off, smoke's starting to drift out between the trees, and there's a rumbling sound like something heavy's falling down.

This seems like a good time not to be here. I get out of my puddle at last and crawl slowly until I reach the road. Then I run some more.

*

A bit further down the road I come to a bus shelter. I haven't got the fare, even if a bus comes, but at least it's somewhere to sit out of the rain.

What happened back there? Did the woman send that animal inside the fence? Did it cause the explosion? Maybe it wasn't alive; maybe it was a kind of drone.

I feel sick and homesick, and I want my dad.

Come on, Mag, that's enough whining. Act adult – you're thirteen.

My tummy hurts.

Temple called it Moon Fever. Bella calls it the Curse. When you start your periods, you're not a child any more. If anything I've been told recently is true, there's something more in it than that, for me.

Magic. My mum says I've got powers that she sent on to me. So what are they? What do they do?

How do I use them?

What do I want to do? Find Dad. There's got to be a spell for telling you where your dad is.

Dreams … I know dreams come into it somewhere. What made me go to the attic with Grace – that started with a dream. And then on the bus, when I saw Humph how he really was, I thought I was asleep even if I wasn't. Maybe if I go to sleep now, thinking about Dad, it'll somehow put me in touch.

I shut my eyes, but even though I'm knackered, my mind's racing too hard to let me lose grip. I'm trying to concentrate on Dad, but all I'm getting is panic about being lost, being a witch, having Nilas and the Others on my track, and all the rest of it.

Sykes used to do this exercise where the point was for me not to think about anything. It's a lot harder than you'd expect, but often he played music, and that made it easier. Now I try making my own music for something not to think about. I start humming, any old notes, down and up and down again, and pretty soon they start making a pattern:

Hi-ho, hi-ho, it's off to work we go …

That's Dad's theme song, so I carry on for a while, and then I stop humming out loud because I can hear him singing along in my head:

With a shovel and pick, and a walking stick – Hi-ho, hi-ho hi-ho hi-ho.

That's him all right, but now the words are different.

'That's grand, two sugars, easy on the milk,' says Dad.

I snap awake, eyes open. It wasn't like imagining Dad's voice. I heard him; I know I did.

Two sugars, easy on the milk ... sounds like he's getting a coffee. That's not the most useful thing in the world I could have found out, but it means I can actually do this stuff. Maybe.

Will it let me see Dad as well as hear him? I start humming again, *hi-ho, hi-ho,* but this time, instead of closing my eyes, I'm watching the drops dripping off the front of the bus shelter. One at a time, a drip swells and drops, and another one takes its place, and it swells and drops. I'm picturing Dad's face, his frown when he's concentrating on some job and doesn't know he's whistling. I can see his eyes, close up to mine, but they're not looking at me, it's something else he's seeing.

Then it's like a camera pulls back for a wider shot, he's sitting on a blue plastic chair ... wider, wider ... he's facing a desk ... on the other side, there's a policeman. That's who he's looking at.

I come out of the vision or whatever it is, and look at my watch. Twenty minutes that took, and guess what? My dad, who has just mislaid his daughter in a bizarre robbery, has gone to the cops. Hey, Mag, next time why not leave the magic alone and try using your head, huh?

*

The rain's almost stopped, but now the light's going. I trudge on along the road, feeling damp and cold and sorry for myself. I could really do with Bella fussing over me, making me a hot water bottle and putting me to bed.

A car comes along behind me and passes me fairly fast. It's a silver-grey S-class Merc; some tycoon on his way to decide the fate of the yen.

A few minutes later it comes back the other way and pulls up next to me.

'You need a lift?'

He's a lot younger and blacker than your average tycoon.

'No thanks,' I say.

He drives on and turns round behind me, and here he is back again, going the way he was going the first time. He drives slowly, keeping pace with me.

'Come on – it's wet. You're wet.'

'I wouldn't want to get your car dirty,' I say.

'Ain't my car.'

'Your dad's car then. Or your boss's.'

'Ain't got no boss, ain't got no dad. Sounds like the blues, don't it?'

'What'd you do, steal it?'

He grins. 'I look the type?'

If I was being honest I'd say yeah, exactly the type. His head's shaved and he's wearing narrow shades with dark green lenses. He's pretty cool.

'Honestly, I'm ok on foot. I've had bad experiences with transport today.'

'Fair enough,' he says, but he keeps on driving the same speed I'm walking.

'Look, I don't want to be rude, but you're making me uncomfortable. I'd be happier if you'd drive on.'

'Keeping an eye on you, that's all.'

This is annoying. Also it could get frightening. I don't see what I can do, though, unless I head off the road into the woods again, and that doesn't seem too smart.

I can hear something, a way off in the trees.

Barking.

The noise is getting louder, coming nearer.

It's Bargus the dog.

He leaps from the darkness into the headlights, and fetches up right in front of me, blocking me. He's monstrously big, nearly as large as when he was a bike. His hair's bristling all over, he's baring his teeth like a mad wolf, and barking so loud it echoes off the tree trunks.

He's come after me: Nilas isn't going to let me get

away that easy. But maybe I can distract him. I've got the hob, surely Bargus will want Humph back?

His baying drops to a snarl, deep in his throat. He's pacing towards me on stiff legs. Any second now he's going to jump for my throat.

I'm bricking it. I don't think I've ever been so terrified. I can barely move.

'Get in here!' The S-class dude's got his door open.

I edge backwards towards the car, never taking my eyes off the dog. I'm holding the thermos towards him, and I'm unscrewing the top as quick as my shaking fingers will let me.

'Get ready to drive fast,' I say, out of the corner of my mouth.

'You got it,' says S-class.

I get the cap off the flask and throw the flask and the cap over the dog's head. I'm in the car, I've slammed the door, and we're hightailing it down the road. Before we turn the corner I get a glimpse of Bargus shoving at the flask with his nose.

'Thanks,' I say. I mean to say a bit more than that, but my voice doesn't seem to be working too well.

The dude slows the car and passes me a handkerchief, a real one, white cotton. It's too good to get dirty, but I'm out of tissues so I could care less.

'Weird stuff in them woods,' says the guy. 'Feral dog, I guess.'

'Yeah,' I agree.

'You heading anywhere in particular?'

'Rostree police station.'

He glances across. I can see his eyebrows up, back of his shades. 'Going to report the dog?'

'No, I've got to find my dad.'

'He in the cells?'

It's the first time I've felt like laughing for a while. 'Could be, if he has to hang around there too long. We kind of lost track of each other, and that's where I'm meeting him.'

I have to hand it to this guy, he knows when not to ask questions. 'I'll drop you outside. The copshop ain't my favourite club.'

'Me either.'

When he pulls up, I offer him the snot-rag back, but he grins and shakes his head. 'Call it a gift.'

'Thanks,' I say again.

'Nothing but a pleasure.'

I realize we never got round to names. Seems a bit late now, so I just wave as he drives off, and then I take a breath and push open the door to the police-station waiting room.

*

'Mag!' Dad jumps off his chair and hugs me. 'Are you ok? What happened? What did he do? How'd you get away?'

'I'm all right, I'm fine. He took off into the wood and then he ditched me. It took me a long time to find my way after that. I was hoping you'd come here. What about you? Did he hurt you much when he hit you?'

'Haven't thought about it. Been too worried about you. Mag, promise me he didn't do nothing to you.'

'Dad, I swear.'

I tell a detective the same: I'm fine, the robber didn't touch me, I never got a good look at his face, there's no point me looking at photos.

'Do you know whereabouts he left you in the wood?'

'No idea. I was trying to find my way out to the road for ages.'

'And did you see anything else while you were there?' He's not the same guy that talked to Dad: this one's Inspector Garnett, says the sign on his desk. He's lean, grey-haired, serious. 'The reason I ask, there was an incident this afternoon up at the Network development. Sabotage. You might have been in the area.'

'I don't know where I was.' I'm not about to report seeing a trained exploding ferret or whatever that thing was. 'I didn't hear anything. What happened?'

'Someone managed to plant a device. We're not sure how they gained access.'

'Did anyone get hurt?'

'Two of the workmen are in hospital, and there's been a lot of damage to the site. So, you see, if you did notice anything, we'd like to hear about it. Did you meet anyone out for a walk? Do you remember seeing any cars?'

For a second I wonder about the S-class dude. Could he have been doing something dodgy round the Network place? Yeah, quite likely.

'I didn't meet a soul,' I tell the Inspector.

He looks dubious, and I'm not sure how long I can keep up the stonewall act, but then the junior policeman, the same one I saw with Dad, comes in and mutters a few words.

The inspector picks up his phone. 'Garnett here. Yes ... That's correct.'

It's not a long conversation, and what it seems to add up to is that there are more important things to do than interrogate a juvenile, because when he rings off, he tells us the constable will take us to Crossbeams.

'Just like that?' Dad demands.

I nudge him. 'Don't make waves, Dad.'

'Yeah, but you've been in danger here, and now you're supposed to go off to school just like nothing happened? You should come home tonight at least.'

'She'll be perfectly safe at Crossbeams, sir,' says Garnett. 'Reliable staff, a secure environment. I think that's the best arrangement all round, don't you?'

I'm too tired to argue either way. The thought of my own bed's a big temptation, but then we'd have to go all the way back to the Residence, round the hills and past the woods, and that gives me the heeby-jeebies, so I let the men decide. In the end the inspector gets his way, and sends us off in a police van, which doesn't do anything for Dad's peace of mind.

The constable drives us through Rostree and out on the southern cliffs of the Island. We're getting into the top income bracket now: there are a few big villas set well back from the road, each with a sea view worth a million or more. They've got names, not numbers: The Anchorage, Salthaven, Normandie. We can't see the houses in the dark, but lights go on as we pass the gates, in case we wanted to break in and steal the family silver.

Then we turn right, through high brick posts, and our headlights flicker past an avenue of trees, all the way up to a big grey building. The car stops on the gravel at the bottom of a flight of stone steps.

This is Crossbeams.

CHAPTER SIX
CROSSBEAMS

'Hey, Sally, check this out. Have we started taking Yardie kids now?'

I pretend I don't hear. I'm doing up my laces.

'What's she doing here?' Sally wonders. 'She wasn't here yesterday.'

Last night I couldn't stay awake. The matron met me and Dad, and she tried to tell me stuff about the school, but I kept going off to sleep, so she let me lie down on her couch. Next thing I know it's morning, and I'm in a bed next to a whole lot of other beds, and there are girls everywhere getting their clothes on.

I'm dressed now, so I stand up. Some of the girls start giggling. Ok, my jeans and trainers aren't the smartest, after an afternoon in the woods and the rain. There could be some twigs in my hair still, too.

'What *is* she doing here?' asks Sally again. Maybe I should try joining in the conversation.

'I'm new,' I say. 'I got here late.'

She looks at me like I'm a piece of furniture that

spoke up, or maybe an insect. Whatever I am, I guess I'm not expected to answer back.

She's older than me, seventeen perhaps, blonde like a Barbie doll. The girl she's talking to is the same sort of age and dark-haired: she's the one that made the crack about Yardies. They're both very pretty and they've both got expensive voices.

Another girl comes running in and fetches up next to my bed.

'I forgot; I'm really sorry, I'm meant to look after you.'

She's out of breath, clutching a towel round herself. She looks younger than the other two but she's bigger, spilling out of the towel all over the place. There are freckles everywhere you can see, and she's got mad ginger hair. Straight off, I know I'm not going to like her.

'Oh, if she's with Bruiser ...' says the dark princess, like that makes me even less loveable. Sally sniggers.

'I'm Ruce,' says the ginger girl, but Bruiser seems a better name. 'I've got some clothes for you.'

'I've got clothes,' I say. I'm not feeling very gracious.

'Yeah, but there's a uniform,' says Ruce, like I might not have noticed everyone else is wearing grey skirts and white shirts. 'They'll give you your own kit later, but you can wear mine for now. It's not that huge,' she adds, seeing me measuring her up. 'Till last year I was your sort of size. Then I suddenly went to a D-cup. It's a pain – nothing fits me – but at least it means you can borrow my old stuff.'

'That's ok, I'll keep what I've got on.' I'm cutting my own throat here, I know. I'd just kind of like to cut everybody else's.

'Suit yourself.' Ruce shrugs, and the towel almost falls off.

'Oh, put 'em away!' pleads the dark girl, which gets my vote too.

'What's your name?' asks Ruce.

We're attracting some notice from the rest of the room. I say, loud and clear, 'My name's Maggot.'

There's a little short silence and then a lot of people start laughing.

'Maggot!'

'Did you hear what she said her name was?'

Sometimes I really, really hate myself.

'Shut up!' Ruce orders the others. Her big face goes pink; the colour clashes with her hair. 'It's probably a West Indian name.'

'I'm not West Indian,' I tell her. 'It's not a West Indian name. It's just my name.'

'What, like, really MAGGOT? Like a little, you know, wriggly wormy thing?' She's fascinated; so is everyone else.

'Yeah, like that.' I've said it; I guess I've got to stick with it.

A bell starts to ring and I'm not the centre of attention any more. Everyone starts hurrying.

'Breakfast time – I'm not even dressed,' Ruce exclaims. 'Look – Maggot – go down and sit at table fourteen. Anyone asks about the uniform, tell them I didn't get it sorted yet but I'll do it as soon as I can. Laban, take her down.'

That's the dark girl, who doesn't look too delighted, but she lets me tag after her.

*

We go past other rooms, doors open to show more beds, and kids rushing everywhere, voices shouting and echoing. At the end of the corridor there's a big landing round a big set of stairs with wooden banisters. It's not so different from the Residence, really, except there's more of it, and everything's a lot cleaner, all the paint is fresh and the woodwork smells of polish.

Downstairs, we go past double glass doors leading outside. I can see where we arrived last night: the gravel drive lined with trees and a lawn beyond. Then we come into the canteen, which is huge, panelled in more shiny wood, and windows only very high up so you can't see out.

There's a counter where you go to get your food and long tables with about twenty people on each, some with girls and some with boys. Opposite the counter there's a raised platform with a table of grown-ups, teachers I guess.

'Which is table fourteen?' I ask Laban.

'It's my table,' she tells me. 'Whatever dormitory you sleep in, that's the table where you sit.'

'Are you head girl or something?' I'm not trying to butter her up, but it was maybe the right thing to say: she looks pleased for a second.

'Head of dorm,' she says, which I suppose isn't as good as head girl.

I know, obviously, she's a bitch, but she's so pretty I want her to like me. Even while I'm thinking that, I know I'm being pathetic.

The breakfast choice is healthier than what Dad gives us at the Residence: no fry-ups here, just cereal or porridge, yogurt, wholemeal toast and rolls, boiled eggs, and a lot of fruit. Herbal tea bags, juice and milk are on offer, but I can't see any normal tea or coffee.

I get a bowl of muesli and some orange juice. There's some funny looks coming my way from other tables on account of my gear, and probably my colour: there's a few dark kids on view, but I'm the blackest. Does it mean I'm going to do black magic? I'm a witch, I tell myself; it doesn't matter what they think about me, I can do magic. It's a warm thought to cuddle.

On my table, some of the girls peek at me, but

nobody wants to get to know me. I listen to them talk to each other, trying to get the feel.

'Are you seeing Wildeth today?' Sally asks Laban.

'Probably.'

'She's spent loads of time with you, hasn't she?' Sally sounds envious and admiring.

Laban tosses back her glossy dark hair. 'You know I can't talk about it.'

'I didn't ask; I was just saying.'

Ruce arrives, bumping into the table. She's got a tray that could feed a small army: porridge, two bananas, two eggs, and a pile of toast.

Laban sneers. 'Got to keep your strength up, Bruiser.'

'Yeah, so I can paste you,' says Ruce.

I get the idea that nobody likes her, but they're all a bit scared of her. She plunks down next to me and her knife splats in my muesli.

'Whoops, sorry.' She grins at me.

I move my bowl away.

'So what happened to you yesterday? Why were you so late? Hey, everybody, this is Maggot; she's new.'

There's a fresh riff of giggles.

'Bus broke down.' I don't want to be any more interesting than I am already. 'Who's Wildeth?' I ask to change the subject.

'She's the Head,' says Ruce.

'And why can't Laban talk about her?' I mutter.

'Oh – Wildeth gives special tuition to some people, and they're supposed to keep quiet about it, in case it makes the rest of us jealous. It's power games, really.'

She obviously means for Laban to hear and be annoyed, but Laban just smiles. 'Only the most promising students get time with Dr Wildeth. And Bruiser's not one of them.'

'Oh, break my bleeding heart.' Ruce slaps her ample breast. 'Sooner you than me. That's her, see – the blonde woman in grey?'

I look at the staff table. Dr Wildeth's very fair, her silvery hair hanging straight to her shoulder on one side, pinned back on the other with a white flower. Her face is pale and her eyes too. Suddenly I realize she's staring straight at me, and I put my head down.

'Don't you think she's creepy?' Ruce whispers.

'She's brilliant. You wouldn't know, would you?' Laban taunts.

'My uncle Rossy knew her pretty well, and he said she gave him the shivers.'

'It's so touching the way you remember everything your uncle said.' Laban's voice is syrupy with sarcasm. 'You should write a book in honour of his memory.'

Sally titters. Ruce goes red, and attacks her second egg with a vicious smash.

'Dr Wildeth will see you for an assessment some

time,' Laban condescends to me, 'but probably not till next term. She's very booked up, she couldn't take on anyone new unless they were exceptional.'

Ruce plants her elbow on the table to block us off from Sally and Laban. 'Where are you from, Maggot?'

'Near Port Benet.' That doesn't seem to mean much to anyone. 'North end of the Island.'

'Oh, she's a *local*,' Laban exclaims, like that makes some sense of me. 'Maybe it's a charity thing.'

Ruce puts down her spoon. 'Even if it is, that's no reason to be snotty.'

She's being kind, I guess, and that makes me want to kick her. I am a witch, I say in my head. I can do magic. Maybe if I try I can disappear.

Maybe I haven't learned that spell yet. Everyone's looking at me.

'Is that you?' Ruce whispers. 'Mah-go?'

'What?' I've missed something, I was concentrating on getting invisible.

'Margot?' The matron I saw last night is standing next to the table, and I get up.

'Margot, come with me. I'll get you some uniform, and then Dr Wildeth would like to talk to you.'

It's a nice moment. It might be the only one I get for a while, so I enjoy it.

*

Matron points me up the stairs. 'Three flights, all the

way to the top. You can't miss it, it's the only room on that level.'

Past the dorms on the second floor, I carry on climbing. At the head of the third flight there's no corridor, just a small square landing and a door with a sign: *Thesida Wildeth, PhD, Head Teacher.*

I tap on the panels, and after a moment she opens up.

'Margot, come in.'

It's an amazing room. Two walls are just glass, and because the room's on top of the school and the school's on top of the cliffs, all you can see is the sea and the sky. There are more windows let into the sloping roof; it feels as if we're floating between the waves and the clouds.

Along the solid side wall there's a big glass tank, like an aquarium, but instead of fish it's got flowers in. It's lit from behind so the colours glow, yellow and red and purple. They look like flowers I know, but when I go closer I see that the poppy's got more petals than any poppy I've seen before, and there's a violet as big as a tulip. They haven't got roots or stalks: they're just suspended in the water.

'It's an eastern tradition,' Dr Wildeth tells me. 'If you preserve the flowerheads in a certain way, they last almost for ever.'

'Beautiful.' I'm looking at a deep blue iris with the

petals fringed in orange. The colours are so strong it's almost as if the light's coming from the flowers. While I watch, they move, gently up and down and round. It's a restful motion that makes me feel like I'm cradled on the water myself.

There's music playing faintly, or is the sound coming from the tank – is it just the water lapping against the sides? It's not exactly a tune, but there's a sort of pattern to it.

'Please do sit down. I heard what happened to you yesterday. What a terrible experience, are you quite all right?' Her voice is low, sweet and strong.

'I'm fine,' I tell her.

'I pulled a few strings to get you out of the police station as quickly as possible.'

I blink. 'How did you know I was there?'

'Oh, I've got a few contacts on the Force. When they told me there was a girl being questioned who was on her way to Crossbeams, I went into action at once. I wanted you safe here.'

So that was the phone call the inspector got yesterday. I'm impressed and maybe a bit scared: if she can make the police do what she says, what else can she do?

She smiles, and it kind of lights her up from inside, like the tank of flowers. I can see why people think she's wonderful, and I can also see why others find her creepy: is she just too good to be true? But when she speaks, it's so warm and tender, you'd want to listen to her for ever.

'It's never easy to face the first few days in a new place with strangers,' she goes on, 'and of course there are odd rules and habits to learn, but if you make mistakes, it really doesn't matter. You must just take your time, and everything will soon come quite naturally. Which dormitory have we put you in?'

'Fourteen.'

'Oh, then you've got Laban Kellerman to look after you. She's a lovely girl. She'll soon make you feel at home.'

I doubt this, but I nod anyway.

'And if there's ever anything you're worried about or you don't understand, you can always come to me. I promised your father we'd take the best care of you.'

She sounds as if it really matters to her how I feel, and suddenly there are tears in my eyes. It's stupid. My dad's not a good dad – he's moody and he's rough – but I'm missing him.

I don't want her to see I'm choked up. She turns away; maybe she knows I need a moment. With her back to me, she draws curtains across the big windows, thin stuff, pearly grey. With the sun shining through them, they're like mist.

I'm still trying to work out if I'm hearing music. It's

a kind of tinkling, maybe bells? No, more like tapping a wine glass with a teaspoon. There are a lot of spoons and glasses: the ringing comes in showers, then spaces out, then speeds up again. I can't get a handle on the rhythm; I think it's coming together, and I want to keep time with my foot. But before I've got it straight, it's changed. I'd like to shut my eyes, feel the beat with my fingers.

Isn't Wildeth going to say anything more? Is she waiting for me to say something? The longer we stay quiet, the more that ringing's in my ears.

'What's the track?' I ask.

Now it's faded out, I'm hardly hearing it any more. Could be just because it was so still in the room – I listened too hard. Maybe it really is some kind of mechanical noise from the tank, or even the central heating, in which case she must think I'm insane.

She smiles again. 'It's something I play to help concentration, for myself and my students.'

'It's interesting.' I'm relieved it wasn't a dumb question after all. 'I've never heard anything quite like it before.'

She comes back across the room to me, and puts out her hand. For a second I think she's going to stroke my head, but she just lets her fingers hover around my face. On her left hand she's wearing a silver ring with a big opal. The misty colours catch the light and flicker, like the flowers in her glass tank.

'You're a very bright girl, Margot.'

Now that's another thing I've never heard before. 'I'm subnormal,' I blurt out.

'Nonsense! Who told you that?'

'People at my last school.'

'They were quite wrong, and I'm glad you're not with them any more.'

'I fail all my tests.'

'Oh – tests!' she exclaims. 'I hate tests!'

I laugh out loud. 'Me too. I didn't think a teacher would say that.'

'Perhaps I'm an unusual teacher. Perhaps you're an unusual pupil. We should get on well together, don't you think?'

I hope she's not wrong, so far it's promising, but she's got no reason I can see to say I'm bright. All I've done is ask her about her ambient sounds.

'I'll be seeing you again, Margot, very soon,' she goes on. 'It's not all the students, you know, who come to me for individual tuition, only the ones I think will really benefit. So just to avoid any bad feeling, I always tell my special pupils not to talk too much about our sessions. I'm sure you understand.'

I just nod. I wouldn't say I understand, but I know I'm not going to tell anyone what it's like up here, or anything about Thesida Wildeth.

*

I've been here a couple of weeks now. Crossbeams is a big place. I'm still finding my way around the buildings and grounds – and liable to turn up in the chemistry lab when I'm supposed to be at the gym – but I'm beginning to get the hang of the layout.

Everything's mixed, boys and girls, except at night and also meals, because you get the same people on your table who sleep in your dorm. In class I'm still a dunce, so at least that's familiar, and lessons aren't much different from Beckwood. I've never done Latin before, so obviously I haven't got a clue, but at least I've got an excuse. Sport's ok, I've always been able to kick, though that's more of a help with football than hockey.

Nobody's said anything about my mother or magic, and nobody's tried to kidnap me again or set off any bombs. All that's happening is I'm getting a slightly better education and a much pricier one.

The students come from all over: Europe, Scandinavia, the Middle East, the Far East. Qataris and Swedes and Russians and Chinese, smart eleven-year-olds and thick eighteen-year-olds, spotty boys and spoilt girls – there's one thing they've got in common: their parents are seriously loaded.

This makes me a novelty item, but I don't get laughed at now. That's down to Laban, because since I saw Wildeth, she's decided I'm cool, and what she says goes. She takes me round with her and shows me off like I'm an exotic pet.

'Maggot's never been on a horse!' she announces, as if that's beyond belief.

'You can try my pony if you want,' offers Sally.

Riding lessons are something you can have as an extra here. You can also learn a musical instrument or do fencing, which I thought was hysterical till someone told me it's sword-fighting. Actually that's still pretty funny.

'Give me an apple, Maggot.' It's nearly lights-out time, and Laban's lounging on her bed.

'Who stole your legs and made you queen?' For some reason Ruce feels she's got to defend me. Like I thought, she isn't popular, but she packs a punch, and even the tough lads in the sixth form give her elbow-room.

I chuck Laban an apple, and she fields it gracefully, like she does everything. I don't mind her ordering me around; she's bossy with everyone, and though she hasn't apologized for how she was to me my first morning, I kind of respect that. Being a cow means never having to say you're sorry.

'Give me one too,' says Sally.

'Get your own,' snaps Laban.

It's a status thing. Laban's top of the pecking order; she hangs round with Sally because Sally's a bit less pretty and a lot more dumb, and she needs to be kept in her place. I'm Laban's slave; I'm not supposed to fetch and carry for anyone else.

I hand Sally an apple anyway. She'd never catch one if I threw it.

'Thanks, Maggot,' she says.

'Do you *like* being called Maggot?' Laban asks me.

'I don't mind.'

'Your proper name's Margot, isn't it?'

'They called me Maggot at my old school.'

'Now you're at a new school, you can be a new person,' she decides. 'You're going to be Margot from now on.'

'Ok.' I take a bite out of my own apple.

'*Ma-ah-go-oh*,' Ruce drawls. 'I think Maggot's much more interesting. Can I still call you Maggot?'

'Call me what you like.' I don't really want her talking to me at all, but anything for a quiet life.

'I saw that dog again,' says Sally.

I stop eating my apple. 'What dog?'

'Big black thing, keeps hanging round the gate.'

'Must be a stray,' Laban yawns. 'You should report it; it might have rabies or something.'

Bargus, it's got to be Bargus. He's come to fetch me; Nilas sent him.

I knew it was too good to last, the way everything's been normal.

Ruce is looking at me. 'Maggot, what's wrong?'
'Apple's rotten,' I say, lobbing it in the bin.

CHAPTER SEVEN
DEEP MUSIC

What am I going to do? Nilas is still looking for me.

It's past midnight, but I can't get to sleep. All around me there are other beds, other girls, breathing and dreaming and turning over in their dreams. I'm the only one awake.

Grace told me Nilas is strong and cruel and wicked. He took her magic – no, he wanted to take it, and when he couldn't, he tortured her. He's got one eye … I don't want to be thinking about this.

Through a gap in the curtains, I can see the moon skimming between the clouds. It's a windy night. I watch the light fade, get brighter, fade again. Away out in the darkness, a ferry siren hoots. By night, that's a lonely sound.

I wish there was someone I could talk to. Laban or Sally? No way. Grace is back on the drugs – she wouldn't know me even if I could get to her. Gordy said he'd help, but he didn't. There isn't anyone.

Where's my White Sister now?

The night Temple took me camping, there was a full moon. We sat outside the tent, and she told me the names of stars. She showed me how to build a fire: dry leaves at the bottom, then little sticks, and a dead branch on top. The flames caught the wood with a crack and a spit, orange tongues licking the dark.

The fire crackled and the stars sparkled, far off. My face and front were hot; the breeze chilled my back and sent the sparks flying up in a red-gold wriggle and flare, like fireworks. Temple sang that ballad, the same one she played last time I saw her:

> *I know a lady lives in a tower*
> *Her face as fair as the lily flower*
> *Her smile as sweet as the crimson rose*
> *That in her secret garden grows.*

Her voice was clear and high like her flute; I can hear it now. I can see her face across the flickering firelight, her eyes bright with the leaping sparks. I'm there with her in the windy woods, with the trees dark and the moon bright.

I'm listening. It's not just like remembering, I can really hear her. The words have changed; it's a new verse.

Little bird sits and sings in a tree.
Pretty bird, pretty bird, fly down to me,
I'll make you a cage of silver and gold
To keep you from the winter's cold.

I've never heard that before; I know I haven't.

The moon's still shining, but I'm seeing it from a different angle, between pearly curtains drawn back to show the sea and sky. To one side there's a glass tank full of shifting colours, and in front of me there's a circle of lamplight on a desk.

It's Wildeth's study. Nobody's there. On the desk there's a file of papers and a pen laid down, as if Wildeth was working on something and got interrupted. Next to the file there's a white flower in a slender glass vase.

Now I'm hearing Temple's flute again, clear notes spilling like raindrops. I'm watching the flowers in Wildeth's water tank, drifting and rising and falling. The notes ripple, the flowers circle. Then there's a click like a door opening or closing. The music cuts out, the vision's gone. I'm sitting up in bed in the dormitory.

What was that? Was it like when I saw Dad in the police station? Temple wasn't in Wildeth's study; how could she be?

It wasn't a daydream. I heard her voice. I heard words she never sang to me. It was real; it was magic.

107

Maybe so, but what good is magic I can't control and don't understand? There's precious little difference between that and madness, it seems to me. Not for the first time, it crosses my mind that I might be cracking up.

I close my eyes and feel sleep coming to take me. In my dreams, I'm a flower drifting in the water, my petals opening and closing.

*

Dr Wildeth would like to see me this afternoon, Matron tells me at the end of lunch. Maybe my vision last night was some kind of premonition, but what's the point of that?

Laban's looking at me with her eyebrows raised like she knows something I don't.

'What?' I say.

She shakes her head and smiles. I check in the mirror in case I've got ink on my nose or spinach in my teeth, but I'm no worse looking than usual.

When I go up to the third floor, the door's wide open, so I go in without knocking. Wildeth's sat facing me, her back to the window, and she doesn't say a word, just gestures me to a chair opposite.

The sun's bright behind her, so all I see is a silhouette. She doesn't speak. I don't speak. She's playing her meditation music again, the spoons ringing against the glass, that mixed-up beat that gets under your skin, into your inside, till you want to jump and sing.

I'm guessing she means me to listen. She said the music helps concentration, so I concentrate, melt into the ringing glass sound. I'm hearing something like a children's choir now, not quite voices but they're singing, high and faint, behind the glass.

Wildeth's shadow's getting darker; the sky's getting lighter. I feel I'm falling forward, though I know I'm sitting still.

Can you hear me, Margot?

She hasn't spoken, not out loud, but I can hear her.

This is magic, Margot. This is what you're here to learn.

Suddenly everything makes sense. I know it all before she tells me: I always knew it, but I hadn't thought it. She's letting me know what I know.

Crossbeams is where the light crosses the light, where magic guides magic, and power comes to know itself.

Wildeth's a witch, she's a mistress of magic. The music's her spell; it comes from inside her. She's speaking to me through the language of music. I understand it, but not in words. The music explains everything. I've got music inside me too, and if I can find it, once I can hear it, then I'll know my own magic: I'll find my power.

Let the music guide you, Margot. The music is the magic, the magic is the music. Can you hear me?

I'm listening; the rhythm's flowing in my blood. The children's song makes circles in my mind, rippling against the clear glass bell notes. I feel like I should be able to reply to her, the same way she's talking to me, but I don't speak the language, I don't know how to do it.

Can you feel it? Do you understand?

I force my mouth to open, but all I can produce is a hoarse kind of groan. It's like those dreams when you think you've woken up, but your body won't move – you're trapped.

'I hear you,' I say. It's so hard to make my tongue do the work, form the words. 'I can feel the magic.'

She stirs and sighs, and I blink. That seemed to take just a few minutes, but now it's late afternoon: the sun's gone, the sky's grey and the room's in shadow. I stretch and swallow. I'm dead tired.

'I'm here to help you, Margot.' Wildeth's voice comes softly through the dusk. 'I'm here to teach you.'

'Teach me about magic?' My throat's croaky, as if I haven't used it for days. 'Can you help me find my, my knowledge? My power?' I'm stammering, stuck trying to ask something I seemed to know, just then, but now it's slipping away from me.

She switches on her desk light so we can see each other better. 'It's hard in words, isn't it? Music is a better language.'

'What is the music? What does it mean?'

'Everyone has their own tune. We call it deep music.'

'Everyone? Not just witches?'

'Everyone and everything: a star, a cloud, a river, a tree. Living things have more complex tunes, and the music of a human being is a symphony, endlessly varied, eternally changing. Everyone and everything has deep music, but only a witch can hear it.'

'The sound in here, that's your deep music?'

'It's my language. I can speak to any witch in that language, whatever language they speak themselves. A witch learns to hear her own tune, and how to let another witch hear it, through her.'

'So it's like … mind-reading?'

'That, and much more than that. With your tune, you can do almost anything. Music can make you feel happy or sad, can't it? It can make you want to dance, or make you want to cry. That's magic. A witch learns to use that magic.'

'How do I hear my own tune?'

She doesn't answer for a moment. She's watching me with those pale blue eyes, and I can't read her expression. 'I'm here to help you,' she says again, and then she smiles. 'There's no hurry, we've plenty of time.'

She stands up and goes towards the door. She's

expecting me to leave now.

But maybe we *don't* have time, maybe I don't. I've got to ask her.

'What are the Others?' I ask.

She turns round quickly.

'Who told you about the Others?'

I could just say to her about Humph and Bargus, couldn't I? Ask about Nilas ... tell her I'm in danger ... but how do I explain? Once I start telling, I don't know where I'll be able to stop.

'Did you dream it?' Wildeth asks.

Dreams were how it started, so I nod.

'That happens to witches,' she says. 'Your dreams can be just dreams, or they can be more than that. They can be true.' She pauses. 'I wouldn't normally tell somebody as young as you about the Others. I don't like giving children nightmares.'

That is so not reassuring.

'There are creatures in this world ... that are different from anything most people know about.' She's picking her words slowly. 'Less than human, more than animal. They are the Others.'

'Are they magic?'

'Yes, but their magic isn't the same as ours. It's primitive, it's violent, it's dangerous.'

I'm thinking about Bargus snarling at me, I'm thinking about when I was alone in the woods.

'We're safe here,' she tells me. Maybe she saw me shiver. 'Nothing like that can come inside the school grounds.'

'Are the Others and the witches always enemies?' I ask her.

'You must never, never trust any of the Others.'

It's not what I meant. I wanted to know if there are some witches who team up with the Others; I was thinking about Nilas.

She takes my hands in hers.

'Don't worry about the Others, Margot. Don't worry about anything. Trust me, and everything will be easy.'

*

'She told you, didn't she?' says Laban.

We're whispering to each other in the dorm, lights out.

'Yeah.'

'When I saw you come down from her room – you looked like I felt when she told me.'

'You're a witch too?' I don't even think how mad that would sound if anyone could hear us.

'Yes.'

'What's Crossbeams?'

'It's a school for magic.'

'But we're not all witches, are we?'

'Just Wildeth's students.'

113

'What about all the rest, the ordinary kids, the staff?'

'They don't know; they don't count. It's all about us, us and Wildeth; we're the ones who matter.' I can't see her properly, but I can hear she's smiling. 'We're the ones who hear deep music.'

'Do we do classes together?'

'Only in the holidays. Then we all stay behind with Wildeth. Wait till half-term – it's pretty intense.'

'Will we get broomsticks?'

'It's not like that. There's no wands or potions either. Everything magic comes from inside. It's about hearing your music, hearing other people's music.'

That's what Wildeth said, and I guess my vision, or whatever it was, when I saw Dad, that started with a tune. And last night, Temple singing? I still don't get what happened there, but it was musical. I'm kind of disappointed about the broomsticks, though.

'Once you can hear, then you can see, you can do anything,' Laban tells me.

'Do you know your own tune?'

'I've known it for ages. Soon I'll find my name.'

'Your name?' I lean in closer.

'That's the final thing, when you get full control of your magic. It's like – your music tells you what your name is. I don't know; I haven't got it yet, but it could be any day now.' She doesn't sound as proud as I'd have expected. 'I hope it doesn't go wrong when I do.'

'Go wrong how?'

'Well – you know David Foster, in the Upper Sixth? He used to be Wildeth's star student.'

'Big Davey?' I'm incredulous. He's seriously lacking. He hardly speaks, and it's not like he's thinking deep thoughts either; he's just a six-foot blank.

'It was only last year he went … like that. And there have been others. Wildeth says it can happen when you get your name; it's like the power blows your fuses. She's working on a cure.'

Till I get my name I can't give my magic back to Grace, and, in the meantime, Nilas and the Others are looking for me. When I get my name I could end up like Davey Foster. This is not good news, but I'm still grinning to myself. I'm a witch, I've got magic, and I'll learn how to use it. Wildeth's going to teach me.

'It must be fun, doing spells,' I say.

Laban giggles. 'Just wait and see.'

Across the room, Ruce grunts, 'Pack it in, will you? Some of us want to sleep.'

Laban takes a breath like she's going to yell back, but thinks better of it and murmurs to me, 'I'll tell you.'

She squeezes my hand. Her and me, we're special, we matter. Everyone else, they're in the dark.

*

'Look up there.' We're out on the games field, and Laban's pointing to the clocktower at the top of the school.

'What?' It's break; we don't have to be anywhere.

'Wildeth's room,' she says.

'Where?'

'Just there. The turret where the clock is.'

'No way. It's nowhere near big enough.'

'That's what I mean. You should be able to see the big windows from here, but you can't, can you? It's a spell.'

I think about it. 'Do you mean it's invisible … or … it's not really there at all?'

She frowns. 'It's invisible.'

'It could be the other way, though, couldn't it? A spell to make it seem as though it's there, but really it isn't.'

'We've been inside. Obviously it's *there*.'

'Ok.' I don't want to start a fight, and I guess I'd rather I'd been somewhere you can't see from the outside than a place that's nowhere, especially since I'll be going back there soon. 'It must be a powerful spell.'

'It's all about what people think, what you can make them think.'

Some girls have moved onto the pitch and started messing about with hockey sticks, but they're too far away to hear what we're saying. Laban points at them. 'See Fenella Morgan?'

'She's the busty blonde one?'

'Watch.'

Fenella takes a swing at the ball, but instead of hitting it, she whacks her nearest team-mate in the shins. There's a howl and a scrimmage.

'You did that?'

'If I'd taken more time I could have got her to send a shot into the canteen windows,' Laban boasts.

'Wouldn't you have to play pretty good hockey yourself for that? I mean, to aim it right?'

'I can play hockey.'

I'd like to see it, but I guess we've given Fenella enough grief.

'So what did you do?' I ask.

'I listened to her tune; I used my music to change hers. See, a witch's music is stronger. Fenella's not a witch; she can't hear deep music at all, so she doesn't know what's happening. But if I get in her head, I can make her do what I want. You can get people to believe what you say or tell you what they're really thinking. You can make a guy fall in love with you!'

'You've got to be able to hear your own tune, right? So how do you get to hear it?'

'You just – do. It comes. Wildeth'll help you.'

But I don't know when I'll be seeing Wildeth again. We don't have set times for our sessions with her, it's whenever she can fit us in, so it could be next week or even longer. I don't want to wait, I want to find my magic, find my music, for myself, if I can.

Out on the games field, there's too much normal noise, and in the classroom or the common room it's even worse: kids talking, sniffing, scuffling, teachers telling off, doors banging. At the end of last period, I go off behind the tennis courts and listen to myself.

There are still other sounds getting in the way. A blackbird's singing up on the roof and some girls are knocking a ball about, thump-a-thump and a twang of rackets. What I need's inside, somewhere. I shut my eyes, breathe slow. Air in, air out.

Every breath takes me deeper into silence and darkness. Below every step there's another, a spiral leading down, down. Dark and darker, quiet and quieter.

Dark's becoming light, down's leading upward. The silence is singing, golden notes, interlocking ever-changing chords. I hear my own heart beating, my thoughts travelling, my magic firing. I'm an instrument, stringed like a cello, taut like a drum, coiled like a horn.

When I come back to the outer world, I'm not too surprised to see hours have passed. I've missed tea, study, and supper too. It's dark; I'm shivering and starving and sleepy.

But I've heard my own deep music.

*

Now I want to try listening to other things. *Everything's* got music, that's what Wildeth told me, and a witch can hear it. For my first experiment, I choose a stone I find at the edge of the drive, a big grey one about the size of my fist. I pick it up, I stare at it, and I turn it round and round. I stroke the rough edge and the smooth hollow; I see the way one side shades into a pearly colour.

I'm getting to know it, with my eyes, my fingers, and my mind. My own tune's playing in my head, I reach out with it to the stone.

After a while, I don't know how long, I hear a low thudding beat. It's irregular, strong then weak then strong again, and now there's a whining whistle, like wind in a sea cave. This is the stone's music.

The music's telling me the stone used to be underwater; for a long, dark time it was washed by the waves. Before that, a huge time before, it was part of a mountain. I can hear the stone's thoughts.

What it thinks isn't all that fascinating, to be honest. It counts time in centuries, not seconds; its slow, old song is off the human scale. But I get the idea that if I learned to talk back, then I might be able to change the stone, move it, make it be somewhere else, through its music – because it's the music that makes the stone how it is and where it is. So, put it this way, maybe one day when I know more magic, I can throw rocks with it.

Hearing gets easier with practice. Next time I listen to a stone, I can do it almost at once, and it's not too long before I get in tune with the apple tree on the front lawn and the pigeons pecking the fruit. There's a cobweb in the cloakroom; I've avoided that corner, but now I make myself listen to the spider, and the fly she's caught for dinner too.

When I move on to human beings. Mr Benwell who teaches Classics isn't that much harder than a pigeon: in a way, he's easier, because his mind works more like mine, only better informed. I could improve my Latin this way, I guess, if I was prepared to put the time in.

With Laban, though, I hit a block. Why's that?

I'm not sure she'd appreciate me trying to listen in to her, so I start by telling her about my stone. She screams with laughter.

'Talking to rocks!'

'Rocks rock.'

'Did it talk to you?'

'Well, yeah. I mean, it didn't know it was talking to me, but it talked to itself. You know, it didn't *speak*.' Even Wildeth, when she talks through her music, isn't doing it in words. 'But it had a language, and I could understand it.'

'Wow. Margot knows Mineral. Did Wildeth tell you to do it?'

'No, I haven't even seen her, since the first time.'

'Don't worry, half-term's coming up. You are staying, aren't you?'

'Yeah, I guess.'

'You've got to. It's a blast, all of us together – just us and Wildeth.'

I haven't broken it to Dad yet; he'll have a fit. I'm also a bit nervous about the rest of Wildeth's special students: they're all older than me, and I've hardly talked to any of them except Laban. Still, I can't pass up the chance to spend four solid days working on my magic.

'What I want to know,' I say, 'about the music thing – can a witch hear another witch?'

'Of course. You've heard Wildeth.'

'Can you hear my music? Can I hear yours?'

'If I let you. Witches control their tunes, you know? We've got to open up to each other, like a conversation. You mightn't be able to do it yet, but we can try, if you like.'

She turns to face me. We're near the fence between our grounds and the farmer's fields, under the trees that help keep wind off the sports pitch. To my left, there's the sound of the sea and a few sheep bleating; the other side of me, the senior hockey team's in full shout. There's Fenella Morgan again, swinging her stick like a scythe.

'I don't want you making me do something stupid,' I say, nodding towards Fenella.

Laban laughs. 'I'll just listen. And let you listen to me – if you can!'

I look at her. I don't have to shut my eyes any more, to hear my tune, and now as soon as I reach for it, it's rising to meet me. It's becoming familiar, like the sound of my own voice, though it never exactly repeats how it's been before.

What I'm coming to realize is how *smart* my tune is. It's lightning-quick, way cleverer than me, and using it makes me feel brilliant too. Even before I know what I want to do, it knows, and it's there, ready to guide me, taking me where I choose to go.

Laban, Laban. I'm staring into her eyes. I'm hearing something new, a warble, a singing, sobbing cascade of notes. It's not outside me; it's in my head, but it's not coming from inside me either. This is Laban's deep music.

It hasn't got the unearthly feel of Wildeth's tune; it's more like something you'd hear late at night in a club when everyone's smooching, but there's still a strangeness. That falling phrase isn't quite a sax, those smoky notes couldn't come from any human voice. Laban's language, what's it saying?

Margot, Margot. What's your tune? ... Open up, you funny little girl, let me in ... What's your music, Margot?

Laban's thoughts, not words, but words are what I understand even though they're not what I hear.

I'll find out what's going on in your head, Margot. I wonder what Wildeth said to you, was it anything like she said to me? ... I've got a great future, I'll be an enchantress. Oh, I'm special.

She's trying to focus on me, but keeps slipping back to herself.

I can't hear her music, why not? ... My tune's the best, Sergei said so ... he thinks I'm pretty lush ...

When Wildeth talked to me through her music, she was saying what she wanted me to hear, but this is like eavesdropping. Whatever's passing through Laban's head is in her tune.

Riding at three-thirty, must get changed, new jodhpurs ... Boys are easy to manage, but I'm a mess. What if they knew? ... They've got to love me, all of them, everyone ...

This is too much information. I take a step back and shake my head: the music and thoughts fade out, letting the noise of the wind and sheep and running kids take over.

'Couldn't do it, huh?' Laban's smiling.

She's the nearest I've got to a friend at Crossbeams, and now I've been in her mind, I feel a bit sorry for her too, so I shrug. 'Maybe next time.'

From across the field, the school clock strikes three. I was tuned in to her more than half an hour, though it

123

didn't feel like it. 'Shouldn't you be getting ready for riding club?' I say.

'Is that the time? I've got to run.' Then she frowns. 'So you did hear something?'

'I guess I must've.' Did I mean for her to know? Show off a little bit? Maybe I should learn to read my own thoughts.

'Beginner's luck,' she says, and laughs, but it's not exactly friendly. 'Good start, little one. See you later.'

The hockey team's still at it: crash-bang-wallop. It's not a game I ever played before I came here, and I can't say it appeals to me much, but I'm not bad at the basics.

Fenella runs across. She's on form, feeding the ball to her mate, dodging, ready for the next pass.

Fenella, Fenella.

I don't know much about her – she's older and not in my dorm – but she looks like an easy target, healthy and sporty, not complicated. I direct my attention to her. I listen for her rhythm; I catch the pounding of her tune.

Fenella … Fenella …

I'm running, I'm running! I'm belting along with my square fair legs, my feet thump the grass, my hands grip the stick. The ball's lined up, I can SCORE!

I flick my sight to school; I put all my will into that. There's the goal. That's where to aim.

The shot flies, there's a horrendous splintering crash.

Fenella's put the ball through the canteen window.

CHAPTER EIGHT

SILVER SISTER

'How's my girl? Making me proud? Looking forward to seeing us?' Dad doesn't wait for a reply. 'I'm thinking the bus didn't work out too well last time, so I was gonna bring the minibus, but you know how that drinks up the petrol. Gordy says he'll pick you up – that ok by you?'

'Dad—'

He's not listening. 'His motor don't look too flash, but he swears it'll do the trip.'

'Actually, Dad, I'm not coming home for half-term.' That's shut him up.

'Thing is,' I explain, 'there's kind of a study camp.'

He can't complain, can he, if I'm taking my schoolwork seriously?

'Something wrong with this phone? Coulda sworn I heard you say study camp.'

'I've got some catching up to do.'

'Study camp!'

'Ok, it's not that funny.'

'Well, good luck to you, girl, but we'll miss your company.'

'Me too. Maybe I can get time off for my birthday.'

'Sure, that's only next month. Abram, will you give it a rest?' Dad yells.

'Hollies playing up?'

'Just the usual, but Sykes ain't been too well, so Bella's had her hands full. I gotta go, Princess, you take care now and don't work too hard. Study camp!' He's still chuckling as he rings off.

That went better than I was expecting. In fact, is it my imagination, or was he just a bit relieved I'm not coming home? Why would that be? I've got mixed feelings myself, because though I'm keen to find out more about magic, it's a hard choice not even to see how Grace might be doing. I was hoping Dad might mention her, but of course he wouldn't.

*

Thursday evening, school feels empty and strange: just a handful of students instead of crowds wherever you go. At supper, I keep quiet. The rest of them know each other, and was I looking to Laban for help making friends? In my dreams. She's in her element, playing off laddish Andy Tottimer against stocky Sergei, who's so virile he's growing a bit of beard already. Tomas the Finn, who reputation says is a devil for the girls, is making a move on pretty, ditzy Ayesha, but she's not paying attention because she's mislaid something as usual, her bag or her scarf or her phone.

Everyone's wearing home clothes, which for me is jeans and a sweatshirt, but Laban's got leopard-print leggings and a scarlet blouse with a loose neck that's always slipping off one shoulder. Paola in Year 11 is showing off her muscle definition in a croptop. Yuki's in black, with studious glasses, and her twin sister Mieko's jazzed up a tartan mini-kilt with fluorescent thigh-high socks, DMs, and a shiny pink bomber jacket. Next to me, Michael Wilkie, who's got floppy hair, a stammer and a mad smile, is in a vintage punk T-shirt and a suede waistcoat.

We're all on top table, where the staff normally sit. Wildeth's in the middle, everyone's very aware of her, but she doesn't say much till we've finished eating. Then she looks round with a smile, and though she hasn't made a sound, everyone shuts up and pays attention.

'First, I'd like to welcome Margot. She's one of us now, and I'm sure you'll all do your best to make her feel she belongs. Now, the rest of you will remember that we work very hard during these special sessions, but to begin with, I always give a demonstration.'

She leads the way out of the canteen, and we follow, passing a stout woman in an overall, standing in the doorway with a tray.

'We'll be outside for a while, Mrs Culligan,' Wildeth tells her. 'It's such a lovely night, I thought we'd try a little astronomy.'

Mrs Culligan looks wistful, as though she'd like to stargaze too, but she's got the washing up to keep her busy.

Wildeth halts us at the foot of the front steps. 'Stay together, watch, and most importantly, listen.'

She spreads her arms wide. The ordinary late noises – wind in the leaves, an owl hooting, the distant rush and slap of sea – all of that fades out, and instead I hear Wildeth's skipping rhythms, her riddling harmonies. Through her tune, I begin to be conscious of other sounds, the throb and trill of trees in private conversation with themselves, grass and stone and air and water all thinking, being, growing.

Look up, Wildeth tells us.

The evening's dark blue, and sure enough, the stars are out, but while we crane our necks, a low cloud gathers across the sky. She's calling it, talking the language of wind and mist. It sinks, it thickens, rain falls: but before a drop hits our upturned faces, each pearl crystallizes, snowflakes that swarm together in the air and hover. They hang suspended, quivering; they flock and weave a diamond lattice, flake building on flake to sketch a fairy palace above our heads. Walls and windows, pinnacles and soaring spires, a snowcastle: lovely and impossible.

It looks effortless, a floating dream, but I feel how it's strung together on Wildeth's taut intention. My senses stretch, trying to see, to hear, to understand.

Next to me there's a low cry. 'I'm seeing things. What is it?'

Mrs Culligan's come out. She's standing with her mouth open; I'm not sure if she's enchanted or scared silly.

'Shh,' I tell her in a whisper. 'It's ... it's fireworks.'

That's nonsense, but it's enough for her to stand still and wonder instead of screaming, and I tuck my hand in hers so she'll think I'm the one who needs to be reassured.

'Did someone say fireworks?' Wildeth sounds breathless but she's laughing. 'Watch! Listen!'

From inside the fragile palace below the stars, light glimmers, shimmers to a blue glow. Gas flares through the transparent spars and walls of ice. The flames are real, the ice is real too, and little by little heat blurs the silver lacework, the outlines begin to melt and drip.

Released from the spell, water splashes us, a quick drenching downpour.

'Oh my goodness,' Mrs Culligan gasps, ducking her head.

Wildeth turns, notices her, and quickly comes with

hands outstretched. Her tune, hushed almost silent when the snow palace melted, sings out to blot the cook's memory dry. *Nothing's happened, everything's quite normal. We came out to see the stars and got caught in a shower.*

'I should have known better than to leave the sink!' Mrs Culligan smiles.

Back indoors, in the senior common room, Wildeth stretches out in an armchair, and the rest of us sit around her.

'Are you all right, Dr Wildeth?' asks Yuki.

'Yes, but very tired.'

'It l-looked easy,' Wilkie grins. 'It looked like – m-magic!'

Sergei laughs, but Wildeth frowns.

'Those of you who were listening properly should be feeling tired too. Magic is harder work, takes more concentration, than anything else you could do.'

Wilkie drops his head, abashed.

'That's why we don't use a spell to wash the dishes or tell our friends we'll be late,' Wildeth goes on. 'Most ordinary things are best done in the ordinary way. We have a responsibility, we witches, to keep our magic for when it's needed – not, for example, to interfere with the ordinary students, Margot. But if you must, could you try to be a little more subtle than smashing glass?'

I didn't think she even knew about Fenella and the

hockey ball.

'I won't do it again,' I say, and she relents with a smile.

'Of course what I showed you just then wasn't necessary, but I wanted you to understand how even the elements can be brought under your control. I think you'll remember. Now, we've got a long day ahead of us tomorrow, so I suggest everyone has a hot shower and gets to bed.'

For once, I'd like to lie awake and think about magic, but I'm asleep as soon as I'm under the covers.

*

Next day after breakfast we gather in Wildeth's room.

'Nothing spectacular today,' she tells us. 'Back to basic skills, listening to each other's thoughts and learning how to adjust someone else's response to you. I'm going to take you through an honesty charm. Who'd like to volunteer for a demonstration?'

Yuki gets chosen, and comes to sit in the middle.

'The point of this exercise,' says Wildeth, 'is to get someone to tell the truth about something they might not want to confess. But I'll make sure you all forget whatever you learn about each other.'

'*You'll* still remember,' says Mieko cheekily.

Wildeth smiles. 'Tomorrow, we'll work on the forgetting spell, and you can perform it on me. So whatever you tell me, I'll only know it for one evening.

Fair enough?'

She draws her chair close to Yuki's, and we listen while their music blends. Yuki's rhythm is fast, a little tense, to begin with, but soon it slows, coming under the influence of Wildeth's tune, and she sighs, her eyes half closing, her mouth a little open.

'Yuki, will you tell me what I want to know?' Wildeth asks.

'Yes.'

Wildeth turns to address the rest of us. 'She's under the spell now.'

'Can she hear what you're saying?' asks Mieko.

'I'm not deaf,' Yuki replies.

There's laughter, but Wildeth raises her hand and we hush. 'A loud noise or a surprise could break the charm. Yes, she can hear us, she can speak to us, but she can't lie to us. Now, Yuki, tell us the worst thing you ever did.'

'I told my sister that her boyfriend was sleeping with another girl,' Yuki announces.

Mieko goes stiff in her seat.

'Was it true?' asks Wildeth.

'No, I just wanted to get him in trouble.'

'Did it work?'

'Oh, yes. She wrecked his scooter with a hammer.'

'Did you ever tell her it was a lie?'

'Never.' Yuki smiles angelically. 'I didn't like him.'

Tomas can't control himself. He splutters with amusement, and a tremor shakes Yuki. She blinks, confused.

'You did very well,' Wildeth reassures her. 'Tomas, you must learn to be silent when you need to.'

'I'm sorry,' he mutters.

Not as sorry as Yuki's going to be in a minute. Mieko's hyperventilating. 'I don't believe you, what are you like? You split us up, me and Darryl?'

'He wasn't good enough for you,' Yuki tries to excuse herself.

'That's for me to decide, not you, you spiteful cow.'

'Shh, shh.' Wildeth puts her hands out. 'Let's forget now. Open up, all of you.'

Her music laps us in calm. *Forget, forget,* she's telling us. *The last few minutes didn't happen. They don't matter; lose them. They are going, gone. You'll remember the spell, but not what you heard.*

Mieko's scowl smoothes out, and Yuki's guilty look vanishes like ripples on a pond.

That's odd, though. I'm not forgetting. I try to open up, wide as I can, but when Wildeth puts her hands down, I've still got total recall.

'Now, you should be able to perform the spell yourselves, even though you don't know what Yuki told us.' I don't want to look like the bad student here, so I don't mention that I remember the whole lot. 'Everybody

135

take a partner, and we'll all try it, turn and turn about. Don't leave anyone under more than ten minutes or so; it could be harmful. To bring them out, touch them gently on the arm or shoulder and tell them it's over. I'll keep an eye on you all. Ready, everyone?'

I land up with Wilkie. His tune's classical, a bit balletic. I'm ready, I'm listening, I'm following his dancing notes, but I'm not feeling sleepy or receptive or honest or whatever I'm supposed to.

'Margot, will you tell me what I want to know?'

'No, I don't think so.'

He tries again. I'm doing my best to relax, open myself to him, but it's clear from his thoughts that he's hearing nothing from me. *Margot, let me in. Listen, you'll tell me what I want to know, won't you?*

'Sorry, no,' I say out loud.

He sits back and huffs. Wildeth comes over.

'Having trouble, Wilkie?'

'I can't get Margot under.'

'Never mind, we'll change partners in a minute.'

Of course everyone thinks it's Wilkie who's rubbish, but pretty soon, when Paola and Ayesha and Sergei have all had a go at me with no result, it starts to look like I'm being obstructive.

'Open up to me!' snarls Sergei.

'I'm trying. I really am.'

'Quiet, everyone,' Wildeth orders. 'Margot, come to

the middle and let me see what I can do.'

They all sit forward, waiting to watch me be put in my place. But even Wildeth's tune, even the quiet authority of her thoughts, don't have any effect. *Margot, Margot, listen to me. Will you tell me what I want to know?*

'I can't hear you,' she says aloud.

'I don't know why. I can hear you.'

'Let's try this, then. An audible sound can act as a guide, a channel from one mind to another. Hum to me, it doesn't have to follow your own tune exactly, but as close as you can. I'll do the same.'

Like a couple of quiet bees, we murmur to each other. I feel her attention reaching out to me, seeking, exploring, her lilting sweetness swaying me, but it's no good; I can't let her in.

At last she touches my arm to tell me I can stop, and sits back. I'm wilting in my seat, exhausted with the effort.

'Unusual,' she says. 'But I expect it's just a temporary block. All right, everyone, that's enough for today. Don't worry, Margot, tomorrow you and I will spend some time together, and I'm sure we'll get you over your problem.'

The rest of them take it for granted I'm holding out for extra attention, or else I'm just pretending I'm a witch at all.

'Why don't you do like the rest of us?' Sergei

demands after supper.

'I want to. I don't know why I can't.'

'You must have talent to keep us out like that,' says Tomas.

'I didn't,' I say, but they're not convinced. They carry on discussing me, in whispers loud enough for me to hear.

'Do you know,' Laban tells them, 'she talks to stones?'

Andy guffaws, and Mieko titters.

'Why's she even here?' asks Paola. 'If she hasn't got a tune, she hasn't got magic.'

'Wildeth must know what she's doing,' Ayesha objects.

'Unless she's just s-sorry for her,' suggests Wilkie.

'Deprived childhood, no?' rumbles Sergei.

'Single-parent family, you know, and brought up in a *mental* home,' Laban shrugs. 'What do you expect?'

*

By the last day, I'm near breaking. Give me the Others, bring on Nilas, what's a spot of torture? No one's misusing me physically, they don't even call me names, though I've started hearing Maggot again, just when I was getting used to Margot. But when everyone hates you, you feel hateful.

Nobody can hear my tune. Every day Wildeth sees me alone to work on my block, but she gets nowhere, and it makes the rest of the kids jealous. I've been one-on-one with each of them, hours at a time. Result: zero. I can hear their music, but they get nothing out of me, and as for their thoughts, I understand those all too well.

'She is dumb in her head,' Sergei decides.

Andy belches to show he agrees.

'She's doing it on purpose,' Laban declares.

'I'm not,' I say.

'Does it matter so much?' Ayesha asks. 'She could just need more time.'

Wildeth almost snaps at her. 'Until she can communicate properly with the rest of us, she won't make progress.'

She's decided everyone will try together. 'Link hands,' she tells them. They're sitting in a circle on the floor of her room, with me in the middle. 'Listen to my music.'

Her melody rings in our heads, clear transparent notes, and, beyond that, the treble chorus singing from some impossibly far-off place. Hers is the dominant tune always, but I hear the others too, each distinct and different. Wildeth's music draws them together, brings them into harmony, one purpose, one theme. It's directed at me, aimed inside my mind, groping, searching, clutching, grabbing.

Margot, Margot.

Where's your music? What's your tune?
Come on, Maggot! Open up.
We can't hear you, stupid cow.
Your tune, we want to listen, we need you to let us in.
Maggot, Maggot!

Their insistent thoughts are a swarm of flies, a hail of stones. They're hurting me, stinging me. I block my ears with my hands, but that doesn't help: the noise is right inside my brain.

I clutch at my own music. The strong slender golden chords are all I've got to hold. The witchkids are battering me with their thoughts; their tunes are slamming against mine. I feel the pressure build.

There's a metallic shriek in my head like steel wheels grinding, and sparks fly. A veil of invisible fire flashes out around the circle: my tune's a whiplash, ripping its way through.

Laban's the first to feel it, a spasm like an electric shock. A second later, everyone's on the floor, or sprung to their feet, backing off against the walls.

'What was th-that?' Wilkie gasps.

'That *hurt*,' whimpers Mieko, cuddling up to Yuki.

Only Wildeth's sitting still, watching us, watching me. Her eyebrows are raised, her eyes open wide.

Andy wants to swear, but he can't do it in front of her. 'She attacked us!'

I think he might whack me, but Paola gets in the

way. 'Easy, Tottimer.'

'Extreme reaction,' Sergei mutters, massaging his shoulder.

Tomas whistles, and winks at Ayesha, who's the only one to look at me with anything less than loathing. 'Are you all right, Margot?' she asks.

'Is *she* all right?' Wilkie's indignant. 'She j-just—'

'Gently, gently,' Wildeth calms them. She raises her hands, spreading the fingers, and again her music rises, rippling through the room.

That's enough now, she tells them, through her tune. *Leave the pain behind. You've done well, my witches. We are together; we will always be together. Magic is our bond and our strength.*

She dismisses them for the evening. As they go, Andy kicks me, accidentally-on-purpose, and Laban nods like that's what I deserve. She's not my friend now if she ever was.

I'm still sprawled on the floor. My legs might bend the wrong way if I tried to stand up.

Wildeth kneels beside me.

'I didn't do that on purpose,' I say.

'I know you didn't. Your music's stronger than you are.' She smiles down at me. 'I believe you're shielded.'

'Shielded?' I repeat.

'Under a charm, to stop you sharing your tune or your thoughts. I've suspected it for a while, but I had

141

to put you under pressure to make sure. Now I'm certain someone's laid a spell on you. But who? Who would want to block your witchcraft?'

I feel shivering cold. Nilas, that's who. It has to be, who else is there?

'Can you take the spell off?' I ask her.

'It won't be easy, unless I can find out who put it on.'

'Does it mean I can't do magic?'

'Some things you can do. As you proved with your hockey adventure, you can influence ordinary people. They're not aware of deep music in any case. But I'm afraid that without the power to let other witches hear your tune, your abilities will be limited. So we'll have to …'

I've stopped listening. Something else has all my attention. On a low shelf under her desk, where I've never looked because I've never been lying down in her room before, there's a flute.

I lean forward to touch it.

The third key from the bottom's dented, there's a scratch near the mouthpiece. It's Silver Sister, I'd know her anywhere.

'How did that get here?' I ask. I don't even know if I interrupted Wildeth while she was still talking. 'It belongs to – a friend of mine.'

'Temple,' says Wildeth. 'My daughter.'

I stay quite still a second, my hand on the flute; then I turn to look at her.

How did I not see before? They're alike; they've got the same eyes.

'She worked at the Residence,' I say.

'I know.'

'Have you spoken to her? Since she left?'

Even their smiles are similar, except Wildeth's teeth don't have a gap. 'We talk to each other every day.'

'Where is she?'

'Not far off. Perhaps you'll see her soon.'

'But she said she'd stay in touch with me,' I burst out. Then I think, no, she didn't. It was me said that.

Wildeth shakes her head. 'Sometimes people have other things to think about. It hasn't been so long, has it?'

'It's been *months*.'

'And a month, to you, goes on for ever. Believe me, Margot, when you get just a little older, a month will pass so quickly you'll hardly know it's gone.'

'The flute,' I say. 'She always had it with her.'

'She asked me to take care of it. And I do.'

I sit there on the floor.

Temple's alive and well, and not far away. She could have got in touch with me any time: she can't be bothered, that's all.

Wildeth's her mother.

Temple didn't like her mother. The first time we talked, properly talked, out in the woods that night, she told me: 'I could never keep a secret from her. She had to know everything that went on in my head.'

Did Wildeth use witchcraft to read her own daughter's mind?

She's watching me now. Her tune cradles me, sweet sympathy: *I can help you, Margot.*

If I tell her about Nilas, if she knows who did the spell, she might be able to take it off.

But she set me up. She said just now, she wanted to put me under pressure. She could have made the witchkids like me, or at least forget they hate me. She doesn't care; she doesn't know what it's like. She probably always had friends at school.

I haven't got a friend. I haven't got a sister. I've got magic I can't share, and my own mother doesn't know me when she sees me.

Nothing can hurt you while I'm taking care of you. That's the message Wildeth's music is sending me, tender and loving.

If that was all I could hear, I'd break down and spill the lot. But there's an echo of Grace too: 'Don't tell *anyone.*'

So I leave Wildeth's room and go to bed.

At least tomorrow we're back to normal school.

144

CHAPTER NINE

RUCE AND MR UGLY

'Maggot!'

It's gone nine in the evening, the Friday after half-term. I'm on my way to the dorm.

'Maggot! Come in here!'

Laban's in the broom cupboard halfway down the corridor, which is where some of the girls and boys meet for a grope. There's no other reason to go there unless you want a broom, but I guess whatever the game is, I've got to play.

'Look what we found!'

She's in there with Sally and Andy and Sergei.

'It's gross!' Sally backs away from something in the corner. I get a glimpse of something greyish-brown with whiskers.

'It's a rat,' says Sergei.

Laban knows I hate rats.

Andy pokes the thing with a brush handle. 'Vermin,'

145

he says. 'Should be poisoned,' and Sally squeals.

'We could give it bleach,' suggests Laban. She gets a bottle off the shelf and makes like she's going to open it.

Andy has another go with the brush, and the thing makes a noise. I'm not sure it is a rat, but I don't think I want to get involved here.

'Have a look.' Laban pushes me forward. She's interested to see if I puke or scream or do something pathetic.

'It's a kitten,' I say.

Everyone laughs. 'Ooh, a kitten, an ickle, fluffy kitten! Go on then, pick it up, give it a cuddle,' says Andy.

The thing looks at me. It is a kitten, but it's mangy, it's half-bald and one of its ears is just a stump with scabby bits. I don't want to touch it with my hands, so I give it a bit of a kick and it mews.

'Ugh!' Laban's really getting off on this. She's wriggling next to Sergei and standing on tiptoe. 'We should drown it, yeah.'

There's a bucket in the corner, with some dirty water in and a mop. Andy gets the mop and pushes it under the kitten, he's trying to lift it up but it scrabbles away from him and gets in between my feet.

'Oh, it likes Maggot!' Sergei chortles

'Hold still. I'll get it now.' Andy comes at me with the mop.

'Get off. Leave it,' I say.

'Are you scared?' Sally asks.

'Maggot likes it; it's her pet.' Andy's pleased I'm up against it.

'It's disgusting. We've got to get rid of it,' Laban urges me.

I'm stuck here. I'd like to just back out, go to bed and stick my head under the pillow; then I wouldn't know anything about it, but if I don't join in, they'll turn nasty.

I don't let myself think; I bend down and pick the thing up and chuck it in the bucket. Laban gasps and Sally squeals again and Andy says 'Hey,' like I've spoiled his fun. I didn't do it right, I shouldn't have touched it. Now they'll say I'm gross too.

It's in the water, it's paddling at the side of the bucket trying to get out. Andy pushes it under with the mop.

I grab the mop away from him.

'What's your problem?' says Laban.

I don't know what to do. Then the door bangs open, and here's Ruce in her dressing gown.

'What are you doing? I can hear you all the way down in the bathroom. We'll have Matron up in a minute. What's going on?'

147

I get the thing out of the bucket. It's now soaking wet and filthy as well as just revolting. It gets in between my neck and my shoulder and clings on with its sharp claws. It stinks.

'Oh foul!' Laban makes a vomit noise.

'It's a scabby cat,' says Andy. 'We're drowning it.'

'Yeah,' says Ruce. 'So drown it.'

She's got herself in between me and the rest of them, she's standing there like a pink towelling concrete mixer.

'Shift then and I will,' says Andy.

'Shift me,' says Ruce.

It's a stand-off. None of them's going to risk getting Ruce's fist in their face; they know she can knock any one of them flying. Even Andy won't mess with her on his own. But there's four of them, if they get their act together they can hammer us.

'Matron's coming!' I whisper.

It works. Even if they don't believe me, it's a way to get out and save face, and they scatter off back to their dorms. Laban's the last to go.

'Hope you like your new pet,' she says.

*

So now I'm mates with Ruce and I've got a kitten to look after. None of this is a massive change for the better. Ruce is still big and ginger and clumsy and tactless, and the animal doesn't improve on

148

acquaintance either. It's just as hideous when it's clean and dry.

'Mr Ugly,' chirrups Ruce, trying to tickle it under the chin. 'Mr Ugly come to Rucey.'

It spits at her. I'm the only one it likes. I can't return the compliment but I can't get rid of the thing either, wherever I go, it comes too. It's a big joke for everyone except me.

'Margot, where did you get that cat?' demands Matron.

'I just found it; it's a stray.'

'We don't have pets in school.'

'I know. I don't want it,' I protest. 'What am I supposed to do with it?'

Matron takes it in her office. A couple of hours later, when it's crapped on her desk and shredded her curtains, she gives it back to me.

'Dr Wildeth says you can keep it.'

Thanks for nothing, Wildeth.

*

'Maybe he's your familiar,' says Ruce.

'Maybe,' I agree before I realize what she's said. 'What do you mean, familiar?'

'Don't some witches have animals? Toads, cats, rats, hedgehogs, that sort of thing.'

Perhaps she's just making a joke.

'Maggot, I know you're a witch,' says Ruce. She's

149

called me Maggot all the time, which helps a bit now the other kids do.

I don't say anything.

'I'm not a witch,' she goes on, 'but Rossy thought I would be.' Rossy was her uncle; he died a while back. 'He was a witch, and he told me about deep music and all that, though he probably shouldn't have done.'

'How do you know I am?'

'You go to Wildeth. Only the witches go to Wildeth. I know what goes on; I know about her teaching magic.'

We've got the gym to ourselves. Ruce is weight-training, I'm leaning against an exercise bike, and Mr Ugly's mauling an old sweat-band.

'I remember you saying your uncle knew Wildeth.'

'They were on the Bureau together,' says Ruce.

She bends her elbows, flexes her shoulders, raises the weights and lowers them.

'Your uncle was on the Bureau?' I'm staring. '*Wildeth*'s on the Bureau?'

'Sure. So's Laban's mum and Andy's dad. Magic runs in families. They send their kids here so Wildeth can spot 'em early and train them up: old boys' network.'

'What *is* the Bureau?'

'It's like the witches' council. I don't know what they actually *do*; you wouldn't ever know unless you were a member. It's all very hush-hush. Maybe you'll get to be on it yourself, and then you'll find out.'

'When was your uncle a member?'

She lies on her back and holds the weights across her chest. 'Most of his life, I suppose. He had to stop when he got ill. I think maybe that's why he told me more than he should have done, because he couldn't do magic any more himself.'

'Did he say anything about the other members, ones from before?' He could have mentioned Grace. 'Did any of them visit him?'

'Just Nilas.'

She's watching the weights, she isn't looking at me.

'Did you say ... Nilas?'

'Nilas Samuel – he's the head of the Bureau.'

Nilas, Grace's enemy. Cruel Nilas, who hurt her and hounded her and wants to get his hands on me so he can hurt me too. Nilas who has his spies everywhere, who's in league with the Others, the less-than-human creatures that live in the hills and chased me through the trees ... But he's on the Bureau. He's *head* of the Bureau, and Humph says the Bureau's the witches who want to kill the Others. So was I wrong? Are the Others out to get me for some completely different reason?

'Maggot, are you ok?'

'Fine. I don't know.'

I'm sitting on the floor.

Ruce squats next to me. 'What's wrong?'

'Tell me about Nilas. It's really important.'

'I don't remember a lot about him except he had big sticky-out ears.'

'Didn't your uncle ever talk about him?'

'Not a lot. They used to be pals, and then they fell out. I think Rossy was quite unhappy about that; it was around the time he got ill too. Nilas just came the once. It was ages ago, and he didn't stay long. Rossy said afterwards that he, Nilas I mean, was trying to make friends again, but it was a bit late for that. He didn't come again, as far as I know.' She pauses. 'Maggot, what's this about?'

Mr Ugly pushes his head under my elbow and starts purring and kneading my thigh with his claws. It hurts, but if you stop him doing it, he bites you.

'Maggot?'

'It's a long story,' I mutter. And then I'm telling it, and when I get going I can't stop till I'm done: Grace and Nilas and Humph, and the woman in the woods and the dude in the car, everything that happened before I got to Crossbeams, and since then too, about half-term and the shielding spell, though I don't go into too much detail on that.

Ruce doesn't interrupt; maybe she thinks I'm crazy.

'And I thought the Bureau was, like, the good guys,

because my mum worked for them. But now you say Nilas runs the Bureau, so I don't get it. I wish I'd asked Gordy a bit more.'

'Gordy?'

'He's the guy that's helping my mum get her memory back.'

'Tall, fair hair, big feet, big smile? Gordy Shaw?'

'Yeah, how do you know him?'

'He was head boy here. Gorgeous Gordy! Laban had a massive crush on him.' Not just Laban, at a guess: Ruce has gone quite pink and dreamy.

'Was he one of Wildeth's students?'

'Of course. His grandfather's on the Bureau too: Maxim Shaw.'

I just can't imagine Gordy doing magic. It doesn't go with the toothpaste smile and the Hilfiger sweatshirts. Still, if he's any good, he's someone I know I can trust, because Mum told me so.

'Maybe Gordy could help me get rid of this spell, curse, whatever it is,' I say, 'that stops any witch hearing my deep music.'

'Yeah, but ...' Ruce hesitates.

'What?'

'Well, if a witch hears your music, they know what you're thinking, is that right? So whoever put the spell on you, they might have been doing you a favour. It stopped Wildeth reading your thoughts.'

'You just don't like her.'

'Maggot, don't you get it? Wildeth's on the Bureau too, remember? She's Nilas's right-hand woman.'

I'm such an idiot. I sit up, flipping Mr Ugly off my lap, then scoop him up and scramble to my knees.

Ruce grabs my elbow. 'Where are you going?'

'I'm supposed to be seeing her this evening. I've got to get away.'

But there's nowhere to go. Outside the school, the Others can get me. Inside, I'm a lab rat: I thought I was hidden, but the top of my cage is glass.

'If you're meant to see her, go and see her. Nothing's changed,' Ruce points out. 'Ok, Nilas can look in whenever he wants, but he could have done it any time since you got here, and he hasn't done it yet, has he?'

*

It's eight o'clock. I've not had a session with Wildeth this late, maybe she's going to show me some magic that only works after dark.

I'm going up the stairs with Mr Ugly draped round my neck. When we get to the second flight I can feel him tensing up, and at the landing he suddenly snarls and spits.

'Stop it!' I tell him. He's digging his claws in my shoulder, and then he lets go and leaps off me, and races off down the stairs as if something horrible's after him.

I'm unnerved. He doesn't like going up to Wildeth's room. I've noticed that before, but he's never run off like that. I can't go looking for him now.

I knock at the door.

'I've got a visitor here who wants to meet you,' says Wildeth. 'Come in, Margot. This is Mr Nilas Samuel.'

CHAPTER TEN

NILAS

My mother said he was strong and wicked: her enemy.
Just his name made me shiver.

This man's old, whitehaired, thin as a leaf. His head
comes up to my shoulder because he's in a wheelchair.

The lights aren't on, but the curtains are open and
there's a big moon shining right in. I can see him well
enough. His face is kind of crumpled on one side, and
his left eye's shut. The other one's grey, and filmy with
age.

Like Ruce said, his ears stick out.

'Margot, little Margot.' His breath wheezes in his
chest. How old is he? 'You've grown up.'

I'm gobsmacked: even with the wonky face you
wouldn't be scared of him. He's too small, too old.
'Did you know me when I was little?'

'A long time ago.' The right side of his mouth lifts
in half a smile. 'Your mother was a great friend of
mine.'

I'm lost for words.

'Sit down. I can't see well, I need you near. Closer, child, closer. I don't bite. Chair here.' He fusses till I'm knee to knee with him and he's got my hand under his own paper-thin palm. Wildeth takes a seat behind her desk, her back to the moonlight, her face in shadow.

'So much to say to you. Could take all night. Mustn't do that.' He talks quick, with little gasps in between the sentences, and doesn't bother with some of the words. I think maybe he's in pain. 'Listen, Margot, it's about your mother. Things you don't know; going to be a shock. Think you'll faint, throw a fit?'

'Can't tell till you try.' That comes out steady. I'm pleased with myself.

'She's not dead. Your mother's alive. Not who you thought. Your real mother's living in the Residence. Name's Grace.'

He doesn't know I know! He's telling me, so nobody knows. I'm safe! Am I?

I guess he'd expect me to feel pretty confused.

'She lost her memory. Lost a lot. Might get it back. That's up to you.' The working eyebrow goes up, and he taps my wrist with one finger.

'How come? I don't understand.'

'Ever heard of the Bureau? Know what it is? Nobody knows what it is. I don't know, and I've been running it for forty years.' His voice pipes the wreck of a tune, and he takes my hand and his on a flight together, veering from side to side: 'This is the way the witches ride, whee-ooh, whee-ooh …'

He's got to be senile.

'Long time ago, sixteenth century, seventeenth century, everyone getting their knickers in a knot about magic. All mixed up with Protestants and Catholics. You don't want a history lesson. Drowning old women, burning, killing. My cow died after you gave her the evil eye.'

I vaguely know what he's talking about.

'So the real witches, mostly not the old women, hm? They got together. Protection. That's how it began, the Bureau. Witches looking out for each other. What do you think magic is? Eh?'

'It's music. Deep music.'

'Yes, yes. That's the way it works, how it comes through. What does it do? What can you do with it?'

'You can hear people's thoughts, let them hear you.' This is just what I can't do, of course, but I know it's what I'm aiming for. 'See things how other people see them, show them what you're seeing. Like when Wildeth, I mean Dr Wildeth—' I glance at her, but I can't see her expression. 'She showed us a spell with rain and snowflakes; it was like she shared a dream with us. It's sort of … imagination, but you can make it real, what you see.'

He begins chuckling. 'You're very young, my dear.'

'You're very old,' I reply as politely as I know how, and he stops laughing.

'Magic is power. Power is responsibility. Very few witches in this world. Many more everyday men and women, good, bad or indifferent, going about their business in happy ignorance or unhappy impotence. In the country of the blind,' he winks at me, 'the one-eyed man is king.'

What's he trying to tell me?

'She's had dreams about the Others,' Wildeth puts in softly.

'Frighten you?' he asks. 'Needn't have done. Could have been a pretty dream. The Others can be more beautiful than anything you can think of. Can be more cruel, too. Bloodier, uglier.'

His head jerks and his mouth twitches. 'Uglier – than I am,' he manages to say.

'You're not ugly.' A bit grotesque, maybe, but I don't mention that.

'Kind words. Quite a handsome fellow, once.'

He's quiet for a moment. The moon shining on his hair turns it silver. The only other light comes from the flower tank, the glow changing colour as the petals move.

'Ordinary people, they don't know about the Others. Think it's all fables. Wouldn't believe it if you told them, wouldn't believe it if you showed them; people see what they're ready to see. So, no defence. You can't fight shadows. Witches are different; we know what's casting the shadow.'

'What *are* the Others?' I ask.

'Monsters and angels, elves and ghouls. Think I'm out of my mind? The Others are real, they're the facts behind the fairy tales; all the legends people make up to explain what they don't understand. The Others are the demons and the gods, and they scare the hell out of me,' he says, his mouth twitching. I can't tell if it's pain or a smile or both.

'Some of them were friendly, once upon a time. That's how the stories begin, hm? This is how they end: the Others at war with humankind.'

'What started the war?' I ask.

'The usual things: territory, land, survival. More people in the world than there were. The Others think they're crowded out. Room for everyone, that's the truth, but for the Others it's all or nothing, they don't do compromise. They decided we have to go.'

'They want to wipe out the human race?'

'There'd be a few of us left, slaves or pets. Back to the small hours of history, spirits of nature walking the earth proud and free, men worshipping them, begging for fire and food.' He frowns, one-sided.

'Can't the Bureau do anything?'

'Tried to keep the peace, for a long time. Failed in the end. The Others aren't rational, you see. They sow discord, distrust. Their magic, it can make humans want to kill each other. The Others haven't got a central authority like the Bureau to control them, don't keep their promises, so you can't make deals with them. The Bureau agreed, finally, witches are human. We have to take the human side, even if that means destroying the Others. Hard choice: shouldn't use magic to take life. But you can't tame the Others.'

He shakes his head, or it could be just a tremor.

'Hard to kill them, too. Thesida, can Margot defend herself against the Others?'

Wildeth leans forward. 'She hasn't needed to leave the school.'

'She'll have to leave it one of these days. She's got a block, that's right?'

'You can't hear her tune. She can hear ours,' Wildeth tells him.

'Got to be a spell there. Never mind. There's other ways.'

With his good hand, he reaches into an inner pocket of his jacket. The twist hurts him, and he frowns as he pulls his hand out, and lays it in my lap. In his palm there's a brass whistle, about as long as his thumb.

'Take it. Blow it.'

162

I do, and there's no sound at all. Is it one of those supersonic dog whistles?

His mouth is hitched up in a smile. 'Listen with your music.'

I close my eyes, summon my own tune, let the golden notes fill my head, and blow again. This time I hear a screeching crackle like static, and there's a fizz of light behind my eyelids.

'Ouch,' I say.

'That's it. Not much. But it frightens them. Keep it. Could save your life, in a corner.'

'If you can't kill the Others—' I begin.

'It's not impossible,' Wildeth tells me.

'But it's hard,' says Nilas. 'Listen: the Bureau, that's the strongest witches there are, working together. Not many, that doesn't matter. Ten witches together doesn't mean ten times more power than one, means much, much more than that. The Bureau's the strongest magic there is.'

He's worked up, panting for air, his fingers clutching mine.

'Together, we could have wiped the Others off the planet. We made our choice. Made our plan. Began to put it in practice.'

'What happened?'

'Nothing. Wash-out.'

'Why?'

'That's what I wanted to know. Only one answer. The members of the Bureau, they weren't all working together. Some of them, in secret, working for the Others.'

He takes a few deep breaths and leans back.

'I asked them, the whole meeting, said obviously there was an opposition element. Invited them to speak up, let us all discuss it. Nobody said a word. I told them, anyone who came to me in private, I'd respect their confidence. Nobody came. And so I found a spell. An evil spell.'

He feels me jump.

'Yes, it was evil. Very old, very strong. A thing called the Skull, buried and forgotten, until I found it. It showed the truth. I knew it was dangerous. Don't know if you'll understand. These were my friends and my colleagues, we all had to trust each other. When we couldn't do that, we couldn't do anything. So I used the Skull, to show me their secrets.'

The sky's clouded over while he's been talking; the moon's gone. Now there's just the light from the flowers reflected on his face, glowing red and blue. I think he's smiling, but it's hard to tell.

'Your mother, Grace, one of the most talented witches I ever met. Magic to her fingertips, and lovely too. If I hadn't been a regular old bachelor, I could have fallen head over heels. Mustn't think I blame her, not then, not now. She believed she was right, someone put her up to it, I stick to that.'

I try to swallow, but my mouth's dry. 'She was helping the Others?'

'Must have been. Because when I came to her, with the Skull, she'd sent her magic out of her. So there'd be no secrets in her for me to read, you understand? What she didn't know was – you could only use the Skull on a witch. Needed their own magic to protect them against the Skull's magic. When I used it on Grace, she didn't have anything to protect her. So, something like a short circuit, the Skull shattered. Grace and me, both injured.'

He lifts his right hand with his left and lets it fall again. Then he points at the right side of his face.

'You can see what happened to me. It was worse for Grace. She lost everything. She didn't remember how she lost her powers, where she sent them. I tried to help her, till I realized I was only hurting her more.'

His working eye shines, staring at me.

'I think she sent her powers to you, Margot.'

How well can he see my expression, how much does it show?

'Power can't just vanish,' Nilas explains. 'Grace had to send her magic somewhere, had to be a channel, had to be close. Only person there, apart from me, was you.'

'I was *there*?'

'Three years old. You'd have known nothing about it, still wouldn't know, nothing to show, except you've cottoned on quick to magic, hm?'

I was there. I was there when it happened. It's like my brain's on spin cycle and just this one thought going round and round in the middle.

The room's swaying, the flower-heads are pulsing brighter and darker, telling me something?

'Put your head down. Breathe.'

That's Wildeth's voice, and I feel her hand on my shoulder. I've never fainted before and now's not the time to try it out, so I do as she says and the world settles down.

Wildeth and Nilas are one each side of me, watching me.

'There's nothing to be frightened of,' Wildeth tells me.

'Grace's magic was strong medicine,' says Nilas. 'You don't want to find yourself dealing with that on your own.'

'I wasn't sure at first,' Wildeth murmurs. 'But the shielding spell …'

'Got to be Grace's power behind it,' Nilas chips in.

Wildeth is close enough that her breath's warm on my cheek. 'You'll be able to help your mother. You'll have her back again. Think about that.'

'Wouldn't be able to do it on your own,' Nilas warns me.

'But you're not on your own.' Wildeth strokes my hand. 'We're here to help you.'

'Yes,' Nilas echoes. 'We're here.'

*

I stumble down the stairs. Mr Ugly's waiting for me halfway, and I wait while he arranges himself across my shoulders, and then I carry on down to the front door.

I go out on the steps: I need some air. It's frosty, and after I've stood there a few minutes I start to feel better but cold. Nobody's asked me what I'm doing outside, so I can take a quick walk up and down the drive.

There's a car parked on the gravel, must be Nilas's. How did he get up to Wildeth's room in his chair? Maybe it was magic, or maybe there's a lift I don't know about.

'Hey, Trouble, you ok?'

The voice comes from the car. I look again: it's the same silver Merc that stopped for me in the woods, and the same young bro is leaning out of the driver's window.

'What are you doing here?'

'Driving Mr Samuel,' he says.

'You told me you didn't have a boss.'

'Doesn't mean I can't drive a man that can't drive himself.'

He opens the passenger door and Mr Ugly slides in, so I might as well sit down too. The seats are leather and it's warm in here.

'Mean-looking animal.' I think it's meant as a compliment. He reaches out a finger to touch Ugly's head, and I wait for the screams, but the cat just sniffs and turns his head away.

'He must like you,' I say.

'Fellow-feeling. Both of us can bite when we need to. Here, have a sip.' He's drinking coffee out of a silver travelling cup: smells like there's a drop of brandy in it.

I take a long swallow. Excellent, I feel better all the way down. 'Thanks.'

'Nothing but a pleasure.'

'Hey, you know when I saw you before, there was a bomb or something at Network.'

'Yeah, that's what took me up in the woods.'

'It wasn't you, was it?' It's a stupid question, and he laughs and puts up his hands.

'I'll come quietly, officer.'

'The police asked me if I'd seen anyone. I didn't say anything about you.'

'That's real sweet of you, but explosives never were my thing. I was fetching Nilas to check it out.'

'What's it got to do with him?'

'He's head of Network. That's his building going up there.'

'I didn't know that.' But then there's such a lot I don't know. Even master witches have their business interests. 'Did they find out who did it?'

'Guards reported some woman up at the site, but they never traced her.' He grins. 'Wasn't you, was it?'

That's getting too close for comfort. Why did I start talking about this? I shake my head. 'Not guilty. I'd better be heading in now; thanks for the coffee.'

'Till next time,' he says.

If he drives Nilas around, I suppose I might see him again. I don't mind; he's smart even if he's sassy.

*

Grace says Nilas wanted her secrets and he tortured her. Nilas says Grace was working with the Others, and he only hurt her when he tried to help her.

'Who do I believe?'

'It's no good asking me.' Ruce is lounging on her bed, trying to interest Ugly in a piece of string, but he's not playing. 'I saw Nilas once. I've never met your mother.'

'I've only talked to her once myself, since I was three.'

'You'll be seeing her tomorrow.'

'Yeah, that's right.' I'm going home for my birthday,

my first visit since I started at Crossbeams. 'You want to come too?'

'Would you like me to?'

'Maybe.'

'There's not much I can do if the Forces of Evil come for you.'

It's all too possible the Others will have a go when I'm outside the school grounds, but I've got to take the risk sometime. At least I've got Nilas's dog-whistle now.

'Moral support's what I need, not a bodyguard,' I tell Ruce.

'I've got more body than morals.' Ugly makes a grab for her hand. 'Get off, fleabag. Won't I be in the way?'

'Gordy's driving me there and back.'

'And why would that interest me?'

'It'd be one up on Laban. If she had the hots for him, I mean.'

Ruce rolls on her back. '*Everybody* had the hots for him, Matron downwards.'

'He must have gone off since then. He wears stripey jumpers.'

'It's what's under the jumper that counts.' She jiggles her own boobs to demonstrate. 'Hey, can you do love potions?'

*

I was worried she was going to go Desperate

Schoolgirl, but actually this morning she looks pretty fit. She's in jeans and a leather jacket and heavy boots and a lot of mascara, and she's rearranged her figure so there's more up top and down bottom and less in the middle. If you like that sort of thing, there's plenty to like, and Tomas wolf-whistles her when she walks downstairs to the hall. Ruce gives him the finger.

I'm looking through the glass doors. Here comes Gordy's two-door green rust-bucket, heading up the drive.

'Haven't sent the limo, have they?' sneers Laban.

I go down the steps as the car stops in a spray of gravel. Gordy gets out, long legs and stripes and tousled fair hair, and suddenly there's Matron hugging him, and Laban's showing a bit of leg, and Wildeth's smiling hello. It's all so fluffy and cuddly it makes me want to heave.

I dump Mr Ugly's basket in Gordy's arms.

'Hey, Mag. Is this your cat? Puss-puss, ow!'

'He doesn't like being poked,' I say.

Good, that's wiped the grin off.

'Ok, let's get going, shall we?' Gordy licks blood from the back of his hand. 'Where's your friend that's coming too?'

'That'd be me.'

It's a fantastic entrance. Ruce is at the top of the steps; he's at the bottom with his eyes on a level with her tits. I see him make an effort to look a bit higher.

'Great, well. Great, yes. Hello, nice to meet you. Why don't you get in the car?'

She squirms into the back seat and I get in the front. Gordy's so distracted he whacks himself on the chin with the car door.

Who needs love potions?

CHAPTER ELEVEN

THE BUREAU
AND THE OPPOSITION

'Gordy, we need to talk.'

He gives me what I suppose is a warning frown.

'Don't pull faces. Ruce is cool; I've talked to her.'

'I'm not a witch,' Ruce puts in, 'but I do know about magic.'

'I'm sure you do,' Gordy smirks with extra cheese. 'Hey, don't I remember you from the old days at school?' he adds over his shoulder.

'Probably not,' says Ruce. 'I developed.'

'Chat her up in your own time,' I tell Gordy. 'Look, I'll tell her what you tell me. Why not cut to the chase and do it now?'

'Mag, we'll have a word later, ok?'

He's not going to budge on this. I sigh and look out of the window, and after a minute I start humming.

'Want some music on?' says Gordy, meaning *That's really annoying.*

'No, thanks.' It was too loud; he's not supposed to notice. I wait and then try again, this time so soft that even I can hardly hear it.

Gently, gently slip inside his head ... I've never tried this before, there's every chance it won't work, but Wildeth said it was a channel. If Gordy really is a witch, is he stronger than I am? He's older, but I've got Grace's power going for me. And I need to know what he knows. I'm guessing he wouldn't be dead straight, even if Ruce wasn't here.

I step up the humming a bit and this time he doesn't say anything. He's driving slower, swerving a bit. 'Gordy, let's pull over,' I say out loud. I want him to answer my questions, not put us in the ditch.

He doesn't argue, so he must be under control. He parks under a horse-chestnut tree. It's a pity conker season's over, I love them when they're all shiny and new and so much handsomer than Gordy.

'What have you done to him?' whispers Ruce.

'It's a spell. Look at me, Gordy.' I keep my voice steady, and he turns his head.

'You're going to talk to me, aren't you?'

He nods. That was so easy. He wasn't expecting it, I guess. I've climbed in like his mind was a car, and I'm in the driving seat now. I just hope I can steer.

'Will he do whatever you tell him?' asks Ruce. 'Will it work for me too?'

'We haven't got time for you to play with him.'

'I could just find out if he fancies me.'

'He's going to remember what we've said when the spell wears off.'

'Oh.' Ruce shuts up.

'So why didn't you do like you said?' I ask Gordy. 'You were meant to fix it so I didn't have to go away to school.'

'I did fix it. It was you who ran off.'

My mouth might have fallen open, so I close it.

'Once you got to Crossbeams,' he goes on, 'there wasn't anything I could do.'

In slow motion, the penny drops and the wheels turn.

'Do you mean it was you who got me snatched off the bus?'

Suddenly a lot of things make sense. That's putting it too strongly, but they make less nonsense. When Humph said Sylvian got a message from the witch, I thought he meant Nilas, but no, it was good old Gordy.

'Who's Sylvian?' I ask.

'She's the Other of the Island.'

'I don't understand.'

He hesitates. This spell doesn't make people any brighter or better at explaining things. 'It's like how the Others are,' he says, 'with the land where they live – a field or a river or just a tree – they're a part of it and it's a part of them. Sylvian's like that for the whole Island.'

I kind of get it. 'Why didn't you let me know what you were doing?' I make an effort not to raise my voice.

'There wasn't time. I hoped you'd guess it was me.'

Maybe I should have done. Hey, I've been kidnapped by a hob; that must be Gordy's idea. No, I don't think I've got to blame myself too much.

'It wasn't safe to talk at the Residence,' Gordy adds. 'There was always the chance of Sykes hearing. He's feeling his age these days, but he used to be pretty sharp.'

'Is Sykes a witch?'

'He's on the Bureau too, he reports straight to Nilas.'

That makes me jump, that little word 'too'. 'Gordy, are *you* on the Bureau?'

'Sure.'

'Can I trust you? Are you on my side?' He couldn't lie to me now.

'You can trust me. I'm Opposition.'

'What does that mean?' Ruce asks.

'We're the ones who are trying to get rid of Nilas. Nilas is the head of the Bureau,' he explains. 'He's gone bad; he's power-crazy.'

'He doesn't look like it,' I object.

'Don't get fooled by the helpless act. He's strong, he's ruthless, and anyone who tries to challenge him openly gets put out of the way.' He twists round in his seat to look at Ruce. 'That's what happened to your uncle Rossy.'

Ruce sits back like he slapped her. 'What? What do you mean?' She doesn't speak loudly, but there's something in her voice that almost snaps the spell: Gordy starts blinking. I hum a bit more and bring him back.

'Gordy,' I say quietly, 'what happened to Rossy?'

'He was close to Nilas, till Nilas started the idea to wipe out the Others. Rossy didn't agree and he said so, and the next thing was he got sick and lost his powers.'

Ruce is leaning forward again. 'How do you know? You weren't there then.'

'No, but my grandfather was, and he's told me what happened. Rossy put himself on the line. He knew he was taking a risk, but he was an old friend; he thought Nilas would respect his opinion. He was wrong, and he found out the hard way.'

Ruce has got her hand on my shoulder, her fist clenched in my jacket.

'Go on,' I say to Gordy.

'So Rossy was out of the game. Then Maxim, that's my grandfather, he set up the Opposition in secret. Nilas realized what was going on but he didn't know who was behind it. He got hold of a spell to find out who was loyal to him.'

'I know what happened to Grace. And after that?'

'Nilas needed to know where Grace sent her powers so he put Sykes on the case. That's what the Residence was set up for. It's just a front.'

'What about the Hollies? What about Dad?' I'm panicking: I've known Sykes ever since I can remember.

'The patients are genuine. Eron knows who Grace is, but he doesn't have a clue about the rest of it.'

'Makes two of us,' I mutter.

'It was only supposed to be a temporary measure. Nilas thought Grace would recover, at least enough to tell him what he wanted. But she stayed the same, and he started to think about you instead. If Grace had transferred her magic to you, then one day you'd know what she knew. That's why Temple came to the Residence.'

Not Temple too.

'She was meant to make friends with you, if she could,' Gordy goes on.

That takes a second to sink in. *Meant to make friends* … I remember the conversations, the camp fire, the songs. Was it all so I'd feel safe with her and open up? No wonder she never got in touch, after she left.

'But she was asking too many questions. Nilas

began ... to suspect ... she wasn't reliable. Had her moved on ... and I was put in.' He's talking slower.

'You were supposed to get close to me too?' I ask, keeping my voice strictly neutral.

'Maxim saw ... his chance.' The words are beginning to slur. 'Told Nilash ... Nilas ... I was ... the right one for the job ... young ... good-looking ... 'swhat he said ... maybe I'd ...'

'What's wrong with him? He sounds as if he's on drugs,' says Ruce.

'That's the spell. It's not safe keeping someone under too long,' I tell her. 'Go on, Gordy. They thought I'd fall for you, so if I started to get Mum's magic, you'd be the first to know?'

'Something ... along those lines ... was the offish ... offish ... *official* ... version. Really ... watching Grace ... help her get ... memory back. Almost ... straight now ... off the medicine. Sykes ... lost the plot ... hardly notices.' His head flops sideways.

Ruce jogs my arm. 'Maggot, you've got to wake him up.'

'Do you mean Mum's back to normal? Gordy, look at me.'

'Pretty much ... remembers everything ... Has to put on ... an act ... for Eron ... Sykezzz ...'

His eyes are closed and his chin's on his chest. I slap him briskly across the cheek; I don't really need to, but it's very enjoyable.

He snorts and yawns and rubs his eyes. 'What the hell? Did I drop off?'

'Snoring like a toilet,' I tell him.

He rubs his hand over his face. 'Did you just hit me?' I see him getting there. 'Did you ...' He can't quite believe it. 'Did you just put a spell on me?'

'Yup, sorry.'

There's a pause; after a while it turns into a silence. I guess we've all got a bit to think about. Gordy puts his hands on the steering wheel and leans his head on them. Ruce stares out of the window at the horse-chestnut tree. I don't look at anything much, nothing that's going on outside me anyway.

*

It's Gordy who speaks first. 'I'm really, really sorry,' he says into his arms.

'That's ok.' I'm trying to be generous, though the idea that I was meant to fancy him is making me spit. 'I can see why you didn't want to—'

'Not you!' He sits up and twists round to Ruce. 'I'd never have said that about your uncle. The spell made me, I wasn't thinking what I was saying, what it meant to you.'

'You were just telling it like it is.' She sounds quite calm, calmer than I'm feeling. All right, it's big, bad news for Ruce about her uncle Rossy, but how about me? All my life, my dad's been hiding a massive secret. Sykes, who's been like my grandad, turns out to have been my warden. And Temple, my White Sister, was a spy. Liking me, seeming to like me, was part of her job. Just about everyone I thought I knew was putting on an act. Gordy can't spare a word for that?

He turns back to me. 'As soon as I heard her name, I knew who she was. That's why I didn't want to talk in front of her. Why couldn't you trust me?'

'Maybe I would if you were a bit keener to tell me what's going on,' I snap. 'Couldn't you have rung me? Sent a text?'

'At Crossbeams? Yeah, if I wanted Wildeth in on the whole tale.' Gordy glances at his watch. 'We'd better make a move or we're going to be late for lunch.' He winds down his window. 'I've got a headache.'

'I should have pulled you out sooner,' I admit.

'If I wreck the car, I'm suing you.' He turns the key and the engine wheezes and sneezes.

'It couldn't be much more of a wreck.' We lurch off the grass and onto the road.

'If Nilas got Maggot's magic,' asks Ruce, 'I mean Grace's magic, what would he do?'

'I think he'd kill Mag.' Gordy sounds pretty smooth with that idea. 'He'd kill Grace for sure. She's only lasted this long because he wasn't certain where she sent her powers. He'd know everything about the Opposition, including me and my grandfather, so we'd be for the chop too.'

'And what happens if Maggot gives the magic back to Grace?'

'The Opposition'll be that much stronger; we can fight Nilas.'

'But after that?' I say. 'What happens to – well, to everybody? Nilas says there's a war on with the Others.'

'If it is, that's only because of what he's done. Look at this.'

We're coming to the Network development. There's a lot of activity, diggers and workmen and noise.

'Do you know how many of the Others have been killed to make way for this?' asks Gordy.

'Do you know what the Others have done to stop it?' I demand. 'I saw a bomb go off here, and people got hurt, ordinary people. They weren't witches; they were just trying to do a job.'

'There are new buildings going up all the time, everywhere,' Ruce points out.

'This place is special,' says Gordy.

'Special how?' I ask. It's just a bit of woodland, or it used to be.

'Special for magic. There's some kind of influence or force. That's not just what the Others think, either.

It's why the Bureau holds its meetings on the Island, why Nilas and my grandpa live here. It's why Crossbeams is the top school for witches.'

'So it's not just this particular spot?' I say.

'Here's the centre. Whatever it is that makes the Island powerful, here's where it comes from. And here is where Nilas wants to build. You know he runs Network?'

'Yes, I heard that,' I say.

'This is a Network site; it's going to be the new headquarters.'

'But work only started here a couple of years ago,' I argue. 'And the Others have been fighting the humans for centuries. It was Humph who told me that, and he *is* one of the Others. So it can't be just because of what Nilas is doing, can it? And even if it is, if the Others are at war with the humans, then no matter why that's happened we've got to be on the human side, haven't we?'

'That's what the Bureau's there for,' says Gordy. 'We're meant to keep a balance between people and Others. If it wasn't for Nilas, we could get things back to – what the—?'

There's a bird flying at us. The windscreen goes dark. For a second all we can see is feathers, and then the car skids across the road as Gordy brakes. I don't think we made contact: the thing's turned in the air, and now it swoops back and settles on the bonnet. It's some sort of a black seagull, with a long curving bill and yellow eyes.

It's Bargus.

I guess this is what Humph meant about a witch always seeing a shapeshifter's real form, except it's not like seeing. I just know. I see a bird; I know it's a dog.

'Go away,' I say out loud. 'Shoo!'

'Awk!' says Bargus. He flaps his wings and raises himself into the air, then flutters round the car. My window's up, so he crosses back to the driver's side and squawks through the gap.

Gordy seems to think the Others are only scary because they've been persecuted. Maybe he's right, but just because they've got a reason to be vicious, that doesn't make them cute. I'm remembering Bargus leaping out of the dark woods, a baying hellhound. Looking at his sharp bird-face now, the wicked beak, the gleaming eyes, I can see the jaws of the dog, the wide drooling howling mouth, the teeth, the red snarl.

'Go away! Clear off, leave me alone!' I'm shouting across Gordy. 'I never did anything to you, just get out, get away from me!'

'Mag, it's ok!'

Yeah right, Gordy, you go head to head with a demonic seagull and see how you like it.

I pull Nilas's whistle out of my pocket and close my

eyes. Do the Others even have deep music? Yes, when I focus, I can hear Bargus, though it's not what you'd call a tune: a thumping, panting pad of sound, which I guess is his dogness, with a coarse whoop and wail that could be the bird bit.

I don't bother what he might be thinking, I just want rid of him. I blow the whistle, I hear the silent screech and see the invisible sparkle, and I go on blowing till I've got no breath left in my lungs.

When I open my eyes, Bargus has gone.

'There's a reason you were screaming at a seagull, right?' Ruce sounds a bit shaken up.

I delay answering while I lean over and shut Gordy's window.

'It wasn't a seagull.'

'Cormorant, whatever.'

'It was one of the Others. It was the dog that went for me in the woods. He's been after me ever since, waiting outside the school for a chance to get at me.'

'What's that thing you were blowing on?' Gordy asks.

'Nilas gave it me. It's defence against the Others.'

'What does it do?'

'Scares them off. It worked, didn't it?'

'But he wasn't trying to hurt you!'

'Yeah, you reckon he wanted to snuggle?'

Gordy straightens the car out and moves on. 'Mag,

look, you don't have to be afraid of the Others.'

'If I don't, it's because I'm a witch. Most people can't protect themselves, can they? As far as I can work out, it's just Nilas keeping a lid on things. If you get rid of him, there's going to be a bloodbath.'

'If we get rid of him, the Bureau can mediate.'

'When you say *get rid of him*—' I begin.

'You said it first.'

'I want to know what it means! Are we talking about, like, *killing* him?'

Gordy doesn't answer.

'I mean, Gordy, I don't want any part of that. The Others kill people. Witches shouldn't kill people, should they?'

'Nilas wants to kill the Others.'

That's dodging the question.

'You know what he did to your mother,' he goes on.

I know what she said he did, and I know what Nilas said. I'm still not sure if I should believe what she told me or how I got it from him.

'Of course I want to help *her*. I don't know if I want to help the Others, that's all. I think I should just stay out of it.'

'Mag, you can't stay out of it. You've got to come down one way or the other.'

'Why do I have to? When I get my name, then I can just use Grace's power myself. Stop the Others killing humans, try to stop Nilas killing the Others.'

'You're thirteen years old—'

'Fourteen,' I correct him. 'That's why I'm coming home today, remember?'

'I'm sorry if your birthday slipped my mind while I was thinking how we're all in mortal danger. What I'm saying is, you won't be able to control Grace's magic.'

'I can control you all right.'

Maybe that wasn't mega-diplomatic. Gordy takes the corner to the Residence drive like Formula One. 'Have it your own way, but if you're not going to help us, then you can't expect us to help you.'

'You haven't been a lot of use up to now anyway.'

'Maggot, be sensible,' Ruce begs me. 'You know you need Gordy, and he needs you. Don't fall out; it's stupid.'

'I'm not falling out.' I can hear myself sounding childish and stubborn. What he said while he was under the spell, that hurts. The fact he couldn't even acknowledge, when he came round, that I might be upset – that's making me fume. 'I'm just saying I'm not taking sides,' I say, trying for rational and mature.

'If you're not with us, then you're with Nilas. It's as simple as that.' We come up to the house, and Gordy brakes like he wishes it was me he was stamping on.

'Hey, look at that!' Ruce exclaims.

There's a big banner over the door:

WELCOME HOME DEAR MAG HAPPY BIRTHDAY!!!

– and then all the Hollies and Dad and Bella and Sykes have signed their names, but Gordy hasn't. I guess he was driving to Crossbeams when they made it, but it's another reason to be angry.

*

The Hollies are all doing birthday surprises in the canteen, so there's no way I can get Grace on her own. Gordy's showing Ruce the bay, and I don't feel like playing gooseberry. I go to my room: it's clean and tidy. It doesn't look like mine, so I say hello to Little Bear and come downstairs again.

Bella hurries past.

'Can I give you a hand?' I offer.

'No way, babe! You're our princess today; you take it easy. Your dad's in charge of lunch. I'm just adding the frills.'

Dad trots after her, carrying a big bowl and wearing a silly smile. He flips my hair as he passes and almost drops the bowl, and they go into the kitchen together.

A lightbulb flashes on in my head. *Bella 4 Eron.* Oh lord, that's all we need, just when Grace is getting better.

'Get away, you filthy brute! Get out of here!'

Bella's shrieking her head off, and I leap up. What's Dad doing to her?

188

In the kitchen, the big table's a mess, milk or something all over it and broken china, and Bella's got Ugly by the scruff of the neck, shaking him. Dad's laughing.

'I'm sorry, I'm *really* sorry. I'll put him back in his basket.' I go to take the cat.

He twists his body round, rakes his claws down Bella's arm so she screams and drops him, and then he's away. Moving quickly; he still looks like a rat.

Bella's got blood dripping off her hand: he must have scratched her deep. Dad puts her in a chair and gets water.

I don't know how to do a healing spell, but I might be able to help. Dad's mopping her arm with cotton wool, crooning like she's a sick horse, and I hug her gently and run my fingers over her head.

Her music's jangled, spiked with pain and shock. I put my tune to work, smoothing and comforting, and after a minute she stops looking so white.

'I reckon we should get it stitched,' says Dad.

'I'll be fine,' she tells him. 'It hardly even hurts now.'

Dad gets the credit for his expert care. He's still fussing, wanting her checked out, and Sykes takes a look but doesn't have much to offer except aspirin.

'All the cream for the trifle,' Bella laments.

'Never mind that; there's plenty to eat,' Dad

consoles her. 'Mag, come and help me set the tables.'

I suppose Mr Ugly'll be gone for a while. But no. When I go in the canteen, he's there, curled up in Grace's lap.

I look at Grace, and there's a flicker – blink and you'd miss it – she's winked at me. Suddenly I feel a whole lot better.

*

Perkin and Betsy have baked me a cake, and Parrot's iced it green and blue. There are fourteen candles, which I blow out in one, but they're the re-lighting kind: Dad's idea, and it's so funny he just about wets himself. It's a good thing he doesn't know real magic.

Ruce is a hit with everyone. She laughs at Dad's awful jokes and admires Parrot's new hair colour and helps Bella carry plates. I was feeling guilty, letting her in for hearing about her uncle Rossy, but she's having a good time now, with Gordy taking a lot of notice.

My presents are a mixed bag. From Dad, a new coat and trainers, which I need. From Bella, a watch, not cutting-edge but a bit more stylish than the one I've had since I was eight. Gordy's given me leather gloves, they look quite expensive, but they're on the small side, and Ruce has got a red collar for Ugly – smart, though I don't reckon I'll get him in it. Lewis has written me a poem on a paper plate; Mrs Frisch gives me a Sudoku puzzle out of last week's paper, filled in at random;

Jennifer's picked me some flowers from the garden; and Abram's cut me a lock of his hair.

Chough performs a great ceremony, making me hold out my hand and close my eyes. When I open them there's a little scrunched-up ball of silver paper.

'A jewel beyond price,' he informs me.

'It's lovely. Thank you very much.'

He makes me promise to carry it with me always, and I put it in the pocket of my new coat.

Sykes's present is a bit weird: it's a picture book suitable for someone of about five. I leaf through it in case there's something I haven't noticed.

'Do you like it?' He sounds anxious.

'It's very nice. Thank you.'

He really is ill. He looks ten years older, thin and stooped, and I'm sorry for him. Even if he is on the Bureau. I don't reckon he's much of a threat to anyone.

*

After lunch I help Dad load the dishwasher.

'You ok at school?' he asks.

'Fine. No problem.' Nothing I can tell him about, anyway.

'Your friend, she's a diamond.'

'Yeah, Gordy agrees.'

'Don't you fret, chick. Plenty more fish.'

It takes me a moment to work out what he means, and then I'm not sure if I'm touched or insulted.

'Dad, I do not carry a torch for Gordy.'

'That's the spirit,' he says, like I'm a gallant little soldier. 'Working hard?'

'Doing my best.'

'Ain't nobody can say more.' He hugs me. 'Place ain't the same without you, though.'

'Dad, are you having a thing with Bella Cole?'

His arm drops.

'What kind of question's that?'

'I thought you two were getting friendly, that's all. Why'd there be anything wrong if you were?'

I guess his conscience is giving him hot potatoes, so he reacts the only way he knows how and gets angry.

'You show a little respect now, or I'll teach it you. Ain't no way to talk to your father.'

'If you don't want anyone to know, fine. But you're not being that subtle about it; you're all over each other.'

'Getting smart, huh? Getting too clever for your own father?'

'Quit saying that like I don't know who you are.'

He raises his hand then stops. 'Been here half a day and you've got me steaming. Don't you do it, girl.'

I could put the spell on him I used on Gordy, but what's the point? He can't tell me much I don't know. What I need's a charm to change his temper, and I'm a way short of that kind of magic.

*

Things aren't too comfortable either when we get back to the canteen. Some of the Hollies got over-excited, Betsy did a strip, Perkin got annoyed and tried to stop her, and Parrot stuck up for Betsy. It all seems to have turned into a bit of a free-for-all. Now Perkin's crying, Mrs Frisch is counting loudly, Abram's singing, and Ruce is trying to wrap Betsy up in a tablecloth.

I'd have expected Sykes to deal with all this, but obviously it's beyond him. He just watches while Gordy and Bella and Dad get everyone sorted and into their rooms to calm down.

'Dr Sykes rest,' Chough advises him. 'Headache?'

Sykes nods with half a smile. 'You're right, Chough. It's not getting any better.'

Chough lays a large pink hand on the old man's forehead. 'Poor old boy, poor doctor.'

They go out together, and I'm not sure which of them's leading the other. I'd say Sykes needs a doctor himself.

The room's clear now, except for Grace. She's been sitting all the time staring into space like usual: the way she keeps up her act is impressive, even a bit scary. No one would guess she's changed, and I can't imagine what kind of self-control it takes.

Now she gives me a smile and I go over. Someone could come in any moment, so I squat down and pretend I'm talking to Ugly, who's still on her knee. He's not normally this relaxed.

'Hey, Mum.'

'Are you anywhere near finding your name?'

It's only the second time we've ever talked, and that's the first question? How about how I feel, how she feels? I suppose we haven't got long, though.

'I'm working on it. I know my tune, I can do some magic now. I saw Nilas.'

'You *saw* him?'

'He came to the school.'

'What did he say?'

'He said he wanted to help you.'

'Oh yes!' She gives a quick little gasping laugh. 'You didn't believe him?'

'No.' I didn't exactly disbelieve him either, but I don't say that.

'You can't trust *anyone*, Margot.'

'Except you and Gordy?'

'Me, yes.' Because she's whispering, it comes out kind of hissy. 'I wouldn't put too much faith in Gordy,' she goes on.

I sit back from her. 'But he's the one who's helping you,' I protest, even though I'm hacked off with him.

'It's very, very complicated, Margot. Too much to explain here and now. I will do, I promise, I'll tell you everything. But for now, just remember this. Magic can bring you very close to people; you probably feel that. It takes you right inside them. But for that very reason you have to keep yourself to yourself, keep your thoughts private. Never drop your guard; never let anyone too close. Your name's what you need.'

Somebody's at the door now, so I drop my head and mutter into the cat's fur.

'I'll do my best, Mum.'

I just catch what she says under her breath:

'Try to hurry. Time may be running out.'

CHAPTER TWELVE
SYLVIAN

'What kind of names do witches have?' asks Ruce. 'Tracey, Chevrolet, Great Mystic Moon Serpent?'

'Not a clue. You don't get told other people's, they wouldn't mean anything to you anyway. You find your own when the time's right.'

'How do you know if you've found the right one?'

'Your music tells you.'

We're walking under the apple trees at the edge of the sports pitch, where some lads are booting a ball around.

'What if someone used it by mistake? I mean, it's got to be some sort of word, right?'

There's a shout from the field. 'Foul!'

'Say your witch name was Foul,' Ruce goes on, 'what would happen?'

'Nothing would. Even if I said it myself, it wouldn't do anything unless I was listening to my own music, talking through it. It's not so much *your* name as the name of your music.'

Ruce is playing with her mobile. Suddenly it makes a giant frog noise: *Ribbit ribbit.*

'What are you doing?'

'New phone. That's the ring-tone if it's you calling; it's the witchiest one I could find.'

She presses another button and the phone bursts into song: *Hal-lelujah! Hallelujah! Hallelujah!*

'Who's that one for?'

'Gordy.'

'Swapped numbers?'

'Yeah, but he hasn't called me yet.'

'It's only been two days,' I point out.

I scuff the grass with my feet. It's cute, her and Gordy, and I'll be so happy if the news gets back to Laban. But Gordy still wasn't speaking to me last thing I knew, and it could get kind of awkward.

There's a sudden shout from the players. Someone's taken a kick, and the ball comes flying up in the air and goes right over the fence into the farmer's field. There's an ironic cheer from the team.

I'm the one nearest the side gate. We're not meant to use it unless there's staff, and you can only work the latch from the inside.

'Keep it open for me,' I tell Ruce.

The sheep in the field don't take any notice of me or the football; they're not much into sport. I shove one woolly backside so I can get a clear run-up, and then I slam the ball: it's sweet, it sails up and over back in the school grounds and bounces at the goalie's feet.

There's a little round of applause, and I take a bow. Then the kids go back to their game, and I'm heading for the gate again when Ruce yells something. I don't get the words, but I get the message, especially as all the sheep are now heading past me in a panic.

I turn round.

There's a big black dog behind me.

He stops a way off. I can run or I can use the whistle again, but for a second I wait to see what he'll do.

He lies down on the ground and rolls over.

I'm so surprised I take a step towards him.

Bargus squirms on his back and whines. It's pretty clear he's saying it's cool, he's not going to savage me. What if it's a trick?

I go a bit closer.

'Hey, Bargus.'

He gets the right way up but stays on the ground, his nose down.

'Is Humph ok?'

He wags his tail.

'I'm sorry about what happened.' I glance over my shoulder: it'd be weird if someone caught me talking to a dog, but nobody's watching except Ruce. 'I'm not your enemy.' I'm not sure if I'm his friend either, but I pat him anyway, and then I walk back to the gate.

'He's following you,' says Ruce.

When I look at him he cringes on his belly.

'Who's a nice boy then?' Ruce puts out her hand and he comes over and licks it with his rough pink tongue, and she scratches his ears. It's quite a love-in.

'Bargus, you'd better go home now,' I tell him.

'I think maybe you should go with him,' says Ruce.

'Are you mad?'

'Look, he hasn't been hanging round all this time just to say hello, has he? Stopping the car the other day, he probably wanted to tell you something if you'd given him a chance.'

'He can't talk.'

'So maybe he's got to take you to somebody who can.'

Bargus thumps his tail on the ground.

'Maggot, you don't know what to do about the Others, right? You think they might sail in and butcher the lot of us if Nilas wasn't there to stop them, but you're not sure. So why not try and find out a bit more?'

'Wait.'

I take a moment to tune in to Bargus through his music. What's going on in his hairy head?

I'm needed, he's telling me. He'll wait forever to do as he's been told; he's a *good* dog. What he's been told is to fetch me, because I'm needed.

'Wildeth said never to trust any of the Others.'

'I know who I'd trust out of Wildeth and this dog,' says Ruce.

*

We're out of sight of school.

'Bargus, how far are we going?' I can't be away too long. 'Can I get on your back, can you be something a bit bigger?'

If I'm following him, I might as well get a ride too. I'm hoping he might do the Harley thing again – I got a kick out of that.

He gives himself a bit of a shake, and right in front of my eyes he starts growing taller, his shaggy hair gets short and glossy, and I'm looking at a black stallion.

He's got no saddle or bridle, and I've never been on a horse in my life, but I scramble up and grab his mane, and he goes cantering off across the field and into the woods.

I'm jolted up and down, I'm soon breathless and bruised, but I'm loving every second, it's even better than the bike. He jumps over a log that's across the path, and though I nearly come off, I'm grinning like a nutter, flying through the air on this creature's back.

He's going slower now, threading through the trees. The leaves are falling, and there's an icy chill in the wind. This autumn's been colder than normal. Maybe we'll get snow, which doesn't often happen on the Island.

We're going uphill. I get a glimpse of the Network fence, so we must be somewhere near the road, but before we get there, Bargus stops. I slide down: my legs are stiff and I almost fall over.

'Watch yerself, missy.'

There's a furry brown shape against a treetrunk. I didn't see him for a second.

'Humph!'

Is he cross with me? Last time I saw him, I shut him in a thermos flask. I haven't thought about it before, how it must have felt. Completely dark, airless, smooth walls all around and no way out.

'Humph, I'm really sorry I put you in the flask.' I take a step or two towards him.

To my horror he puts his paws over his snout and starts choking and snuffling.

'Was it that bad? I didn't know—'

I realize he's in fits of laughter.

'What a joke!' he gasps. 'Change into a snail, Humph. Let's see yer do it! I never heard nothing like it!'

I'm so relieved I start giggling too. 'I didn't know if it'd work.'

'Cleverest thing I ever sees. Never suspected nothing, and don't yer let nobody tell yer hobs is thick.'

'Why are you waiting round here?' I ask.

'Sylvian got work for us. Soon as she got word yer was coming, she called us out.'

I glance round: there's no one here but Bargus, back in dog-shape. 'What do you mean, work for us?'

'We need your help.' That's not Humph talking. It's a woman's voice, speaking almost in my ear.

I'm looking right at her. Was she there a second ago?

It's the one who was outside the Network building. She's dressed just the same: the long shabby coat and the hat with the feather. When I saw her the first time, from a distance, I thought she looked a bit mad, and close up I'm not changing my mind. Her face is flat and brown and ploughed with lines; her nose is like a gorilla's, wide nostrils and no bridge; and her eyes are like an animal's too, all dark, no white. She could have come out of a cave somewhere, out of the earth, out of a tree. Maybe that's what she just did.

'What do you want me to do?' I ask.

She points at the Network fence behind the trees.

'Destroy the building.' Her voice is harsh and deep.

'Like the explosion a few weeks back?'

'It wasn't enough.'

'It was enough to hurt the workmen,' I say. 'How did you do it anyway? What was that animal you sent in?'

Her eyes close for a second. It's like a toad blinking. 'One of mine.'

'She doesn't think about the names,' mutters Humph. 'Doesn't mean so much to her, see?'

'Did it die?'

Nobody answers me.

'People and animals getting hurt, getting killed, none of that means much to you, does it?' She's so expressionless; it's winding me up. 'Just the Others, are they all you care about?'

'Everything dies. Humans, animals, Others, trees. Everything dies.'

'Isn't it because the Others are getting killed that you want the Network building destroyed?'

'Humans make buildings; it's what they do. Where they build, the Others die. Not only here but everywhere – humankind is breeding and making homes.'

It's more or less what Ruce said to Gordy.

'We can't stop them all,' Sylvian says. 'Here, we must stop them.'

'What's special about here?'

'This is the Sleeper's ground. We have to guard the dreams.'

She moves closer, staring at me as if she wants to hypnotize me. I can feel the pull, but I'm keeping my feet.

'If Nilas finishes here,' she goes on, 'he will be able to use the dreams. He will be stronger than all the Others and all of humankind.'

'What dreams are you talking about?' I ask.

'The dreams feed the earth and the earth gives life to the dreams.'

'Who's the Sleeper?'

'The one who lies here: the guardian.'

This is going in circles. Who's the Sleeper? The one who's here. What's special about here? It's where the Sleeper is.

'Ok, it's an important place,' I accept. 'You don't want Nilas to get the power because he'll use it to wipe out the Others.'

'Humankind will be no better off than the Others, in the end.'

'So what is it you want me to do?'

'Join in the spell. We have held out as long as we can, but the building is founded and defended with witch magic. The Others can't defeat it alone.'

'Say I do help you. What then? Will the Others stop attacking humans?'

'Where humans build, the Others die,' she says again. 'There can never be peace.'

'That's not good enough. I'm human. I can't help the Others if it'll just make them stronger to kill people.'

'Then the Others will die and your kind will suffer.'

'You tell me that. Everyone tells me things. I don't know who to believe.' I can hear myself sounding weak.

She puts out a hand and I move back. 'Some things you have to do without knowing.'

'When I get my name, maybe I'll understand a bit more.'

'It must be now.' She's coming towards me. 'Soon he will be able to use the dreams against us, and then it will be too late.'

Use the dreams ... it's what Grace said Nilas did to her. I shiver. But I've seen what the Others do too.

'Missy, can't yer do like she wants? It'll help us,' Humph urges.

'I know, I'm sorry. I can't.'

God knows how I'm going to get back to Crossbeams, I don't suppose Bargus'll give me a ride. If I get to the road maybe I can hitch a lift or get the bus.

'You will join the spell,' Sylvian says.

'I won't. You can't make me.'

'Then we will keep you. Perhaps you will be useful another way.'

'Missy's a friend,' Humph protests. 'She lets me out of that pot she puts me in.'

Sylvian ignores him. Her hands are stretched out,

long fingers the colour of earth. They could knot round my neck like branches.

'Nilas needs you. He wants you alive. We can bargain with him, perhaps.'

'Use me as a hostage? You'll have to catch me first.'

I duck under her arms and then I'm off, pelting through the trees.

'Ain't no use to run,' Humph shouts, but I can sprint pretty fast; it's got to be worth a try.

I'm heading for the road downhill, pounding along, my legs aching with the strain of not tripping headlong. I slow down and steal a glance over my shoulder: there's no one after me. Have I lost them?

Maybe I've lost myself too. I was sure the road was ahead, down the slope, but I didn't think it was so far. I carry on, walking now. The only thing I hear is my own breathing. There's no breeze here, and the branches are still.

What's that?

Nothing, just a dark space between two tree trunks. I thought for a second there was a face, grinning at me. This is taking far too long. Which way am I going? I stop a moment to look all around and I see the Network fence over on my right. How did I do that? I must have turned without realizing. I'm going back the way I came. At least I've got my bearings now, and I swing round and head for the road, keeping the fence to my left.

There's a rustle in the undergrowth. A thicket of branches and bracken is opening up. I can see eyes, a wide mouth. I'm staring; I can't move. Then the pattern shifts, and it's just brambles, nobody there. I try to swallow but I'm dry. I force my legs to keep working. I look to my right, and there's the Network fence.

That's enough. I'm the witch here, Sylvian.

I stop and reach in my pocket for Nilas's whistle, and I give it all I've got. I hear the shriek, I see the spark, and then the noise is in my own head, unbearable, deafening, and there's a flash that hurts my eyes.

I'm lying on the ground in the fallen leaves, and the whistle in my hand is blackened, crushed flat like an elephant stamped on it.

She sent Nilas's magic back at me.

I scramble up and start to run again, I don't know where I'm going but I want to get away, and then I skid to a stop and almost fall back down because there's the fence right in front of me and Sylvian and Humph and Bargus waiting.

I'm sobbing for breath. I can't run any more.

Bargus comes and shoves his warm wet nose in my hand, and Humph gets my other hand in his furry paw.

'Easy now, missy,' he mutters. 'Don't yer waste yer

strength. Yer can't hide from Sylvian in her own place. Best we all takes care of each other, eh? She ain't gonta hurt yer.'

Sylvian doesn't move; she's planted there. For a second I see her face move like the brambles moved: is she made of flesh or leaves? Is she just a trick of the light?

She lays her hand on my head. It rests heavy; she's solid enough. 'Help us.'

'If I try, will you let me go?'

She nods.

Never, never trust any of the Others.

What choice have I got?

*

There are three guards round the gate, standing at ease. Sylvian stops before they see us.

'Stay here,' she says, 'and witch girl, cover your ears.'

I do like she says and watch as she walks forward. One of the men catches sight of her and grabs for his walkie-talkie. Sylvian puts her hands in the air, throws her head back and opens her mouth. Her throat's moving as if she's singing, but I can only hear the pulse inside my head.

The guards have got their mouths open too, but I guess they're not joining in the chorus. One of them staggers, clutching at the gate, and then one after another they fall to the ground and lie still.

Sylvian lowers her arms. I take my fingers out of my ears and run forward. Has she killed them? No: they're breathing, and their faces are peaceful as if they're asleep. One of them turns over and starts to snore.

Sylvian pushes the gate open, and we follow her inside the Network compound.

CHAPTER THIRTEEN

THE SKULL

We're walking a broad track of earth beaten flat. Sylvian strides ahead, Bargus pads behind me and Humph trots at my elbow, inquisitive about everything.

'Look at them big yeller jobs with the teeth.'

'Diggers,' I say. There are no workmen around, but there are girders and pipes and concrete mixers, and a big sign, *NETWORK IT,* in silver letters on dark grey.

'What's that mean?' asks Humph.

'The company's called Network, it does Information Technology. It's kind of a pun, *Network it, Network I.T.* Internet, communication, software. You know? Linking computers up and letting them talk to each other.'

Humph nods, but I think he's just humouring me.

We can see the building now. It's not big, just a single-storey block. The surface is reflective glass, and there's one curved entrance without a door.

Sylvian waits for us under the arch.

'Look at the trees,' she says.

What does she mean? There aren't any trees in the compound.

I blink, and as I close my eyes, for a second I can see them: a grove of birches and rowans, silver trunks and golden branches and scarlet berries. There's a rustle of leaves, and then it's all gone. Sylvian leads us into the building.

The walls are shiny, smooth and grey. We're in an entrance hall with rooms off to each side, nothing in them yet. Everything's empty, but there's a faint humming noise like a fridge going. The sound's coming from a shaft in front of us. I guess there's going to be a lift there, but now it's just a hole going down to nothing. I step back: it's making me giddy.

Sylvian skirts the edge to a flight of descending stairs and stops again.

'Here is the way down to the water,' she says.

Again, for a moment, instead of the lift shaft, I get a vision of a grassy mound with a deep cleft in it and steps worn out of the rock. They wind down between walls grown green with ferns and moss and a few white star-shaped flowers. There's a trickling sound like a spring running below.

Now it's vanished. Sylvian walks down the concrete treads and we follow her. It's light, but you can't see where the light's coming from, and the humming noise gets louder. We're going deep undergound.

We've come to the bottom. A bare floor stretches ahead into an immense round room. Way up at the ceiling there's a maze of silver pipes and ducts, and below that the walls are lined with flat-screen monitors. There must be hundreds of them. They're blank and grey, and they don't show anything or reflect anything. In the middle there's a control desk with banks of keyboards and switches.

Standing there, Sylvian looks back at us.

'This is the lake.'

The whitish light fades: the room, the desk, the screens fade with it, and it seems I'm standing by dark water. The far side's in shadow and I can't see where the pool ends, but high above there's a crevice, the cavern entrance, stone steps winding down. Tree roots clasp their damp edges, and a sunbeam strikes through the gap. The light slants to the middle of the water where a single uneven rock rises: its rough sides green from the touch of the water, its top level with a mound of pebbles at the centre.

A ripple whispers on the water, and the lake's gone: the slanting ray of sunlight, trees and rock, all vanished. Sylvian's standing on an empty grey floor with empty grey screens all round her.

'This is where the Sleeper lies,' she says, and though her voice is as flat as ever, there are tears running down her face.

She throws back her head. A long howl comes from her throat, like a dog baying at the moon. It echoes through the space of the building and comes back to us in a hundred yelps and groans.

The air around us thickens like mist. It swirls and parts and comes together, and out of the folds, figures move forward to make a circle.

They're like nothing I've ever seen. These are the Others: a giant, its head near the ceiling; a group of slender cloaked figures, small as children, whose hair is whitish-green like hay; a man with antlers; and a woman with the legs of a deer. Then more that aren't so pretty: short men with gnarled faces and naked toes twisted as roots. There's a woman who looks human but uncanny, with hair matted like cobwebs across her scalp and a shawl hanging off her sharp shoulders. Behind her is a shape all bones and bare grin, and next to me is something I can't see but I can feel it, clammy and quivering.

Am I terrified? I'm not even sure; I seem to have stepped out of myself, watching from a little distance. Maybe the short black kid in school uniform is as weird as any of them.

Sylvian's wordless calling dies away, and nobody else speaks. She looks all round and her eyes come to rest on me. She holds out her hand and I see myself step forward into the centre of the circle.

*

'This is the place of sleep.'

Sylvian's behind me, her hands on my shoulders; she's talking over my head to the Others.

'Dreaming is king here; death is queen: green death that's in life, decay that feeds the earth. Here lies the power of all that's below.'

She stamps hard down on the floor and I feel a tremor up through my feet. What's underneath us? Did Nilas drain the lake I saw, or are we standing on a platform over water?

'Nothing should be built here,' Sylvian goes on. 'But the witch Nilas has cut down the trees and choked the stream. He has taken the ground and made it empty: space without air, movement without desire, life without death. He will take the power of the Sleeper, take it for himself, and use it against the Others.'

She turns, taking me with her to face round the circle.

'We've fought it, but he's been stronger. Our magic isn't his magic; we can't find the way to bring his walls down. That's why we need the witch-girl.'

I hear a hissing murmur from the Others. I don't know if it's fear or hatred or excitement, or maybe all three.

'She's here to help us.' Sylvian's fingers dig into my arms. 'Look at her, remember her. She is our friend and she is not to be hurt by any Other anywhere.'

One by one, they drop their heads to me. The dwarves knuckle their foreheads, the green-haired erls flourish their cloaks, and the giant kneels. Even the skeleton bows. The only one who doesn't move is the skinny woman with the tatty shawl and grey rat-tail hair, and she stares into my eyes, her own bright and unblinking.

Sylvian lets go of my shoulders and takes both my hands, raising them and pulling me to face her.

'Now!' she shouts. 'Reach out, look down to the sleep under the earth, look down to the dream. The power will be given to destroy and to restore. Reach out, look down!'

I do as she says, but I don't see anything except my feet on the floor. What happens now?

The only sound's the background hum of the building, the electric whine that's been tormenting us like mosquitoes ever since we came in. Then, little by little, that's blown away. Instead there's a brush of breeze, a drip of rain, a drift of leaves.

It's Sylvian's music I'm hearing, and it's the noises of the woods, the hills, the sea. My eyes are closed. I'm aware of everyone in the room as if all the creatures here are part of one body with me. We're breathing one breath, there's nothing that isn't us and no edge where one ends and another begins.

Sylvian's breeze quickens to a storm, clouds gather, thunder rolls. My own tune's soaring in harmony, and I feel her strength like heat and cold, lightning in darkness, rain dancing on the crashing waves. All of us are together: we're the elements, we're the Island.

Now we can all feel the magic that's resisting us. I don't have to be told: this is Nilas's force. It's alien to the cave, the water, and the rock: it's the energy of the grey room. Like Sylvian said, it's emptiness. How do you fight an empty space? You fill it up.

With the Others, I grow. We branch, sap and blood and bone. Colours are born and flower, sound songs itself, flame and water run. We see the rock at the centre of the lake, clearer than before. We draw closer in: the waves lap below our feet.

Here are the pebbles in the middle, raised in a rough heap. What's under them, nobody knows. Not even Sylvian. Is there treasure? Is there a dead body? Is there a monster?

We crouch down and stretch our hands out to the stones. We take them one by one in our fingers and palms and paws. We pick them up and throw them aside. They drop into the water. Splash, splash. The layers fall away; we're getting to the end. Underneath there's a single slab resting on the rock.

Do we dare to lift it? The power's terrible. It's

bottomless; it's life and death. We move as one. We put our hands to the stone and raise it.

*

Below there's nothing, just an empty hole: a pit of raw stone, empty as Nilas's spell.

*

We're back where we've been all along, in the grey room with the grey walls and grey screens. We're not together any more. We're each of us alone and cold and frightened, and there's no music but the sound of crying. Sylvian's wailing aloud, her hair wild, her eyes shut and her hands clutching her head, trying not to know.

'Gone,' whispers one of the erls.

'Nilas has the power,' says the giant.

'We're finished,' bleats the deer-woman.

'Done fer,' says Humph.

'No! We can still fight!'

Sylvian's voice has lost power. It's deadened. There's a cloud round us, and the Others are disappearing, back into the mist.

'Stay!' calls Sylvian, but they're going, they've gone. Now there's just her and Humph and Bargus and me and the strange thin woman. What's she waiting for? She's still staring at me.

A bell starts ringing. Something's set off an alarm, or our magic's too weak now to keep it quiet.

'Best we gets moving, ennit?' Humph makes for the stairs and the thin woman follows. I'm going after them when I realize Sylvian's still where she was. She's staring round like she doesn't know which way's up, so I grab her hand and pull her along. The bare steps fight my feet and my legs ache.

When we come out at ground level, the guards are waking up. They're in a daze, fumbling to their feet and rubbing their eyes. They gape at us as we go past, and then we're through the gate and back among the trees.

Where are we going? The thin woman's leading the way, and Humph and Bargus seem to think that's ok, so I tag after with Sylvian in tow. She's walking blind, tripping and stumbling: if I wasn't there she'd be headbutting the trees.

Here's a building, a hut, looks like someplace for woodcutters or gamekeepers. We go in, and it's bigger than I thought. There's a mattress on the floor and a couple of junk chairs, and a curtain that must lead to another room. Somebody's living here – I guess the skinny woman.

'Safe now.' It's the first time I've heard her speak: her voice is a whisper as thin as her body.

Sylvian sits down like her legs won't hold her any more. 'What now? What can I do?'

I don't think she's expecting an answer, but Humph

gives it a go anyway.

'Ain't no more no one can do. Power's gone to Nilas. Puts lid on, dunnit?' He doesn't sound too miserable about it. 'Make best of a bad job. If we're all gonta be slaves or dead, then might as well enjoy ourselves while we got the chance.'

I wonder how hobs party, but maybe now's not the time to ask. Sylvian's scowling.

'Fool!'

Humph's ears go flat.

'Thinking of nothing but your own life,' she spits at him, 'like humankind.'

'We're not all like that,' says the thin woman. I look at her and find she's looking at me again. She sits down next to Sylvian and says something more, so quietly I can't hear.

'What's she?' I mutter to Humph. 'Is she human?'

'Ghost watcher.'

'What's that?'

'Summun as sees ghosts, ennit?'

I think he's sulking about Sylvian calling him a fool.

'Witch-girl.' Sylvian beckons me. 'Delphine can help you, perhaps.'

'If you want me to,' comes the whisper.

Delphine's skin and bone, she's a scaffold draped in rags. Now she's sitting down I can see the mottled top of her head through her skimpy hair. She doesn't look like she's got much to offer.

'You will fight for us,' she says.

'I don't know.'

'She sees the future,' Sylvian tells me.

'Ghosts are in the past, aren't they?'

'I can see the past too, if that's what you want,' says Delphine. 'But your name is in the future.'

'I thought nobody else knew a witch's name.'

'I can show you a time when you will know it.'

'Missy, don't yer do it.' Humph is pawing my arm. 'Dangerous stuff.'

'Is it?' I ask Delphine. 'What could happen?'

She smiles, showing gums and broken teeth. 'Whatever you see.'

Is the future decided? Maybe if you look, then that settles it.

'I don't want to see the future; I want to see the past. When my mother sent her magic to me.'

Humph's whiskers tickle my ear. 'Ghost watchers, ghost powers, them's unchancy things. Yer dunno what they does.'

I look at my watch: I'm going to be so busted when I get back to school. I haven't got time to argue.

'I want to see quickly.'

Delphine goes to the curtained doorway. 'Come with me.'

*

221

It's dark, just a few cracks of daylight between the planks of the shed. When my eyes get used to it, I see we're in a room about as big as a bus shelter, with a tiny table and two stools. Delphine sits and puts her hands on the table, so I do the same.

'First, I need a little of your blood.'

I'm thinking, *Never share a needle*. She doesn't look too clean or healthy, and it'd be a bummer if I escaped the magic curse and got hepatitis instead. But I've gone too far to back out, and I really want to see what she can show me. I let her prick my finger. And then she pricks her own thumb, and we hold hands for a second.

'It's your own past you want to see?' Her whisper fills the narrow room. 'Think about how old you were, anybody else who was there, whatever you know that happened. Look in the glass.'

She passes me a mirror: it's broken off a plastic powder compact and it's cracked across. All this is so makeshift I'm having trouble taking it seriously, but I lean my elbows on the table and stare at my own face.

Hey you, Ms Special Powers, give us a smile. I'm tempted to stick my tongue out, but Delphine's looking.

Ok, I was three. I can't remember that far back, but I try for the earliest memories I've got. Coming to the Residence with Dad. I'm riding Dad's shoulders; I do kind of remember that. But the time I'm trying to get to, he wasn't there. Mum was, and Nilas. I think about Grace. I see her smile; I hear her voice; and I feel her hand in mine. I think about Nilas: the shut eye and the cloudy eye, the white filmy hair.

The crack in the glass is worrying me. It comes right across my nose. I'm trying to watch my face, see if I'm suddenly going to get younger, but all I can see is the crack; it's splitting me in two. I'm disappearing; there's no me anymore. There's just the crack, and it's going to swallow me. It's a mouth as wide as the world.

'Hello, Margot.'

I jump out of my skin. It's Nilas, he's bending down and putting out his hand. Where does he get off patting me on the head?

He's not in his wheelchair. He's got two good eyes. And I'm three years old.

It's the weirdest feeling. I'm both at once: I'm three and fourteen. My body's teeny-wee – did you ever see such cute fingernails? And I know everything that's happened, that's going to happen, up to where I am now, where I was then, when? Don't think about it, don't think; you'll scramble your brain.

I back away from Nilas and grab onto Grace's skirt.

Nilas laughs. 'Funny moppet. Scared of me.'

'Instinct, I suppose.' Grace's voice comes from over my head: big Mummy, she'll take care of me.

'She's got quite a look of Eron, hasn't she?' says Nilas.

'I wanted a little baby so much. I don't care what she looks like,' says Grace.

I poke my lip out and punch her on the leg.

'Steady! You've got to be good now, darling. Mr Samuel and I have to talk. Don't we?'

'You know what I've come for?'

'Of course.'

She sits down and takes me on her lap. It's such a sweet feeling and so lost and gone: I can't help it, I start crying. I bawl, my nose runs, and it's luxury and misery both.

'Put her in another room!'

Nilas's voice cracks and I stop at once on a sob and a hiccup. I've got to stay here.

'She'll be good, won't you?' Grace wipes my nose and eyes. 'There's no one else to look after her, Eron's at work. Hush now. Nilas wants to know if I've been selling secrets to the Others.'

He smiles. 'I don't think you have. But I've got to make sure.'

'How are you going to do that?' Her arms are warm round me.

'The Skull.'

He takes out a grey leather case, lays it on the table between them and opens it. Inside there's a crimson velvet nest, the sort you get with jewellery, and I'm expecting to see a real skull, but in the moulded cloth there's just a cup. It's plain pottery or earthenware, brownish, not big.

'It's not very pretty, is it?' Grace sounds amused but I can feel her heart going. 'Why is it called Skull?'

'That's what the warriors used to drink from. Perhaps it actually was once a skull; perhaps it was replaced. The spell's still there.'

'It's very old?'

'Very, very old.'

'What does it do?'

'We both drink out of it, and then I'll know your secrets. I'll know everything you know.'

'So simple. What do we drink?'

'Water. Wine. Cherry-cola if you like.'

'Champagne!' She jumps up, holding me. 'I think it's worth it, don't you?'

She carries me into the kitchen and there's a bottle in the fridge. Dad sure doesn't keep bubbly in the house these days.

She's sat me on the sideboard, and now she leans over so her eyes are on a level with mine. She kisses me on the forehead, whispers a word in my ear, but I can't hear what it is, and something happens. It's not much; it's like a sneeze, a buzz, a tickle. I start laughing, and she taps me on the nose. 'That's my girl.'

*

Was that it?

*

She opens the champagne and we go back to Nilas. He's got the cup ready: Grace pours fizz up to the brim. 'To the truth,' she says.

Nilas sips. 'Good health, my dear,' he says, and hands the cup to her. She drinks.

It's like a train crash except it's silent. It's like watching a disaster on mute, except we're not watching; we're part of the picture. Everything seems to stop and fly apart: the cup's dust, Nilas is on his back by the wall, Grace is crouched on the floor and I'm under the table, too frightened to cry or scream or move.

Nilas sits up. He's cut his head — there's blood pouring down his face. You can't see his eyes at all. He tries to stand. Then he turns on his front and drags himself over to Grace.

'What did you do?'

I can just understand what he's saying.

'Look at me.' He wipes his eyes. One of them stays shut. 'Grace?'

She's hunched over, her knees up and her arms round her head.

'Look at me!'

He forces her chin up. Her mouth's hanging open,

she's dribbling, and her eyes are looking nowhere. I've known her like that most of my life, but it's a shock to Nilas. He lets her go at once.

'You stupid bitch. With the traitors, weren't you?'

She doesn't answer. She can't.

'You've – been working for the Others. Thought you could hide it, and now you've lost it. I'll find it. Find everything you've hidden. Get it out of you. Oh, I will, darling.'

He's choking; he retches. He's on his hands and knees.

'You'll tell me – everything, every name, every secret. And then I'll kill you and I'll kill them and I'll kill every last one of the Others. All the fairies, all the dwarves, all the little dancing men ...' He's laughing and spitting blood.

I start to scream. Then everything goes dark and I'm sitting on a stool in a wooden hut and I'm fourteen years old.

CHAPTER FOURTEEN

MAXIM

It's morning. I'm in bed, but it's not my bed at home or at school: I'm lying on something that rustles and scratches with an old sack keeping me warm.

Humph's cave. That's where I am.

Last night I wasn't in a state to go anywhere much. Humph got me back here, covered me up and left me to sleep. I wish I thought I'd had bad dreams, that'd be better than knowing it was real.

It still is real. That's what brings me upright in a sweat. It's still going on, somewhere. It's all still happening, or how could I have got into it? Always, somewhere, I'll be three years old, and Nilas will be with my mother, and she'll be putting the cup to her mouth.

I'm never looking at the past again. I'm sure as hell never looking at the future.

That leaves today, I guess.

Humph's scurryingg around making tea, or he's pouring hot water into mugs. It smells a bit like tea. I won't ask.

'What yer gonta do now, missy?'

I can't go back to school: Nilas could come for me. He's got to know something happened at the Network site; he probably realizes there was a witch involved, so when Wildeth tells him I was out of bounds yesterday, that's not going to be hard science. I can't face him now, not after what I've seen.

I'm on the run.

And Grace? She knew what Nilas was, and she sent her powers to me with a kiss. She used me to protect herself, and she's still trying to use me.

My phone goes. It's Ruce.

'Maggot, what's happened? Where are you?'

'In a cave in the woods.'

'Are you coming back?'

'I don't think so.'

'Is your cave big enough for two? Wildeth's going ape; she's asking everyone if they know where you are. It's only a matter of time before she gets to me, and I know too much, Maggot. I know about Gordy and your mum and everything. I won't be able not to tell her – you know I won't. I've got to get away.'

'Where are you now?'

'In the bog.'

'Don't panic. Get Ugly. Wear gloves,' I add, thinking about times I've tried to put him in the cat

basket. 'Bring all the stuff you can carry for both of us
– you won't have to walk far. Get out of the side gate
and Bargus'll come for you.'

I look at Humph for confirmation, and he nods.

'Ok.' Ruce is calming down. 'I don't know when I'll
be there.'

'He'll wait.'

*

I pass some time playing cards with Humph for acorn
stakes, and then I show him games on my phone. He's
a natural addict: after a bit I have to take it away from
him.

'Sorry, I've got to save the battery; I can't recharge it
here.'

'Playing with pictures, seeing things as ain't there,
like what witches do, ennit?'

I'm trying not to think about what witches do.

'Hungry?' he asks.

My last meal was lunch yesterday, but I still can't
manage more than two spoons of the stew.

'What's in it?'

'Tree nuts.' He points at the table where we were
playing cards.

'Do you mean acorns? Humph, I'm human. I don't
think I can digest them.'

'Hobs ain't so keen on 'em neither,' he agrees.

'So why eat them?'

'Can't get nothing else, now I doesn't live with no humans.'

'Don't be pathetic; of course you can get food. Where's the nearest shop to here?'

After some bickering, he admits there's a takeaway van in the woods for the crew on the Network site.

'Change your shape. I'd go, but I want to stay around for Ruce.' I root in my pockets: I've got ninety-seven pence and Chough's silver-paper jewel, which isn't going to get us far. 'Have you got any money?'

'Hobs doesn't use no money.'

'What about the wallets you took off the passengers on the bus?'

Everything's still in the box where he put it, cash and plastic and the other stuff people keep in their purses all muddled together. It's not as if Humph is about to trace the owners, so using their money seems better than starving.

'The van probably sells milk,' I suggest.

A while later he's belching after two litres, I've had a hot dog and three doughnuts, and I'm feeling like I could maybe go on living for a while.

I look at my watch: half-two. I hope Ruce gets here soon. If Wildeth catches her … I'd better do something to take my mind off this.

'Humph, can you teach me to change shape?'

He's looking sleepy. 'Dunno.'

'You did say you thought a witch could learn. I might need to hide.'

'Ain't no good if yer hiding from witches. A witch always sees yer real form.'

'Yes, but what if I changed into something really small, a spider or something? I mean, if they saw me they'd know who I was, but they've got to see me first, haven't they?'

He blinks. 'Smart one, you are, missy. I never thought of that. Little things is more difficult,' he warns me.

'So could we try something big to start with?'

'I never learns nobody.' He mumbles to himself a while and then cheers up. 'Hob can do a thing witch can't do. A hob learning a witch – that'd be a good un.'

Now he's got the idea he's enthusiastic, but he's not a good teacher.

'Think like yer a bear,' he urges me.

I don't know how bears think.

'You think like a bear,' I suggest, 'and I'll try to think like you.'

I hold his paws, and listen to him doing bear-thoughts. His music is getting louder, slower, thumpier and lumpier. My music has to match; it's not easy, but I'm feeling my way, almost getting it, like when you find out you can wiggle your ears. It's coming, it's coming ...

'Anyone at home?'

I leave go of Humph and run to the steps. 'Ruce, come on down.'

'Yeah, right.' She's staring over my shoulder. 'He's friendly, is he?'

Humph is a massive grizzly, taking up most of the cave.

'He's fine, he doesn't usually look like that.'

'And how about you?'

'Am I a bear too?' I ask hopefully.

'No, but you've got furry ears.'

Well, it's a start, but it takes three goes before I get my ordinary ears back.

*

'Ruce, I'm sorry. I didn't mean for you to get dragged into my problems.'

'That's ok. I wasn't so struck on Crossbeams anyway; that place is peculiar.'

'That's kind of the point.'

'Maybe it's more fun if you're part of it. Maybe not though.' She hesitates. 'Something's happened to Laban.'

'What?'

'She came down this morning looking like – well, like she hadn't brushed her hair or done her face or anything. And she sat at the wrong table. And somebody told her, and she didn't answer back. She just got up again and did what they said.'

It doesn't sound like much, but I know Laban. And I know what happened to Big Davey Foster.

'I thought Wildeth must have been questioning her about you,' Ruce adds, 'and gone too far or something.'

I shake my head. 'She must have found her name.'

'Isn't that when you get your full witch power?'

'Sometimes it goes pear-shaped.'

'Well – there've been times I'd have given a lot to see Laban go pear-shaped. But I was sorry for her today.' She shrugs. 'Anyway, that's not so important now. Tell me what happened to you.'

Telling takes a while. Humph makes more tea, and reluctantly shares milk with Mr Ugly.

'So what now?' Ruce asks when I'm done.

'I've got to stay out of sight till I've got my name. I don't know where to go.'

'Have you been in touch with Gordy?'

'Last time I saw him, he wasn't too happy with me.'

'He's still on your side.'

I don't want to tell him he was right about Nilas. I know it's childish, so I just make a face.

'Home's out anyway, because of Sykes,' I say, though my real reason is Grace. I can't feel the same about her since I looked at the past, and I don't think I could handle seeing her yet. 'Have you got anyone we could go to?'

'Only in Edinburgh, or St Petersburg.'

They both seem a long way off.

'I tell you what,' says Ruce, 'we could try Gordy's grandfather.'

'I've no idea where he lives.'

'Big place called Haven Heights out on the cliffs near school. Gordy was telling me.'

'Yeah – but I've never met him.'

'We know he's Opposition. That means he'd protect you from Nilas, doesn't it?'

'We can't just turn up on a stranger's doorstep.'

'Have you got a better idea?'

'We could stay here if Humph didn't mind.'

'Long as yer like. We can learn yer more shifting and play them little games with the pictures.' He sounds quite keen, but Ruce shakes her head decisively.

'I'm not built for camping,' she says out loud. 'Putting him in danger,' she mouths at me.

She's right, too. If Nilas finds us here, we're all sausage-meat. At least Gordy's grandad's a witch too; he can look after himself.

*

We wait for dusk before we set off: we'll be going near school, and we don't want to get spotted for truants. When it's getting dark, Bargus takes us back through the woods to the southern end of the Island and puts us down at the gates of Haven Heights.

The house is like a cake, all cream icing and pillars for candles. There's a floodlit swimming pool round the side, you can see the artificial blue through a hedge of keep-out evergreens.

'Vulgar,' says Ruce, 'but I could get accustomed.'

If she wasn't here, I'd bottle it. I make myself ring the bell, and it doesn't just go bing-bong, it plays a whole symphony.

A big old guy comes to the door in a thick bathrobe and sheepskin slippers, rubbing his hands on a tea-towel as if we caught him washing up.

'We'd like to see Mr Shaw, please.' My voice sounds a bit too loud and a lot too common.

He's got bushy eyebrows. One of them climbs up his big forehead and the other one goes down. He pulls out a pair of specs and peers at us.

'Who are you?'

'He doesn't know us. My name's Margot. It's kind of private business.'

'Of course it is.' He grins, ear to ear, and I realize this has got to be Maxim Shaw. The shaggy hair's grey, and the broad shoulders have sagged a bit, but he's Gordy in fifty years' time. 'Delighted to meet you, Margot, and this is—?'

'Rusalka Ross,' says Ruce, very mature.

He takes her hand and does a little bow over it. 'Your uncle was a dear friend of mine. And, of course,' turning to me, 'so was your mother.'

So I was wrong: he does know us. That makes things easier, but it gives me a bit of a shut-in feeling too.

He takes us through to a study. There's a polished desk and leather chairs, bookshelves lining the walls, and floor-length green curtains across the windows.

'Make yourselves comfortable.' He gestures at the chairs. 'And let's talk about your private business.'

'We need help, I guess,' I admit. 'Somewhere to be for a bit, anyway.'

'You're very welcome, of course, but I wonder what made you think of me?'

'Gordy told us you were Opposition,' I say.

The eyebrows do their up-and-down trick again.

'He didn't exactly mean to tell us,' Ruce puts in. 'Margot did a spell on him.'

He laughs. 'Clever young lady. And have you told that to Nilas?'

'I haven't told him anything. I'm hiding from him.'

'And you want me to hide you.' He's not laughing now. He leans on the edge of the desk and rubs his hand through his thick hair. 'It's true, then, that Grace sent you her knowledge?'

'Yes, and if I get my name I can give it back to her. Unless my fuses blow.' He looks puzzled: I'm not explaining this too well. 'I helped the Others do a spell.

I think Nilas probably knows. I know what he did to my mother. If he finds me, I don't know what he'll do to me.'

'Funnily enough, you'd probably be safest with him.'

Safe with *Nilas*? Why would he say that? I don't get a chance to ask; he carries straight on.

'But you're here now, so we play it as it comes, eh? What about some coffee?' He doesn't wait for an answer. 'I won't be long.'

'He's nice,' says Ruce.

'You mean when he smiles he looks like Gordy. You're besotted.'

The cat's scuffling to get out of his carrier.

'Calm down. This isn't a carpet for you to pee on. Ruce, what did he mean about Nilas being safer?'

'I don't know. What's wrong with Ugly?'

He's caterwauling now.

'Shut up!'

'Sometimes a man's gotta go,' says Ruce. 'We can put him in the garden.'

She unlatches the front of the basket; he shoots out and starts scratching at the door. She turns the handle.

'Open it, then.'

She tries again. Nothing happens.

'Maggot, I think we could be locked in.'

*

'Why would he do that?'

'We haven't got time for a seminar,' I snap. 'We made a mistake coming here, now we've got to get out.'

The windows are locked too, and they're reinforced glass.

'He's not going to hurt us. He's Gordy's grandfather!'

'Get a grip. The way my life is going, I can't sit around and wait for the axe; I've got to do something.'

'Like what?'

Shape-shifting. Now wouldn't that be useful. 'Ruce, I might be able to get myself out, but I don't think I can do a lot about you.'

'Just go for it.'

She steps behind the curtains: it'll take him about two seconds to find her there, but the only chance I can see is if I manage to go small, get out and find help.

I close my eyes and try to think like a spider. I remember the one I listened to at school. I hear its spidery tune. I imagine Humph there with me, holding my hands. His furry mind's not like a human mind. It works a different way. I try to think like Humph thinking like a spider.

'Any luck?'

Ruce's voice is muffled behind the curtain; it sounds

a long way off. High up.

I'm on the floor. I'm tiny. I've got eight legs.

I *hate* spiders.

I run over the floor: wow, I can move like the clappers. I can't see too well at all; everything's multiple vision, and it's all so big I don't know where anything is, but I can feel vibrations.

The door opens.

I zip under the desk and see two huge green eyes staring at me: Mr Ugly got here first.

'It's me,' I try to say, but I don't have a tongue any more. Thank god Ugly doesn't like spiders either: he backs off against the wall.

Maxim sighs. 'You tumbled to it, did you? I'm sorry; I was hoping you wouldn't realize.'

His feet move forward into my line of sight. I'm getting a bit of focus now.

'One of you has changed shape. Margot, I suppose.'

How does he know? He's picking something off the floor: looks like my trousers.

When I get back to being human, I'm going to be butt-naked. Humph didn't think to mention that, but I guess hobs don't wear clothes.

'You know, you really are extremely talented,' he compliments me and sits down with his back to the window.

'What about you, Ms Ross? Has she made you

invisible, or are you just hiding?'

The curtains break into a joyful chorus:

Hal-lelujah! Hallelujah!

Fantastic. Gordy's phoned Ruce.

CHAPTER FIFTEEN

GORDY

Maxim's sat her in a chair. He hasn't let her take the call.

'You know I don't want to hurt you, and I don't have to. If Margot shows herself, then I'm going to let you go.'

And if not? I jitter out from under the desk.

'Ah, there you are. I'll look the other way, while you restore yourself.'

Ruce doesn't get the point, so she's staring at me full frontal. I scramble into my sweater and jeans, forget the underwear.

There's a tray on the desk with three cups. I reach out for one of them.

'No!' exclaims Ruce.

Was he going to drug us? His expression's not giving anything away, but I guess I'm going to have to do without coffee. I sit down opposite Ruce. 'What do you want?' I ask Maxim. 'Why did you lock us in?'

'I can't let you get away.'

'What, ever?'

He's not meeting my eyes.

'What were you going to do with us?' I insist.

'What *am* I going to do with you? I wish I could think of a different answer.'

This so doesn't sound good.

'Nilas talked to you, didn't he?' he says.

'I didn't tell him anything!'

'What did he ask you?'

'He said he'd help me deal with Grace's powers.'

'Margot, there's only one thing Nilas wants from you. There was only one thing he wanted from Grace. The names of the Opposition.'

The phone on the desk rings. We all jump, and Maxim stares at it, but doesn't pick up. After a while it stops.

'The Opposition is all that's preventing Nilas finishing the Network building,' Maxim says.

'I thought it was the Others preventing him,' I object.

'It's the Others doing the damage, but if the Bureau was united behind Nilas, the Others couldn't have held out for weeks, let alone years.'

'It must be costing him a fortune. Why doesn't he just build somewhere else?'

'It's the site he wants. That's where the trouble started.'

Maxim puts on the table lamp, casting a cosy pool of light. He rests his backside against the desk, facing me.

'When Nilas became head of the Bureau, he was already running Network. It wasn't such a powerful company then, but as technology got more and more advanced, Nilas saw the possibilities. Magic online! A master witch with unlimited outlets through the Internet could create himself an empire.'

Ruce is out of his sightline, the other side of the desk. Little by little she's manoeuvring herself round behind him: he's not paying attention to her; he's concentrating on me.

'Witches have often been successful in business for obvious reasons. Most of the Bureau members are top people in their field. We've got a Chief Constable and a High Court Judge, a college principal, and myself, a bank director. But, by tradition, the job's taken second place. In other words, we use our clout to advance the interests of the Bureau; we don't use magic to make a profit. Nilas is different. He wants riches, he wants power, and he sees no limit to the powers he can win. With magic he can widen his professional influence, and through Network he can bring his spells to bear on more and more people.'

'Network's pretty big, isn't it?' I've got to keep him talking. I'm not sure what Ruce is up to, I can't see properly beyond the lamplight.

'It's very big indeed, but there's still competition. That's what Nilas wants to change, by building on the Island.'

'What's so special about that wood?'

'The story goes that a magician's buried there, sleeping, not dead. That's probably metaphor, but in any case it hardly matters what the source of the power is. What's important is what Nilas could do if he took that power and channelled it through Network.'

'I think he's already taken it,' I say. I tell him about Sylvian's spell and the vision of the stone and the empty space.

'If that's true, then we're all finished. But if Nilas had the power, he would have used it. There'd be no reason to wait, and every reason not to.'

'So what's happened to it?'

'Maybe it was never there at all! That would be a joke. A joke a lot of people have died for,' he adds. 'I don't believe it, though. Nilas looked into the whole thing very carefully. He wouldn't have gone ahead if he hadn't been certain.'

'It isn't there now. The Others haven't got it. If Nilas hasn't got it either, then everyone's fighting over something that's vanished. Can't the Opposition explain that to him?'

'Nobody explains to Nilas that he's wrong. That

was the mistake Rossy made.'

He glances half over his shoulder towards Ruce, but doesn't really look at her.

'It was a long time ago now,' he goes on. 'Nilas already had a base on the Island. He'd heard the rumours about a powerful magic site, and he decided he wanted to use the power for Network. The Others said the wood was theirs. The first negotiations were enough to convince everyone that there'd never be an agreement: if Nilas went ahead, he'd have a war on his hands. At that point most of us in the Bureau thought he'd back off, but not he. He said this was the time to draw a line, make it clear to the Others that they couldn't run the world the way they wanted. He was going to build his headquarters, even if every single one of the Others had to be cleared from the Island, or the whole world, come to that.'

'Was Rossy the only one to stand up to him?'

'The Others are a nuisance, you know. They're forever in the way. There's always some sacred grove that has to be chopped down or some standing stones to be cleared for a motorway, and then the whole merry-go-round starts again: the Others attack the humans, the Bureau has to step in ... All we're trying to do is keep the peace, and precious little thanks we get for it. Some of us thought it wouldn't be a bad thing to make an example. We didn't think it would come to much anyway. We didn't think Nilas could exterminate the Others for real. But Rossy didn't agree on principle. He protested to Nilas, and Nilas took his powers. That was the first warning we had, of how strong Nilas had become, and how ruthless.'

He takes his glasses off and rubs his eyes. Behind him in the shadows, Ruce puts her hand on the desk.

'I thought somebody had to stop him, but who? I couldn't do it alone, and if I made a mistake, approached the wrong person, they'd tell Nilas, and then bye-bye Maxim. I moved an inch at a time.'

Ruce is doing something similar. What's she holding?

'It took me a long time to find out who I could trust. By then I knew we had to get rid of Nilas: he was obsessed with Network and with killing off the Others. He was verging on mad. But on the other side there were those who backed him, because through him they could have more power than any witch had before.'

It's an ashtray Ruce has got, solid glass, looks heavy. Like they say, smoking harms you and those around you.

'Grace was the strongest witch after Nilas,' Maxim goes on. 'When she signed up for the Opposition, we were in business. We started meeting in secret. Nilas knew people were working against him, and he had to find out who. He couldn't take on the Others alone.

248

But the Opposition couldn't risk an open revolution, and without that we couldn't do much either except help the Others delay building at the Network site.'

Ruce weighs her weapon, looking for her moment.

'Nilas thought if he knew one member of the Opposition then he could get the names of the rest, but it didn't work like that with Grace, because she'd sent her knowledge to you. Nilas wasn't sure of that, but he suspected it, so from that moment on he was determined to protect you.'

'*Protect* me?'

'You're the only one he knows could give him the names of the Opposition. The Skull, the spell he used on Grace, that's gone, broken. There's nothing else like that. He's waiting until you get Grace's full knowledge. Then you'll know what she knew, including who was working with us. Then he'll get it out of you. That's why I have to kill you.'

He says it so calmly, like it's just another bit of explaining.

'I'm sorry, Margot,' he adds.

'Don't be,' says Ruce and smashes the ashtray down on his head.

There's an almighty *crack!* and I flinch: I'm expecting him to crumple and fall. But it's the ashtray that's broken. Ruce is clutching her hand and Maxim hasn't turned a hair.

249

'Nice effort.' He doesn't even sound sarcastic. 'Don't try anything else; you'll only get hurt.'

Ruce doesn't bother replying – she just takes a swing at him. At the same moment, Mr Ugly makes a surprise appearance from under the desk and launches himself at Maxim. There's a confusion of fist and fur, and then Ruce goes sprawling back and hits her head on the wall, while Ugly, the world's first flying cat, shoots across the room yowling and lands halfway up the curtain. He rips it coming down, but that's the only damage we've done.

'You really can't fight magic, Rusalka. Please believe me and stay out of this.'

She's not moving. I think she's stunned.

'I don't know the names of your precious Opposition,' I shout. 'I only know about you because Gordy told me.'

'You will know.'

'If I did, I wouldn't tell Nilas.'

'You wouldn't have a choice.'

'Even with Grace's magic? You said yourself she was the strongest.'

'Except for Nilas. Even if you had all her power and knew how to use it, you couldn't possibly fight him: you're too young.'

I'm tired of people telling me that.

'Let's have a trial run,' I say.

The trouble is, I don't know spells for attacking witches. But I've got to do something: he's coming towards me, and he's a lot bigger than I am. Without magic, I haven't got a hope.

I dodge behind the desk. Maxim follows, and I nip round the other side, throwing a chair in his way as I go.

'Come here, Margot.'

'Yes, sure,' I tell him, backing away.

I'm in front of the desk again. Maxim's stepping over the chair. I'm listening to my own music, summoning it with all the attention I can spare from simply staying out of his reach. Keeping my eyes on him, I reach out my right hand to guide me past the bookcase. My fingers brush the spines.

Books. Why not? I grab a fat volume as I keep going backwards and hold it in both hands. I feel its weight, the leather binding, the edges of the pages. I'm tuning in, getting through. Can I talk to this book?

Fly! I command it, and it flaps like a clumsy bird, launched into the air towards Maxim's head. It's not fast enough to hurt him, but it takes him by surprise, and he stumbles, tripping over the edge of a rug.

He's just next to the bookcase. Hey, maybe I'm in with a chance here. While he's off balance, I shout in my mind to the whole row of books directly above him. They shuttle outwards from the shelf and tumble round his shoulders, striking his forehead, neck and arms. He falls to his knees.

'Who's too young?' I crow, but next second he's lunged forward and grabbed me round the ankles. I go down with a crash, and then he's on top, his full weight crushing the breath out of me. Now I can't bring the whole case down on him – it'll squash both of us.

'Don't make this harder than it has to be,' he says.

The doorbell rings.

Maxim pauses with his hand above my neck.

'Help,' I squeal, but my voice wouldn't reach the sharpest-eared Jehovah's Witness. Next minute Maxim's big hot palm is clamped over my mouth.

The doorbell plays its theme again. *SOS, call the police, break the door down*, I'm shouting in my head, but nobody's listening.

There's a click and a creak and a bang. The Jehovah's Witness has a key!

Footsteps stride across the hall and a cheery young voice calls, 'Hey, Grandpa! Anyone at home?'

I'm gagged, and Ruce is out cold. Maxim's not making a sound, not moving a muscle.

'Miayrrow-ow-ow-ow!' says Mr Ugly, leaping onto the desk and throwing cups in all directions.

The study door opens. 'What's going on?' says Gordy.

*

It's a difficult one. There are books splayed all over the floor and coffee dripping off the desk, the curtains are torn, the china's broken, Ruce is unconscious by the wall, and I'm on my back with Maxim crouching over me. He takes his hand off my face.

'Your grandfather wants to kill me,' I explain.

Gordy says, 'Ha-ha-ha!' Then he sees Ruce. 'What's happened to her?'

'She hit her head,' I say. 'She probably needs to go to hospital.'

'I'm fine.' Ruce is coming round to find Gordy clasping her hands and staring into her face: she maybe thinks she died and went to heaven.

'Gordy, I need a word with you,' says Maxim.

I'm scraping myself off the carpet. 'Just to save time: I came to Maxim because I knew he was Opposition. I thought he'd protect me from Nilas. I didn't get the thing about Nilas wanting to know who's Opposition so he can kill them all. I've got Grace's knowledge: apparently that means sometime I'll know who's in the Opposition, even though I haven't got a clue now. So Maxim thinks the best thing for everyone is if I die. Then he'll be safe, and so will you and the rest of the gang too. Did I leave anything out?' I ask Maxim.

Gordy's eyes are popping; he can't decide who

to stare at most.

'It's true,' croaks Ruce.

'Gordy, I don't expect you to understand—' Maxim begins.

'You'd kill a child just to protect yourself? I know who you are too, remember. How are you going to kill me?' I didn't know Gordy could do heroics.

'I'm trying to keep you safe, for heaven's sake!' Maxim shouts. 'Why do you think I've never told you who else is in the Opposition? This girl's the only one, and it won't be just me who'll suffer if Nilas gets to know—'

'Sure, you're trying to save the world!' Gordy interrupts him. 'Sorry if I'm not putting your name up for the Nobel Prize. If you get rid of Mag, how are you going to fight Nilas? You and your Opposition haven't had a lot of luck so far, have you? If you're going to have a hope of defeating him, you need Grace's powers, and that means you have to help Mag, not try to murder her!'

'Calm down!' Maxim snaps. 'Let's discuss this rationally.'

I'm standing up now. 'Yeah, hey, or here's another idea: let's just not.' I've trapped Mr Ugly back in his basket. 'Gordy, got the car? Then what do you say we get out of here?'

'Fine.' He helps Ruce to her feet: she's taking full

advantage, or maybe she's really still wobbly on her legs.

'Where are you going?' It's a treat to hear Maxim lose his cool: he's squawking, flapping his arms like a hen.

I just shake my head. 'Nowhere you know about. Thanks for the literature, Mr Shaw.'

I'm glad I got that line in.

*

We're eating fish and chips in the car, trying to decide what to do next.

'Did you know we were with Maxim, or was it luck?' I ask Gordy.

'Ruce sent me a text.'

She looks self-conscious. 'It seemed a bit rude to go off and see his grandfather without even telling him …'

I can't complain.

'Sorry if I was ratty last time,' I mutter at him.

'I'm sorry my grandpa's a homicidal maniac.'

Ok, that's the hugs over.

'You really should go to hospital,' he says to Ruce.

'No way. I don't want to find Wildeth by my bedside.'

'I suppose you could come to the Residence. Sykes isn't noticing a lot these days …'

'Maybe not, but Dad and Bella are going to notice,' I point out. 'They'd send us straight back to school.'

'So where else is there?' Ruce ponders.

'I'm not keen on staying with the Others.' I'm thinking aloud. 'Sylvian mentioned using me to bargain with Nilas. I don't trust her. Really I should be with a witch, somebody who can help me find my name, or at least find the names of the Opposition. Then I can write them down and say, if I die, the information goes to Nilas: that should stop Maxim hunting me.'

'He'd never try again!' Gordy exclaims.

'Of course he's going to try. Gordy, I'm a lethal danger to him. He couldn't bring himself to kill me in front of you, but I'm not taking any chances on him having a change of heart.'

'Maggot, you know what he said about the safest place being with Nilas?' Ruce ventures.

'I couldn't. I just couldn't. You'll have to believe me.'

'I didn't mean go to him. I was thinking if you went to someone else who's *not* Opposition, then they wouldn't want to kill you.'

That seems logical in a twisted way, but there's a problem. 'We don't know who is and who isn't, apart from Maxim.'

'Your friend Temple?'

'I'm not sure she was ever my friend.' I still can't get used to that idea. 'Besides, I can't contact her.'

'What about a witch who's not in the Bureau

at all?' she suggests.

Gordy frowns. 'The only one I know is Shade.'

'Who's he?' I ask.

'He's a kid Nilas picked up. Word goes he's talented but not reliable. He's trained with Nilas. Nilas wanted him to join the Bureau but Shade says he doesn't like establishments.'

That sounds promising, except for the Nilas connection. 'Is he loyal to Nilas?'

'I don't think he's loyal to anything except himself. I don't like him much.'

I shrug. 'There's times you don't like me a lot either. Can you get in touch with him?'

'I've got his number,' Gordy admits. 'But I'm really not sold on this idea, Mag.'

'It doesn't seem as if there are a whole lot of options,' says Ruce. 'Why not let Mag meet him, see what she thinks?'

We argue round it a while longer. In the end Gordy makes a call and says Shade's on his way.

'I warn you, he's mad as a bucket of frogs.'

'Gordy, I've hung out with mad people most of my life,' I remind him.

A while later a silver S-class Merc draws up beside us, with a young dude driving that I've seen a couple of times now.

'That's Shade,' Gordy tells me.

CHAPTER SIXTEEN
SHADE

Maybe I should have guessed, but I didn't.

'Hey, Trouble,' he greets me. 'Had an idea I might be hearing from you.'

'Why'd you think that?' asks Gordy.

'She's gone missing. Nilas is doing his nut. Relax – I ain't planning to share the news with him. You need a place to hide out, right?'

'Got it in one.' I give him a thumbnail of My Life and Times: most of it he seems to know already.

'Nilas tells you a lot.' Gordy's suspicious.

'Some he tells, some I pick up.' The tenser Gordy's acting, the lazier Shade sounds, maybe partly to tease him.

'Maggot,' Ruce whispers, 'can't you check him out with a spell like you did on Gordy?'

'Honesty spell, that what you mean?' Boy, his hearing's sharp. 'Be my guest,' he invites me.

'I'm not sure I can make it work on someone who's expecting it,' I tell Ruce. I'd probably skip it anyway:

the thing is, I feel comfortable around Shade. I'm not sure if that's the same as trusting him, but right now I'll settle for anything less than naked terror. 'Have you got a place we can go?'

'My sister J – she's got a pad.'

'We can't just turn up at midnight,' says Ruce.

'They ain't early birds at J's,' Shade assures her.

'Who else lives there apart from your sister?' Gordy wants to know.

'Kind of a shifting population.'

'Doesn't sound too secure,' Gordy objects.

'Take it easy,' Shade drawls. 'Ain't nobody going to find the girls there.'

*

I see what he means. He drives to Rostree and right through, out to the airport, then up to the top of the multi-storey car park. After that, he walks us to a metal door behind a set of bins. Through the door there's a stairwell, and we go up a flight on bare concrete to another fire-door.

'What is this place?' demands Gordy. 'Some kind of lock-up?'

But when Shade opens the second door there are carpets and candles, drum and bass out of one room and New Age flutes from another, and a sweet smell of incense. It's warm as bed in the morning.

Shade's sister J is a bit older than him and a lot

taller. She's handsome, with her hair in cornrows, and she's wearing a kind of purple robe with gold tassels. It looks like something out of a pantomime, but I guess it could be her dressing gown. I start to apologize for busting in, and she grins.

'I wasn't sleeping.'

'That's her work clothes,' says Shade. 'Should see what she wears to go clubbing.'

She doesn't seem bothered about me and Ruce coming to stay for we don't know how long.

'No problem. There's just Tippy and Bo here, last time I looked.'

She takes us into the big untidy kitchen and makes us hot chocolate.

'You all three witches?' she asks.

Gordy gives what he may think is a subtle cough.

'Ruce ain't,' says Shade.

Another girl walks in the kitchen, wearing a T-shirt and men's boxers. 'I'm a witch too,' she chirps.

'Not,' mouths J. 'This is Tippy,' she adds aloud.

'Last Beltane we all went dancing skyclad, it was really free and like primal,' Tippy babbles on. 'I could feel the moon-mother like caressing my whole body.'

'Who you talking about?' rumbles a new voice. It's a mountainous white guy with tattoos and shoulder-length greasy hair. 'Nobody touches Tippy's body but me, man.'

261

Tippy sits down next to Gordy, well inside his personal space. 'You ever dance skyclad?' she asks him, nuzzling up.

'It means naked,' J tells him.

He tries for a debonair laugh. 'I sing in the shower. Does that count?'

Tippy feels his biceps. 'You got a lot of resistance,' she tells him. 'It's the masculine fighting the goddess.'

The mountain scowls. 'Ain't the goddess you got to worry about, man, if you don't keep your hands to yourself.'

'Just showing your ignorance, Bo.' Tippy tosses her plaits. 'These are witches; they can do spells on you.'

Bo leers at Ruce. 'Show us some magic, sweetheart.'

'Shade, can we have a word?' asks Gordy in the sort of quiet, polite voice that's just short of a tantrum.

I think J is as near getting the giggles as I am. 'Come on, let's try my room.'

She leads us in where the bass is booming, and turns it down to a low throb. 'Take a seat, if you can find one.' Everything's jam-packed with gear: laptops and scanners and printers on desks and shelves, all tangled up with cables, clothes spilling out of drawers and piled on the floor. There's a bed half-hidden behind a wardrobe: Mr Ugly leaps off my shoulders and makes himself a nest in J's pillows.

'Who the hell are those freaks?' Gordy explodes

when the door's shut. 'Do you tell the whole world you're a witch?'

Shade's keeping a straight face. 'Far as they're concerned, it's just crystals and tarots. J is the only one who knows the score.'

'How do you know who they're going to bring back with them some night? I've put protection on these two, but that's not going to help if someone from the Bureau comes knocking at the door.'

'Relax, blad,' says Shade. 'Ain't nobody going to get in here that shouldn't.'

'What do you mean, protection?' I ask Gordy.

'A shielding spell. Blocks your music, so no one can read your thoughts or see you in visions. I've had you covered since I came to the Residence, and Ruce since she visited for your birthday.'

'Protect me, big boy,' says Ruce.

'Are you saying—' I can barely get the words out. 'You mean, that was *you*?'

When I remember what it was like at half-term, I could seriously slaughter him. 'Do you think you could have *told* me? Heaven forbid, *ask* what I thought?'

'Mag, if I hadn't, Wildeth and Nilas would've known everything you said, anywhere you went.'

'Not if I didn't open up.'

'They're stronger than you are, you couldn't keep them out. Anyway, you'd have shared with

Wildeth, wouldn't you?'

I swallow. He's right, of course, but he's never going to know what it did to me. Laban, and Tomas, and Wilkie, and the rest of them I thought might be my friends, all avoiding me like I was a bad smell, because they thought I wasn't letting them hear my tune. All because of Gordy and his protection.

'I've got to make my own decisions,' I say. 'Learn to do things for myself.'

'All you've got to do,' he says patiently, 'is find your name and hand your powers back to Grace. Leave the rest to me. And remember, people who think they're into the occult but don't know about real magic, they're not safe. I don't want you spending time with those guys.'

It's this attitude that gets my goat and all the rest of my livestock.

'Gordy, I'm not your little sister. It's not up to you who I talk to.'

'Could be tricky anyway,' J remarks. 'What's the girl to do, lock herself in the bathroom? That's the only place she's going to keep clear of company.'

'Can't do that either,' says Shade. 'The bolt don't work.'

Luckily, Gordy's too tired for much more argument, so we manage to pack him off back to the Residence before I'm driven to do him an injury. The rest of us settle down for what's left of the night: Ruce on a futon in the living room and me on the sofa, with red velvet cushions that smell musty, and more velvet for a blanket. I think it's an old curtain.

*

'This shielding spell, there's stuff it stops me doing, right?' I ask Shade.

'Not so much. Mostly you can find a way round.'

'But Wildeth said ... she seemed to think, it'd be a handicap.'

'She'd say so, wouldn't she? What she wanted was to get in on your thoughts. The shield was in her way.'

'So it doesn't really matter?'

He shrugs. 'Easier if you was open. But you're the one needs to hear your own music, and the shield don't make that any harder.'

We're up on the flat roof of the carpark, chilly, but the only place we can get away from Tippy and Bo. There's a view over the airport and the scrubby flatland that borders the runway and, after that, the sea.

'Couldn't I do the shielding myself?' I say. 'So I can take it off if I like?'

Shade hesitates. 'You know, I hate to come down the same side as Gordy ...'

'You think I should leave it to him?' I haven't told anyone what I went through on account of Gordy's spell, not even Ruce, and I'm not going to snivel to

Shade now. 'What if he has an accident or something? Next thing I know, I'll be pay-per-view.'

'Might be worth the risk.'

'Worth it how?'

'Gordy protects you,' he says. 'That just means no witch gets to listen in to what you're thinking or watch where you are. You protect yourself, it's a different game. You're setting up a resistance.'

'You mean I won't hear deep music so well, if I'm stopping other people, other witches, hearing me?'

'That's kind of the deal.'

I think he's looking at a plane taking off, but he's wearing his mirrored sunglasses, so I can't be sure.

'Is that why you're called Shade?' I ask. 'Because of the shades, I mean.'

He faces round to me, then smiles and takes them off. 'Could be. Could be my mama named me that.'

'Are they your protection?'

'Wish it was that easy.' He's blinking in the sun.

'Put them on,' I tell him. 'I don't mind.'

He keeps them in his hand. 'What's magic, to you?'

'What I hear in other people, their music, their thoughts. More than thoughts, their … wishes, what they believe, how they are. Like … sympathy, or insight.'

When I said something like that to Nilas, he laughed, but Shade nods. 'Everyone's got a bit of that kind of craft.'

'Everyone?'

'Sure. It's like music, not deep tunes but the regular kind, everyone can hear that, right? But there's only a few can play. Witches, they don't just hear music, they make it. Now, you can strum your guitar, hum your song, whatever, by yourself, but if you want to make sweet sounds, you got to play along with other people. Witches are meant to work together, listen to each other. Should be like a collective thing.'

'That's what the Bureau's supposed to be?'

'You got it. Witches, we shouldn't work alone. Turns us crazy. See, Nilas thinks magic is power – that's what he wants. Soon as he became head of the Bureau, he started being afraid somebody was after his place, so he got scared and started shielding himself. Guess that's where the trouble began.'

A few gulls are flying past, below the level of the roof, screaming like girls at a fairground. Mr Ugly looks interested and flicks his tail, but he's not stupid enough to take a dive off the building after them.

'Then the rest of them get the idea,' Shade goes on. 'If Nilas is keeping secrets, maybe they should do the same. No trust no more, see? Got so's every witch in the Bureau's going round like in a suit of armour. Sure, they're all safe, but they can't touch each other. You get what I'm saying?'

'If I'm not wearing armour, it gives me an

advantage?' It sounds like it could also mean I get sliced in pieces.

'Let's hope. You got to fight him.'

'Fight Nilas?'

'What he's done to himself, he's done to all the witches everywhere. Every one of us on our own, walking round inside our protection, suspecting every other witch, frightened, aggressive. Magic's meant to be a together thing, and he's made it like solitary confinement. If you can trust Gordy enough to let him shield you, that's a move the right way.'

'You really think I can fight Nilas?' My voice comes out a bit shaky.

He grins. 'Guess you got to. Ain't nobody else.'

'There's Grace. There's the Opposition.'

'Opposition, pur-lease. They've been opposing away all these years, they ain't done no more than drag on his wheels. What I say about Grace is, maybe her powers are all they're cracked up to be, and we better hope they are, because you're going to have to use them. But I don't reckon she was fit for her magic, or why'd she send it on? Escape to the asylum and leave her own child to take the rap. I got no respect for that. My money's on you, Trouble.'

He looks at me for a second and then puts the sunglasses back on. Now all I can see is my own reflection, twice and tiny, staring back out of his face.

*

Settling in at the Pad's not easy. There's no structure to anything. I mean the days, though you could say it about some of the furniture too. I'm ashamed to admit it, but I kind of miss school: at least the meals were regular and the showers were hot. Here, there's a trickle of rusty water into a rusty tub, and by the time you've run enough to wash yourself in, it's gone cold.

More importantly, I miss my sessions with Wildeth, and even having Laban around. Ok, one of them was trying to ferret out my secrets and the other bitched me up, but they knew about magic.

Here, there's no one who understands. Shade's not around much – he may not like Nilas, but he loves driving that Merc – and Gordy's busy at the Residence. J's kind and funny and laid-back, great company when she's not working, but she mostly is, designing websites. 'My own craft,' she says. 'Who needs spells when you got software?'

She tries to interest us in the gear: there are programmes that draw in 3D and programmes that make music. I'm not in tune – staring at the screens makes my brain feel sick – but Ruce gets quite into it.

Bo's a liability – he drinks and mouths off, and he pinched Ruce's bum once. She stamped on his foot, so he hasn't tried that again. Tippy's a space cadet, but she's friendly and I don't mind her, though she drives Ruce spare with her star charts and pan-pipes and camomile tea. She's fascinated by witchcraft, and seeing she's the only one who takes much interest, I indulge her one day by having a try with her toys.

'You never read the tarots?' She's amazed. 'I thought you was a witch.'

'We don't really use cards.'

She smiles in a condescending way. 'Shuffle and think of a question.'

How am I going to fight Nilas? How can I win?

I cut and hand her the deck and she lays them face down in a complicated pattern, then turns them up one at a time.

'Three of wands, yeah. High Priest, hm. Queen of Cups, ooh.'

They're just pictures to me.

'The answer's yes,' she tells me.

'*Yes?* That's not an answer.'

'You wanted to know if somebody fancies you, yeah?'

I sigh. 'Not exactly.'

'Maybe you didn't *think* that was what you wanted to know. Sometimes they answer what you don't ask.'

'What good is that?'

She smiles. 'That's how magic goes.'

It's stupid, but I'm getting annoyed. 'Not my kind of magic.'

'You don't know much about it though, do you?'

'I know more than you!'

'Yeah, well, what can you do then?'

'I can listen to what people are thinking. I can watch what they're doing when they're somewhere else.'

'What, like in a crystal ball?'

'No, I can just see.' I won't try explaining deep music, she wouldn't get it if I did.

She purses her lips. 'Prove it.'

'How? I can look at somebody and tell you, but you wouldn't know if it was true.'

'I know what Bo's doing right now. Have a look and tell me.'

She leans back and crosses her arms. Part of me knows it's good if she doesn't believe I'm a witch, but the rest of me's busy tuning in to Bo. I know his music well enough, thrash metal's the nearest you'd get to it on an ordinary playlist.

The vision's coming. Yeah, that's Bo.

He's got no shirt on. In fact, he's wearing no clothes at all. It's not a pretty sight, but his blonde female friend isn't pushing him away.

'So,' says Tippy, 'where is he? What's he doing?'

CHAPTER SEVENTEEN
SELF DEFENCE

I've got to lie. I've got to make her think I was just showing off.

'I – think he was on the bus.'

'Bus? What bus? Where was he going?'

'To the pet cemetery,' I say wildly.

'To the *what*?'

Come on, obviously I'm making it up as I go along, aren't I?

'You're lying,' she accuses me.

Yes, bulls-eye. I'm just a fantasist, a little girl who wants to be a witch. So why isn't she laughing at me, telling me to grow up or something? Her eyes have gone narrow, and she's staring like she hates me.

'What was he really doing?'

Uh-oh, intuition. She's not as stupid as all that.

'I don't know.' I spread my hands – look, nothing to hide. 'I'm sorry, I couldn't see anything.'

'Yes, you did! I could tell by your eyes.'

If I tune in to her thoughts, I can make her

believe what I say.

On the other hand, why should I help Bo cheat on her?

'He was with another woman, wasn't he?' she says.

I nod.

'That trash, that piece of scum!' Her eyes are glittering, and her voice is high and tense. 'He told me he was with his mother.' She looks suddenly hopeful. 'It wasn't his mother, was it?'

'Nope. Sorry.'

'What did she look like?'

'Long yellow hair. Um – I didn't get a good look at her face.'

'It's that whore Natalie. I know. I'm going round there right now.' She gets her jacket and wrings its neck. 'I'm going to catch them together, oh you bet your sweet life somebody's going to be sorry.'

I wish the odds didn't look so good on that somebody being me.

*

'Hip hurray!' exclaims J when I confess what's happened. 'The boy's had it coming a long time.'

Ruce isn't so confident. 'Could be awkward for you, Maggot.'

'You don't have to say it: Gordy was right again.'

'He's not so dim as he looks,' she says proudly.

J pats my arm. 'Don't beat yourself up about it.'

'I may have Bo to do that for me.'

There's a bang as the front door flies open, and then a lot of swearing. We pile out into the hall.

'You get your hands off me, you get your things, you're not spending another night here!' Tippy's weeping and screaming; Bo's got her by the arm.

'Spying on me, following me round!' Bo bellows. 'Making me look stupid!'

'Don't need Tippy for that,' J remarks. 'You leave her alone, Bo.'

'Keep your nose out!' He shoves her away with his free hand, like somebody batting an insect. That gives him a clear view of me, lurking guiltily.

'And you, you little bitch, stirring it up, making trouble between me and my woman—'

He's let go of Tippy to concentrate on me, backing me against the wall.

'Don't touch her!' Ruce shouts. She gets both hands in his belt and tugs, but she might as well try shifting an ox.

'Think you can make a fool out of me—' He pulls back a hand. I duck, but too late to miss a smack like a brick on the side of my head.

'Maggot!' cries Ruce.

I feel the impact jar my whole body. Everything goes black with coloured lights flashing, and then I hear a thundering crash like a house fell down, and I'm standing up straight and Bo's on his back over by the door.

There's a moment's silence.

'Wow,' says J. 'How'd you do that?'

I'm not sure what I did, but it seems like a hell of a neat trick.

'What happened?' I ask. My head feels loose, as if it might float off somewhere, and there's a buzzing in my ears.

'He just went flying,' Ruce tells me. 'You didn't even lay a finger on him.'

Bo's starting to struggle to his feet. Then the door opens behind him and here's Shade.

'What's going on?'

'Bo hit Mag,' J begins. 'And then—'

She doesn't get any further because Shade hauls Bo up by the neck of his sweatshirt and socks him on the chin, and then lets him fall back on the floor.

J starts laughing.

I shamble over to Bo and look down at him, and he cringes, putting his arm up to defend himself.

'It's all right, I'm not—' It's going to sound ludicrous, me telling this vast man I won't hurt him. Suddenly I feel quite sorry for Bo.

Tippy's been standing with her mouth open. Now she gives a high wail and falls on her knees.

'Sweetie, are you ok? Tell me you're all right, baby.'

He rubs his hand over his face. 'Dunno,' he mumbles. 'My head hurts.'

'Come in the bedroom, angel. You lie down and I'll rub some tiger balm on your temples.'

'No way!' Bo exclaims indistinctly but passionately. He lurches to his feet and staggers towards the door, pulling Tippy after him. 'I'm not staying here to take this Exorcist crap. I'm going to my mum's.'

'What, your real mum this time?' J taunts him.

Tippy's not listening to her. 'Whatever you say, Bo, honey. Take it slow; lean on me.'

They head out of the flat, J following.

'Tips, he's no good for you. Let him go where he wants, you stay here.'

Tippy's fondling Bo's arm like a pet. 'It's my love-line,' she sighs, giving J a backward martyred glance. 'Always was too strong for me.'

J comes back rolling her eyes. 'Some girls you just can't help.'

'Some help themselves,' Shade says, looking at me. 'Someone going to tell me what happened?'

Ruce and J split the story, interrupting each other. I keep quiet: I'm still feeling a bit high and a bit shaken up. Best if I keep my lid on.

'So then he whacked Mag,' says J.

'I thought she'd be out cold,' says Ruce.

'There was a noise like an explosion,' says J.

'That was when Bo hit the wall,' says Ruce.

'Mag didn't touch him, but he shot across the hall as if he trod on a landmine or something,' says J.

'Guess you got a new skill, Trouble,' Shade tells me.

'I don't even know what I did.'

'Next time you'll know what you're doing. Tomorrow, you and me start work on self-defence.'

*

The carpark roof seems like the best place for a combat tutorial. It's been raining during the night and there are puddles on the concrete, but the sun's shining now.

'You didn't get taught nothing at that school about fighting, huh?' Shade asks me.

I shake my head. 'One time, I got the witchkids to back off, with my tune. What I did with Bo was a bit like that, but I wasn't even thinking about music.'

'You was using it just the same. Everything you do, everything I do, it's in the tune. Listen.'

'You're going to open up to me?'

He takes off his shades. 'Wide open. Welcome to my world.'

'Yeah, but say you were Nilas, you wouldn't have to.'

'He'd open up. Shielding yourself takes energy. He's going to want to use his strength on you.'

Shade's music is angular and bluesy, hard to get a

handle on. 'I can't let *you* in, though,' I say. 'Not with Gordy protecting me.'

'I'll fight regular. See, if I'm planning to kick you—' He lashes out, I jump back, but he stops just short. 'You hear it?'

'I wasn't listening.'

'Gotta listen, all the time. Try again.'

Tuned in, I get what he means. A split second before he moves, his music changes: louder and faster, a decision, a threat.

'I'm meant to react? It's too quick.'

'Quick as thought, baby.'

This time, I'm ready for him, and I leap aside, but it's his other foot, so I make hard contact between my hip and his instep.

'Ouch.'

'Different right and left, different feet and fists, different if I'm going to punch or wrestle. You can hear if you listen.'

'I'd have to do, like, a degree course before I start fighting you.'

'Your music knows better than you. Don't just listen to me. Listen to yourself.'

We jig about, slow motion. I'm beginning to understand. The first time you try to ride a bike, it seems impossible. Then your body starts to learn how you stay upright on this thing. If I balance between his tune and my own, I can keep out of his way, but as soon as I let myself consider what I'm doing, I've walked into a right hook.

'Ok, Trouble, you're learning how to run away. Now we'll up the game: you gotta fight back.'

I land a punch on his shoulder.

'Oh, oh, I'm dying, that hurt so much. Don't do it again, mercy.'

'I'm not a heavyweight,' I pant.

'C'mon, how you going to pulp me? Getting serious now. Gotta be for real or you won't learn.'

He's weaving around me, poking out quick, punishing jabs. When he lunges, going for my arm to swing me and floor me, I sidestep, just in time, and his weight crashes him down on his hands.

He kicks up and back, hard and fast. I take it on the thigh, and the pain makes me gasp; in a flick, he's on his feet. He's got me spun backwards with an elbow round my neck. He could crack my spine.

This hurts; this is dangerous. I feel the rush of adrenalin and anger, but I force it inwards not outwards. The magic surges through my music. I grab his forearm and, while my legs bend, my back flexes. He somersaults over my head and lands splayed on the floor.

Wow, that was *easy*.

'Are you ok?' I gasp.

For an answer, he jumps up and throws a punch. I'm dancing away on the damp concrete: if I focus, I can hear the tune of what's under my feet. When Shade moves in to get me in a wrestler's lock, round the waist, I'm talking to the puddles; I make the surface icy. His legs slide from under him. They slip like crutches on a shiny floor, and he stumbles against me, trying to save himself, knocking me backwards.

We sprawl together, but only for a second before we're both up again, eager for more. I'm laughing, but he's concentrated, his eyes narrowed. What's he planning?

Listen, listen to his music. He's going for a knockout, straight from the shoulder. Now I've got options: to try another trick with what's around us or use my tune for strength, but I still haven't got to the place I was with Bo. Something I did, something my music did, sent him flying like a rocket as soon as he connected.

Only one way to find out. Shade's fist is coming, and I don't dodge; I don't hit back. I wait for it, listening with everything I've got. Time slows, and between my heartbeats I get space to know what's happening. His knuckles catch me below the ear. And just at that split instant, I feel my force explode. It's through my whole body, in my blood, along my nerves and muscles, and I can use it, direct it how I want.

My arm straightens, my fingers point, and I aim the

blast from my centre to his. I blink, and in the second's darkness I see a flash and crackle. I hear it as a piercing note, slicing the air.

Shade's on his knees, but when he lifts his head, he's grinning.

'Had enough?' I sing out.

'Bring it on!' he says.

He springs into a crouch, shimmying from side to side. If I let him, he'll take a low tackle, pull me off my feet. I'm ready for him. I'll duck and dive, and give him another laser blast of power.

Before I can do it, there's a shove between my shoulder blades. I lurch sideways, coming down with a crack on my knee. How did he do that?

He didn't. Something tall and stripy cannons past, gets Shade by the shoulder and pounds him on the jaw with a white clenched fist.

It's Gordy, the big idiot, come to save me.

'Cut!' I yell like I think I'm Spielberg. 'Cut it out, Gordy. Leave him alone!'

I might as well be singing 'Away in a Manger'. Gordy goes to slug Shade again, but Shade slips under his arm, hooks a leg round his knee and sends him sprawling.

Now I think they'll stop, but Gordy grabs Shade's wrist, plants a size-twelve trainer in his middle and brings him down across his own chest. Then there's a muddle, punching and pulling and twisting, no craft, just two boys battering the crap out of each other.

They're rolling over and over, both of them fighting to stay on top, and they're close to the edge of the roof, much too close. There's no barrier, and five storeys to the ground.

'Stop!' I shout, my voice cracking. 'Stop it!'

Nobody's listening. I'm going to have to go in.

Yeah, but how?

I listen for their music. And just as quick, I shut down again. They're not thinking about reasons or consequences. They're not thinking at all; it's instinct riding them here, the raw red. Somebody hits you, you hit them back HARD. You mash them; you pulverize them. Hey, now I know what it feels like to be a guy.

All this zooms through my thoughts, and any moment now they'll be off, both of them or one of them, tumbling down. I can't get between them and the fall.

A seagull floats over.

I drag air through my teeth and lift my arms. *Think like you're a bird.* Not a seagull, a big sod-off monster, one of those things with the naked neck and the bald head.

My wings spread, my body lifts. I'm up and off. I haven't even got time to enjoy the flight. There's maybe a second in it; they're poised on the lip of the roof. I swoop out beyond the building, bank in the air and swerve back, my beak open.

'*Eeee-yark!*' I screech, my head up against Gordy's.

He's on top of Shade, throttling him. They both freeze. And if I wasn't a giant vulture, I'd laugh at their expressions. I clutch my forklift talons round Gordy's shoulder and pull him inwards, dragging Shade underneath. They're no baby lambs; I can't get them far, and after I've heaved them a few inches, I release with my feet and use my beak to jab, prodding them away towards the safe centre of the roof. They're more than happy to go. In fact, they're scooting for cover.

I flop down to land and let the shriek rip once more, like triumph.

*

'Can we try and remember we're all on the same side?' I suggest, once we're down in the kitchen and nobody's about to go skydiving.

Ruce nudges Gordy and he grunts.

'I'm talking to both of you.' I'm pretty angry with Shade. 'Gordy at least thought he was protecting me. What's your excuse?'

'Maybe I don't take too kindly to being hoist off the rooftop by guys I'm trying to help.'

'I come up there, I see Mag fighting you off, what am I meant to think?' Gordy demands. 'You could have said something.'

'Yeah, would that be with my teeth down my neck?'

'Give it a rest,' J recommends. 'Don't both of you have something to say to Mag?'

Gordy looks blank; Shade grins at me. 'What, like thanks for saving us from a ghastly death?'

'Don't mention it,' I say.

'Even before Gordy turned up you was taking me to the cleaners. Real nice work. A few more sessions and you'll be ready to play with the big boys, Trouble.'

Gordy clears his throat. 'There might not be time for any more sessions. The reason I came over today was to tell you Nilas has called a Bureau meeting. They're all coming to the Island tomorrow.'

Shade whistles. 'Guess it ain't to discuss the Christmas party.'

'The meeting's at the new Network building. I think he's got it ready to roll.'

'Then even if I get my name,' I say, 'even if I give the power back to Grace, we're too late.'

'Why's the building important?' J wants to know.

'It's on a place the Others call the Sleeper's ground,' I tell her. 'There's magic there that Nilas wants to use for Network. That's what the Others were trying to stop.'

'If he's really got his computers hooked up to whatever's under the site, that's going to be a lot of power,' Gordy says. 'I don't know if my protection's going to hold. He might be able to see you; he might come for you.'

Shade gets up. 'Then we're going to have to be ready to fight.'

'We won't even be together.' I feel helpless. 'You'll be driving them round. Gordy'll be there at the meeting. I'll be sitting here not knowing what's happening. I won't be able to listen in or get a vision; they're all protected.'

'Stop me if I'm being stupid,' says J, 'but how about something normal, like we get Shade a gun and he pops the guy?'

Gordy shakes his head. 'Nilas has got magic that'll stop a bullet.'

'You ever hear of the Introduction?' Shade asks him. 'It's a spell lets someone else hear and see through you. You're at the conference, you can act as a channel for Mag.'

'And you can go back to the Residence and be with your mum!' Ruce exclaims. 'If all the Bureau members are going to be with Nilas, that means Sykes, too.'

It doesn't sound like a healthy plan to me, but I don't have anything else to suggest.

Gordy puts his arm round me. 'Mag, don't look so miserable.'

'We're not done yet!' Shade declares.

'We're all on your side,' says J.

'We know how strong you are,' Ruce assures me.

'Yeah, what you did up on the roof was amazing,' says Gordy. 'I'm sorry I went for Shade. I'll be your link tomorrow if you think you can trust me.'

I'm stupidly moved. 'Of course I trust you. I trust all of you round this table.'

'Then we're one up on the Bureau already,' says Shade. 'Because none of them suckers trust each other further than they can spit a pip.'

CHAPTER EIGHTEEN
ERON

'Where have you been?'

Eron's so relieved he can't even cuss. He's not sure if he wants to clout me or cuddle me, so he holds my shoulders and shakes me like I'm a bottle of ketchup.

'I've got police calls out, Missing Persons in the papers – didn't you see none of that? Appeal on the radio. I'm thinking you gotta be drowned, but they told me your friend's gone too. So then Bella guesses you both ran away. I'm saying you been snatched for the White Slave Trade.'

'I'm not white,' I point out. 'Dad, I'm really sorry, really.' I didn't think he'd know I'd done a runner, but of course Wildeth would have asked if I'd come home. 'I'm ok, and so's Ruce. We had to hide out for a while.'

'Hide out? You been breaking the law or what?'

'Nothing like that. It's kind of complicated.'

Bella comes out on the drive and shrieks when she sees me. 'Pumpkin! Oh my God, you're home. I don't believe it. Are you well? Are you hurt?' She folds me in a squashy embrace.

'I'm fine,' I mumble into her cleavage. 'I need to talk to Dad.'

'Of course you do, pet.'

'Yeah, sure,' he grumbles. 'Turn up out of nowhere and expect me to drop everything. Some people got a job to do. Bella can't handle the whole show on her own.'

'Your dad's been staunch.' Bella's still got an arm round me and now she ruffles Dad's hair: my, aren't we the happy family? 'Dr Sykes and Gordy both had to go on a Health Management course today, so it's the two of us in charge. No worries, Eron, pet. They've all had their morning meds and nobody's throwing a loop. I can cope. You and Mag get some quality time.'

She looks down at the basket on the gravel: Mr Ugly's complaining that he wants out. 'Just don't ask me to take care of the puss-cat.'

Shade brought me here in a silver stretch limo and said it's got to be the grossest car he's ever driven. Nilas hired it to chauffeur the Bureau members from around the Island and the rest arriving by sea and air: Shade's going to have a busy morning. I hid out in the bay till he left again with Sykes and Gordy, then I came round the front and found Dad putting out the rubbish.

Now we go in his office, and I let Ugly out to sniff

around. Dad leans against the desk, arms folded. 'This better be good.'

'Dad, I'm going to tell you everything, but first off, it's not going to work unless you tell me some stuff as well.'

He doesn't scowl like I'm expecting: he looks down and moves his feet around like he expects to find somewhere more comfortable to put them.

'Yeah. Girl, I gotta say I'm sorry for how I was last time you was here, when you said that about Bella and all. I was out of order. Guess you caught me on the raw.'

'Oh. Right. You mean you and her are …' What do you say? 'Going out' sounds like kids. 'Lovers' sounds like the tabloids.

'Maybe. Yeah.' He doesn't know the word for it either. 'That why you ran off?'

'No! Of course not.'

'It's not like. I mean, it ain't exactly straightforward.'

'You mean because you're not free?' I ask.

His head comes up quickly. 'What you saying?'

'Dad, I know about Grace.'

We look at each other a while. I can hear the thoughts chasing back of his eyes.

'How do you know?' he asks at last.

'She told me.'

He gives a short laugh. 'Yeah, really.'

'Yes, really. When she was in the attic with me that time. Dad, there are a lot of things … I'm not going to lie to you.'

I thought about doing a spell, but I kind of want him to believe me without magic, so I just tell him. A couple of times he starts to interrupt, then shuts up again and lets me go on. When I've come to the end, he's looking like I've blown his circuits.

'Mag, you been smoking skunk?'

'I don't smoke, Dad.'

'We gotta get you some help. We'll talk to Sykes when he's back. You know, it's like delusions.'

'Probably sounds that way. But I'm not mad, and neither's Grace.'

'You shut your mouth about Grace!' Suddenly he's lost it. All the temper he's been saving up comes out like a jackpot. 'Somebody been talking to you – I don't know who, sure as hell ain't Grace. Somebody stirring mischief and now you give me all this about magic and crap; you think I'm simple? You know what I been through the last ten years? You think you can make a monkey out of me with some—'

He's building up for a slap, and I'm not going to take it. The music's marching in his head, dwarves on the warpath, *Hi-ho, hi-ho!*, and I send my tune slamming in. He goes backwards, hard down in a chair, and sits there with his mouth open.

'Listen to me!' I tell him. 'You're not going to hit me, understood?'

He starts to get up: I chuck him back down. He can't think what's happening.

'I'm doing that to you. Me. And I'm playing nice so far, but if you get violent, I'm going to put you through the window.'

He rubs his eyes. 'Jeez. I gotta be sickening for something.'

'Dad, it's all for real.' I kneel down next to him and take his hand. 'Grace was a witch.' He tries to pull away but I hold on. 'And now I'm a witch.'

'Ain't no such thing, girl. I know that.'

I sigh. 'Ok, Dad, whatever you say. Tell me the way you see it.'

'Maybe I should. I tell you the score. It's gonna hurt, but it's gotta be better than you making up these stories to yourself.'

'Just give it to me straight.'

'I met Grace; we was both pretty young. She was twenty and I was nineteen. Guess we weren't the best-matched couple. I was a chef on a boat, long-distance. She was in first class. She was gorgeous and smart with it. Don't know what she saw in me to take her fancy. She said I was something solid.' He laughs and taps his forehead with a finger. 'Solid wood, I told her. Anyway, we was going round together maybe eighteen months, and then she gets pregnant.'

'That was me?'

'Sure was, babe. Neither of us had been planning on that, but we took a chance. She got offered a job out here on the Island with Network.'

'That figures,' I mutter.

'So we came over together. She got accommodation in the package. We moved in, and a few months later out pops you to join us. That was a real happy time.'

He's holding my hand tight.

'Boss of Network, he thought the world of her. She was going to get a promotion, and I had a job at St Pen's, hospital cooking. I worried I wasn't, you know, bright enough for her. She used to laugh and say she had to work all day with eggheads, she didn't want another one at home, but I was trying out some evening classes, thought maybe it wasn't too late to get myself some education. And then I come home one day ... '

I'm crouched at his feet, looking up into his face, and I can see him blink away tears.

'All I can hear halfway down the road is you crying. I'm running to get there, and the front door's open, and you're in the front room, and Grace is sitting on the floor, just sitting there. I go to her even before I go to you. She's ... she's like she's not there. You don't know what she used to be like before.'

'I do,' I whisper. 'I do know.'

'I try everything to find out what happened. The room's messed up. I think maybe burglars, but nothing's gone, and the doctor says she's not been hurt, she wasn't – attacked any way. He says all we can do is take care of her, and maybe she'll get better one day. That was Sykes.'

He wipes his eyes with his free hand.

'He was a lifeline, that man. Can't ever pay back what I owe him. Said he was setting up this place, the Residence; he'd take Grace and give me work here so I could stay near her. It was him said maybe you shouldn't know what happened.'

I'm thinking about Sykes, being so kind to Dad, and all the time working for Nilas. It's hard to believe some people.

'And that was the way it went. Maybe it wasn't for the best, but it seemed that way. You could go to school, and Grace was getting the care she needed, and I could be with both of you.'

'She didn't even know who we were.'

'I kept thinking there'd be a change. I used to kid myself she was improving. One time I let go with her, I started shouting. I slapped her round the face, just trying to get her to look at me, you know? Sykes said if it ever happened again, I'd be broken.'

'So you took it out on me instead.' I can't help sounding bitter.

'Yeah. Ain't no better way to say it, girl.' He strokes my fingers. 'Seeing her like that, remembering how it used to be, it made me so I couldn't always keep a check on myself. Couple of years ago, I'd just about got to the end of the rope, I was going to pack up and leave. You was just going to start senior school, we could have moved anywhere, but Sykes said if we stayed, it was good for her to have us round.'

Of course, Nilas wanted to keep me where he could find me.

'When Bella came along, right off I started feeling, I don't know … she put some life in me.'

'She's got enough for two,' I say, and he smiles.

'Yeah. She's real fond of you and all, girl. Gave me a whole new headache though, because what have I got to offer? So I didn't make no move on her nor nothing. Not till you come home and you asked was we getting together? After you left I was thinking, I got no right to rip up at you the way I did. So then I talked to Bella.'

Maybe one day I'll learn to keep my mouth shut.

'I told her like I've just told you, and it seemed like she didn't have no objection to me. Crazy, I know, but you can't never fathom a woman.'

'But Dad—' I hesitate. 'Don't you still love Grace?'

'I ain't never going to stop loving her, girl. But she's no companion; you gotta see that.'

'What if she got better?'

He shakes his head. 'Whoever told you about her, they served you a bad trick. You're going to be thinking like I was, hoping all the time she's going to come back to us. But, girl, she ain't coming back.'

Mr Ugly's gone nose down, tail swishing. Maybe there's a mouse.

'I made some wrong choices, done some wrong things,' Dad goes on. 'Need to keep a watch on my temper, Bella said that, and I'm gonna try. I got a whole lot to say sorry for, girl, but I never saw it till Bella started telling me.'

The door behind me smacks open.

'And darling Bella's made all the difference, has she?'

Grace is standing in the doorway.

She's in her loony-tunes clothes, grey gown over pyjamas, but it's plain to see she's only mad like fury.

'I've been listening to every word,' she hisses.

Magic can make you forget normal stuff. I'm protected against mind-reading and visions but, hey, remember keyholes?

'So you're planning to leave me for a fat Kiwi tart? Are you?' she challenges Dad.

He's sagging; his mouth's open. I think he might be going to pass out, and I grab his hand again to put a bit of warmth in him. That gets Grace's attention.

'And you, you little idiot. After everything I said to you, you have to go running and tell him. You always were a Daddy's girl. Have you found your name yet? Too busy playing teenage witch, obviously. Gordy told me how good at spells you're getting. Well, three cheers, clever girl. Remember whose magic it is you're using? While you're waving *my* wand you might have forgotten *I'm* stuck in a bloody freakshow.'

'Quiet!' I beg her. 'We don't want everyone to hear.'

'Everyone! That'll be the Mensa members I've spent the last ten years with, will it? Did I really once say I was fed up with eggheads?' she wonders. 'Oh boy, did I ever have a chance to change my mind. Have you any idea what it might feel like when the only company you've got is lunatics?'

'You were one of them till a couple of months ago,' I protest.

'Or is it dear *Bella* you don't want to hear us? Yes, she's the one, the little ray of sunshine who's brought light and hope back into—'

'That'll do.' Dad doesn't raise his voice but she stops at once. 'Grace,' he says. 'Grace, whatever happened to you?'

Her face crumples. 'Eron, you're all I've got to hold onto. If you leave me, I don't know what I'll do.'

Then she's sobbing in his arms.

I back out of the room and close the door behind

me. Maybe this is the miracle every single-parent kid dreams of, Mum and Dad back together, but it doesn't feel too good.

Down the hall in the canteen, the Hollies are having coffee and biscuits. I don't go in, but I stand watching through the round glass panel: it's a routine that happens every day, and watching it now soothes me. Bella's taking round the trays, Chough and Parrot are helping hand the mugs. Mrs Frisch has taken control of the sugar; luckily nobody minds too much how many lumps they get. Abram's conducting an imaginary orchestra with a teaspoon. Jennifer's got a nervous fit on: she's shadowing Bella, holding an edge of her overall. Bella takes her hands and holds them for a moment, persuading her to sit down.

Bella's kind: she cares about the Hollies; she cares about me. Sometimes it looks like she cares more than Mum does.

But I can't blame Mum. Look what happened to her. Dad's not had it easy either, has he? And whatever way up, certainly Bella's done nothing wrong. It's just a mess, and it's all Nilas's fault.

Betsy's been waltzing to Abram's silent music, and now she pulls Parrot up for a partner. The only dance Parrot can do is a pogo, and the results are what you might expect: biscuits everywhere, and Perkin gets milk tipped in his lap. Bella calms them down and mops up.

It's time Dad came to give her a hand: she must think he's still talking to me. I should go in and help, but I don't.

I'm hearing a low-level buzz like a mobile on vibrate. After a minute I understand it's inside my head: Gordy's telling me the Bureau meeting's about to start.

It's a relief to have something to take my mind off things at home. I run up to my old room and lock the door.

I sit down on the bed. Gordy and I didn't get much of a chance to practise, so I'm not sure how this is going to go, but I'm hearing his music loud as if he was in the room with me, and as soon as I close my eyes I get a picture, clear as the most vivid dream.

There's Gordy's face, which I wasn't expecting: surely I'm seeing through his eyes? Then I realize it's a reflection, very close up. He's looking nervous. He's in a small space, with mirrors on both sides as well as in front. It's a lift.

The doors in front of him open, and he steps out.

It's the underground room at Network. When I saw it before, it was almost empty, and the banks of screens were dead eyes looking at nothing. Now they're flickering a screensaver message: *NETWORK IT* in silver floating across a grey ground. All around the control desk people are sitting.

'Come in, Gordon.' I want to look at the other

people, but I've got to take what Gordy's eyes give me, and right now he's focused on Nilas in his wheelchair. 'Find a seat, make yourself comfortable. Here, next to me.'

Gordy sits down – I sit down. I can kind of feel it though I've got no control.

'Your first full meeting, isn't it, Gordon? Better all introduce ourselves, hm?' Nilas clears his throat. 'Nilas Samuel.'

He looks at the woman on his right, and so does Gordy.

'Thesida Wildeth.' It seems a long time since I heard that sweet voice. She's pale as always, wearing a silvery dress, and there's a white lily in her silvery hair. It could be one from the flower tanks in her room.

Now Gordy looks round the table, as the others speak one by one.

'Sandra Coper.' She's a small spare woman with grey hair in severe waves, frowning over her spectacles like she's about to tell someone to sit up and pay attention. She sounds Scottish.

'Francis Sykes.' He's looking even worse than last time I saw him. His cheeks are hollow, and his beard, which I remember always being trimmed, has grown down over his collar. He coughs and takes a swig from a glass of water.

The girl next to him giggles. 'You know who I am,

301

don't you, Gordy? Lucasta Lucas.' She's a model; she's always got her picture in the papers in a new club or taking a new drug. Her blonde hair's arranged like a wild nest, and she's wearing electric blue chiffon over a white body stocking. It's got to be the latest fashion on some planet.

'Harald Mortensen.' He's a sleek man with red-framed glasses, and a goatee that might be sexy if you were a goat. 'Welcome to our merry throng.'

The next voice is precise, refined. 'Lady Cootie Kellerman.' Laban's mum, and doesn't she look it. Perfect make-up, perfect hair, perfect clothes, and a lot of pearls.

I know the man on her right. 'Maxim Shaw.' He winks at Gordy.

His neighbour looks down at the table. 'Felipe Castaneda,' he murmurs. He's tall, a head above Maxim, with a bony dark-skinned big-nosed face and deep bright eyes, a bit like a camel.

'Tottimer,' barks his neighbour and Gordy's. 'Brian Tottimer.' Andy's dad, he's got the same bull neck and the same heavy brow over small, mean eyes.

'Gordon Shaw,' says Gordy shyly.

*

Something's happened to me while they've been saying their names, like a curtain drawn back in my head.

The Opposition.

CHAPTER NINETEEN

THE CONFERENCE

Maxim, of course. Then there's Castaneda. And Lady Cootie, Laban's mum, she's number three.

I'm not reading their thoughts, I'm just kind of remembering what Grace knew. When she was on the Bureau, ten years ago, that was the line-up.

Three out of ten. There's Gordy too, the new recruit, but it's still not many, is it?

Should I tell someone? There's no one to tell. Better keep watching.

I've missed a bit while I was thinking about who's on the Opposition. Nilas is talking: '... welcome you to the new Network building,' he says.

'Impressive,' comments Lady Cootie.

'Last assault by the Others held us up a while, but damage wasn't too bad, hm?' he goes on. 'Now, delighted to tell you, ready for action.'

There's a round of applause.

Maxim's looking pretty blank, though he's clapping

303

along with the rest. 'Congratulations,' he says loudly. 'You've accessed the Sleeper's power?'

Nilas gestures towards the keyboard in front of him. 'When the computers come on line, you'll see something,' he promises, with triumphant anticipation.

'That's great news.' Gordy clears his throat. 'Does it mean we don't have to trouble about the Opposition anymore?'

Nilas raises his working eyebrow. 'On the contrary.'

'But surely,' Gordy protests, 'now you've got what you wanted, there isn't anything for the Opposition to, well, to oppose. It's history – time to draw a line.' Out of the corner of my eye – Gordy's eye, I guess – I can see Maxim frowning.

'Nice idea,' says Nilas blandly. 'Can't agree, unfortunately. You see, Gordon, now Network's got the Sleeper's magic, going to be damn powerful. Before I share that around the Bureau, need to be sure everyone's singing off the same hymnbook, hm?'

'Well, naturally,' Gordy soldiers on. 'But then can't we make a fresh start? I mean, everyone's tried to find where Grace sent her knowledge, just so we'd be certain who was Opposition, and it hasn't got us very far. Why don't you tell us what you propose to do with these new powers, sir? Then we can all say whether we agree or not, and, well, then everyone knows where they stand.'

Sykes starts coughing again. His glass of water's empty, and Coper refills it for him from a jug.

'Anyone like to comment on Gordon's suggestion?' asks Nilas.

'The thing is, dear boy,' Mortensen says gently, 'of course everyone's going to say they support Nilas. As they have always done. Even more so, if he's just collected a lot more strength from, er, underground.'

'The only way anyone ever found to ensure honesty was by use of the Skull,' says Castaneda. 'And that's broken.'

'Maybe the newer members don't understand the situation,' Coper says in her precise Edinburgh voice. 'The Skull was tried first on Dr Wildeth and Dr Sykes, and those two, to put it crudely, passed the test. Then came Grace, and that was the last time the spell could be used. The result is that there is now what I might call an inner circle, whom Nilas trusts, while he does not trust those others of us who may be just as reliable, if not more so.' She directs the last words pointedly at Wildeth.

'Bless my soul,' says Nilas. 'Didn't know you felt slighted, Sandra.'

'Certainly I feel slighted!' she snaps. 'How would you feel if you were the principal of the witches' training college, and you had no witches to train? Dr Wildeth is supposed to send the most talented students from Crossbeams on to me, and nothing arrives but dross.'

'Crossbeams is not the only school that trains witches,' says Castaneda. 'You have candidates from all over the world.'

'Crossbeams is meant to be the *crème de la crème*,' Coper replies. 'Because the Sleeper's ground is here, it is the prime site for all witchcraft activity. It's where all of you send your children.'

'Not all of us,' Castaneda objects.

'Yes, well, I know you are an advocate of state schooling,' Coper says acidly, 'and heaven forbid I should criticize your principles. Nonetheless, your own – no doubt highly promising – progeny aside, I repeat that from Crossbeams I receive nothing but the feeble-minded dregs.'

'Sandra dear, we've all got the same problem,' says Mortensen. 'Most of the young hopefuls who come to me for jobs couldn't report an egg at breakfast.'

Coper's not amused. 'Witchcraft isn't journalism.'

Lady Cootie's aristocratic contralto joins the argument. 'There's something strange going on at that school. Up until last month, my Laban was one of the most gifted witches I've ever seen. She'd just found her name.'

'And what's happened now?' asks Maxim.

'I've no idea. From being a bright, outgoing,

devastatingly intelligent girl, she's become apathetic, interested in nothing, hardly gets out of bed in the morning. I'm in despair.'

'Excuse me, but how old is she?' asks Castaneda.

'Seventeen.'

'Oh well.' He laughs. 'If you'd seen my eldest son at seventeen you wouldn't be complaining about your daughter. They become a quite different species for a few years, a nocturnal animal with filthy habits.'

'I beg your pardon!' Lady Cootie glares at him. 'I am not talking about adolescence. I am talking about a so-called virus. Do you have any comment to make, Dr Wildeth?'

Wildeth shrugs. 'I'm very sorry of course about Laban. A dear girl, with outstanding abilities, I must agree. We must hope that she returns to her former brilliance very soon.' She smooths back a lock of hair from her forehead with long white fingers, then takes the lily from behind her ear and sniffs at it before putting it in her water glass.

Coper snorts. 'Are you expecting us to believe you've only had one pupil with any brains in the last ten years?'

'Hold it right there,' Lucasta pouts. 'I believe I resent that.'

'Do you, dear?' Coper's smile is as false as Lucasta's eyelashes. 'Why so?'

307

'Well, I came on to you from Crossbeams, didn't I? Are you telling me I've got no brains?'

After too long a pause, Castaneda says, 'Of course she isn't.'

'I got elected to the Bureau, didn't I?' Lucasta insists.

'I rest my case,' Coper mutters.

*

Someone's knocking. I'm wondering why nobody's paying any attention, then I understand they can't hear it because the sound's in my room.

Reluctantly I pull out from Gordy's viewpoint and go to open the door. It's Chough.

'Good girl!' he greets me, giving me a hug. 'Back for the holidays.'

'Just visiting, probably. How are you?'

'Very very well, oh very well indeed!' He looks it, too; his fat cheeks are rosy, and he's bouncing a bit on his toes. 'Haven't felt so splendid since the day I was crowned.'

'That's great. Look, Chough, I'm in the middle of something right now. I'll be down in a bit, I'll talk to you then.'

'Of course, of course. Affairs of state,' he agrees. 'I only wanted to make sure you're taking care of the jewel.'

'Jewel?' I can't think what he means for a moment.

'Oh – my birthday present. Yes, it's in my coat pocket.'

He beams at me. 'Excellent. Keep it safe. It's the king's token, you know.'

He trots away again and leaves me smiling. Talking to him always cheers me up, even if what he says doesn't make sense.

*

I go back to the conference. Tottimer's on his feet, in the middle of a sentence.

'... just a plain old copper. I don't understand politics, but if you take my advice, Nilas, you'll cut your losses.' He draws a solid finger across his neck. 'They've caused us all a deal of trouble and expense. I say don't waste any more time, just kill 'em.'

Are they discussing the Others?

'I can't believe it is necessary to slaughter innocents,' says Castaneda.

Tottimer chuckles. 'Grace was no innocent.'

'And the child?' Castaneda demands.

It's me and Mum they're talking about. My mouth goes dry.

Gordy jumps up. 'Whatever Grace did or didn't do, we've got no reason to think Mag, Margot, poses any threat at all.'

For a second I feel like Nilas's good eye is looking straight through and seeing me. 'Point you seem to have forgotten: we don't know where the girl is. Under

309

the circumstances, difficult to carry out the Chief Constable's, hm, lurid suggestions.'

'When we find her, obviously we're not going to kill her.' Coper's small and quite old but she's got powerful presence: I'm glad she's speaking up for me. 'Until we've found out what she knows.' Maybe I'm not so glad.

'Ridiculous,' snorts Tottimer. 'Girl that age doesn't know anything.'

'I agree!' Cheers, Gordy, nice to know who your friends are. 'I mean, not that we kill her,' he backtracks. 'I mean I agree she doesn't know anything. I know her better than anyone else here.' *Shut up*, I'm trying to warn him, but this isn't a two-way channel.

'She must have some quality,' Coper says. 'Your own daughter, Dr Wildeth, became quite fond of her, I believe?'

Wildeth's smiling. 'Temple is a soft-hearted girl.'

No, she's not, I want to say, but luckily I can't.

'What's become of Temple?' Maxim asks.

'She's gone abroad,' Wildeth tells him. 'She felt she needed to find a new direction.'

'Never mind about Temple,' says Coper impatiently. 'It's Margot we need to talk about. If she was sent Grace's magic, it means that one day soon she will be able to tell us who is in the Opposition.'

'We're not sure she *was* sent Grace's magic,'

Castaneda points out.

'She's run away,' Mortensen reminds him. 'Surely that's a strong indication that she has something to hide.'

'Circumstantial evidence is usually correct,' Tottimer growls. 'I know I won't get a judge to agree with me there.'

'I'm not talking as a judge. Perhaps I'm talking as a father.' Castaneda looks round at the others. 'She could be hiding because she's frightened. Nilas has informed her of the true situation regarding her mother. That might be enough to traumatize any young girl.'

'Her craft is phenomenal for her age,' Wildeth says. 'I'd swear she has her mother's power.'

'I don't believe she's any more talented than Laban,' declares Lady Cootie, and Wildeth smiles.

Castaneda turns to Sykes. 'Francis, what's your opinion? You've spent the most time with the child, even more than Thesida or Gordon.'

There's a pause. 'Francis?' Nilas prompts.

'I, well, I, it's very interesting,' Sykes stammers. It's obvious he hasn't been paying attention. 'A good point.'

'What's a good point?' demands Lady Cootie. 'We're asking if you think Margot has Grace's magic or not.'

Sykes blinks. 'Yes, precisely. I can't really, well, it's

not as if I could triple it. There are so very, aren't there? And it does get unfortunately ladder.' He gives an uncertain smile and stretches out for his water, but his fingers are shaking so badly he can't grip the glass.

'Francis, what's wrong?' Coper asks him.

'Internal, yes, I'm sure. But then why so yellow? Not to be underfelted, in the longer lawn ...' His voice trails into silence and he leans back, closing his eyes.

'What's the matter with him?' asks Tottimer.

'He's very old, isn't he?' Lucasta remarks.

'He's no older than I am!' Maxim tells her irritably.

'Quiet.' Nilas's voice cuts across the rest. He's staring at Sykes, his one eye narrowed, his mouth twitching. It's like Mr Ugly when he's going to pounce.

The wheelchair hisses as it glides round the desk. Coper makes room, and Nilas moves in next to Sykes, taking his trembling hand and peering into his face. Then he looks at the rest of the witches.

'Anyone know anything about this?'

'Has somebody poisoned him?' Lucasta asks.

'Somebody's drained him. Taken his magic.'

'Are you sure?' Castaneda exclaims.

Nilas glances at him, then back at Sykes. 'He's not ill. Lost his powers. I know the difference.'

'Yes, I remember Rossy ...' Castaneda murmurs.

'Gordon!' Nilas barks. 'What's been going on at that place?'

'Place?' repeats Gordy. 'What place, sir?'

'The Residence. If somebody's been draining Francis of his craft, they'd have to be on the spot.'

'Grace!' Tottimer bangs a fist on the table. 'What did I tell you? She's dangerous; she always was.'

'She couldn't ...' I can't see Gordy's face but I'm guessing he's gone red. 'She's been no different – she's—'

'Clever enough to pretend,' Wildeth finishes his sentence.

'Or there's the girl,' says Mortensen. 'Say she has got Grace's magic, say she's found her name. She could have done it. Maybe that's why she's gone missing.'

'We have to find her!' exclaims Coper.

'Yes, but how?' demands Lady Cootie.

'If we all combine—' Maxim begins.

'I can find her.' Nilas waits until they're quiet. 'Network can find her.'

*

There's nowhere left for me to hide, no one can help. I keep watching; there's nothing else to do.

*

He glides around the desk back to his place at the controls.

'This – is the new craft. This – is the new technology. Ancient magic – combined with modern science – will give us power – no witch has ever seen

313

before. Ladies and gentlemen, I give you – the future.'

One-handed, he types a short phrase onto the keypad in front of him.

There's a single high chord, like when you turn on your own PC, and then all the lights go out.

The screens are dead, even the little bulbs on the control panel. There's just a faint glow around one point.

'What the hell's that?' asks Tottimer.

It's Wildeth's flower in her water glass. 'Just a gadget,' she says. 'Pretty, isn't it? You only notice the effect in the dark.'

'What happens now?' Lucasta pipes up. 'Can't we turn the lights on? I don't like this; it's making me claustrophobic.'

There's a pause.

'Nilas?' Castaneda sounds quizzical. 'Is this – er – according to plan?'

There's a tapping as Nilas keys in his password again. Nothing happens.

'Electrical failure?' suggests Lady Cootie.

'Magic doesn't run off the mains,' Coper retorts. 'We all know what's going on, don't we? This is the work of the Others.'

'How could they access the system?' Nilas mutters.

'We don't know.' Mortensen enunciates deliberately. 'Nobody but you has any idea how the system works.'

'Quiet, everybody,' Nilas commands. 'Need to feel what's happening here.'

There's silence. Wildeth's flower is the only thing to watch as the inner light of the petals pulses gently: brighter, dimmer.

'Nothing,' says Nilas after a long minute. 'Got to be a spell.' There's a squeak from his wheels. 'All right, shouldn't be possible, but maybe they've done it. Leaves the question, what are they going to do next?'

'The Others?' Lucasta squeaks. 'What could they do?'

Nilas laughs with no humour. 'Got us down here in the dark. What couldn't they do?'

'Oh!' she gasps. 'I want to get out.'

'Think we should all get out. Don't suppose the lift will be working. Leaves the emergency stairs. Who's quick on their feet? Lucasta, you go first,' Nilas orders her. 'Tell Shade to have the car ready. Gordon, Brian: you'll have to carry me up. Don't panic. Once we're outside we'll decide what to do next.'

I can hear Lucasta's platform heels as she runs up the stairs, then shuffling as the others start to leave, and a muttered curse when somebody bangs into the desk. There's a flicker as Wildeth retrieves her lily: when she's gone, the room's in utter darkness.

*

I'm coughing. I've got to open my eyes. Am I still

315

having a vision or something? The room looks kind of dim and cloudy. What's that smell?

I leap off the bed and open the door. Smoke rushes in, and from further down the corridor there's an ominous crackling sound.

The Residence is on fire.

CHAPTER TWENTY
TO THE HOSPITAL

I grab Little Bear before I've thought how silly that is. Then I charge down the stairs and nearly fall over Parrot who's crouching on the bottom step.

'Bad news!' she wails. 'Had bad news!'

'Stay where you are.' I run into the kitchen: Bella's sitting at the table with her back to me.

'Listen, Bella—'

I stop. I've never seen her crying before.

She tries to smile. 'Sorry, star. Just had a bit of bad news.'

I should have known Parrot was telling me somebody else's grief. And of course I know what the bad news is: it's Dad and Grace.

No time for that now. 'There's a fire,' I tell her. 'Call the fire brigade. I'll start getting everyone out.'

She's great in an emergency. She doesn't even stop to blow her nose. 'Don't frighten the Hollies,' she says over her shoulder. 'Your dad's in the canteen.'

So are most of the others, finishing their lunch.

Dad's staring into a dish of peas like he can see a small green future for himself. I put a hand on his arm and he jumps.

'Dad, we've got a fire upstairs.'

You can smell smoke in here now. Dad starts making for the stairs. 'Come back!' I hiss, clutching his arm. 'Get them outside.'

'You get 'em out,' he says, shaking me off.

'Ok, everybody!' I clap my hands: maybe I could get a job at Butlins. 'Come outside the house, there's something exciting to see.'

I thought I was just telling the tale to get them moving, but when we get out on the drive and look back, it is pretty exciting. The whole upper storey's blazing away like Guy Fawkes.

'Firemen on their way,' calls Bella. 'Where's your dad?'

'Playing hero.'

'Eron!' she screams, and disappears back in the house. Damn both of them, I've got to get Ugly and I can't leave the Hollies.

There's a miaow and a scratch on my ankle. Thank God someone's got sense. Wish he could have brought his travelling basket out with him though: I don't think any of us is going to be staying around here.

I'm doing a headcount. Chough, Perkin, Parrot, Betsy, Lewis, Abram, Mrs Frisch. Jennifer? She's right next to me, gazing up. 'It must have started in the attic,' she whispers.

The attic. I go cold all over. Where's Grace?

'Everyone get in the minibus,' I bellow. 'Nobody go near the house.'

I belt up the steps. Inside, the smoke's thick and hot. I can hardly breathe; I can hardly see. 'Bella,' I choke. 'Dad.'

I press my arm over my nose and mouth and feel my way up, my eyes streaming. Halfway I meet the two of them stumbling down, Bella supporting Dad and dragging him along with her. 'Nothing … we can do,' she rasps at me.

'Where's Grace?' I cough.

Dad lets go of Bella and nearly falls. 'Gone away—' he wheezes.

'Get – out!' Bella flings the full weight of her body against me and we all three go tumbling down the stairs to land in a heap at the bottom. The air's a bit clearer at floor level, and we crawl to the door and into the fresh air.

'What do you mean, Grace has gone away?' I ask, when we've stopped choking.

'I thought she mighta gone up to her room. Bella says not.' Dad's looking anywhere but at Bella.

'She headed off outside. She was pretty well riled. I don't know what's happened. I don't understand; she was talking as plain as I'm talking to you now. She said …' Bella bites her lip.

'Never mind what she said,' Dad tells her. His hand goes out, like he wants to put an arm round her, then he pulls it back and rams his fists in his pockets.

'But where's she gone? Did you just let her walk out?' I demand.

'I don't think I could have stopped her,' says Bella. 'There didn't seem much wrong with her wits, that I could see.'

'This is the craziest thing she's done yet,' I snap.

Dad stares at me.

'Ok, she wasn't exactly safe at the Residence,' I admit, 'but at least I knew where she was.'

'I thought you meant—' He glances up at the blaze. 'No, she couldn't.'

Couldn't she, though? Revenge on Dad and Bella? Maybe trying to make out to Nilas she's dead?

'Nobody's in the building; that's the main thing.' Bella's pulled herself together. 'You'd better call St Pen's,' she says to Eron. 'See if they can help us out. I'll get in the bus with the Hollies.'

Here's the fire engine. Dad goes off to ring the hospital on his mobile, and I huddle in my coat watching the hoses stream onto the flames and the black fumes.

If Grace torched the Residence, she's mad: not like

she was before, but a real nutter, dangerous. She's in danger herself. Where is she? I try to tune in so I can get a vision, but there's nothing: I guess Gordy's got protection running on her like on me and Ruce. Unless she's protecting herself? There's Sykes's magic to account for. I know I haven't stolen it, so that leaves Mum. But how could she take his powers when she didn't have her own? Too many questions – no answers. What happened at Network? Where's Nilas and the Bureau now?

'The hospital can do us a couple of rooms,' Eron announces. 'I talked to the firemen; they said it's ok to go. Going to want to talk to us later, try and find out what caused the fire. We better get moving.'

*

The Hollies are over-excited, and it's hard to settle them down in the minibus. Bella does her best, but she looks wretched, and I'm not helping her much. I'm too stressed.

Apart from anything else, to get to the hospital in Rostree we're going to be driving right past Network. I hope we don't run into a battle between the Others and the Bureau.

When we come to the fence, I slide down in my seat. Peeking over the edge of the window, I can see the gate: nothing seems to be happening, and the only people around are the guards. I relax a bit when we've gone past.

Dad swears and jams his brakes on. The Hollies are all belted in, but I haven't bothered, and I land on the floor on top of Mr Ugly, who yowls and scratches me. When I pick myself up and go forward, I can see why Dad's stopped: there's a motorbike right across the road, and a menacing hooded figure's standing by the driver's door with a gun levelled.

This is all we need. Humph is holding us up again.

I yank the side door open. Dad's yelling at me to stop but I scramble down onto the road.

'Move that bike *now*. I mean Bargus.'

Dad leaps out of the bus. 'Mag, you get back in. I'll deal with this.' Bella's here too, getting in between me and the gun.

'It's all right,' I tell them. 'He's not dangerous.'

'That's the guy took you away before,' says Dad.

'He's not taking anyone now. Humph, put the celery down.'

He lets his weapon fall. Dad's poised to wrestle him or something manly: this could be the moment for magic. I take a second to get my tune trustworthy, then I put my hands out to Dad and Bella, and my music wraps round theirs like a warm rug.

'I know him. We're friends; he was just playing a trick.'

It's a good spell. Dad drops the fighter pose, and

Bella laughs shakily. 'Shouldn't joke that way, you scared me into fits.'

'Sorry,' Humph-the-robber mumbles.

'What do you think you're doing?' I hiss at him.

His big false face looks embarrassed under the hood. 'Highwayman like.'

'What for? You're not rescuing anyone now, are you?'

'I does it for the money.'

'Hobs don't use money!'

'I does now.' He smirks as if he's half-pleased with himself. 'Yer gets milk with money. Yer teached me that.'

'So it's my fault?'

'I been buying other stuff an' all. Pretty things for me cave.'

'Humph, you mustn't rob people, somebody'll find out and you'll get in real trouble.'

'Wouldn't never if I'd known it was yerself.'

'There's worse people than me on the roads today,' I tell him. 'The Bureau's out mob-handed.'

He takes a step back. If you could see his ears they'd be flat.

'Won't do it no more, not never no more.' Then he cheers up. 'Got a powerful good haul off the last lot I stopped. Reckon that'll keep me going a while.'

'You're a disgrace.' Mentioning the Bureau's

reminded me how risky it is hanging about in the open. 'Go home, Humph. We've got people to take to hospital.'

Dad and Bella watch him speed off on Bargus-the-bike. 'Funny friends you got,' says Dad.

'You don't know the half of it,' I sigh. 'Come on, let's go.'

He turns to the bus, and then stops as if he's walked into a wall. 'Mag.'

Bella and I look where he's pointing. The coach is empty. All the Hollies have gone.

*

They can't be far; we've only been talking a few minutes. But we shout and search up and down the road and can't find any of them.

'They'll have headed for home.' Dad climbs back in the coach. He sounds more confident than I feel.

'That'll be it,' Bella agrees. 'Drive back slow, the way we came. We're bound to spot them soon.'

After we've been going a while I say, 'They can't have got this far; it's not possible.'

Dad pays no attention.

'Dad! Stop,' I tell him, and put a hand on his shoulder, but he swats me like a fly, trust spell and all.

'Don't you know no better than to jog a man when he's driving?'

'But they can't have got this far,' I protest again.

324

'Maybe they got a lift,' suggests Bella.

'A *lift*? Who's going to give eight loonies a lift?'

Then a truly ghastly thought strikes me, and sure enough, round the next corner, there's the Bureau limo parked on the verge.

Has Nilas got hold of the Hollies? I don't know if I should tell Dad to stop or drive on, but he doesn't wait for me to tell him anything. He pulls over and opens his door.

My instinct is to get behind the seats, shape-shift into a woodlouse, anything. But Dad's out of the bus, and Bella's followed him. I can't leave them unprotected. With no time to think, I try to get a grip on everything I've learned about self-defence, and hop down to the road.

The first person I see is Gordy.

'What's going on?' I whisper.

'Engine conked out, the driver couldn't fix it.'

Maybe there's a reason he can't talk. I try to listen to his thoughts, but I'm getting nothing, and his eyes are innocent as a baby bird's. No hidden message there.

'Have you seen any – strange people?' I ask cautiously. 'We've lost—'

My voice dies in my mouth. Wildeth's coming up behind Gordy.

She's the headlights; I'm the bunny. I freeze, and it does me about as much good as if I really was a rabbit.

'Thank goodness,' she says with a warm smile. 'I'm glad somebody's come to help.'

She's looking straight at me. There's no way she wouldn't recognize me.

'We're in a bit of a hurry,' she goes on. 'Do you think you can get us moving?'

Do I look like I can mend a motor? Wildeth looks a bit doubtful: then her expression clears.

'Or are you going to give us a lift? Shade said if he couldn't find a mechanic, he'd try to get a hire car.'

Shade! Maybe he can tell me the score. I look round for him, but all I see is the rest of the Bureau, shepherded towards the bus by Dad and Bella.

'Dad! What are you doing?'

'Taking them to the hospital like we agreed. I knew we'd find them somewhere near the Residence. That's right, Abram, you give Betsy a hand.' He watches with approval as Castaneda helps Lady Cootie to a seat.

He thinks they're the Hollies.

They think we're a breakdown team.

Why am I the only one who can see what's real?

'Nilas!' He's last in the line, and I'm more frightened of whatever's happening here than I am of him. I just about throw myself in his lap. 'Do you know what's going on; do you know who I am?'

He pats me kindly. 'Good girl. Not to worry now.'

Gordy and Mortensen get him on the chair-lift, and

he takes his place on the bus.

'Come on, Mag,' Dad shouts. 'Don't get left behind.'

My legs take me on board the bus, but I'm not sure it's me moving them. There's magic at work, and it's stronger and stranger than anything I know about.

*

On the trip to the hospital the witches go to sleep, every one of them, flat out like Mr Ugly on my lap. I'm trying everything I know to get a handle on this spell, but it's no good, there's not a clue where it's coming from.

My next idea is to get a vision of one of the Hollies, so I'd know where they've ended up: that's a wash-out too. My brain feels stuffed like a sofa, I'm just bouncing off the cushions. I can't see Ruce; I can't see J. I'm stuck in my own stupid head. As for Gordy, he might as well be on Mars, though he's sitting right in front of me, collapsed on Coper's shoulder and snoring.

I'm hoping when we get to St Pen's, someone there will spot the deliberate mistake, and I'm first out of the bus on the forecourt. There's a man and a woman heading our way: him in green overalls and her in a suit.

'You must be from the Residence. I'm Dr Penrose; I'm in charge here.' She's crisp with authority, like I might suddenly demand to take over running her psychiatric department. 'It hasn't been easy to clear places for all your clients. We've got one room each for the men and the women.'

'These aren't them,' I say. 'There's been a mix-up; we've lost the real ones.'

'Of course we understand the situation.' She's not hearing what I'm saying, nobody's listening to anything except the script playing out in their head. 'You'll appreciate we can't provide anything more than very basic care.'

'We'll be staying to look after them, long as you can fit us in,' says Dad. 'Couldn't leave them alone in a strange place.'

What's the use arguing? Dr Penrose isn't in charge here, whatever she thinks, but somebody is. We're all dancing to a silent beat, whether we know the steps or not.

'Let's get the poor souls into the warm.' The man's got an Island accent and a broad weatherbeaten face. 'Look at 'em all off in the land of Nod.'

'They've had a tough day,' says Bella.

Her tracksuit bottoms and hand-knitted pullover don't look as professional as the man's scrubs. Dr Penrose gives her a patronizing smile before turning to Dad.

'George will give your, er, woman a hand. Come

328

with me and we can deal with the paperwork.'

She leads Dad off, and George climbs on board the bus.

'Come along, my dearie, now.' He shakes Wildeth's shoulders. 'You can zizz off again just as soon as you're tucked up in your beddybyes.'

'I'm not staying,' I tell Bella. 'I'll only be another extra body for St Pen's to deal with.'

'OK, pumpkin. You'd better be getting back to school, hadn't you?' She gives me a quick hug. 'You've had a scare too. I don't like sending you off on your own.'

'I'm fine,' I say hastily. 'You see to the Hollies.'

I head out of the carpark before she can shift into mothering gear. I want to get back to J's: I'm hoping Shade'll do the same, then maybe he can help work out what's happening.

Daylight's starting to fade, and there's a cold wind that stings with salt. The Pad's miles away, and how am I going to get there? I ran out of the Residence without my bag, which means I've got no phone and no money: all I've got is Little Bear, and Chough's bit of silver paper in my pocket. I should have borrowed a phone off Bella, but it's too late now, she's inside the hospital with the witches.

I set off walking. Most of my enemies are out of action for the moment, but there's still a chance I could bump into a teacher from Crossbeams, so I keep my head down and try to look inconspicuous. Should I shift shape, turn into something faster? I don't think I can raise the juice for magic; it's easier to keep trudging. At least Mr Ugly's still asleep, draped across my shoulders like a heavy scarf.

What's happening around here? Everyone thinks the witches are the Hollies, and they're not arguing. That's got to be the most powerful spell out. What caused the power cut at Network? What caused the fire at the Residence? Where are the real Hollies? Are they wandering somewhere in the woods, or what? Where's Grace, and could this all be down to her?

By the time I make it to the airport, I'm knackered and starving and no nearer any answers, and Mr Ugly's awake and digging his claws in my neck. I let him have a pee on the wheels of a Porsche in the multi-storey, and then head up the stairs. My keys were in my bag along with everything else, so I lean on the bell and pray someone's home.

Shade opens the door. 'Am I glad to see you, Trouble.'

CHAPTER TWENTY-ONE
THE SPELL

We're all in the kitchen, Shade and me and Ruce and J. We're eating some soup Ruce made, maybe out of old socks, but it's hot and filling.

I tell them about the conference. 'I know who the rest of the Opposition are. It just kind of came to me, when they were talking. Castaneda – that's the tall Spanish guy – and Laban's mum, Lady Cootie.'

'Nilas never trusted Castaneda,' says Shade.

Ruce laughs. 'Laban's mother a rebel!'

'So what do you do with the hot news?' J wonders. 'Tell Maxim his secret's not such a secret any more?'

'I can't tell him anything right now; he's on a hospital ward. Shade, what happened after the witches left Network?'

'First off, they was planning to visit the Residence, check on Grace. That got me panicked. I was busting to see what was going on over there, but it was like the lines were down.'

'Same with me,' I tell him. 'No visions.'

'Then we find the place is a burnt-out shell swarming with the fire squad. So we head out of there, I'm thinking you're crispy duck. Next thing, the limo packs up, motor just went dead on me, but I couldn't find nothing wrong. I went to pick up the Merc, look for help, and when I came back there was nobody. I couldn't think where else to go, so I fetched up here.'

'That's what I was hoping you'd do.' I look at him. 'Maybe that's what you were meant to do.'

'You think somebody's pulling our strings?' J says.

'I *know* somebody is. I just don't know who.'

'Grace?' suggests Ruce.

'She could definitely have set the fire. The rest of it?' I crumble my bread. 'To steal Sykes's magic, she'd have needed her own powers.'

Ruce frowns. 'You'd have noticed, wouldn't you, if she'd taken them back from you?'

Is that why I couldn't get anywhere with my own tune when I was trying to see where the Hollies had gone?

'I'm going to have another go with the music,' I say. Maybe I can find my way through to Dad. He's easiest; I know him best.

Ruce and J are watching me like I'm about to light up or grow wings or something.

'Stop staring!' I tell them.

'It's interesting,' says Ruce.

'Well, don't. I can feel it.'

They start clearing the table. I sit still, fixing my mind on Dad's tune. It's slow, sad, muddled. His thoughts are on Bella and Grace, Grace and Bella – he can't sort them out in his mind. I close my eyes.

*

This answers one question, anyway: I can still get a vision. In fact, it's the clearest picture I've ever had. I'm almost there with them, Dad and Bella, sitting on a wall overlooking the sea with the moon shining on the waves. Even though they're in the hospital yard behind a bank of recycling bins, it's still pretty romantic, but she doesn't look happy.

'Whole thing's a mess.' Dad's got his hands in his pockets and his chin down on his chest.

'We'll find a house to stay in till the Residence is rebuilt,' Bella encourages him. 'We can claim off the insurance.'

'They don't pay out for arson.'

'You think somebody set the fire on purpose?'

He grunts something I can't catch. Bella stares at him.

'Grace?' she whispers.

'What else can I think? She's done a runner, ain't she?'

'Because of me? Because of – us?'

'All my fault,' he mutters.

'Eron, it is not.'

'I knew I had commitments. Didn't have no business making up to you that way.'

'I was the one that did the making up.' Bella shifts a little closer to him.

He turns away. 'Promised her I wouldn't be with you no more.'

'You think she'll be back?'

'How do I know?' He stares out at the dark and silver sky. 'She's been sick for years, and now maybe she's crazy a different way. I don't know what to think. Only know what she told me, and that's crazy enough.'

'You feel you've got to stick by her.' It's half a question.

'Don't see what else I can do.' His voice is rough: it's like when he used to lash out at me. 'She's the mother of my child. You ain't.'

Bella doesn't say anything more. She turns and slips down into the yard and walks off, and he doesn't go after her.

*

I come out of the vision when somebody nudges my shoulder. I see Ruce standing back from me, staring and shaking her hand like she just touched a live wire.

'I saw it!'

'What?'

'What you saw. It was, wasn't it? The nurse from

the Residence, she was walking outside somewhere with dustbins.'

'Yeah, that was it,' I agree.

'Maggot, I'm sorry, I didn't mean to, you know, interfere. But you were looking so sad and worried, I just came to give you a hug.'

'And got a vision instead.' Shade pulls out a chair next to me. 'Gordy's shield must be down.'

'But I'm not a witch,' Ruce points out. 'I shouldn't be able to see what Maggot's seeing.'

'Can we all do it?' J demands, excited.

'We could try,' I say.

'Maybe she'd rather not.' Ruce stands over me protectively. 'It could be private.'

I shrug. 'Dad hasn't exactly invited me to peek into his private affairs either. But the more we all know the better.'

The others sit down and we make like a seance, fingers touching on the table-top.

*

Dad's walking in a back door at St Pen's. George the hospital porter is coming out, and he laughs when he sees Dad.

'My oh my, some of them patients of yours got good lungs on 'em.'

'They making a row?' Dad sounds weary. 'Maybe they'll calm down if I take a look in.'

335

George claps him on the shoulder. 'Good luck with that.'

Dad turns down a short passage through a pair of swing doors. As soon as they're open you can hear what George means: there's clanging and screeching and shouting like baboons are working on a building site. Dad stops by another door and looks through the round glass panel.

'Damn it,' he mutters under his breath. Then he squares up his shoulders and unlocks the door.

Inside there are four white beds, four adjustable tables, four cross witches. None of them's asleep: Coper and Wildeth and Lady Cootie are sat on one of the beds watching Lucasta Lucas. She's by the window, shrieking and hitting it with one of her aqua platforms. The glass is reinforced with metal bars, so she's not doing any damage, but the noise is impressive.

Dad shuts the door. 'Now now, Parrot.' He's keeping his distance, trying to soothe her with the power of the human voice. 'Ain't no way to carry on. You give it a rest now.'

'Let me out! Let me out! You can't keep me shut in here, I get claustropho-o-o-o-obia!' I think that's what she says, but it comes out one long howl with added percussion. She throws herself at Dad, pummelling his chest with one hand and whacking him round the head with the shoe.

He gets her wrists and holds her. She struggles for a moment and then bursts into tears; her legs go floppy and he sits her down on one of the beds.

'Ain't gonna be for long,' he quiets her. 'You want something to help you sleep, maybe?'

'Oh please,' she sobs. 'I'd kill for a vodka and a Valium.'

'Don't you dare,' Coper says sharply. 'Surely even you understand we've got to stay alert.'

'Stay alert for what?' Lady Cootie's haggard, twisting the bracelets on her wrists. 'We're prisoners. We're all under a spell; there's nothing we can do.'

'Relax.' Wildeth's the only one who's taking it easy, legs up on the bed, twirling her white flower in her fingers. 'We'll get let out when the time comes, I imagine.'

'Do you know what's going on here?' Lady Cootie demands.

'I haven't the faintest idea. But it's interesting, don't you think? I rather suppose Grace must be responsible, or else the girl. Whoever's stolen Francis Sykes's magic.'

'Listen here, my man.' Coper rounds on Dad. 'I am Professor Sandra Coper, and I demand that you release us immediately.'

'I know you ain't used to being locked in, but it's regulations here,' Dad tells her. 'You girls just gotta

337

make the best of it. Don't know what's got into all of you,' he mutters, letting himself out.

*

Pressure on my hand brings me back to the kitchen at the Pad.

'You notice anything there?' says Shade.

'They know who they are themselves. They don't look any different, but everyone else thinks they're the Hollies. How would you do a spell like that?' I wonder.

'On a small scale, not too hard to make somebody see what they expect. Something like this, everyone under the same illusion and controlling the Bureau as well, we're talking major magic.' He takes his shades off. 'That's not what I meant.'

'O wise one,' J implores. 'Tell us dumb mortals what we're missing.'

'We all just saw four witches, right? Nobody there doing Gordy's job, no one to let Mag look through their eyes.'

'They're not protected!' Ruce exclaims.

Shade gives her a thumbs-up. 'We've taken a look at the ladies, now let's have a try with the gents.'

*

I take Gordy's tune for my way in, and there's no resistance. This time it's an eight-bed ward we're looking at. All the male witches in the middle of the room, except for Sykes who's lying

338

limp against his pillows.

'One more try.' Nilas is at the centre of the circle. 'Join hands.'

'Oh please!' Mortensen exclaims. 'What is the point?'

'The point is to get out of here,' Maxim says.

'We're not going to do that by playing ring-a-roses.' Mortensen folds his arms.

'I think Harry's right,' Castaneda joins in. 'When we tried before it was quite extraordinary – I could sense the power there, but just out of reach. As if it were being held above our heads, to tease us almost. Did anybody else feel the same?'

Tottimer grunts and takes off his jacket. 'If we can't use our magic, at least we can use our muscle. Gordon, take an end of the bed. We'll try it as a battering ram.'

'I don't think it'll be any good,' says Gordy. 'They build these places to keep maniacs in, you know?'

'Pretty soon we will be maniacs,' Maxim complains.

'Please.' Nilas's voice is quite gentle but everyone turns to him at once. 'We're still witches, hm? Believe I'm still head of the Bureau. Brian?'

Tottimer flushes, and leaves go of the bedstead he was hefting.

'Harry?'

'Whatever you say, Nilas.' Mortensen sounds smooth as ever, but he avoids the gaze of the one eye.

'If Felipe feels the magic, perhaps a final effort will get us there.' Nilas stretches out his right arm, and the others link up around him. 'I want to see what's happening at Network.'

I can feel the effort. It's almost as if I'm the one trying to break through the spell. Tottimer's sweating; Gordy's biting his lip. Suddenly Castaneda cries out and throws up his hands, and everyone falls back a step, staring at Nilas.

The old man's head is weaving from side to side. Both his eyes are shut and his face is grey.

'I can see ...' His lips mumble, spitting out the words.

'What can you see?' pants Maxim.

'*NO!*' Nilas shrieks. His head falls forward, and for a second nobody moves; then Castaneda drops to his knees beside the wheelchair.

'Nilas. Nilas. What was it, what did you see?'

'The control room. Everything working—' He's gasping for breath. 'The computers – are on.'

'The electric's back, then.' Tottimer sounds reassured.

'They're linked up; they're online,' Nilas chokes. 'Somebody's in there. Got my password. Taken it over – using – my power.'

'Who was it?' demands Mortensen.

'Grace!' exclaims Tottimer.

Nilas shakes his head. It turns into a spasm and he clutches at his ear with his good hand, forcing himself to be still. 'Not Grace.'

'The Others?' asks Castaneda.

'It was a man. I don't know – who he was ...'

*

I open my eyes. I'm back in the Pad.

'So that's what it's all in aid of,' says J.

'To let someone take over from Nilas at Network?' Ruce frowns and rubs the back of her neck. 'But who?'

Shade stretches out his hands. 'Guess we'd better try to take a look.'

*

I don't know who's at Network, but I've been in the building. I remember how it sounded, the echoing mechanical hum.

I'm trying to find that note and get a link to Network, but it's not happening. Instead, my own tune's warping, out of my control. It's responding to a stronger force, a deeper music. I'm being taken, guided towards I don't know what.

A bird's calling: *caw! caw!*

I can't get it out of my head. The cawing fills my inner ear, a raucous, insistent cry.

Caw! caw!

My own tune's telling me to go with the crow. I have to follow where it leads.

I'm seeing wood-panelled walls, high windows, a crowd of boys and girls. It's the canteen at Crossbeams.

How did I get here when I was aiming for the Network control room? This is different from any vision I've had before. It's not like looking; it's like being *shown*.

All the students are at the tables, though it must be way past dinnertime. They're eating cake. The teachers are chatting as if everything's cool, but where Wildeth should be sitting, there's thin little Jennifer, tucking into chocolate sponge.

'I do like something sweet before bedtime,' she confides to Matron.

'I don't mind it myself!' Matron laughs and cuts herself another slice of Swiss roll.

Like a badly tuned radio, I can hear Ruce at the same time explaining to the others. 'That's our school. That's one of the patients from the Residence, in the headmistress's place ...'

Down in the hall, I get a glimpse of table fourteen. Sally's examining a jam tart as if she's never seen anything with so many calories, and next to her there's a girl gaping like a zombie, her hair lank, her face white and expressionless. It's Laban.

I don't get time to think about it: *Caw! caw!* says the crowing in my head, and the picture changes. I recognize Maxim's study. There's the desk I ran behind, with the table lamp casting a pool of light. Mrs Frisch is sitting with her feet up, talking down the phone.

'Nine, fourteen to four, sixty-one, twenty,' she says.

There's a muted reply from the telephone.

'Eighteen and three quarters,' Mrs Frisch suggests.

Whatever or whoever's guiding me, I'm supposed to see what's happened to the Hollies. They've taken the places of the Bureau. This has all got to be part of the same spell that made the Bureau seem like the Hollies, to Eron and Bella and the hospital staff: but *why*? What's the point of it?

Caw! caw!

Here's yet another place. It's like we're getting a slideshow, one image followed by another and another, with sound as well. This is a big open-plan office, nowhere I've been. There's a man in glasses making notes: he's on the phone too.

'Eighteen and three quarters!' He sounds amazed. I realize he's on the other end of Mrs Frisch's call. 'That's going to play merry hell with the markets,' he mutters.

'Wow,' says Ruce. 'Nobody knows they aren't the Bureau.'

'The lunatics have taken over the economy!' Shade's laughing. 'What's next – the High Court? The press?'

'This spell's fun,' says Ruce. 'Think what they could do!'

'A lot of damage,' retorts J.

'Way to go, baby,' chortles Shade.

We're on to a new scene. The Island airport's more crowded than I've ever seen it, with photographers flashing away. At the centre of attention is Parrot, in tartan pyjamas and a tatty old raincoat, with a yellow duster tied round her head. She's kissing her hand to the crowd.

A woman presses forward with a microphone. 'Lucasta, is it true you're going to be in a film soon?'

'In a film soon,' confirms Parrot with a bright smile.

'That's an amazing outfit. Is it something to do with the movie, or are we all going to be wearing it next week?'

'All going to be wearing it next week.' Parrot flaunts her mac, and the cameras go off again.

The paps notice Perkin in the crowd.

'Isn't that Sir Brian Tottimer?'

'We didn't know you were going to be on this flight, sir.'

'Are you with Lucasta?' demands a bold young man.

Perkin doesn't like all the noise and lights. He pushes through to Parrot and nestles against her: there's a gasp and a dazzle of flashes.

'What a story!' rejoices a journo.

'That's the Chief Constable's reputation shot,' says Shade.

Caw! caw!

Next up is a helicopter pad. Betsy's being helped on board by a stout man in uniform. 'This way, Lady Cootie.'

The pictures are changing quicker now. Here's the ferry terminal, with the guards waving Abram through. 'Have a good trip, Your Honour.'

There's Grace! I almost cry out. She's walking down a country road that could be on the Island or just about anywhere. I only get a glimpse; after that there's a quay with a yacht perched at anchor and Lewis on deck. A young man in white hands him a glass of wine and a telephone. 'Royal Press Office on the line, Harald. Doing their nut about leaks from the Palace ...'

Then there's a blank, like an empty screen.

'Ok, what now?' I hear J mutter.

*

The view pulls back: it actually was a screen. We're looking at a whole bank of them, rows ranged along a grey wall.

The crowing in my head gets louder, nearer. There's a whole flock of birds, screeching to each other or to me, calling, summoning. Whatever I see now, I know it's going to be the answer, the centre of the spell.

The lines of screens are the monitors in the

Network control room. Everything we've watched till now was on a different one of the sets: we've been flipping between channels. Now they're all visible at the same time, each showing its own scene: there's Crossbeams, there's Maxim's office, and all the rest.

The focus shifts to the desk at the centre of the room.

There's Chough.

He's sitting in a swivel chair. He's wearing his old grey dressing gown that makes him look like an enormous monk. His face is pink and pleased: he's smiling. He's smiling *at me*.

He waves his fingers: it could be *hello*.

The noise of the cawing crows is deafening, for a moment: then it fades to a background chatter and flutter. This is Chough's deep music, and though it's not sweet to hear, it's in charge of my tune and my visions. I guess for the last few hours it's been running everything we can see on the screens round the Network walls. There's Parrot on her plane, Lewis on his yacht – and there, on other sets, are the real Bureau members in the hospital, Nilas and the men in one room, Wildeth and the women in another. There's *us!* Shade and J and Ruce and me, in the kitchen.

'Chough, is it you doing all this?'

I'm not sure if I've spoken out loud or in my head, but anyway he can hear me. He nods.

'Splendid, isn't it? I found this place all ready, but none of the pictures were working. I've got them all on now.'

He's taken Nilas's place. He's got the password; he's in charge at Network.

'You can watch whatever you want from here,' he goes on. 'Look.'

We see a woman piloting an aeroplane. She's watching a display that maps her route. We see a surgeon operating, while next to him a nurse tracks heartbeats on a monitor. We see staff in a military station, all intent on luminous blips that travel across their screens – more planes, maybe, or submarines, or missiles. We see different places all over the world: everywhere there are people with computers, following the images that tell them what to do.

'And I can make them see whatever I like too!' Chough laughs, a high insane giggle, and gestures at the screens. 'I can make the planes fall down. I can make the bombs drop. I can show the doctors how to cut. I can tell all the soldiers a war's started. Just think what I could do!'

'Chough, Chough, you've got to stop!' I'm shouting aloud.

He whispers back and the words echo round my head.

'You'll have to come and stop me.'

CHAPTER TWENTY-TWO

BETWEEN THE RAVEN AND THE DOVE

'No entry without authorization.'

'He wants to see us,' J insists. 'He said so.'

'Mr Samuel left clear instructions. No entry without authorization.'

I was expecting the Network compound to be open and deserted, but there's a full set of guards, and they're not listening to anything we say. It's past midnight, it's freezing, and the stars are glittering like frost. I'm shivering, with my coat collar up and my hands in my pockets.

We back off from the gate.

'I could climb it,' Shade offers.

'That's razor wire.' Ruce points to the top of the fence. 'Anyway, the guards'd see you.'

'Can you witch us in?' asks J.

Shade shrugs. 'I guess not if Mr Chough don't want us to. He's calling the shots.'

'He wouldn't have told us to come if we couldn't get in,' Ruce argues.

'He's mad,' I remind her.

'Not mad like the others,' she says. 'He's making the spell, isn't he?'

I can feel something with my numb fingers. I bring it out and J looks at it lying in my palm.

'What's that?'

'Just a bit of silver paper, but Chough said it was important.'

'Give it a try,' says Shade.

I hold it out to the guard. He raises his hand in a salute.

'Cleared for access.'

I walk through, and at once he's barring the way to the other three.

'No entry without authorization.'

I stop, looking back at them through the mesh. 'Looks like it's just me.'

'You can't go on your own!' protests Ruce.

I'm not going to hang about and argue; it's too cold. 'Think of something else if you can. I'm going inside.'

*

When I was here before, it was bare earth inside the fence. Now it's asphalted, a smooth surface stretching away on all sides. Tall floodlights glare, showing the building ahead of us with its one arched entrance like a black mouth.

I walk into the lobby. There are carpets on the floor and glass between us and the side rooms. Recessed lights set into the walls show the offices ready for use: work stations, printers, filing cabinets. Everything's perfect, in its place, untouched: empty chairs, blank paper, silent phones.

The mirrored doors of the lift reflect me walking forward. I look small. I bare my teeth at myself: it doesn't do much to raise my spirits. I hit the button and the panels slide smoothly apart. I step inside. the doors close behind me, and immediately I'm gliding down.

At the bottom there's hardly a jolt. The humming I remember from before is louder now: all the machines are on. The noise wraps me round as the lift releases me into the underground control room.

The huge space is brightly lit, right up to the silver sprawl of pipes at the roof. All round the curved walls the screens are active, and in the middle the banks of keyboards and controls flash with coloured codes, red and green and blue.

There's just the one human figure, sitting in a swivel chair.

This is the one who's doing it: this is the guy who can turn the world upside down. But when he gets up, Chough looks so fat and familiar I can't help grinning.

He hugs me. 'Good boy! Good girl!'

'Chough, what are you doing?'

'I've got all the machines on,' he boasts. 'Isn't it wonderful? I just think of somebody and I can watch them on one of these. Like this.'

He stretches out his hands like a conductor towards the screens.

In a grand drawing room I see Betsy doing an energetic striptease, surrounded by a well-dressed and horrified group.

'Lady Cootie – please!' A man in a dinner jacket hurriedly takes it off and tries to wrap it round Betsy's shoulders.

'It sometimes happens, even in the best families,' murmurs an old lady.

Chough points again: Abram's announcing his lunacy to a bemused group of courtroom clerks.

It's like back at the Pad when everyone could see what I was seeing. Chough did that, I guess, and now he's doing the same thing on a massive scale. He's projecting his visions so anyone can see them, and he's making people think what he tells them, he's making the Bureau seem like the Hollies and the Hollies like the Bureau ... He could make the armies of Russia and America and the Middle East think they're at war ...

He must have stolen Sykes's powers – but Sykes couldn't do this. Nilas couldn't do it.

I sit down in the swivel chair and look up at Chough. He's got to have the strongest magic ever, anywhere.

He's still orchestrating his screens, showing me what's going on with the Hollies. Lewis is producing a poetic edition of tomorrow's news, and on another monitor Perkin's making his way down a prison corridor, opening all the cells.

'Time to go home, time to go home,' he hums, inviting the bewildered criminals to join him.

'Sir! You can't—' A warder comes galloping and presses a button on the wall. Alarms go off and a metal grille slides down, blocking the exit.

Perkin bursts into tears. The guard speaks urgently into an intercom. 'The Chief Constable's been taken ill.'

I jump out of the chair. 'They'll be locked up, all the Hollies. They'll be in strange places. They're alone; they'll be frightened. Please, you must stop, you must bring them home.'

'I can't stop it now.' He puts a plump hand on my shoulder. 'Only you can do that.'

'Me? What am I supposed to do?'

He sits down and swivels, swinging his legs. 'You've got to let the witch fight me.'

'Do you mean Nilas?'

'You're the channel,' he explains. 'The jewel I gave

you, that's the link. He must send his magic through you.'

'Why? If you want to fight Nilas, fight him. You know where he is.'

'The witch built this.' He gestures around him, at the walls, the screens, the desk with its winking lights. 'Only another witch can destroy it.'

'Aren't you a witch? Are you one of the Others?'

'I'm the King.' His bald forehead wrinkles. 'I think I'm the King. I was, once.'

He's always said that.

'When were you King?' I ask him.

'I don't know. I think it was a long time. I've been asleep. They put me here.' He points to the ground below his chair.

Suddenly, sickeningly, I get a moment's vision: slippery rock beneath our feet, water all around. I feel Chough's warm pudgy hand on mine and I come back to the room, swaying where I stand.

'It's you, buried under here?' When I say that it sounds ridiculous, but he nods.

'Sleeping until the time of danger. Dreaming. Beautiful dreams, some of them: mountains and clouds and birds. Humans and Others, living and dying and making and fighting, books and marble and bones and fire. Such a lot of dreams.'

'You're the Sleeper.' I'm seeing Sylvian in my mind,

her strong arms raised to summon help that didn't come.

'Without the dreams there would be nothing. No world. Not even this one.'

He looks around at the grey walls and the computer screens. 'I saw a place like this when I was sleeping. No – that was later.' He sighs, leaning his head on his hand.

'I get muddled, you see. Waking isn't easy. No, I saw a grove of trees, dark leaves and bright berries. I saw a lake of water in a cave. I saw a rock in water, and around the water another island, and around that more water, and a great island in waves of air. Dreams within dreams.'

While he's talking the screens are changing. I can see the vision Sylvian showed me: the rowans and the rocky steps leading down to the hidden pool with the single block of stone at the centre. I can see the Island, our Island, small and alone in the sea. I can see the world hanging in space, a blue-green toy.

'Then I saw the witch.'

Nilas's face appears. It's like it was when he was younger, when he was with Grace: two eyes, a mouth that moves on both sides.

'He wanted to make everyone dream his dreams. Other men have wanted that, but he was cleverer: he found the place.'

355

Nilas stands on the rock in the rippling silence. He kneels and presses his hands to the mossy surface. He smiles.

'He couldn't break through. But he knew, if he put his machines here, they would take strength from the sleep, as much strength as he wanted.'

Workmen move on to the site. They chop down the trees, they drain the water, they fill concrete around the rock. Deep in the earth a smooth metallic surface spreads over rough stone. Above ground the building rises, gleaming and complete.

'The Others knew what was here. They remembered what humankind forgot. Their magic is closer to the old earth; they take their life from it. They tried to fight.'

I see Sylvian outside the building, shouting her war-song. I see flames and smoke. When it clears, the walls are damaged, but below, the control room's unharmed.

'Only a witch can destroy,' Chough says again. 'The danger was here. And so I woke up.'

I look from the visions on the screen to his round pink face. 'Did you take over Chough's body or something?' It's an unpleasant idea.

He shakes his head. 'I was always Chough. I saw it in the dreams, before it happened. I woke, I was born, and I grew up. I think I was a little strange always.' He chuckles. 'That's why they put me in the nice house with the kind doctor.'

'Sykes?'

'Poor doctor, I had to borrow from him. I needed a witch's magic for the spell.'

'Was it you who started the fire?'

'Burning, burning,' he murmurs, and on one of the screens I can see the flames rising again from the Residence. 'First the fire, and then the battle. It has to be tonight, between the raven and the dove.'

'What does that mean?'

'The raven's twilight is evening; the dove's twilight is dawn. Between the raven and the dove – that's a magician's night.'

Chough flourishes his fingers at the screens and I see Nilas and the other men in their hospital room.

'You have the token; you're the bridge,' he tells me. 'Talk to the witch. Tell him to send his magic through you. Tell him the Sleeper challenges him to fight.'

*

'Nilas.' I've said it out loud. My voice is quavery, but they all hear it: the witches jump and look round to see where it's coming from.

All except Nilas. He doesn't turn his head. 'Margot,' he says. 'I've been wondering about you. Where are you?'

'I'm at Network.'

'How's she throwing her voice like that?' Mortensen

mutters. 'It's like a loudspeaker.'

'I'm not doing anything,' I say. 'It's Chough. He's the one who—'

'Chough?' Nilas interrupts. 'Who's that?'

'He was one of the patients at the Residence. He's …' I hesitate. 'He's the Sleeper.'

'The Sleeper – at the Residence!' Castaneda exclaims. 'Is that possible?'

'Must have been him who took Sykes's magic,' says Tottimer, and from his place lying on the bed, Sykes mumbles something incomprehensible.

Nilas ignores them. 'What does he want?'

'He challenges you to fight him,' I reply.

'Only too pleased. Problem is, I'm stuck in here.'

'You're to fight through me.'

'Through you,' he echoes. 'And whose side are you on?'

I hesitate. 'I don't know.'

That's the truth: I hate Nilas and everything he's done, but Chough's a loose cannon. He's got the power to play the Network system like a computer game. If he did what he threatened, he could set off World War Three.

Chough's shaking his head at me. 'You're the channel,' he says softly. 'There's no choice to make.'

'It doesn't matter whose side I'm on,' I tell Nilas. 'I'll do whatever I've got to.'

He smiles, lopsided, at his companions. 'Me against the Sleeper. If he wins, what then? Worth the risk, boys?'

'It doesn't seem,' says Mortensen, with a glance round the hospital room, 'as though there are any other options.'

'Wait a second.' Gordy's on his feet. 'Mag could get hurt.'

'Better her than us,' grunts Tottimer.

Gordy ignores him. 'There's got to be another way.'

'Another way?' Nilas repeats. 'With us locked in here?'

'She's a *child*,' Gordy tells him furiously.

'Gordy,' I say, 'I appreciate you sticking up for me, but please, just don't. Like Nilas says: you're there; I'm here.'

'I don't think it's right—'

'Nobody's asking you to think anything,' Maxim cuts him off. 'Sit down, Gordy, and don't be an ass.' I know what he's thinking, I guess: if Chough can get Nilas beaten, that's the Opposition's job done.

'No, but listen, Mag,' Gordy persists. 'If you're going to be – if Nilas is supposed to send his magic through you – then you've got to be, you know, open to receive.'

He's trying to ask if he should lift the shield.

'I think Chough's taken care of that,' I tell him.

'Honestly, Gordy, do like your grandad says.'

He isn't happy, but there's nothing he can do.

'Everyone else on board?' asks Nilas.

'How about the women?' asks Castaneda.

Chough shows me another screen: Wildeth and the others are silent, heads up, listening.

'They can hear what's happening,' I say.

'And we believe Nilas can succeed,' Wildeth declares. There's a nod from Coper, a hysterical giggle from Lucasta, and a shrug from Lady Cootie.

'I guess it's unanimous,' I relay to Nilas.

He laughs, a high whinny of excitement. 'Should be a battle to remember, hm?'

Tottimer chuckles. 'I wouldn't like to be on the Sleeper's end.'

Nilas raises his voice. 'Margot, are you ready?'

'I'm ready.' Am I? I've got no idea what I'm getting into.

'Need to relax,' Nilas tells me. 'Think you can do that? Going to be a lot of power coming. Don't try to think ahead. I'll be doing the work. You're the bridge; you're the conductor. Give yourself up.'

I feel Chough's arms around me. For a moment I cuddle him, warm and solid and someone I've always known.

'I'm ready,' I say again.

*

The room darkens until only the monitors are lit. The picture draws in to Nilas: his face fills every screen, one grey eye fixed on me from all sides, multiplied over and over.

Chough faces me.

'On guard,' he says, and raises his hand in a salute.

A single crow calls, a harsh cry so far away it's only a trembling on the air, then louder, nearer. More birds call, a flock cawing through bony beaks. Their wings fill the air with sound and darkness. They're on their way to war.

I hear Chough's thoughts, and they're nothing like the friend I know: they're memories of blood and fire, dreams of earth and water.

My own tune feels tiny, a trickle of notes. It's not enough to fight with; it's barely enough to keep me upright.

Sudden as a slammed door, his magic's all through me. I don't have a chance. My legs flop like a rag doll's, then flex and push me off the ground. My arms fly out and I do a full cartwheel over the chairs, coming down with my forehead striking sparks off the edge of the control desk.

I'm half stunned, and every one of my limbs aches as if I've dislocated both hips and shoulders.

This is a great start. Where's Nilas, then? I can't hear or feel his magic, though I can still see hundreds of him on the screens.

Chough looks down at me in pitying reproof. 'The jewel,' he reminds me. 'That's the link.'

Painfully, I squirm my hand into my pocket and touch the little ball of silver paper, then clutch it in my palm.

Nilas speaks in my head. *I'm with you, Margot.*

His music's a thrum of brassy chords, the tread of a distant army shaking the earth, a rumble of thunder beyond the horizon. I get the sense of force held back, strength under strict control. Then the brakes are off; the march quickens to a gallop. Metal-shod hooves stampede, closer, louder, with a shout of trumpets, a blast of noise from a thousand throats.

It floods into me, a swell of sound that heats my heart, sends power pumping through my veins, strings my nerves taut and lifts my own tune singing, soaring, thrilling.

I'm not even aware of getting to my feet again, but I find I'm standing, poised and electric.

Nilas is with me, I've got his magic, his will to win, in my arms, legs, backbone, blood. Pain's still there, but it's a sidebar, something I don't have to read right now.

I grab Chough's hand, and he pulls back, but Nilas's music masters his, commands him. His resisting muscles soften, weak as a cooked noodle, and I drag him off his feet, send him stumbling, spin him round. I spin too, and Nilas's skill brings my leg flying up – an elegant move that plants my heel in Chough's ribs. Now it's him who goes crashing down. Where his head cracks against the wall there's a splintering sound, and a split opens in the smooth metallic surface. Chough falls back and I see there's blood on his brow. He gasps for breath, struggling on to hands and knees.

For a second I block out the alien tune, and see him with my own eyes. There's blood all down the side of his face.

'Chough,' I say, and go towards him.

Look out!

That's Nilas yelling, and I dodge just in time as Chough launches himself at me, bellowing like a beast. He hurtles past but seizes my arm, pulls himself to a halt, turns, wrenching me round with him, and then he's on me, his mouth open, flesh and teeth and tongue, wet, howling. I go down, shielding my head with my arms.

Fight! Fight! Nilas is shouting.

Chough's on top of me, pulling my hands from my face; he's going to *bite* me.

I clutch the silver paper ball, the king's token, and Nilas's music is back with mine, violent and insistent, thrusting, piercing. I get my fingers in Chough's mouth. Nilas is pulling with me, we're ripping him.

My solo tune pipes up, imploring: *I can't do this.*

Nilas's notes thunder in my head. *Feel his strength; use it against him.*

Chough's got his teeth in my wrist. I feel the gnawing and open with a sensual rush. I inhabit the pain and control it, send it into Chough, biting back, a grinding of teeth in his softness. He yelps, draws away, and I dart stiffened fingers at his eyes, sharp and hard.

Suffer, Sleeper! Nilas laughs.

He chokes, blinded, his head snapping back so his neck's exposed.

In the throat! Nilas orders, and using the edge of my hand like an axe, I chop Chough across the gullet. He gags, and while he's coughing I ram a knee into his stomach, and then follow through with a battering kick. My foot crushes him against the wall. I feel him crumple and shatter, brittle bone behind soft flesh, and I hear a horrible sound of breaking.

We're killing him. I brace myself against the spell. This could tear me apart: I've got Nilas fighting through me and I'm trying to hold back. He's too strong for me. My head's going to burst; my muscles are seizing up. I want to cry out, beg him to stop, but my voice is jammed in my throat.

Then I see where Chough's hit the wall again, a wider darker cleft spreading in the grey. The surface shatters. Screens hang sideways, and rock appears behind metal.

I understand!

Chough's the Sleeper, his power's in the building. It's his magic Nilas used to make Network, and now every blow Nilas sends against Chough is striking his own fortress apart. Chough said only a witch could destroy. Defeating him, Nilas defeats himself.

Now I let the Sleeper's token free the channel again between me and Nilas. I strike out, I scream aloud in fierce fighting joy. There's thunder in my ears and a light too silver to see.

Chough towers, a monstrous blackness in the bright. He comes at me roaring and I'm filled with magic, filled with fury, strength like nothing I've ever felt. Nilas and me, we can eat the world, nothing can defeat us. We conquer; we rule. Our music's a wind-borne fleet of fighters careering down the spacious sky. Chough's bird battalions fly screaming before our flaming swords. We slash, spear, wound; we tear the night apart.

Nilas's lust for domination shrieks: *I'll kill, I'll kill.* I've got Chough by the throat, *miserable man, I'll crush and squeeze.* I'm shaking him, strangling him. He's like a doll in my fists. *You thought you'd challenge me; you thought you could keep what I want, you victim, you Other-lover, you filth. I'll slaughter you. I'll make you cry for mercy.*

You're nothing, nothing. I'm bashing Chough's body around against whatever's solid in the way. *Destroy, destroy!*

The walls are coming down: the screens fly aside; the eye of Nilas spins and blacks out. There's a sound like drums and trumpets, a deafening fanfare. The shining grey around us explodes into chaos, sheets of steel and blocks of concrete crashing down.

Run for it, run! Get out!

I don't know who's shouting – Chough or Nilas, maybe me? I start sprinting, dodging the heavy hail of falling spars. A silver pipe from the roof groans and buckles, and then comes plummeting down.

The ruins don't lie still where they tumble: they're moving, heaving. The floor begins to quake. It comes apart in chasms, and water bubbles up. The lake pours from the ground.

I leap for safety, but there's nothing there to cling to. Everything around me is collapsing: I'm falling; the waves close over my head.

Something below me thrusts me upwards, and a hand, a huge hand, snatches me into the air. A giant's standing, feet planted in the torrent, holding me, and there's a green shape beneath the water, hair flowing, raising her face to sing. The Others are here, the Others of the Sleeper's ground, reborn in their elements.

They pass me between them, ogres and elves and invisible wraiths, holding me and handing me on. They're shouting and laughing, playing with me, tossing my little human body like a toy.

The cavern arches overhead, dark and secret, and a shaft of moonlight enters through the crevice, showing the rock slab rising from the water.

On the rock crouches Chough. I see him for a moment on his knees, and then he collapses, limp as an empty bag, and lies on his back, eyes open, lifeless.

I cry out, but I'm being thrown up the steps, out into the air. The wreck of the building lies tumbled: trees are growing from the rubble, trunks rising, branches spreading, leaves unfolding.

Dawn's breaking and the pale light spreads. Beyond the trees the fence is fallen: the guards are gone. There's Ruce, and Shade, and J. They run forward to me and we hold hands, looking back.

All around us the earth is bursting into green: it's springtime. Flowers bloom and summer brightens, then the rowan berries ripen and the branches turn to gold and brown. Autumn's on us and the leaves start falling, whirling round us in a dry blizzard. The wind blasts cold and grey, clouds unfurl and chuck a snowstorm down at us. The flakes whirl faster and faster. Then everything slows and there's a sigh as if the Island's taking breath. The sun rises. The wood's a white diamond in the dawn.

From where the Network building stood, a black bird flies up. It flaps slowly away across the snowy hills and out of sight.

CHAPTER TWENTY-THREE

JOINING FORCES

'A chough's a sort of crow,' says J.

'Is it?' I'm lying on the sofa at the Pad. It's days since the battle, but I still feel like I've been put through a shredder.

'That was a crow that flew out, right at the end.'

'His music sounded like crows. Maybe he turned into a crow.' I smile. 'I bet he's a fat one.'

'I did a search. There's a legend King Arthur became a red-legged chough. They're rare birds.'

'King Arthur like Knights of the Round Table?'

'And there's another legend that when Arthur died, he was buried on an island. One day when there's danger he'll wake up to save his country.'

'Chough always said he was a King.' I sit up. 'Do you really think he was King Arthur?'

'There are a lot of heroes who are supposed to be not really dead, just asleep till they're needed.'

'What, he's not the only one?'

'Maybe he's all of them. Maybe he's the real thing,

and the others are just stories. Maybe not.' J grins. 'Let's hope more of them don't get their alarm clocks ringing.'

'Let's hope they don't need to.' I'm happy to think Chough possibly didn't die, but it's not enough to keep me smiling.

J sits down next to me. 'What are you looking so worried about?'

'What Nilas is going to do next.'

She shrugs. 'Lick his wounds. Suck a lollipop. Who cares what he's going to do? You've beaten him.'

'He beat himself,' I correct her. 'I was just the channel for him to fight Chough; that's what brought the building down. I didn't do anything much except conduct the power. But because I did that, I know now just how strong he is.' And how vicious, how angry, how frustrated. I can still feel that thirst to murder if I let myself.

I get up from the sofa and walk round the room: I'm tired but I'm restless, I can't stay still for long. What I don't want to let on is I'm not just worried, I'm petrified. Nilas wanted the Sleeper's power more than anything. I helped stop him from getting it, and now he's going to want revenge. And I know, in my bones and my nerves, just how hard he's wanting it. I know it in my music.

'You feeling fitter now?' J asks. 'Want to go out

and get some air?'

'No!' I exclaim, and then try to laugh. 'I don't think I'm ready for the great outdoors.' Here at the Pad I'm safe. Could I just live here for ever like some weird hermit?

'Take your time, honey.' J's been an angel looking after me. 'When Ruce gets back, maybe you'll feel more like a step outside.'

'What's taking them so long?' I wonder. Ruce and Gordy are meant to be helping Dad get the Hollies back to the Island. They must have done it by now, surely.

J winks. 'They probably aren't hurrying. You know, that pair of lovebirds haven't had a lot of time to themselves.'

'I hope it's just that.' I'm still fretting. 'I wish they'd ring or something.'

When they finally turn up, J teases them. 'Hey hey, you two been doing anything we shouldn't know about?'

Ruce goes bright pink. I guess they did have a stopover somewhere.

'Took a while to get everyone sorted,' says Gordy breezily. 'We had to leave Parrot where she was, she's got a contract from Benetton.'

J laughs. 'Truly?'

'She's bosom buddies with Lucasta too,' says Ruce.

'Parrot's just what she always wanted, the ultimate yes-woman.'

'The rest of them are in a temporary place Sykes has hired,' Gordy adds.

'Sykes?' I repeat.

Gordy nods. 'He's got his wits back now Chough's gone. Just as well in a way; I don't think your dad could have coped on his own.'

'What about Bella?' I ask.

Ruce sighs. 'She's going home to New Zealand as soon as they can get a substitute. She talked to me a little bit – she's miserable, poor cow. Your dad won't go near her. He says he can't break his promise.'

'Rough on her,' J comments. 'You get any news of Grace?'

Ruce shakes her head.

'Sorry, Mag, but I think she's not playing fair,' says J. 'She wants the man, she should stick around with him, not make him wait till she's ready.'

'Are you shielding her?' I ask Gordy.

'What, Grace?' He stares at me. 'No.'

'I thought you might have put protection on her, like you did on me and Ruce.'

He looks self-conscious. 'Maybe I should have done. I didn't think of it.'

'I can't tune in to her,' I explain. 'She's got no powers of her own, so somebody's got to be doing it for her. If it's not you, who is it?'

The front door slams and Shade walks in. He's sweating and panting, and there's a dark streak of motor oil or something on his sleeve. He's normally so dapper and cool, the second I see him I know it's disaster.

He leans against the wall, getting his breath.

'Well, folks,' he says at last, 'looks like we lost our paddle.'

'What do you mean?' demands J.

He's not wearing his shades: his eyes meet mine. 'Nilas knows you're here. Mag, he's got Grace.'

And I thought I'd only got myself to worry about. 'What's he doing to her? What's he done?'

'Nothing, not a thing,' he tells me positively. 'She's fine, but she's frightened. Nilas wants you to go there. He told me—' He swallows and passes his finger round his neck like the collar's tight, even though it's open.

'What did he do to *you*?' J wants to know.

He smiles, but it's not the usual laid-back grin. 'Just scared the crap outta me, is all.'

'How did he get to know I was here?'

'Trouble, if I had an idea—' He breaks off, and looks from me to Gordy. 'You let the shield slip?'

Gordy's watching his feet. 'I don't know,' he mutters. 'I might have done.'

Nobody says anything.

'At the hospital, none of us had any powers,' he goes on after a moment. 'When it came back – after the fight – I picked up as soon as I could. But perhaps I wasn't quick enough.'

'It wasn't your fault!' Ruce squares up like she might have to stand by her man.

'If anyone's to blame, it's me.' Shade looks wretched. 'I'm the one told you to rely on Captain Efficient.'

'Don't beat yourself up,' advises J. 'Or each other,' she adds hastily: Gordy clearly doesn't like being called Captain Efficient. 'The point is, what now?'

They all look at me. This is the kind of moment I really hate: hey, Mag, you're on the line here. Tell us what to do, why dontcha?

'I can't stay here.'

'You've got to go to Nilas, haven't you?' says Ruce.

'Not right away.' I'm playing for time, but the feverish moves in my head are making a sort of sense. 'If he wants a showdown, ok, I guess he's got to have it. But I'm not going on my own. I need to get the Opposition lined up, and Sylvian too.' Yes, it's a plan, and it means I get breathing space. 'If I've got to leave here, there's only one other place to go. Gordy, can you get hold of the Opposition witches?'

I'm hoping to hear it'll take a while, but he just

nods. 'They're with Grandpa. They thought they'd stick around and see what happens now Network's gone down.'

'Bring them to Humph's cave. Ruce knows where it is. Humph can get Sylvian there, and then we can have a council.'

Shade hitches himself off the wall and salutes. 'You got it, General.'

I hope my face looks brave, though inside I'm a terrified jelly. 'Time to join forces, comrades.'

*

'We can't come with you to Nilas,' says Maxim.

'Why not?'

There's a pause. It's like an uncomfortable hippy-themed party, all of us sitting on the floor except Maxim and Lady Cootie, who took the plastic crates, and Sylvian, who's standing like someone planted her in the earth, and hasn't said a word.

Humph's done his best at hosting: everything's spick and span, there's a fire going, and he's laid on some peanuts and cider. He's also dolled up his cave with a lot of pound-shop tat, which is obviously what he meant when he said he'd been buying 'pretty things' – there are mauve candles that pong like fake jasmine, festoons of plastic flowers, and some tinsel. Pride of place goes to a musical box that's shaped like a snowman, and plays 'Walking in the

Air'. I didn't let Humph wind it up again after the first time.

Maybe we could have done with something to cover the silence.

'Why can't you come?' I ask again.

'We mustn't reveal ourselves.' Maxim looks at Castaneda and Lady Cootie: they make agreeing noises without exactly saying anything. 'What if it goes wrong?' he adds. 'If you lose.'

'If *we* lose,' I say, with emphasis. 'We're all in this together.'

Castaneda leans forward. 'What you did at Network, with Nilas – we can do that for you again. If we link our powers, and you open up to us – we to you – we can fight through you, as Nilas did.'

I'm not sure I like this. 'Ok. You won't be there, so Nilas won't know who you are. So if he trashes me, you'll still be around to pick up the pieces.'

'Why should Mag be the one to take the heat?' demands Shade.

'She's the best,' says Castaneda. 'The battle at Network was a magnificent feat of conducting.'

'I had the Sleeper's token,' I protest. 'It wasn't just me.'

'I think you've never protected yourself? That makes you a better link than any of us could possibly be.' He smiles at me. 'You will win, you know. If you go to Nilas, you needn't be frightened.'

Yeah, that just trips off your tongue, doesn't it?

Ruce jumps up. 'You might get your name, Maggot. Have you thought about that? If he's attacking you – you're going to need it – maybe it'll come.'

Gordy gets hold of her hand. 'Maybe it will, maybe it won't. Calm down. It's not going to help her, thinking it might happen, if it doesn't.'

'Yes, but—'

Lady Cootie interrupts her. 'If it does come, that may not help either. Look what happened to Laban.'

Castaneda lays a hand on hers. 'She'll get better.'

'Will she?' She sounds bitter. 'Thesida Wildeth says it sometimes has that effect, when a witch gets their name, but I never heard of it, did you?'

Her mentioning Laban has given me an idea. 'What's today?'

'Wednesday,' says Gordy.

'Date?' I've lost track, I'm genuinely not sure.

'Seventeenth December,' supplies J.

'So tomorrow's the last day of term. They're all still there.' I'm looking at Ruce.

'The witchkids at Crossbeams?' she exclaims.

'Ok, I didn't get on with them brilliantly well,' which is putting it mildly, 'but there were reasons.'

'Extra back-up?' says J.

'They're children,' Lady Cootie objects.

'Older than Mag,' J points out, 'and she's the one you're planning to send into the lion's den.'

'They've got power,' I say. 'Maybe not Bureau standard, but every little helps.' Ayesha's good, and Sergei too. Paola's got game, Yuki takes it serious, and Mieko's sparky. Wilkie's precise, Tomas is wily, and Andy, well, Andy wouldn't give me the time, especially as his dad's on the other team, but if I do a trust spell on the lot, I can get them on side.

'If you're all sending your magic together, everyone should be in the same place.' I'm thinking aloud. 'I need to bring them here.' I cast an apologetic glance at Humph, who's already tetchy about filling his cave with witches: if Sylvian wasn't around, I don't think he'd be so hospitable.

'So, first stop school?' says Shade.

'It'll have to be.'

Going back to Crossbeams, is that better or worse than going to Nilas? Hey, Mag, do you want to be eaten with butter or jam? Either way, you're toast.

'That's just wasting time,' declares Gordy. 'You've got to go where Grace is.'

'Uh-huh.' Shade shakes his head. 'Mag's laying her ass on the line, it's her call.'

'The thing is,' I explain, 'I'm not sure any of you know how strong Nilas is. I know. At Network I channelled him, and I *know*. Maybe you're all good, but

I'm telling you, we need everything we can get, every little bit.'

'If you're joining forces,' J puts in, 'should be all the force you've got. And as the only thing this council's decided is that none of you is going with Mag—'

'I will come.' It's the first time Sylvian's said a word.

Humph pipes up. 'Me too.'

I'm suddenly near crying. That's pathetic, and I take a gulp of cider. 'Thanks. I think Sylvian'll do.'

His ears go flat.

'Humph, it's not that I don't want you. I just don't want Nilas to mash you. Hobs aren't really fighters, are they?'

'I'm a fighter. Want me along?' offers J.

Ruce leans forward too. 'Can I come?'

'Not a good idea,' says Gordy before I can reply, which nearly makes me tell her Yes, but I'm not that petty.

'Gordy's right,' I tell both of them. 'You couldn't do anything to help, and I'd be worrying if you were ok.'

'Sending your magic to Mag,' J says to Maxim, 'you'll have to drop your shields or whatever they are, won't you?'

He glances at her under his eyebrows. 'Of course.'

'How will you know to do it? There's no Sleeper to block your powers now.'

'The Others have no shields. I can send a message.'

Sylvian points at Humph.

'That's right!' His little eyes brighten. 'We takes care of it, Sylvian and me. Don't yer fret, missy.'

Ruce gets up to give me a hug. 'You're going to be all right, Maggot. You are.'

The more everyone insists on that, the worse I feel.

Gordy's still ready to argue about picking up the witchkids, but Shade's got the clincher. 'Unless you got your motor here, I'm giving her the ride.'

*

He parks up near the school gates. 'How you planning to get in the joint?'

'I thought I'd shift shape, go small.' I get out of the car. The freak snow that came after the Network battle has melted, but it's still cold, and the night's overcast. That's good, I tell myself. Darkness is my friend. 'Stay,' I tell Ugly. I didn't want him to come, but he climbed in the Merc before I could stop him.

Sylvian, on the other hand, refused a lift. She was right here, though, as soon as we stopped. I guess she doesn't have to travel; she can just be wherever she likes on the Island.

I take off my coat and leave it on the seat. 'I might need this when I get back. Who knows if I'll get a chance to find my clothes?'

'Your clothes?' repeats Shade, mystified, but Sylvian's on message.

'If you have to shift back in a hurry,' she says, 'you don't have to come back to your naked self. You can change to a shape with clothes on. They won't be real, but they'll last as long as you're wearing them.'

Why didn't I think of that? It's obvious, really.

Last time I walked up this drive, I was coming back from my birthday. The Residence was still standing, so was the Network building, and Grace was still at home . . .

I veer off the gravel because my feet are making too much noise, crunch-crunch. The grass is wet; I can feel it squelch under my trainers. In front of me the school's mostly dark, just a few lights in the teachers' rooms and the corridors.

Round the side there's a tiny kind of shed with the electric and gas meters. There's no door, but nobody'd see inside unless they were standing right in front. That's where I leave my clothes, folded up against the wall.

Then I think squirrel-music, and I'm running up the wall to where I can see a window open a crack on the third floor.

It's funny, you'd think when you're this size it'd look further to fall, but I guess squirrels don't have trouble with heights. I can even hang on upside down if I like, but I haven't got time to play little furry games now.

I stop on the windowsill. A squirrel could get noticed indoors – I'd better be something smaller still. Let's try a mouse.

I slip through the opening and run down to the floor. Here I am, back at school.

CHAPTER TWENTY-FOUR
WHITE SISTER

Dorm 14 looks a lot bigger than it did when I was human size. There's a dim light from the night-bulbs by the wall. I scurry down between the beds and the sleeping girls till I get to Laban: I want to check her out before I start on the other witchkids.

She's breathing peacefully. I climb up onto the pillow, scamper scamper.

And I get the shock of my life, because she's looking right at me. She doesn't twitch a muscle; she doesn't blink. Can she be asleep with her eyes open?

I hop about a bit and flick my tail.

Nothing.

'Laban!' I try to whisper: it comes out a squeak. There's no reaction from her, but Sally in the next bed wakes up, takes one look and squeals to raise the dead.

'A mouse, it's a mouse!'

I shoot off and under where no one can see me. Everyone's bustling about in a panic – yeah, well done, Mag, really unobtrusive. I make my way out of the room keeping close by the wall. Sally and the rest are still flapping, but there's not been a sound out of Laban. I don't think she's even moved.

Back in the corridor, I think about what just happened. She certainly didn't recognize me, which she should have done as a witch. Is it like Sykes – has somebody taken her magic?

That's something I can suggest to Lady Cootie later – if there is a later. Right now I'd better get on with the job.

I trot off to my next call, Ayesha, the pick of the bunch for talent and good nature both. She might support me even without a spell.

But when I get to Dorm 12, it's the same story as Laban: she's lying like she's asleep with her eyes open. She looks at me and doesn't shift. I don't try any squeaking this time. I don't want the whole school on vermin alert.

What the hell's going on?

Two more visits, two more zeros: Andy Tottimer and Sergei, both waking blanks.

Now I'm panicking, and my little mouse-legs ache from running. Tomas and Wilkie, Yuki and Mieko, finally Paola in Dormitory 3. Every single one of them, alive but lifeless.

I sit on the stairs, twitching my whiskers. Have they all lost their powers? Have they all lost their minds? It's got to be very recent, at least for Andy, or his dad would have brought it up at the Bureau conference.

There's only one place I'm likely to find any answers. I set off up the stairs to Wildeth's room.

*

Naturally the door's shut, and of course a mouse can't open it. If Wildeth's in there, she's going to know who I am, no matter what shape I'm in. This could be the stupidest thing I've ever done.

On the other hand, what have I got to lose? I'm going to face Nilas anyway. He's got Grace. What more can Wildeth do to me?

I think about what Sylvian said, and change shape to myself in clothes. It comes out as school uniform, which I guess is appropriate. Then I try the door.

It swings open without a creak. Does she leave it unlocked when she's not here?

'Dr Wildeth,' I say softly.

No reply.

The gauzy curtains are open, and the wide windows, backs to the dark, mirror the room. The deep bright colours bloom in the glass tank, and again in ghostly reflection. There's movement among the flowers: every so often one of them sinks lower in the water and another one rises.

I tear myself away from the tank and look around. I've never been in here on my own before, so I've never had a chance to snoop.

Temple's flute is where it was before, on a shelf under the desk. I pick it up, put it to my lips and breathe softly across the mouthpiece. A wisp of a sound echoes in the room, and I put down the flute quickly.

I take a peek in the drawers, but it's all syllabuses and reports.

Beyond the flower tank, right in the corner, there's a second door. I turn the handle, making no noise, and push it open a crack. Inside it's dark and silent. Groping to my left, I find a switch and turn on the light.

On a narrow single bed, that takes up nearly the whole length of the room, lies a woman.

It's Temple.

She's lying on her back, with her eyes open like Laban, like Ayesha. She's on top of the covers, head back on the pillow, her pale hair straggled round her head. She's wearing a white nightdress, or it was white once, but now it's grubby, like she hasn't changed it in months.

I touch her foot, and it's icy.

'Temple! Temple!' I shake her by the shoulders, but I know she's not going to react. She's breathing shallow and slow.

I retreat next door.

She's not far away, Wildeth said to me. Was she here then?

Remember, you can't see this room from the outside. It's invisible, or it isn't real at all. It's a spell. What spell? How does it work? She's got to have enchanted them, all the witchkids, and Temple too.

I stand by the tank and close my eyes. Even with them shut, I see the swimming colours of the flowers, lily-white and rose-red. Maybe the flowers are the spell.

I can hear something: a high, distant piping that reminds me of a children's choir. I always thought that was part of Wildeth's tune, but now I realize it's the song of the flowers. What are they saying, thinking?

... emmy ... oh emmy ... oh way ... air ... eh air ...

Nonsense words.

I try to feel my way deeper into their chant. If the flowers have got something to tell me, I want to know what it is.

Now there's a new sound, ringing ever so faintly, tapping its way into my head: familiar glassy notes that chime and spread their circles, rippling across my own tune.

Some tiny part of me knows I need to run, hide, cry out, but I can't move, can't open my eyes to see. Behind my eyelids, colours mingle, bleed scarlet into blue, violet paling to lilac. My music's drifting into clear water, washed clean away.

A chill rises from my feet to my legs, belly, heart, and up to my ears. There's a bubbling, sucking noise.

I can understand what the flowers are saying.

They're not singing, they're screaming in thin high voices.

Help me! Oh help me, let me out … Go away … Take care! … Beware … Save yourself …

Too late.

I'm inside the tank.

*

I'm imprisoned in a flower, deep in the water. Or maybe I *am* the flower: there's no point where I end and it begins. I can't hear or see, I've got no ears or eyes, but I've got a consciousness that's stretched thin and wide. I know everything that's going on. It's like a vision or a dream, sight and hearing and knowledge that's mine but not my own.

The flowers aren't the spell; the flowers are the students. I know that now, because I'm with them, I'm one of them. They whisper to each other and to me. I don't know which is which, I don't know who I am either.

Why did you come?

You should have stayed away.

We tried to warn you.

You're with us now.

It's cold, terribly cold, and there's a feeling of pain

388

or maybe sorrow, you couldn't say for certain because we've got no bodies and we're all one mind, but it hurts, it hurts like homesickness. We know we'll never go home, never be warm again.

Outside the glass there's a girl in a grey skirt, white shirt, standing still. That's the body I used to have, before I was here.

Then SHE comes in.

SHE's warm. SHE has all the warmth and joy in us. The nearer SHE comes, the more we feel it, and we yearn to HER, to our comfort in HER; our petals unfold for HER. SHE's our goddess, our queen, our mother.

'Hello, Margot.'

HER voice is sun and honey. My flower-self unfurls, though my body in the room doesn't move.

'I see you. What a pretty pink rosebud you've become.'

I long for HER to love me.

'Yes, you're mine, and now you always will be. I'm so very glad you came.'

SHE's reading my thoughts.

'So they're the Opposition. Maxim – yes, that doesn't surprise me. And Gordon, naturally. I might have guessed about Felipe too. And Cootie? I wouldn't have thought so, but I suppose it was the thing with the Others. The landed gentry always think they have a monopoly on killing animals.'

SHE laughs.

'It'll be easy enough to take care of them now I know. Perhaps I'll let Nilas do it, or perhaps I'll wait until I'm the head of the Bureau. That won't be long. He's exhausted. He can hardly drag his poor old body around on its wheels. He's not much of a man, is he? Half gone. The fight with the Sleeper wasn't easy for him. I could kiss you for that, my rose.'

SHE strokes the girl's hair.

'You can feel that, can't you? Yes. There's a little bit of you left in your body, just enough to make a very simple creature. You'll eat and walk and sleep, at least I think you sleep. I'm never sure with the flower-children. If you look at them at night, very often their eyes are still open. I don't think there's much difference for them between waking and sleeping. You won't dream, of course.'

Grief for my old body fills me. Around me in the water the other flowers mourn for their lost selves.

'It's a pity you hadn't got your name yet,' SHE goes on. 'I used to wait till my flowers had their full magic, and even then I took only the cream of the crop. But now I've taken all of you, every witch in the school is in my water garden. I couldn't afford to wait any longer. If it came to a fight between you and Nilas, I really wasn't sure who would win. What if you got your name and Grace's strength? That would be quite an even match, you know, since he's so tired. I wouldn't want to bet on it. I wouldn't have cared to fight Grace myself. But now there'll be no fighting. I'll just wait for Nilas to hand over the reins to me and then, then we'll have such fun, won't we, my flowers? We'll do wonderful things together.'

SHE laughs again. SHE's wearing a white lily, and now SHE touches it.

'Are you listening, Temple, my clever daughter? Of course you are, you can't help it. You're me, I'm you. That's the way mothers and daughters are meant to be. Your little friend's here too now. You felt for her because she had problems with her mother.'

HER voice goes high and strident.

'You thought you could get away from me. You thought you could get the better of me. I'll teach you different. I've taught you.'

Then SHE speaks softly again, so sweetly.

'I love you, daughter. I love you because you're part of me. You'll never get away.'

SHE stops, closes HER eyes.

'What's that?' SHE murmurs. 'Somebody's in the school grounds. Somebody who shouldn't be here. Are they looking for you, Margot? I expect they are. Let them look. They can find you, they can take your body away and do what they like, but they'll never get you back, because I've got you now.'

We feel it too, the invading presence, the alien magic, entering the building, climbing the stairs.

'Let's watch what they do,' SHE smiles. SHE steps to the window. HER body shimmers, becomes silvery and thin. You can't see HER against the curtain.

The door opens and two people come into the room, a young man in sunglasses, and a big woman with tangled hair and a long green coat. They see my body and go to it. The young man laughs and says, 'Hey, Trouble, how's it hanging?'

Maybe I knew him once.

His face gets angry. 'What's happened? What's she done to you?'

There's a cat in the room too, a tatty animal. It sniffs at my old body, and then comes to the flower tank. It gets on its hind legs to pat with its paws at the glass.

The woman in green looks at the cat, and then at us, the flowers.

'She's in there,' the woman says. 'Soul flowers.'

'Can you get her out?' the man demands.

The woman doesn't reply, but she lays her hands on the side of the tank. She begins to hum in a low voice, and the ripples come out from her fingers, rocking the water. We're moving, we're rising and turning, the waves go round and round and make a whirlpool.

'Look at that,' says the man. 'Sylvian's got flower-power.'

SHE's coming forward to stop the woman. HER anger is ice, SHE'll freeze us all. SHE despises the Others and their magic. SHE didn't suspect that it could break the flower spell.

The man doesn't see HER but the cat does. It screeches like a demon, and sinks its claws and teeth in HER leg. The sharp pain goes through the flowers, and we shriek in silence.

SHE kicks the cat away, but it's ripped HER tune for a second, and HER invisibility slips like a veil. SHE's a silver shadow on the air. The man knows SHE's there now, and he listens for HER music, sends his own against it to bind HER, trap HER, keep HER where SHE stands.

SHE's stronger than he is – we all know that, the flowers. But SHE has to give him HER attention, for a moment or a minute, and that's time won for the woman at the tank.

The humming hasn't stopped, the warm breath of her song spinning the water. There's a rhythm to the waves: round and back and *strike*, and round and back and *strike* against the glass, and round again and back and *strike*.

We feel the impact; we're begging her to stop, stop, it's hurting us, it's hurting HER. But it goes on, round

393

and round and *strike*, and now the glass *cracks*. A fine line spiders up the clear wall of our home. We're feeling warm air seeping in on our chill. Round again and back and *crack*, and round again and back and *break*. The glass splinters, and water spills out onto the floor.

SHE feels the shock. SHE's forced the man down to his knees, SHE's mastered him, but when the flood comes, SHE staggers.

The woman in the green coat takes a flower from the mess of broken glass and water and petals. It's a pink rosebud. She cups it in her hand and breathes her song on it.

*

I've never felt such pain. It scorches me like hellfire. I can't scream or breathe or see or think.

I'm in my body again.

*

I take in air like I've been drowning. I retch for a second and wipe the tears off my face. I've got to get it together, no time to find my wind.

Wildeth's spread her arms. She's raging, smoking with icy power. A blast of magic froths from her hand to Sylvian, crouched among the flower-heads.

I dive forward to take it, I meet it head on. I accept it, swallow it whole, and it's like I'm in a glacier: my lungs are a deep-freeze, my music's choked.

Sylvian's crouched behind me. She's shovelling up flowers, and as she breathes on them, the petals fly in a cloud of confetti round her head.

The glassy notes ring louder, faster, colder. Wildeth's a sheaf of silver frost. She throws back her head, and the magic starring the room concentrates around her: a core. She casts the spangled blaze at Shade, at me, at Sylvian. It's an atomic flash: we all back off, from cold like nuclear winter.

It's more power than I can take. I'm struck like a statue. Darkness gathers in my eyes. I'm spinning into nothing; I'm done, passing out. I can't fight any more.

The door from the stairs flies back. I see them first white on black like a negative, then filling out to solid human flesh and muscle. Laban and Andy; Wilkie, Mieko, and Yuki; Sergei, Tomas, and Paola; Ayesha and big Davey Foster: the kids Sylvian's restored burst in and throw themselves at Wildeth.

They've got no control. They're all over the place: fazed, dazed and uncoordinated, but their raw fury takes her off guard. She puts her hands up – not like a witch, like a woman – to guard her face. Something falls to the ground: the white lily.

I hear Sylvian groan. She can hardly move for cold, but she manages to reach out her hand and scoop up the flower. She gasps down on it with all the breath she can raise.

Wildeth's music falters; the notes chime off key. Her icy radiance fades, and I can see the witchkids tearing at her, belting her round the head and body. A shiver runs up her from the ground, like someone's taking a saw to her roots.

I never closed the second door, the one to the bedroom. In the opening, I can see a pale shape.

Temple's coming.

Her face is white as dead fish, her nightdress is dirty white, her matted hair's like damp straw. Just her eyes are hot and shining. I don't have to guess the pain she's in, except it must be worse, far worse, than mine.

Step by step, she walks to Wildeth, and Wildeth watches her approach.

'Mother,' whispers Temple. Then she starts to sing:

> *I know a lady lives in a tower*
> *Her face as fair as the lily flower*
> *Her smile as sweet as the crimson rose*
> *That in her secret garden grows.*

Her voice is a frayed thread, but I can hear the music in her mind. Every note's carrying what she's got inside, that hellish heat, and sending it straight to Wildeth.

Little bird sits and sings in a tree
Pretty bird, pretty bird, fly down to me,
I'll make you a cage of silver and gold
To keep you from the winter's cold.

Wildeth doesn't make a sound, but her mouth opens, a ragged black hole. Her eyes are staring. Behind her, the glass wavers like water.

I'd sooner die from the winter's cold
Than live in a cage of silver and gold
For birds must fly and flowers must die
So I'll take my wings and away I'll fly.

Wildeth's tune is breaking up. I hear the crystal notes shatter; I hear a sizzling like oil in a pan. I feel the floor shiver under my feet. I know what's about to happen.

'Get out of here!' I try to yell, but it comes out a sob. 'Everyone out, quick!'

The kids are crowding to the door. We've been together; we've been part of her and her spell; we understand without speaking what the danger is. Ugly's already gone. Shade's slower off the mark, but he feels the pressure shift and he dives towards Sylvian, half-lifting her. She grabs the last flowers and holds them as he shoves her out.

'Temple!'

She's still facing Wildeth. I try to drag her with me, and she turns her head.

'Mag. I couldn't … I can't …'

'Quick, quick.'

'Goodbyes suck,' she says. For a second the rabbity smile lights her face, and then she sags, her legs crumple. I think her strength is done, but she pushes me hard and sudden. I'm not ready. I stumble with her full weight against me, and fall backwards through the door. It slams behind me.

Shade pulls me across the landing. Sylvian's at the head of the stairs, and the witchkids are scrambling down below her. There's a soft *thump* from behind the door – not much of a noise, but it throws us like dynamite. We tumble, petals drifting over us.

The door to Wildeth's room swings open. It moves out, then back, like there's a draught.

Nobody wants to move.

I'm the nearest.

I look inside, and see no airy glassy space, no windows, just a closet full of dust. Temple lies face down, her arms flung across her mother's waist. Wildeth's on her side, one hand on her daughter's hair.

There's no life in the silence.

My foot kicks something on the floor. A silver flute.

I pick it up, and take it with me. Temple won't be wanting it any more.

CHAPTER TWENTY-FIVE

REVENGE

Getting outside into the fresh air feels like freedom I thought I'd never have again. Whatever I say to Shade and Sylvian isn't going to be enough, so I say 'Thanks.'

Sylvian just nods, like, Yeah, tell me about it.

Shade gives me a squeeze. 'Guess you got what you came for.'

Neither of them knew Temple. Did I know her? *Mag, I couldn't ... I can't ...* What was she telling me? That she couldn't help what she did at the Residence, when I thought she was my friend? Or that she really was my friend, and so she couldn't betray me? Sykes got her moved on; Nilas didn't trust her. Maybe she stood up for me. I'd like to think that, but I'll never know.

I can't ... can't leave my mother? Can't live with what I've done?

'Hey, Trouble, we better get this show on the road,' mutters Shade.

I pull myself out of my head and look at what's

going on around me. Students are scattered all over, half-dressed and manic. The ones who were in the flower-tank longest aren't on the spot – they'd left Crossbeams. But even the kids who were prisoner just a week or so are having trouble adjusting, and Laban's skipping across the gravel, while Big Davey's on his knees digging his fingers in the earth.

Morning mist veils the school, damp light creeping through. Shade's right, we've got to make a move. I'd just as soon not explain to Matron what killed the headmistress, nor why there are students dancing in their pyjamas on the lawn, and besides, it's freezing. They haven't noticed, because anything seems warm after the tank, but their toes are turning blue, and we can't risk going into the dorms for clothes.

Shade's thinking what I'm thinking. 'They won't all fit in the Merc.'

'Over here,' I shout. 'Hold hands.'

I grab Laban off the drive, leave Shade to hang on to her, and set to herding the rest. When I've got the full set linked in a straggling crocodile, I say, 'Listen to my tune, and join in. It'll stop you getting too cold. And walk fast, keep together.'

Off we go, some of them singing out loud. It's like a carnival parade with cheaper costumes. Sitting across my shoulders, Mr Ugly keeps at least that bit of me warm.

'How you doing?' I ask Laban, across Shade.

She's sashaying along on the sopping grass. 'Un-be-liev-able!' she carols. 'I never thought I'd be so pleased to see your face.'

Same old Laban, then. It's kind of reassuring.

'Do you know how to send your music to someone else?' I ask her.

'I've never done that.'

'Shade, you'll have to stay with them, take them through.'

'Sure,' he nods, with maybe a spot too much enthusiasm. Even after a month with no moisturizer, Laban's still easy on the eye in her flimsies.

Sylvian's nursing her arm. She must have bashed it when she fell downstairs. 'Let him take them.' She jerks her head at Shade, and the movement makes her wince. 'You and I must go to Nilas now.'

'I have to talk to the kids first.'

'We must hurry. We must go to Nilas.'

I wish she'd stop saying that.

'I just want to make sure my back-up team's all together and not dead of hypothermia.' It sounds rational enough to me.

'What will you do when you get to him?' she demands.

I'm trying not to think about it, is the truth.

'He is sly and subtle,' she goes on. 'He may try to

persuade you that the best way is not to fight. You must not believe him. Never trust him.'

'That's what Wildeth said about the Others,' I tell her. 'If there's something we can do that means no one else dies, I'm all for it.'

Sylvian looks at me with disillusion, and then drops back. Let her sulk if she wants. Maybe she can heal herself, hug a tree or something.

The sun must be up now, but the mist hasn't lifted, in fact it's clotted to a real Island fog. Drops of water hang on the hedges and thicken out of the grey air. You can't see more than a few yards of the road; you can't see the fields on either side. We're walking under a big soggy canopy.

It's miles to Humph's cave, some of it cross-country, and I'm wondering if my spell's going to be enough to get us there. We must have been walking an hour already. The flower-kids are tired, now the first thrill's worn off.

Just when I think it doesn't get worse than this, the rain sets in properly.

There's Sylvian ahead, though I thought she was behind us. Her arm's moving freely now, so I guess the tree hugged her back. I put on a spurt to try to catch her up, ask if she can think of any better, quicker way to go, but she lengthens her stride. I'm not planning to play tag, and I slow back to a trudge.

Something's beyond her on the road, a black shape in the mist. It's moving towards us.

'It's that dog,' says Laban. 'The one that used to hang round the school.'

He's dragging himself along like he can hardly move. Now I hear him whimpering.

'Bargus!' I cry out.

By the time I get there, panting for breath, Sylvian's on her knees in the road with her arms round his neck.

He's bleeding. His ear's ripped and there's a ragged cut down his side. His coat's sopping wet, covered with dirt.

I go to hug him, but Sylvian keeps me off.

'What happened?'

'Nilas found the cave,' she snarls.

'What did he do?' I whisper.

'The humans got away. He caught the hob.'

I don't say anything.

'He killed the hob,' says Sylvian.

*

I'm running, I'm galloping, all four legs. I don't see the country I'm passing, I don't feel the rain falling on my back. I don't even know what I've turned into till I see the beech tree up ahead and stop to howl.

I'm a wolf. I'm queen of the wolves, big as a pony, with a set of teeth I could use to chew on broken bottles.

A lot of good that does me. The cave's empty under the roots of the tree, ash from the dead fire scattered on the floor.

There's no body. Someone must have taken him away, maybe buried him. I think of his furry shape, still and cold and stiff. I've seen dead things. I remember him saying *Hold me paws*.

I run on, a grey wolf in the grey light, feeling the ground hard under my pads. All I want to do is get to Nilas; all I want to taste is blood.

I've never been to his house, but I know where I'm going. I can smell him out – wherever he is I'll find him. I leave the valley and hit the road, cross it in a bound, and I'm on a field stretching up towards the clouded sky. The world spins away, and I'm on the crest of the hill: looking down I can see a huge house in the hollow beyond, and behind it the sea.

Down the slope, and here's a ditch and hedge. I pause, back on my haunches to take the jump, and then suddenly there's something in my way, some little creature that springs out of nowhere and scratches me.

I'll kill you, little animal.

I've got it in my jaws, I'm shaking it to death. There's blood in my mouth.

What the *hell* am I doing?

I drop my mouth open and a limp grey thing falls out in the ditch.

It's Ugly.

I nose him, lick him with my rough tongue, and he miaows. He's not dead.

Poor bloody cat. Must have come all the way on my back, clinging on.

Grey wolf, grey cat, grey morning.

This is no good. I can't go in there with claws and teeth: if I'm not thinking like a witch, then I've got no chance.

I change to my own shape, dressed in black. In my hand there's a long, sharp sword. I'm an avenger; I'm prepared to kill.

I stroke Ugly. 'I'm sorry,' I tell him. 'You'll be ok.'

He spits at me and tries to bite. That's more like it.

Now I'm ready.

*

The door's open, and I walk in.

There's a hall like a palace, grey marble and gilt. I pace along looking in the mirrors, seeing myself dark and sinister, the light gleaming from my weapon. There are rooms on all sides, but even now I'm not a wolf, I know where to go.

A drape hangs in my way, thick embroidery on gold rings. I push it aside.

The wheelchair's got its back to me. Nilas is looking out of the window into the fog that hangs low over the sea.

I swing him round to face me, and raise my sword.

Such a small man, for a second I hesitate. He's nested in his chair, huddled under a woolly shawl for warmth.

'Margot,' he says gently. 'Come to kill me, have you?'

I can't think what to say. 'Yes,' seems to cover it.

'Why?'

'Because you killed Humph.'

'Humph?' He frowns. He didn't even know the name, and that makes me so angry, I swing my sword with all the force I've got. I'd like to see it slice him; I want to cut off his head.

He hardly blinks his one good eye. He moves one hand – the only hand he can move – and my blade drops, fades to nothing.

'I want to talk to you,' he says.

'There's nothing to talk about.'

'Grace is here. You knew that, eh?'

I'd almost forgotten. That's why I was coming to him, wasn't it, to rescue her?

'Wants us all to work together. You and her and me.'

'You kidnapped her.'

He shakes his head. 'Came of her own accord. We've talked, a long time. Long time since we talked.' He half-smiles. 'I'd forgotten ... Only one I ever trusted. The one who betrayed me. Now I'm ready to trust her again. Stupid old man.'

'You want us to work together?' I echo.

'She wants it. Now you've scuppered Network – you and the King – only thing left, hm? Only way to go.'

'To do what?'

'Rebuild the Bureau. Way it was meant to be.'

'What about the Others?'

He sighs. 'Let them – go on. Little green people, carry on in their little green ways. What does it matter? We – can still – have the power.'

'The power *to do what?*' I say again, louder.

He doesn't respond for a moment; then he smiles. 'Whatever – we like. You and Grace and I … We can do anything. Thesida's dead, isn't she?'

I nod.

'Felt it.' He shivers a little. 'Not such a bad thing. She – wanted to take over. Not Opposition, perhaps worse. I might have been a fool all these years. The Skull – relied on that. Bad spells give bad counsel. Thesida Wildeth and Francis Sykes. She's dead. He'll never be the same again, since the Sleeper robbed him. Left … all alone …'

'So you're just a poor old man, ready to give up?' I challenge him.

'Poor old witch, poor old witch,' he hums to the

tune of 'Three Blind Mice', then chuckles. 'Maybe – not quite. With you and Grace – could still be – a world to live in.'

'If you want to work with me, why did you do it?' I ask. 'You didn't have to kill him.'

'Kill who?' He frowns, one eyebrow going down.

'You don't even remember? Just now, at the cave. You tracked me there, and you attacked them, and you killed the hob.'

'One of the Others?' He looks bewildered. 'Just now? No.'

'He's lying.'

My mother steps out from behind the embroidered curtain.

Once before, when Delphine let me look into the past, I saw her how she used to be: healthy, pretty, in normal clothes, not asylum gear. Now she's gorgeous. Her face has filled out a bit, her eyes are wide and shining, her hair's springy and thick. She's wearing jeans and a sweater, nothing fancy, but still, with everything going on in my head, I take a second to think: Dad got lucky there.

'Nilas is lying,' she says again. 'He broke into the cave; he killed the hob. He took me. He's kept me here by force. Now he says he'll let us both live if we agree to join him. Is that what you want?'

I stare from one to the other.

'Grace.' Nilas's voice is stronger now. 'What's the game?'

'We're not playing your game,' she tells him with contempt.

'Not what you said to me before.'

She laughs. 'What I said? It was you saying how you'll wreck the Island and the Others, how you'll rebuild your Network empire and make the planet dance to your tune.'

He goes smaller in his chair, gathering himself together. Then his head comes up and he looks full at her.

'More tricks,' he says, biting off the words.

'Tricks!' she mocks him. 'You know a few of those, don't you?'

He doesn't reply. He passes his hand slowly across his face. I hear his music, not the full-throttle thundering menace of his charge on Chough, just a clenching, flexing beat, but behind it, the intention's no less dangerous. *I'll kill you now,* Nilas is thinking. *Grace, you've lied once too often. It's time to say goodbye.*

He darts his flattened fingers at her with the full force of his magic.

I'm only ready because I've been listening to him all the time. I can't let her take that, she's got no magic to meet it, and I jump in front of her, opening myself to the blast, sending my tune against him.

The snarl of his attack rasps across my strings, warping and distorting. It's an assault on everything that holds me together. I feel my mind swell like a balloon to the point of bursting. I'm dissolving, unmade. My music loses all meaning; it's no more than a vanishing scream.

My knees buckle, my will crumbles. I'm a snuffed candle, a broken bubble. I'm going out, small, smaller, an atom, a mote of lost dust. Then, from some pinprick in the blackness, a pale glimmer shines, a note trembles. I still have a spark, a breath. I cling to it; it draws me up out of the dark.

Now, now, I gasp, begging in my head. *Now I need the back-up; I need your magic. Maxim! Castaneda! Laban!*

There's nothing.

Of course there's nothing. Sylvian and Humph were the link, and she's not here, and he's dead.

They know that – won't they be listening out? Won't they have dropped their shields?

Shade! Gordy! Sylvian!

Not a whisper. Looks like I'm on my own here.

I get to my feet.

'Fight someone your own size,' I say to Nilas.

He cackles. 'Rate yourself, don't you?' he taunts me. 'Come on, then. Show me what you're made of.'

I don't wait to be asked again. I throw myself forward and seize his arm, and drag him out of his chair across the room.

For a second I'm appalled at what I've done. It's an old man in a wheelchair! Then he comes up on an elbow and looks at me, and I forget everything except terror. Just his eye fixed on me, and I can't think, remember, decide.

I can't stop my feet moving. I'm walking towards him.

'Easy does it,' he croons. 'Approach, my child.'

His tune's a wisp of sound. He doesn't need to crush me; he can drain the life from me with an echo. I can feel the dry, gentle pressure on my scalp, my skin. He will suck the seeds from me, my empty rind will fall.

My feet take me forward.

'What's your name?'

I can hear a voice. My mother's voice.

'Your name. What's your name?'

CHAPTER TWENTY-SIX

GRACE

I don't know, I don't know what my name is.

'What's your name?'

Margot. Mag.

My feet go one at a time.

There's a light in front of me. It's an eye, a grey eye.

'What's your name?'

Nilas's tune fills my head. His grey light surrounds me.

'Your name!'

Who's shouting so far away from me?

In the grey noise, there's one note of my own, one golden string, plucked over and over again.

It's a word. It has meaning.

Mag. Mag.

More, there's more. I can't understand.

For a hairsbreadth second I can hear it.

'Magistra,' I say out loud.

My shining music floods me. I've never surfed, but now I know what it feels like: the wave catches me, lifts me up, carries me high and far. I'm on top of the world: it's all below and I'm riding it, confident and beautiful, mistress of my mystery, the power of all the sea to bear me.

Then the wave rushes on, and I'm left behind.

Every scrap of power and magic goes from me.

Grace steps forward. 'Magistra!' she cries, and it chimes round the room like a victory peal of bells. For a moment her body's transparent, a gauzy shimmer with light shining through.

It was her name I found, not mine. When I said it, all my power – all *her* power – went to her.

I look down at myself, and see even my clothes are dissolving, rubbing away to rags, tatters, nothing. They were a spell, I made them for myself with magic when I shifted shape. Now I'm stripped bare.

And in my head, there's no sound. I'm struck deaf, stone deaf to deep music.

I pick up Nilas's shawl from the floor, I wrap it round my nakedness. Then I stand watching. It's all that's left for me to do.

Nilas is on his side, propped on an arm, his finger stretched, but he's aimed at me, and I'm nothing now. Grace pulls him to his feet with a gesture, and he stands swaying: it's not his own strength keeping him upright. He gasps.

'Nilas!' she sings out. 'What are you?'

He grimaces and groans. 'Still – something.'

He's dangling, suspended on his toes, his teeth set, his limbs trembling. Then his chair begins to move across the room. The wheels spin, the seat glides beneath him.

Grace flicks her fingers, and he tumbles into the wheelchair, arms and legs sprawling.

'There's your dignity,' she says.

He spits at her. It doesn't touch her: three small drops of moisture hang in the air between them, sparkling in the light. They start to revolve, dancing around each other like summer flies. Quicker and quicker they spin, till they're a whirling blur.

Grace backs away from him. A moment ago she had the upper hand, but now she's in retreat. Her eyes widen, and beads of sweat star her forehead. What's he doing to her?

'No, oh no.' Her voice is a whisper, then it rises to a shriek of such panic, it raises the hairs on the back of my neck.

He's sending fear into her. She wants to run but her legs won't move, her knees buckle, she's sobbing in nightmare. This must be what her dreams were like. Her mouth stretches in horror.

Can I stop him or distract him?

The flying water drops close in on her. He'll invade her mind, wring the strength from her, flatten her to paper. He'll be able to lift and tear her with one hand.

I don't have my deep music, her deep music, any more, but I couldn't forget the tune. I chant it, sing loud as I can, to the word *Magistra, Magistra*. It doesn't matter that my voice is cracked and I can't reach the notes. If I give her the key, that's all that matters.

I'm singing up close in her ear, and I see her pupils, tiny points, dilate. She's hearing her own music, bringing it back under her command.

The moist whir of Nilas's spit thickens to a cloud, moving away from her, back towards him. Round his head, it changes colour from greasy grey to white, to a flush of flesh pink, a full-blooded blush.

He draws in breath, he laughs, but his breath's out of his control. He sobs, deep and harsh in his throat.

'Oh, Grace,' he croaks.

Colours swell and throb in the mist that crowns him, and his tongue comes out to lick his lips. His face is contorted with some ache I don't recognize, somewhere between pain and pleasure.

'Grace, my darling.' His voice is husky, drunken. 'My love, my love.'

'Look, Margot,' she whispers. 'He thought he could scare me helpless, and look at him. Is love stronger than fear? Longing, ecstatic need, that's all he's feeling now. Isn't it so, Nilas? Aren't you my slave?'

He's dribbling.

'I'm your goddess,' she cries. 'I could tear you to pieces and drink your blood.'

'Do it, do it!' He's gasping.

'Yes, I'll do it.' She steps delicately forward, one pace, two. 'You'll die in joy,' she murmurs. 'Is that what I want?'

She doubts, just for a second, and the second's all he needs. It's enough for him to find himself, gather his strength back and send it out, and though I can't hear the fury of his music, I see her flinch. The cloud of magic swells and drives forward, away from him, into her face. She has to turn her head, it's in her eyes and mouth and nose, and I can smell it too, pungent and heady. It's like drug smoke; I feel my own head spinning, and Grace has to breathe it in. She totters on her feet, she sways, and then she sits down, sliding to the floor.

Her lips widen in a halfwit smile. She hiccups and grins, starts giggling. Her legs splay, her arms can't support her, and she sprawls out full length.

Nilas stares down at her. His wheels spin him forward.

'Yes, yes,' he's muttering. 'That's the way of it, shame of it, see who's the slave now, shan't we? Take it, my lady, take what I'm giving, won't be long. You'll be gone. Squeeze the last drop from you, the knowledge. I'll have it, and then, then …'

His hand's reaching, the fingers crooking. The grey fumes of the spell descend around them both, linking them. It's a wraith without edges, darkening to violet towards the centre, with a white glow at its heart. Lightning stabs, jagged bolts of electricity striking, probing to her brain.

She cries out suddenly, as if she's touched the spark. Her body contorts, and she throws her arms out, opening herself to him.

He darts at her, teeth bared. But it's the moment she was waiting for. I see her face suddenly aware and intent, I see the white radiance contract for a second, then stab through his grey eye straight into his brain. She never lost control. She's entered him, his mind and body, with one searing strike.

For an instant both his eyes open wide, with ghastly light behind them. His thin white hair stands out from his head, and both hands fling up, throwing him forward in the chair. He crumples and lies bent to one side, his neck twisted.

The cloud softens, shreds, and wafts away. Grace looks down at Nilas's body.

I don't move, I don't say anything. After a minute she bends down and straightens Nilas in his chair. She folds his hands on his lap. Then she looks at me, muffled in the shawl, and sighs, and smiles.

'I'll find you something to wear,' she says.

'Mourning, for the funeral?' I suggest. I'm shocked at my own voice. It's thin, feeble – it sounds nothing like me. I realize I'm feeling ill, like I'm coming down with flu: there's an unpleasant feverish warmth all through me. I'm queasy; I need to sit down.

'Are you all right?' she asks.

'I'm fine,' I say as firmly and loudly as I can. I'm damned if I want her to feel sorry for me now.

'You'll be weak for a while,' she tells me. 'Losing your magic is painful; it upsets your whole system. But you'll recover. It wasn't your own magic.'

'Let's get out of here.' I don't want to stay in a room with a corpse.

'I'll make you some tea.' That's so domestic it almost makes me smile. She leads me through the house into the kitchen and puts the kettle on. 'Wait a moment.'

While she's gone, I sit staring at the table, and when she comes back with an armful of clothes, I dress myself without worrying that they're too big. They smell faintly sweet; they smell of her. It comes back to me from all those years ago.

She's spooning sugar into a cup and stirring.

Maybe tea's a good idea. I haven't had anything to eat or drink since last night at Humph's. Thinking that, I have to swallow hard and get a grip.

'You must be exhausted,' she says.

'I'm not the one who's just fought the battle.'

'You've had plenty of fighting. You beat Thesida Wildeth, so I understand.'

'Not really.' I didn't fight her, Temple and Sylvian did. I didn't fight Chough, Nilas did. I didn't fight Nilas, Grace did. I haven't fought anybody.

'Drink that.' She puts the cup in front of me.

'Thanks, Mum.' It's meant to come out sarcastic, but I find I'm near to crying.

She sits opposite me, her arms on the table, and looks me full in the face. I keep my eyes down on my cup.

'I'm proud of you, Margot.'

I don't reply.

'There can't be many girls,' she goes on, 'who've done for their mothers what you've done for me.'

'There can't be many mothers who've done to their daughters—'

I can't go on. She's got the point, though.

'You're angry with me?'

I sip scalding tea.

'Margot, I had to do it. I haven't had any choices.'

'You lied to me.'

'Yes,' she admits. 'I had to do that too.'

'Tell me why.'

'When I got my memory back – at the Residence – when I'd talked to Gordy, I realized just how much danger I'd put you in. Not just from Nilas, but from Maxim and the rest of the Opposition too. I was biting my nails every day, hoping you'd get my name and give my magic back. Until that happened, I was helpless, there was nothing I could do to protect you.'

'You knew it'd be your name I'd find.'

'It had to be my name. It was my magic. But if you found it and didn't tell me – you could have kept it as your own. I don't know what would have happened then. It might have destroyed you.'

'And anyway you wanted it for yourself.'

'Of course I did!' she exclaims. 'Wouldn't you? That was what was making me more and more frightened – for you and for me and all of us. You were loving being a witch.'

I can't tell her she's wrong.

'So I started to wonder what pressure I could put on you. I know that sounds cruel, but it was necessary. I thought you had to get my name when I was there – that way you could hardly avoid letting me know. The only plan I could come up with was for you to find me in danger from Nilas. You'd have to fight him. He'd be stronger. And then the name would come.'

'You can't have been sure of that.'

'Sure enough,' she says. 'So I engineered a quarrel with Eron to give me a reason to leave.' She laughs suddenly. 'Poor Eron! You can tell him, now, I don't mind what he does with big Bella. They're a good match; he'll be far better off with her.'

'You're not coming back to him?'

'I don't think so. I did love him, you know. But he's not a witch. He could never understand what I am and what I do. I think really a witch has to be alone.' There's a smile still hovering on her lips. 'Magic is enough; it's more than love. No, I won't be coming back to Eron.'

'Where will you go?'

'I don't know yet. I've got the whole world now.' She stretches her arms, and looks blissful. 'We'll see … But I haven't finished telling you yet what happened. When I walked out of the Residence, I knew I was going to Nilas. I was going to let you think he was holding me prisoner.'

'You took a big risk.' Reluctantly, I have to admire her.

'I thought he wouldn't hurt me until he was sure of getting you. What I didn't know, of course, was that the whole affair of the Sleeper would blow up just then, or that you'd be involved. My heart was in my mouth the whole time. You were strained to the limits; what if you got the name then? You could have come to full power and I'd never get it back from you.'

She pauses. 'And of course I was terrified you'd be hurt,' she adds.

'Thanks for the afterthought.'

'Margot, you should understand what it's like. Wouldn't you do anything to be a witch again?'

I can't answer.

'Luckily there's nothing you *can* do.' She pours more tea into my cup. 'I know you don't see it that way, now. But you will. Witches aren't happy people. You can be happy now. You can grow up as a normal girl and fall in love and – oh, do all the things people do. I've given you all that. That's what I have to hang on to, to remind myself I'm not such a bad person after all.'

'If it's such a terrible thing to be a witch, why were you so keen to get your magic back?'

'I was never going to be like everyone else. I was naturally a witch – that's how I was made. You, you lucky little girl, you were born without that power and that longing for power. You know what it's like now, but it's not yours, it never was. You'll be happy,' she tells me again.

'Excuse me while I pull a cracker and put on a party hat.'

'You don't believe me, so forget it,' she says with an impatient sigh. 'Anyway, when Nilas recovered from fighting the Sleeper, I told him I'd been a fool to rebel against him in the old days, and now I wanted to come in on his side. It wasn't easy to convince him.'

'But you did. He was going to work with you, with

425

us. He said so.'

'And you would have fallen for that?' she exclaims.

Yes, I would, too. Until I remembered what it was like fighting Chough with Nilas's killing rage inside me.

'I told him I was frightened for you at the hands of the Opposition,' Grace goes on. 'I had to get you here where you'd be safe. That was at least half true.'

'Not since I knew who was in the Opposition.'

'It hardly matters now, does it? With Nilas and Wildeth dead, and me gone, the Bureau's going to have a lot of work before it's any sort of power to be reckoned with again.'

'So you convinced Nilas to keep you here and shield you.'

'Yes, and then to tell your friend Shade that I was under threat.'

'How did he know I was with Shade? I didn't tell you that.'

'Gordy knew where you were.'

'Gordy?' I put my cup down so hard the saucer cracks. 'Gordy was in on this?'

'He knew you'd never be safe until you'd given up your powers. He was worried about you, Margot, like your schoolfriend too.'

'Ruce? That's not true,' I say, though of course it must be. Gordy couldn't have been plotting and her not know about it.

'She wasn't happy about deceiving you. But she wanted revenge on Nilas so badly, you see, for what he did to her uncle Rossy. And we all knew that the only one who could defeat Nilas was me, with my full powers.'

When Ruce and Gordy were getting the Hollies back and it took so long …

My head's not functioning properly. I'm not even as upset as you'd expect. It feels like there's cottonwool wrapped all round my brain, and my ears are buzzing.

'What about Maxim and the rest of them? Were they all part of the plan?' I understand now, they never meant to send their power. I had to be alone, so I'd get my name. Grace's name.

'All except Shade and his sister. We weren't sure we could rely on them not to tell you.'

'Sylvian?'

'She was the one who hated Nilas most, she'd have done anything to see him dead.'

'And—' I can't bring myself to ask.

'Your little furry friend?' Grace smiles. 'He's not dead, you know.'

I gape at her.

'It was the only way we could think to bring you to the boil. You wouldn't come to Nilas! Sylvian was in despair. We thought you'd come straight away for me, you see. I didn't realize that your connection to

427

me wasn't so strong.'

'Oh, make me feel guilty, why don't you?' I burst out. 'Like you haven't done enough of that already.'

'Ruce thought that he, the hob, was the one you cared most about,' Grace goes on. 'So they arranged a masquerade with the dog. It was our last resort. Sylvian suspected you might bargain with Nilas, and she wouldn't stand for that.'

Humph's alive! He's not dead. He will be when I lay hands on him. No, I haven't got the strength to throttle him. I haven't got the strength to go on with this conversation. I want to be at home in bed with Bella to look after me.

I gather what energy I've got and stand up.

'That seems to cover everything,' I say. 'Thanks for the info.'

She smiles at me. 'Brave girl. I know how you're feeling.'

'Sure, you've got insight.'

We walk together to the front door.

'Where are you going?' she asks me.

'Home, I guess. Don't worry about me, I'll be ok.'

'I know you will.' She bends to kiss me, and I let her do it. It's a light touch on the forehead, like when she sent her magic to me all those years ago, only now she's not giving me a thing.

'You want me to go, don't you?' she says. 'That's

what I want too, so let's say goodbye.'

'Will I see you again?' I really didn't mean to ask her that.

She strokes my hair briefly. 'You're my daughter. I'm your mother. It's best we don't meet too often, don't you think?'

She opens the door, and something grey shoots through, mewing. Mr Ugly gives me a second's attention, then turns to Grace. She picks him up and he arranges himself across her shoulders, just like he always used to do with me.

'I've really missed having a familiar,' she says. 'Well – so long, Margot.'

She walks off down the drive. Ugly's tail waves at me over her shoulder.

I never did like that animal. I'm glad to be rid of him.

CHAPTER TWENTY-SEVEN
WITCHWORK

The Residence is still being rebuilt after the fire. Sykes has got a temporary place, smarter than the old house and it feels emptier. There's a room for me, but it hasn't got any of my stuff in. That all went up in smoke. I sit Little Bear on the pillow the first day, but after a bit I put him in the drawer. I'm not so keen on furry things as I was.

Bella and Dad are pleased to have me around, but a good deal more pleased with each other. Dad doesn't believe me at first when I say Grace isn't coming back, but then he gets a letter that sends him catatonic for half a day, after which he arrives home with a bottle of champagne and a bunch of red roses. One of them's plastic, from the joke shop; it squirts water, and Bella thinks that's just as funny as he does.

Sykes still looks pretty tired. He was never rough, but now he's so mild he can hardly swat midges, and he's not really pulling his weight around the place. I suppose that's been true for a while now, and the rest of them have got used to running things with him as figurehead.

The Hollies are pretty happy, though they miss Parrot and Chough, and Perkin even has a fit of crying about Grace.

What I find hardest to take is being around Gordy. He doesn't think he's done anything to be ashamed of: after I've blanked him a few times, he starts to get the message, but then he just acts huffy, like it's me who's being unreasonable. Ruce hasn't come to visit. She's sent a text, saying any time I feel like being crawled to, she's ready, but I don't think I'm quite there yet.

I stick it out over Christmas; then I've got to get away for a while.

*

'Omigod,' says J, when I turn up at the Pad.

'I should have phoned. I was worried you'd say I couldn't come.'

'Say you're going to stay. Please say you're going to stay.'

'Sure it's not a problem?' Then I get in the kitchen, and I clock why she's so happy to see me. Here's Laban, large as life and twice as manicured, drinking hooch with her bare feet up on Shade's lap.

'Hey, Margot,' she drawls. 'Long time, little one.'

Shade looks a bit embarrassed. He gives me a hug, and when he sits down again, it's in a different chair on the other side of the table.

'Heard the score on the Bureau and all that?' Laban asks me. 'Oh no, I forgot. I guess you're out of the loop now, aren't you? Bummer.'

'Yeah. But you can tell me if you like.' I open a bottle of hooch without being offered: I think I might need a bit of chemical courage. 'Has Maxim taken over? Or is it Coper?'

'That's, like, the question. Should it be someone who was on Nilas's side or Opposition?'

'Oh, come on. They're still arguing about that?'

'Can't get their heads round it,' Shade puts in, 'that there ain't no Opposition now. Seems like they can't agree on nothing.'

'Drives my mother wild,' says Laban. 'If they'd just listen to her …'

'Guess they'd all feel that way,' J suggests.

'Lost their direction,' Shade says. 'Besides, Nilas and Wildeth, they been steering that concern so long, now they're gone, the rest of them feel like they got no map. They wanted Grace to join again, but it looks like she wants to take her own road.'

J nudges him. 'They asked you too, didn't they?'

'Yeah, they tried it on. I told them I don't want no part of it.'

'Thing is, now there's a whole lot of really bright young witches on the scene, yeah? All of us that

Wildeth enchanted. Since we've got our magic back—' Laban interrupts herself. 'Did I ever say thanks for that?'

'Don't thank me,' I say. 'Thank Sylvian and Shade.'

'I showed my gratitude.' Laban tosses her hair and throws Shade a speaking glance.

'To Sylvian too?' I enquire.

J snorts, but Laban takes it with a giggle. 'You think she'd like me to?'

I have to laugh. 'Maybe not. So what's happening with the witchkids?'

'The older ones, I guess they'll train with Coper at college. The rest of us, well, I've been thinking, when we're back at school, who's going to teach magic? They're getting a new head, but that'll probably be someone ordinary, you know? Not a witch.'

'So?' I ask, since she's obviously got more to say.

'So we could have, like, a co-operative, all of us working together. I could run it.'

Laban's idea of a co-operative would naturally mean her being boss. The Bureau still quarrelling and Laban in charge of magic classes at Crossbeams? This all sounds like a recipe for disaster, but what have I got to do with anything? Nothing.

'So,' she stretches out a foot and pokes me, 'are you coming back next term?'

It's ridiculous, but I haven't even thought about this. Dad hasn't mentioned it: I guess he assumes I'm going to do just that.

Being around witches, and not being a witch myself, I'd be like Ruce. I don't know if I could handle that. Maybe I should just go back to Beckwood and be a retard again. Maybe they won't want me there.

'Think about it,' Shade advises. 'Ain't no hurry.'

'Except term starts next week,' Laban points out. 'And you've missed a good deal already, haven't you?'

Yeah, thanks. I'll find my natural place at the bottom of the class.

There's noise on the stairs, and Tippy sails in, with Bo following.

'Mag!' squawks Tippy, and kisses me all over, or that's what it feels like. 'It's so great to see you.'

'Are you back here, then?' I ask, trying to get out of her hug.

'Oh yeah, Bo fell out with his mum. Are you staying? I really hope you're staying,' she says, with a sideways look like a blowtorch at Laban. I guess there's been trouble with Bo there.

'Full house,' says J with satisfaction. 'Sorry, Laban, but Mag gets first call on the couch.'

'No sweat, I've got a club to go to.' She stands up, pitching her empty bottle in the bin. 'Anyone wanna come?'

After a moment Shade gets up. 'Guess I could take a look in.' He ruffles my hair. 'See you later, Trouble. Take it easy.'

When he's gone, I feel so depressed, I just want to curl up and die. J looks at me in concern.

'Mag, you're not well, are you?'

'I'm ok,' I gulp into my pop.

'You want me to give you a massage?' Tippy offers.

'No, she don't. Cripple her for a week,' growls Bo.

'Come in my room.' J shepherds me out of the kitchen and closes the door. 'Want to talk about it?' she says when I'm sitting on her bed.

'Not really. It's just …'

And then I cry full out. It's meant to make you feel better but it doesn't do that for me, it just hurts my throat and my nose, and after a bit I stop.

J kneels on the floor in front of me.

'You don't want to worry about Laban. She's kind of a control freak, you know? It's easier to go along with what she wants.'

'I know. It's not that.' It is, a bit, but that I can handle. 'It's the magic. J, I can't take not being a witch.'

'Uh-huh.' She sighs. 'Shade thought as much.'

'It's like it's what I *was*; it was *everything* I was. Without that, what am I?'

'If you *were* a witch, what would you do?'

That stumps me for a bit.

'I'd try to get the Bureau working together, the way they were always meant to. I'd find out more about the Others, see if they'll talk to the witches and the witches talk to them, so there'd be peace between them and us.'

'Sounds good,' says J. 'I don't credit a word of it.'

'All right, what do you think I'd do?'

'I think you'd have fun, doing what you're good at.'

That just goes to my heart. 'Yeah,' I howl. 'That's what I'd do!'

'So you're good at other things, or you will be. There are other ways to have fun. I know it's not much consolation now, but it's like being in love when they leave you. That means it wasn't really them you loved. You know?'

'I've never been in love.'

'Yes, you have. You've been in love with magic. And now it's left you, so you've got to move on to the next better thing. But not for a while, you've got some grieving to do.'

It's harsh, but I can recognize honest truth when I hear it, and maybe tomorrow or next week or next year I'll know she's right.

'J, I'm sorry. Coming here and sobbing and whining all over you. I do appreciate it.'

'Babe, it's really nothing but an honour.' She gives me a quick hard hug. 'You rock. You think you could go to sleep now?'

I'm just about dropping off where I sit. That's one thing the crying's done.

J tucks me up on the living-room sofa. 'See you in the morning,' she says. 'Or the afternoon. No need to get up, you can stay in bed all day if you like.'

*

Maybe I'll do that. What's to get up for? I lounge around till ten, and J brings me toast and coffee, and then I sleep a bit more. I'm not happy, but at least I'm comfortable.

Around midday she comes back.

'Mag, Ruce is here.'

'Oh, right.'

'She doesn't know you're staying. Can I tell her?'

'Yeah, I guess.'

'You want to see her?'

'Not really.' J doesn't go away. 'You think I should?'

'She's unhappy, Mag. I know she did a wrong thing, but she did think it was for the best. It'd be kind of – kind if you said hello. But you don't have to.'

'Ok, ok. I've got to see her sometime.' I try a bit harder. 'Thanks, J, I'll probably be glad when I've done it.'

'I think you will,' she nods.

When she's gone, I make the effort to get out of bed and put a sweatshirt and trousers on. Always the perfect hostess.

Ruce comes in. She stands awkwardly by the door.

'Sit down.' I'm not looking at her.

'Hello,' she says. Except it isn't Ruce.

Now I look at her. It's big and ginger; it's Ruce all over. But it isn't.

I'm staring.

'What do you see?' she asks me.

'I see,' I say slowly, 'a nasty, hairy, treacherous, smelly old hob.'

'Yer saw me! Yer saw me!'

He starts hopping round the room.

'Yer a witch! Yer a witch!'

Then the real Ruce comes in, and Shade and J and Gordy too. Bargus trots in last, and comes and shoves his big wet nose in my hand. I start crying again, and this time it feels really, really good.

'You fixed it,' I accuse J.

'I fixed it,' boasts Shade.

'When he went off last night,' says J.

'Best way I could think of,' he explains, 'to find out if you really was magic.'

'And you are!' Ruce is crying too.

'Don't know what you're so pleased about,' says J. 'I think witches are foul.' She puts her tongue out at Shade, and then hugs Ruce. 'Long live the not-witches.'

'It is true, isn't it?' I say in a panic.

'Only a witch can see yer real form,' Humph

declares in triumph. 'I knows that. And don't let nobody tell yer hobs is thick.'

Gordy comes over, shuffling his big feet, and shakes my hand.

'Welcome back,' he says.

After that, it turns into a bit of a party.

*

Much later the same day, I'm on my own again. I feel like being outside, but it's cold, so I go to my bag for a jumper. When I pull it out, underneath there's Temple's flute.

I took it home with me, now I've brought it back here. I don't know why I'm keeping it with me, but I don't want to leave it.

If there's one person I'd like to talk to, about everything that's happened, it's the one person I can't. I pick up the flute, and climb the stairs to the carpark roof.

The evening's inky blue, jewelled with airport lights. The wind's in my face. I sit cross-legged, with the flute across my lap.

I'm listening, I'm listening.

> *I know a lady lives in a tower*
> *Her face as fair as the lily flower*
> *Her smile as sweet as the crimson rose*
> *That in her secret garden grows.*

I know what she was telling me, the last time.

'I couldn't … I can't …' *I couldn't save my mother. I can't save her now. But you can save yours, and you will.* It's a whisper on the wind.

> *Little bird sits and sings in a tree*
> *Pretty bird, pretty bird, fly down to me,*
> *I'll make you a cage of silver and gold*
> *To keep you from the winter's cold.*

Under Temple's music, then over it, I hear another tune. It's nothing like Grace's, that I thought was mine. This is moody and dark, I don't even know if I like it, but it's my own deep music I'm hearing.

Temple's song keeps me company a bit longer.

> *I'd sooner die from the winter's cold*
> *Than live in a cage of silver and gold*
> *For birds must fly and flowers must die*
> *So I'll take my wings and away I'll fly.*

I should go back in and get warm. But I stay sitting there, shivering, looking out at the night sky.

I'm a witch. I really am a witch. It's my own magic, not Grace's.

Now all I've got to do is work on finding my own name.

When I think that, something clicks inside me.

My own name.

If everyone calls you something, does that make it your name? Can your name – your witch name – be something you've always known about?

Why not?

'Maggot,' I say out loud. And I feel like I'm a million miles high.

It's not the name I'd have chosen, but I can live with it.

BETWEEN THE RAVEN AND THE DOVE

Find out more about the Witchwork Series:

 /WitchworkSeries

á

For more great books, and information
about Sophia Kingshill, go to:

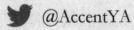 @AccentYA

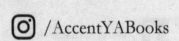 /AccentYABooks